ALSO BY LJ SHEN

All Saints
Pretty Reckless
Broken Knight
Angry God

PRETTY RECKLESS

L.J. SHEN

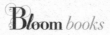

To first loves and to famous last words.
And to Sarah M. Qattar, who fell in love with Penn and
Daria before they had the chance to fall with each other,
and Ariadna Basulto, the real California Girl.

Copyright © 2019, 2023 by L.J. Shen
Cover and internal design © 2023 by Sourcebooks
Cover design by Antoaneta Georgieva/Sourcebooks
Photo credits by Chrizalyn Dimarucut/EyeEm/Getty Images,
andipantz/Getty Images, Olga Siletskaya/Getty Images
Internal design by Tara Jaggers/Sourcebooks

Published by Bloom Books, an imprint of Sourcebooks
P.O. Box 4410, Naperville, Illinois 60567-4410
(630) 961-3900
sourcebooks.com

Originally self-published in 2019 by L.J. Shen.

Cataloguing-in-Publication Data is on file with the Library of Congress.

Printed and bound in the United States of America.
WOZ 10 9 8 7 6 5 4 3 2 1

THEME SONG

"I Feel Like I'm Drowning"—Two Feet

PLAYLIST

"Too Young"—Zeds Dead
"Cute Without the 'E'"—Taking Back Sunday
"Who Knew"—Pink
"Solo Amigos"—Maniako
"Right Above It"—Lil Wayne
"Killing in the Name"—Rage Against the Machine
"If You're Feeling Sinister"—Belle and Sebastian
"Tainted Love"—Soft Cell

PROLOGUE
DARIA/PENN

It started with a lemonade
And ended with my heart.
This, my pretty reckless rival, is how our
screwed-up story starts.

DARIA, AGE FOURTEEN

The tiles under my feet shake as a herd of ballerinas blazes past me, their feet pounding like artillery in the distance.

Brown hair. Black hair. Straight hair. Red hair. Curly hair. They blur into a rainbow of trims and scrunchies. My eyes are searching for the blond head I'd like to bash against the well-worn floor.

Feel free not to be here today, Queen Bitch.

I stand frozen on the threshold of my mother's ballet studio, my pale pink leotard sticking to my ribs. My white duffel bag dangles from my shoulder. My tight bun makes my scalp burn. Whenever I let my hair down, my golden locks fall off in chunks on the bathroom floor. I tell Mom it's from messing with my hair too much, but that's BS. And if she gave a damn—*really* gave one, not just pretended to—she'd know this too.

I wiggle my banged-up toes in my pointe shoes, swallowing the ball of anxiety in my throat. Via isn't here. *Thank you, Marx.*

Girls torpedo past me, bumping into my shoulders. I feel their giggles in my empty stomach. My duffel bag falls with a thud. My classmates are leaner, longer, and more flexible, with rod-straight backs like an exclamation mark. Me? I'm small and muscular like a question mark. Always unsure and on the verge of snapping. My face is not stoic and regal; it's traitorous and unpredictable. Some wear their hearts on their sleeves—I wear mine on my mouth. I smile with my teeth when I'm happy, and when my mom looks at me, I'm always happy.

"You should really take gymnastics or cheer, Lovebug. It suits you so much better than ballet."

But Mom sometimes says things that dig at my self-esteem. There's a rounded dent on its surface now, the shape of her words, and that's where I keep my anger.

Melody Green-Followhill is a former ballerina who broke her leg during her first week at Juilliard when she was eighteen. Ballet has been expected of me since the day I was born. And, just my luck, I happen to be exceptionally bad at it.

Enter Via Scully.

Also fourteen, Via is everything I strive to be. Taller, blonder, and skinnier. Worst of all, her natural talent makes my dancing look like an insult to leotards all over the world.

Three months ago, Via received a letter from the Royal Ballet Academy asking her to audition. Four weeks ago, she did. Her hotshot parents couldn't get the time off work, so my mom jumped at the chance to fly her on a weeklong trip to London. Now the entire class is waiting to hear if Via is going to study at the Royal Ballet Academy. Word around the studio is she has it in the bag. Even the Ukrainian danseur Alexei Petrov—a sixteen-year-old prodigy who is like the Justin Bieber of ballet—posted an IG story with her after the audition.

Looking forward to creating magic together.

It wouldn't surprise me to learn Via can do magic. She's always been a witch.

"Lovebug, stop fretting by the door. You're blocking everyone's way," my mother singsongs with her back to me. I can see her reflection through the floor-to-ceiling mirror. She's frowning at the attendance sheet and glancing at the door, hoping to see Via.

Sorry, Mom. Just your spawn over here.

Via is always late, and my mother, who never tolerates tardiness, lets her get away with it.

I bend down to pick up my duffel bag and pad into the studio. A shiny barre frames the room, and a floor-to-ceiling window displays downtown Todos Santos in all its photogenic, upper-crust glory. Peach-colored benches grace tree-lined streets, and crystal-blue towers sparkle like the thin line where the ocean kisses the sky.

I hear the door squeaking open and squeeze my eyes shut.

Please don't be here.

"Via! We've been waiting for you." Mom's chirp is like a BB gun shooting me in the back, and I tumble over my own feet from the shock wave. Snorts explode all over the room. I manage to grip the barre, pulling myself up a second before my knees hit the floor. Flushed, I grasp it in one hand and slide into a sloppy plié.

"Lovebug, be a darling and make some room for Via," Mom purrs.

Symbolically, Mother, I'd love for Via to make my ass some room too.

Of course, her precious prodigy isn't wearing her ballet gear today even though she owns Italian-imported leotards other girls can only dream of. Via clearly comes from money because even rich people don't like shelling out two hundred bucks for a basic leotard. Other than Mom—who probably figures I'll never be a true ballerina so the least she can do is dress me up like one.

Today, Via is wearing a cropped yellow Tweety Bird shirt and ripped leggings. Her eyes are red, and her hair is a mess. Does she even make an effort?

She throws me a patronizing smirk. "*Lovebug.*"

"*Puppy,*" I retort.

"Puppy?" She snorts.

"I'd call you a bitch, but let's admit it, your bite doesn't really have teeth."

I readjust my shoes, pretending that I'm over her. I'm *not* over her. She monopolizes my mother's time, and she's been on my case way before I started talking back. Via attends another school in San Diego. She claims it's because her parents think the kids in Todos Santos are too sheltered and spoiled. Her parents want her to grow up with *real* people.

Know what else is fake? Pretending to be something you're not. I own up to the fact I'm a prissy princess. Sue me. (Please do. I can afford really good legal defense.)

"Meet me after class, Vi," Mom says, then turns back around to the stereo. Vi *(Vi!)* uses the opportunity to stretch her leg, stomping on my toes in the process.

"Oops. Looks like you're not the only clumsy person around here, Daria."

"I would tell you to drop dead, but I'm afraid my mom would force me to go to your funeral, and you legit aren't worth my time."

"I would tell you to kiss my ass, but your mom already does that. If she only liked you half as much as she likes me. It's cool, though; at least you have money for therapy. And a nose job." She pats my back with a smirk, and I hate, *hate*, **hate** that she is prettier.

I can't concentrate for the rest of the hour. I'm not stupid. Even though I know my mother loves me more than Via, I also know it's because she's genetically programmed to do so.

Centuries tick by, but the class is finally dismissed. All the girls sashay to the elevator in pairs.

"Daria darling, do me a favor and get us drinks from Starbucks. I'm going to the little girls' room, then wrapping something up real quick with Vi." Mom pats my shoulder, then saunters out of the studio, leaving a trail of her perfume like fairy dust. My mom would donate all her organs to save one of her students' fingernails.

She smothers her ballerinas with love, leaving me saddled me with jealousy.

I grab Mom's bag and turn around before I have a chance to exchange what Daddy calls "unpleasantries" with Via.

"You should've seen her face when I auditioned." Via stretches in front of the mirror behind me. She's as agile as a contortionist. Sometimes I think she could wrap herself around my neck and choke me to death.

"We had a blast. She told me that by the looks of it, not only am I in, but I'm also going to be their star student. It felt kind of…" She snaps her fingers, looking for the word. I see her in the reflection of the mirror but don't turn around. Tears are hanging on my lower lashes for their dear lives. "A redemption or something. Like you can't be a ballerina because you're so, you know, *you*. But then there's *me*. So at least she'll get to see someone she loves make it."

Daddy says a green Hulk lives inside me, and he gets bigger and bigger when I get jealous, and sometimes, the Hulk blasts through my skin and does things the Daria he knows and loves would never do. He says jealousy is the tribute mediocrity pays to genius, and I'm no mediocre girl.

Let's just say I disagree.

I've always been popular, and I've always fought hard for a place in the food chain where I can enjoy the view. But I think I'm ordinary. Via is extraordinary and glows so bright, she burns everything in her vicinity. I'm the dust beneath her feet, and I'm crushed and bitter and *Hulky*.

Nobody *wants* to be a bad person. But some people—like me—just can't help themselves. A tear rolls down my cheek, and I'm thankful we're alone. I turn around to face her.

"What the hell is your problem?"

"What isn't?" She sighs. "You are a spoiled princess, a shallow idiot, and a terrible dancer. How can someone so untalented be born to *the* Melody Green-Followhill?"

I don't know! I want to scream. *No one wants to be born to a genius. Marx, bless Sean Lennon for surviving his own existence.*

I eye her pricey pointe shoes and arch a mocking eyebrow. "Don't pretend I'm the only princess here."

"You're an airhead, Daria." She shakes her head.

"At least I'm not a spaz." I pretend to be blasé, but my whole body is shaking.

"You can't even get into a decent first position." She throws her hands in the air. She isn't wrong, and that enrages me.

"Again—why. Do. You. Care!" I roar.

"Because you're a waste of fucking space, that's why! While I'm busting my ass, you get a place in this class just because your mother is the teacher."

This is my chance to tell her the truth.

That I'm busting mine even harder precisely because I wasn't born a ballerina. Instead, my heart shatters like glass. I spin on my heel and dart down the fire escape, taking the stairs two at a time. I pour myself out into the blazing California heat. Any other girl would take a left and disappear inside Liberty Park, but I take a right and enter Starbucks because I can't—*won't*—disappoint my mom more than I already have. I look left and right to make sure the coast is clear, then release the sob that has weighed on my chest for the past hour. I get into line, tugging open Mom's purse from her bag as I wipe my tears away with my sleeve. Something falls to the floor, so I pick it up.

It's a crisp letter with my home address on it, but the name gives me pause.

Sylvia Scully.

Sniffing, I rip the letter open. I don't stop to think that it isn't mine to open. Seeing Via's mere name above my address makes me want to scream until the walls in this place fall. The first thing that registers is the symbol at the top.

The Royal Ballet Academy.

My eyes are like a wonky mixed tape. They keep rewinding to the same words.

Acceptance Letter.

Acceptance Letter.

Acceptance Letter.

Via got accepted. I should be thrilled she'll be out of my hair in a few months, but instead, the acidic taste of envy bursts inside my mouth.

She has everything.

The parents. The money. The fame. The talent. Most of all—my mother's undivided attention.

She has everything, and I have nothing, and the Hulk inside me grows larger. His body so huge it presses against my diaphragm.

A whole new life in one envelope. *Via's* life hanging by a paper. A paper that's in my hand.

"Sweetie? Honey?" The barista snaps me out of my trance with a tone that suggests I'm not a sweetie nor a honey. "What would you like?"

For Via to die.

I place my order and shuffle to the corner of the room so I can read the letter for the thousandth time. As if the words will change by some miracle.

Five minutes later, I take both drinks and exit onto the sidewalk. I dart to the nearest trash can to dispose of my iced tea lemonade so I can hold the letter without dampening it. Mom probably wanted to open it with Via, and I just took away their little moment.

Sorry to interrupt your bonding sesh.

"Put the drink down, and nobody gets hurt," booms a voice behind me, like liquid honey, as my hand hovers over the trash can. It's male, but he's young. I spin in place, not sure I heard him right. His chin dipped low, I can't see his face clearly because of a Raiders ball cap that's been worn to death. He's tall and scrawny—almost scarily so—but he glides toward me like a Bengal tiger. As if he's found a way to walk on air and can't be bothered with mundane things like muscle tone.

"Are we throwing this away?" He points at the lemonade.

We? Bitch, at this point, there's not even a you to me.

I motion to him with the drink. He can have the stupid iced tea lemonade. Gosh. He is interrupting my meltdown for a lemonade.

"Nothing's free in this world, Skull Eyes."

I blink, willing him to evaporate from my vision. Did this jackass really just call me Skull Eyes? At least I don't look like a skeleton. My mind is upstairs with Via. Why does Mom receive letters on her behalf? Why couldn't they send it directly to Via's house? Is Mom adopting her ass now?

I think about my sister, Bailey. At only nine, she already shows promise as a gifted dancer. Via moving to London might encourage Mom to put Bailey in the Royal Ballet Academy too. Mom had talked about me applying there before it became clear that I could be a Panera bagel before I'd become a professional ballerina. I begin to glue the pieces of my screwed-up reality together.

What if I had to migrate to London to watch both girls make it big while I swam in my pool of mediocrity?

Bailey and Via would become BFFs.

I'd have to live somewhere rainy and gray.

We'd leave Vaughn and Knight and even Luna behind. All my childhood friends.

Via would officially take my place in Mom's heart.

Hmm, no thanks.

Not today, Satan.

When I don't answer, the boy takes a step toward me. I'm not scared, although…maybe I should be? He's wearing dirty jeans—I'm talking mud and dust, not, like, purposely haphazard—and a worn blue shirt that looks two sizes too big with a hole the size of a small fist where his heart is. Someone wrote around it in a black Sharpie and girlie handwriting *Is it a sign?—Adriana, xoxo* and I want to know if Adriana is prettier than me.

"Why are you calling me Skull Eyes?" I clench the letter in my fist.

"Because." He slopes his head so low all I can see are his lips, and they look petal-soft and pink. Feminine, almost. His voice is smooth to a point it hurts a little in my chest. I don't know why. Guys my age are revolting to me. They smell like pizza that has sat in the sun for days. "You have skulls in your eyes, Silly Billy. Know what you need?"

For Mom to stop telling me that I suck?

For Via to disappear?

Take your pick, dude.

I shove my free hand into my mom's wallet and pluck out a ten-dollar bill. He looks as if he could use a meal. I pray he'll take it before Mom comes down and starts asking questions. I'm not supposed to talk to strangers, much less strangers who look like they are dumpster diving for their next meal.

"Sea glass." He thrusts his hand in my direction, ignoring the money and the drink.

"Like the stuff you get on Etsy?" I huff.

Great. You're a weirdo too.

"Huh? Nah, that shit's trash. Orange sea glass. The real stuff. Found it on the beach last week and Googled it. It's the rarest thing in the world, you know?"

"Why would you give a total stranger something so precious?" I roll my eyes.

"Why not?"

"Um, hello, attention span much? Weren't you the one who just said nothing in this world is free?"

"Who said it's free? Did you get all your annual periods today at once or something?"

"Don't talk about my period!"

"Fine. No period talk. But you need a real friend right now, and I'm officially applying for the position. I even dressed the part. Look." He motions to his hobo clothes with an apologetic smile.

And just like that, heat pours into my chest like hot wax. Anger, I find, has the tendency to be crisp. I really want to throat punch him. He pities me? *Pities.* The guy with the hole in his shirt.

"You want to be my friend?" I bark out a laugh. "Pathetic much? Like, who even says that?"

"Me. I say that. And I never claimed not to be pathetic." He tugs at his ripped shirt and raises his head slowly, unveiling more of his face. A nose my mom would call Roman and a jaw that's too square for someone my age. He's all sharp angles, and maybe one day he will be handsome, but right now, he looks like an anime cartoon character. Mighty Max.

"Look, do you want the lemonade and money or not? My mom should be here any minute."

"And?"

"And she can't see us together."

"Because of how I look?"

Duh.

"No, because you're a boy." I don't want to be mean to him even though, usually, I am. Especially to boys. Especially to boys with beautiful faces and honey voices.

Boys can smell heartbreak from across a continent. Even at fourteen. Even in the middle of an innocent summer afternoon. We girls have an invisible string behind our belly button, and only certain guys can tug at it.

This boy...he will snap it if I let him.

"Take the sea glass. Owe me something." He motions to me with an open palm. I stare at the ugly little rock. My fist clenches around the letter. The paper hisses.

The boy lifts his head completely, and our eyes meet. He studies me with quiet interest as though I'm a painting, not a person. My heart is rioting all over, and the dumbest thought crosses my mind. Ever notice how the heart is *literally* caged by the ribs? That's insane. As if our body knows it can break so easily, it needs to be protected.

White dots fill my vision, and he's swimming somewhere behind them, against the stream.

"What's in the letter?" he asks.

"My worst nightmare."

"Give it to me," he orders, so I do. I don't know why. Most likely because I want to get rid of it. Because I want Via to hurt as much as I do. Because I want Mom to be upset. *Marx, what's wrong with me?* I'm a horrible person.

His eyes are still on mine as he tears the letter to shreds and lets the pieces float like confetti into the trash can between us. His eyes are dark green and bottomless like a thickly fogged forest. I want to step inside and run until I'm in the depth of the woods. Something occurs to me just then.

"You're not from here," I say. He is too pure. Too good. Too real.

He shakes his head slowly. "Mississippi. Well, my dad's family. Anyway. Owe me something," he repeats, almost begging.

Why does he want me to owe him something?

So he can ask for something back.

I don't relent, frozen to my spot. Instead, I hand him the lemonade. He takes it, closes the distance between us, pops the lid open, and pours the contents all over the ruined letter. His body brushes against mine. We're stomach to stomach. Legs to legs. Heart to heart.

"Close your eyes."

His voice is gruff and thick and different. This time, I surrender. I know what's about to happen, and I'm letting it happen anyway. My first kiss.

I always thought it would happen with a football player or a pop star or a European exchange student. Someone outside of the small borders of my sheltered, Instagram-filtered world. Not with a kid who has a hole in his shirt. But I need this. Need to feel desired and pretty and wanted.

His lips flutter over mine, and it tickles, so I snort. I can feel his warm breath skating across my lips, his baseball cap grazing my forehead and the way his mouth slides against mine, lips locking with uncertainty. I forget to breathe for a second, my hands on his shoulders, but then something inside me begs me to dart my tongue out and really taste him. We're sucking air from each other's mouths. We're doing it all wrong. My lips open for him. His open too. My heart is pounding so hard I can feel the blood whooshing in my veins when he says, "Not yet. I'll take that too, but not yet."

A groan escapes my lips.

"What would you have asked of me if I took the sea glass?"

"To save me all your firsts," he whispers somewhere between my ear and mouth as his body brushes away from mine.

I don't want to open my eyes and let the moment end. But he makes the choice for both of us. The warmth of his body leaves mine as he takes a step back.

I still don't have the guts to open my mouth and ask for his name.

Ten, fifteen, twenty seconds pass.

My eyelids flutter open on their own accord as my body begins to sway.

He's gone.

Disoriented, I lean against the trash can, fiddling with the strap of my mother's bag. Five seconds pass before Mom loops her arm around mine out of nowhere and leads me to the Range Rover. My legs fly across the pavement. My head twists back.

Blue shirt? Ball cap? Petal lips? Did I imagine the whole thing?

"There you are. Thanks for the coffee. What, no iced tea lemonade today?"

After I fail to answer, we climb into her vehicle and buckle up. Mom sifts through her Prada bag resting on the center console.

"Huh. I swear I took four letters from the mailbox today, not three."

And that's when it hits me—*she doesn't know.* Via got in, and she has no idea the letter came today. Then this guy tore it apart because it upset me...

Kismet. Kiss-met. Fate.

Dad decided two years ago that he was tired of hearing all three girls in the household moaning "oh my God," so now we have to replace the word *God* with the word *Marx*, after Karl Marx, a dude who was apparently into atheism or whatever. I feel like God or Marx—*someone*—sent this boy to help me. If he were even real. Maybe I made him up in my head to come to terms with what I did.

I open a compact mirror and apply some lip gloss, my heart racing.

"You're always distracted, Mom. If you dropped a letter, you'd have seen it."

Mom pouts, then nods. In the minute it takes her to start the engine, I realize two things:

One—she was expecting this letter like her next breath.

Two—she is devastated.

"Before I forget, Lovebug, I bought you the diary you wanted." Mom produces a thick black-cased leather notebook from her Prada bag and hands it to me. I noticed it before, but I never assume things are for me anymore. She's always distracted, buying Via all types of gifts.

As we ride in silence, I have an epiphany.

This is where I'll write my sins.

This is where I'll bury my tragedies.

I snap the mirror shut and tuck my hands into the pockets of my white hoodie, where I find something small and hard. I take it out and stare at it, amazed.

The orange sea glass.

He gave me the sea glass even though I never accepted it.

Save me all your firsts.

I close my eyes and let a fat tear roll down my cheek.

He was real.

PENN

Question: Who gives their most precious belonging to a girl they don't know?

Answer: This motherfucker right here. Print me an "I'm with stupid" shirt with an arrow pointing straight to my dick.

Could've sold the damn thing and topped off Via's cell phone credit. Now that ship's sailed. I can spot it in the distance, sinking quickly.

The worst part is that I knew nothing would come out of it. At fourteen, I've only kissed two girls. They both had enormous tongues and too much saliva. This girl looked like her tongue would be small, so I couldn't pass up trying.

But the minute my lips touched hers, I just couldn't do it. She looked kind of manic. Sad. Clingy? I don't fucking know. Maybe I just didn't have the balls. Maybe watching her three times a week from afar paralyzed me.

Hey, how do you turn off your own mind? It needs to shut up. Now.

My friend Kannon passes me the joint on my front porch. That's the one perk of having your mom live with her drug-dealing boyfriend. Free pot. And since food is scarce these days, I'll take whatever is on the table.

A bunch of wannabe gangsters in red bandanas cross our side of the street with their pit bulls and a boom box playing angry Spanish rap. The dogs bark, yanking on their chains. Kannon barks right back at them. He's so high his head might hit a fucking plane. I take a hit, then hand Camilo the joint.

"I'll lend you fifty so you can make the call." Camilo coughs. He is huge and tan and already has impressive facial hair. He looks like someone's Mexican dad.

"We don't need to call anyone!" my twin sister yells from the grass next to us. She is lying facedown, sobbing into the yellow lawn. I think she is hoping the sun will burn her into the ground.

"Are y'all deaf or something?! I didn't get in!"

"We'll take the money." I ignore her. We have to call the ballet place. Via can't stay here. It ain't safe.

"I love you, Penn, but you're a pain in the ass." She hiccups, plucking blades of grass and throwing them in our direction without lifting her head. She'll thank me later. When she is famous and rich—do ballerinas get rich?—and I'm still sitting here with my dumb friends smoking pot and salivating over lemon-haired Todos Santos girls. Maybe I won't have to stand on street corners and deal. I'm good at shit. Sports and fighting mainly. Coach says I need to eat more protein for muscle and more carbs to get some body fat, but that's not happening anytime soon because most of my money is spent buying Via's bus tickets to her ballet classes.

I tag along because I'm hella worried about her riding on that bus alone. Especially in winter when it gets dark early.

"I thought you said your sister's good? How come she didn't get in?" Kannon yawns, moving his hand over his long dreads. The sides of his head are shaved, creating a black man-bun. I punch his arm so hard he collapses back on the rocking chair with a silent scream, clutching his bicep, still hardy-har-harring.

"I think a demonstration is in order. Chop-chop, Via. Show us your moves." Cam puts "Milkshake" by Kelis on his phone, balling a gum wrapper in his hand and throwing it at the back of her head.

Her sobs stop, replaced with catatonic silence. I turn around, scrubbing my chin before twisting back to Camilo and swinging a fist at his jaw. I hear it unlock from its usual place and him *harrumphing*.

Darting up from the grass, Via runs into the house and slams the door behind her. I'm not sure what business she has sitting in the living room when Rhett is home, griping about being tired and hungry. She will probably get into a screaming match with him and return to the porch with her tail between her legs. My mom is too high to interfere, but even when she does, she chooses her boyfriend's side. Even when he uses Via's leotards, which her teacher buys for her, to shine his shoes. He does that often to get a rise out of her. On days she shows up to class in her torn leggings and hand-me-down shirts, she spends the bus ride sobbing. Those are usually the days when I rub his briefs on the public toilet seats in Liberty Park.

It's incredibly therapeutic.

"Hand me the fifty." I open my palm and turn to Cam, who slaps the bill into my hand obediently. I'm going to buy myself and Via burgers the size of my face, then top the credit on her phone so she can call Mrs. Followhill.

I charge down my street to In-N-Out, Camilo and Kannon trailing me like the wind. Cracked concrete and murals of dead teenagers wearing halos line the street. Our palm trees seem to hunch down from the burden of poverty, leaning over buildings that are short and yellow, like bad teeth.

But twenty minutes later, the satisfaction of clutching a paper bag filled with greasy burgers and fries is overwhelming. Via's gonna forget all about her meltdown when she sees it. I push the door to my house open, and the first thing I see makes me drop the food to the floor.

My mother's boyfriend is straddling my sister on the couch, his jiggling belly pouring out on her chest. He pummels her face, his sweaty, hairy chest glistening and his arm flexing every time he does. His ripped jeans are unbuttoned, and his zipper is all the way down. She is wheezing and coughing, trying to breathe. Without thinking, I dash toward them and unplaster him from her. Her face is bloody, and she's croaking out weak protests, telling him that he's a cheap bastard, and he keeps yelling that she is a thieving whore. I grab Rhett by the collar of his shirt and pull him from her. He swings with the momentum, falling on the floor. I punch his face so hard, the sound of his jaw cracking echoes around the room. He whips his head back, hitting the floor. I spin back to Via, and all I see is her back as she slides through her own blood, tripping to the door. I grab her wrist, but she wiggles free. Something falls between us with a soft click. I pick it up, and it looks like a tooth. Jesus fucking Christ. He knocked her tooth out.

"I'm sorry," she says, her voice muffled from the blood in her mouth. "I'm sorry. I can't, Penn."

"Via!" I cry out.

"Please," she yells. "Let me go."

I try to chase her, slipping in the trail of blood she leaves behind. My hands are covered in it now. I stand and start for the still-open door. A hand snatches me back and throws me on the couch.

"Not so quick, little asshole. Now's your turn."

I close my eyes and let it happen, knowing why Via has to run. *Geography is destiny.*

It's been three days since Via ran away.

Two and a half since I've last managed to stomach anything without throwing it up (Pabst counts, right?).

After Rhett beat her up for stealing his phone and trying to call London, I'm not surprised she ain't back. I know better than to fuck with Rhett. Via is usually even more cautious with him because she's a girl. It was a moment of weakness on her part, and it cost her more than she was willing to pay.

On Friday afternoon, I find myself loitering outside her ballet class, hoping she'll appear. Maybe she's crashing at her teacher's house. They seem close, but it's hard to tell since Via puts on a mask every time the bus we board slides into the city limits of Todos Santos. The fact she hasn't touched base yet makes me heave when I think about it. I'm telling myself she has her reasons.

At six, pink-wearing girls start pouring out of the building. I dawdle by the shiny black Range Rover with my hands in my pockets, waiting for the teacher. She comes out last, waving and laughing with a bunch of students. Another girl walks beside her.

The girl I kissed to be exact. The girl I've been obsessing over for a year to be super-exact. She is beautiful like the shit hanging in the museums. In a really sad, distant, look-but-don't-touch way. I trek toward them, and they meet me halfway. The girl's eyes widen, and she looks sideways to see if anyone else is here to witness us talking. She thinks I'm here for her.

"Hi." She tucks hair behind her ears, her gaze traveling to Mrs. Followhill in a silent I-swear-I-don't-know-this-guy plea.

"Hey." I kill the butterflies in my stomach because now's not the place and definitely not the time, then turn to the teacher. "Ma'am, my sister, Via, is in your class. I haven't seen her in three days."

The teacher's eyebrows pinch together as though I just announced I'll be taking a shit on the hood of her vehicle. She tells the blond to wait inside the giant Range Rover, then tugs at my arm, heading toward an alleyway. Sandwiched between two buildings, she sort of forces me to sit down on a tall step (dafuq?) and starts talking.

"I've been calling her five times a day and leaving messages," she whispers hotly in my face. "I wanted to let her know she'd been accepted to the Royal Academy. When the letter never arrived, I called them to check. Everything is in motion now. As I said before, you needn't worry about the tuition. I'll be paying the fee."

My nostrils flare. All this in her future, and she could be lying in a ditch right now. Goddamn Via. Goddamn all pretty, volatile fourteen-year-old girls.

"Well, ma'am, thank you for the gift she'll never be able to cash in on since *we* can't find her," I respectfully mock her. But *we* is just me. Mom is out of it—she never really bothered bouncing out of her first drug binge some years ago—and Rhett is probably happy he has one less mouth to feed. When the truancy officer called from school earlier, I told him Via went to my aunt's, something my mother later confirmed when he showed up on our doorstep. Mom, wild-haired and sucking on a cigarette as if it were an oxygen mask, never once asked if it was true. If I call the police, they'll dump both our asses in foster care. Maybe together but probably not. I can't let that happen. I can't be separated from Via.

Mrs. Followhill stares at me with an expression as if she just realized she caught a stomach bug. She is probably wondering how I dare speak to her like that. Usually, I'm a bit more user-friendly. Then again, I don't usually have to deal with a missing sister. I clean my mother's puke from the walls and close the bathroom door on Rhett when he falls asleep on the toilet seat. I don't look at grown-ups with the same air of reverence her daughter does.

"Whoa." That's all Mrs. Followhill says.

"Thanks for the insight. Have a nice life." I stand and swagger toward the street. She catches my arm and yanks me back. I twist around to face her.

"My daughter..." She licks her lips, then looks down, looks *guilty*. The girl is leaning against the Rover, staring at us, chewing on her thumbnail. "My daughter and Via haven't been getting along. I tried to encourage them to communicate, but the more I pushed them together, the more they seemed to dislike one another. I *think* I had a letter go missing last week. A letter that could have been... important. I don't even know why I'm telling you this." She lets out a breath, shaking her head. "I guess I just...I don't want to know, you know? I hate the fact that my mind is even going there."

But maybe it should.

The flashback crashes into my memory.

The paper that hissed in her little fist.

Me taking it from her.

Tearing it apart.

Throwing it into the trash can, watching her face blossom into bliss.

Pouring the lemonade on the remains for good measure when her blue eyes twinkled the request.

Setting my sister's dreams on fire.

Kicking this entire nightmare into motion.

My jaw flexes, and I take a step back. I throw one last glance at the chick, filing her into memory.

Archive under: Shit List.

Revisit document: When I'm able to ruin her.

"So Via's not with you?" My voice hardens around the words. Like tin. I'm desperate. I have no lead. I want to rip the world apart to find her, but the world is not mine to destroy. The world just continues turning at the same pace, because kids like Via and me? We disappear all the time, and no one notices.

Mrs. Followhill shakes her head. She hesitates, touching my arm. "Hey, why don't you come with me? I'll drop Daria off at home, and we can look for her."

Daria.

I turn around and stalk toward the bus stop, feeling stupid and hateful and alive. More alive than I've ever felt. Because I want to kill Daria. Daria made everything fade into the background the first time I saw her, and while I was busy admiring, everything around us burned.

You look like you could use a friend, I told her. Stupid boyish faith. I mentally throw it onto the ground and stomp on it on my way to the bus as it slides to the curb.

Daria was right. I was pathetic. Stupid. Blinded by her hair and lips and sweet melancholy.

Making a beeline to the bus stop, I hear Mrs. Followhill yelling my name behind me in the distance. She knows my name. She knows me. Us. I don't know why it disturbs me. I don't know why I still give a fuck that this girl knows I'm poor.

I hop on the first available bus, not sure where it will take me.

As far away from the girl but not far enough from myself.

The burn in my chest intensifies, the hole around my heart growing bigger, and my grandmother whispers in the back of my mind.

Skull Eyes.

CHAPTER ONE
DARIA

The night before senior year
I spotted you on those bleachers.
You looked adorable.
Your heart cracking for a guy
Who would love to smash a foot in it and
crush it into pieces.

ALMOST EIGHTEEN

The snake pit is crowded tonight.

It always is when Vaughn fights, and Vaughn *always* fights. He breaks noses almost as well as he breaks hearts. Breaking hearts, in case you're wondering, is his second-favorite art. At least six girls have moved to different private schools just to run away from the misery of seeing him gliding through the hallways since he got into All Saints High. He has three more years here, and parents across town are locking their daughters up and shaking with fear.

Every popular guy at All Saints High and our rival school, Las Juntas, in San Diego fights at the snake pit as a rite of passage. This is not my usual scene, but Blythe, Alisha, and Esme dragged me here on the night before school starts. They're avid Vaughn observers. The jerk spent summer vacation in a studio in Italy sculpting and returned two days ago, so now they need their fix of his beautiful, listless face.

The truth is, Vaughn is too cruel to fall in love, in lust, or even in like. This, however, is a lesson they'll learn the hard way. I'll have plenty of fun watching even though I'll do the whole OMG-sweetie-he-is-so-not-worth-it act.

Side note? He *totally* is.

"How can someone so violent create such delicate art? He is fuckable to a fault." Blythe munches on her *Little Mermaid* red hair as she stares down at Vaughn, who is pacing back and forth on the field, his tattered black clothes clinging to his lean muscles.

Legend claims the snake pit, a deserted football field on the outskirts of San Diego, got its name after a snake plague caused it to be abandoned. The faded, chipped blue bleachers are where the guys are slumped drinking beer. We, the girls, sit with our legs crossed, sipping expensive wine from the bottle and vaping. The Las Juntas crowd sits on the bleachers opposite of us. They don't wear Swiss brands and drive German cars. They pass half-empty bottles of tequila and rolled-up cigarettes.

"Gross, Blythe, he's a sophomore." Alisha, part African American, part Dutch, and all gorgeous, makes gagging noises beside me.

"Shut up, you would take a full-time job as his reusable condom if he'd have you. You didn't come here to watch sweaty nobodies get whipped."

"Who is he fighting, anyway?" I pop my fruity bubble gum, rearranging my dark green velvet minidress on my thighs. My ten shades of shiny blond hair is half tied into a silky black bow, and I look Instagram-ready. My winged eyeliner is on point, and my pout is red and matte, creating the perfect film-noir effect.

I'm Daria Followhill.

Cheer Captain.

Rich Bitch.

Little Miss Popular.

See something you like? Too bad. I don't do boys. Men, on the other hand…

"No idea, but I don't envy him. The fights today have been brutal so far, and Vaughn is the best fighter in the pit, so they usually save him for last." Alisha examines her manicured fingernails.

"Here comes the meat," someone hollers three rows down, and we all stand and crane our necks to check out the unfortunate soul going against *the* Vaughn Spencer. I rise on my tiptoes as the crowd on both sides erupts in barks, pumping their fists. The scent of sweat, alcohol, and dried blood from the previous fights lingers in the air like a cloud. The twang of human desperation hits my tongue.

I see a tall, well-built figure zigzagging toward Vaughn on the dead field. He is clutching a bottle of what looks like something alcoholic, and his ear-length dark-blond hair—or is it light brown?—falls across his forehead. I can't see his face, but I don't need to. There's a hole in his red shirt, right where his heart is, and my hand goes straight to the small piece of sea glass hanging at my throat.

Don't faint, bitch. You're wearing a super-short dress.

For the past four years, I've become a pro at avoiding Penn Scully. A miracle, considering he is a star football player and I am a cheer captain at schools of the same size and in the same county. So far, we've played against each other twice each year. Our teams always make the playoffs, and All Saints is always on the losing end.

I couldn't face him after everything blew up with Via. Every time we had a game against Las Juntas, I either faked period cramps or slipped into my car before the game was over.

"Someone pinch me." Blythe claps her hands excitedly. She is wearing a nude-colored cropped shirt to match her pointy, nude-pink nails. "Penn Scully, Las Juntas's wide receiver, is the hottest thing in SoCal. I've been wanting to sit on his face for a while now too. Tonight's my lucky night."

"From what I hear, you're in the business of parking your ass on anything it fits on. Just a heads-up, Vaughn doesn't like his food fast."

Knight chuckles behind me. I twist my head to face him, arching a brow. I'm just trying to pretend seeing Penn doesn't make my heart twist in my chest, unchaining itself from its arteries.

A chick I don't know is sitting in Knight's lap, trying to hoover his ear into her mouth with her arms slung over his broad shoulders. His legs are spread lazily, and he is wearing a vintage Gucci jacket and white Air Jordans. His jeans are tailor-made for him, and his haircut costs more than my upmarket tote bag.

Knight is gorgeous, and not only does he know it, but he would also advertise it on a billboard if it were possible. Hooded green eyes, dimples as deep as his Casanova gaze, pouty red lips, and a jaw you could cut cheese with. His chestnut-brown hair is softer than medieval-themed porn, and everything about him screams hedonism.

We all live on the same cul-de-sac in the same neighborhood, and our parents are best friends. Knight and Vaughn are the closest to each other, practically brothers, which is weird because they are also like fire and ice. Vaughn is a crazy artist with psychotic tendencies, and Knight is the definition of a popular jock.

One is Edward Scissorhands; the other is Zac Efron's prettier, long-lost brother.

"Is your girlfriend going to get pissy when she realizes you came home with crabs? They make pretty useless pets." I bat my eyelashes sweetly at him. Luna is not his girlfriend although he would die trying. That's why I never really liked Luna Rexroth. She is the original Via. The girl who created the Hulk inside me. The girl who Vaughn always smiled at and Knight followed blindly. Daddy once laughed that Luna is like a Sicilian nun. Once a year, the nuns appear behind lifted curtains so their families can see and adore them because they miss them so.

"That's Luna. When she appears, everything stops."

Yup. And I cease to exist.

"Suck a saggy cock, Dar." He clamps his joint between his teeth, cupping his hand over it to light it, then blows a chain of gray smoke straight into my face.

"Is that an invitation? Because there's a pill for your Q-tip of a dick." I jerk my chin up.

"Baby, my cock is too hard for you to take. The only pills you'll be needing are three Advil to handle the aftermath of having me inside you."

"Inside me? In your dreams, Knight Cole."

"Hard no. In my dreams, I have Luna's legs wrapped around my waist, and the rest is NC-17. No offense, Tiffanie." He pats the girl's ass with the hand holding his Zippo.

"Stephanie."

"Don't make it awkward, babe. I forgot you were in my lap until Elsa here pointed it out." Knight motions to me and laughs.

"Too bad you're a sophomore, and Luna is a junior. She'll never date you." I'm just egging him on. I mean, Luna probably wouldn't date him, but it's not because of his age. She's trapped in her own little universe. She is the sun, and he is the Earth. Always circling around her and getting an inch closer every lifetime even though the burn could ruin him.

He cocks his head to the side, his smile so wolfish, his teeth look pointier than usual.

"Oh brother, if you knew how many of your senior friends gave my cock mouth-to-mouth when they were juniors, you'd have a heart attack."

A loud, shrieking, "Whoa!" interrupts our banter.

The crowd winces in unison, and we all snap our heads back to the field, watching Penn fall to the ground on his way to the center of the pit. My Marx. They haven't even fought, and he's already knocked down on his ass. He looks super drunk. Vaughn is going to kill him before he realizes where he is.

I turn my attention back to Knight.

"You need to tell Vaughn the fight is off."

"Look who's got her thong in a twist. Why? You placed a bet with Gus tonight?" Knight is rubbing the girl's ass, but he's not into it. He never is. I go crimson, my head so hot it might explode. My hands ball into fists beside my body. I don't want Penn to end up in a hospital tonight even though he hates me and probably wouldn't want my concern. Guilt swirls in my stomach as the memory of him tearing up his sister's acceptance letter plays in my mind.

"Whatever. As if I'd ever talk to Gus voluntarily. But this loser is obviously drunk. Vaughn's going to slaughter him."

"He is a huge-ass football player on a team consisting of straight-up gangsters. He can hold his own," Knight shoots back darkly.

As the starting quarterback of All Saints High, Knight's had the dubious pleasure of playing against Scully. Rumor has it, Penn is the best wide receiver in the county. Maybe even the state. Principal Prichard has tried to offer him a scholarship several times so he could join our team, but lucky for me, Penn is the loyal type.

"Knight." My voice breaks, falling off the cliff of indifference. I'm begging. The girl in his lap shoots daggers at me with her gaze. "Vaughn could get into real shit if this goes south."

His face morphs from bored to annoyed. He pushes the girl off his lap and hands her the remainder of his joint.

"I'm not going to break it apart because you're being a vagina, but I'll go downstairs to make sure these two dicks keep it clean." He swipes his tongue over his lips, and his tongue ring pokes out.

I look back at the field, and both guys have taken off their shirts. Knight is right. Penn is a far cry from the emaciated boy who gave me the most precious thing in the world four years ago. Muscled, sinewy, and imperial, he has zero percent body fat and bulging arms. A prominent V points down to his holy grail, and by the way my fellow cheerleaders sigh beside me, they've noticed it too. Vaughn is skinnier in comparison. Not that it matters. He has a feline patience you cannot help but admire, and when he's in his element, I've seen him take down guys triple his size without breaking a sweat.

They circle each other, quiet and deadly and serious. Vaughn is expressionless, as per usual. Stoic and calm. Penn looks out of focus, wearing a loony smile on his lips. The glass bottle slips from between his fingers and rolls on the ground, and people burst out with laughter that echoes in my heart.

"Does he fight here often?" I ask no one in particular.

"Nope." Gus, our football captain who sits two rows down, takes a pull of his beer. His friends beside him are passing a clipboard with names written on it between them. They've been placing bets on the fights all night, and this one takes the cake. Gus snatches the clipboard and pushes it into his duffel bag, balling his varsity jacket and stuffing it on top to conceal it. Guess he still thinks it's a secret that he runs a betting ring. Rumor has it, he makes a small fortune running these bets, and Vaughn—the guy who hates money and everything it represents—gets a cut. Everyone knows what he does with it. Saving so he can open his own studio without touching a dime of his parents' wealth.

"Penn's not the get-drunk-and-fight type of dude, and I've partied with his school plenty. Something's up." He finishes his bottle and rubs his hands together.

Something's up.

I need to stop this guilt-fest. I'm not responsible for his problems. A different girl—a brave girl—would have faced him by now. Not me. He knows what we did that day and how it led to his sister's disappearance. I never asked for his forgiveness because—let's be real—I don't deserve it.

My breath catches deep inside my throat as the two measure each other on the dead field, their body language a perfect mirror. Vaughn is the first to throw a punch in Penn's face. It's a heavy blow, and Penn's nose bursts with blood. People shriek and suck in a collective breath. Penn stumbles backward, laughing and shaking his head as if he dodged the hit. He licks the blood on the corner of his upper lip, then pounces on Vaughn in a way I've never seen before.

Bengal tiger.

I almost forgot how quick and graceful he was. *Is.* Just like his sister.

Penn jams Vaughn to the ground, locking his knees on either side of Vaughn's torso, then rains sloppy fists down on his face. Some hit. Some miss. I want to throw up. The crowd is screaming. This hasn't happened before. Vaughn has taken some serious beatings over the past couple of years, but he's never been thrown to the ground. Vaughn knows better than to squirm and waste his energy. He learned jiujitsu before he was kicked out of three different classes for being disobedient.

"Spencer! Spencer! Spencer! Spencer!" All Saints High students chant from our side of the bleachers, throwing empty cans of beer to the sidelines. Students from Las Juntas, the other school, remain silent but no less intimidating. They are less prone to public gestures, but I know better than to think they're any less loyal to their football star.

Vaughn has a busted lip and a black eye before he manages to roll on top of Penn and mount him, kneeing his ribs. Penn pushes Vaughn clumsily, and before I know it, they're stumbling back upright again. Vaughn is toying with an obviously plastered Penn, but his fists are precise and accurate. I see Knight striding along the sidelines of the football field, running his fingers through his hair, exhaling sharply.

"Let's wrap it up, V. Asshole's more sauced than a cliché abusive dad in a teen film, and you're bleeding like a chick on her period."

"Which is why I'm not going to kill him and just teach him a valuable lesson. He'll thank me." Vaughn winks, spitting a lump of blood as he circles Penn again. He's in a mood when he fights.

Vaughn sends a roundhouse kick to Penn's chin. Blood sprays across the dirt, shooting from his mouth like a rainbow. He falls, a beaten and bloody mess, and doesn't move.

One second.

Five seconds.

Ten seconds.

Get up. Get up. Get up.

A scream erupts from my mouth before I can swallow it down and rings in my ears. Blythe, Alisha, and Esme tug me down the bleachers. Knight enters my periphery, wrapping his arms around me quickly.

Knight is hurling people left and right with his shoulders as kids pour out to the field in what looks like a massive fight between the two schools. Knight ushers me to the parking lot and shoves me into his powder-blue Aston Martin Vanquish Volante. His back seat doesn't have much space, and I'm forced to sit straight and slap a hand over my mouth so I don't puke. He twists a bottle of water open and hands it to me. I take it, but my hands shake too hard for me to take a sip without spilling it all over.

"Puke in my back seat, and it's game over for you, Followhill."

He circles the convertible, then hops over the driver's door into the seat without opening it. Like a summoned demon, Vaughn appears from the chain link entrance of the field, wiping his face with the hem of his black shirt. His jeans are torn, and his makeshift belt consists of his army boots' laces. Knight throws a finger in Vaughn's direction as his engine roars to life.

"You're high if you think you're getting into my car looking like Carrie after the bucket scene."

Vaughn fires a paper-dry look.

"Calm your tits, Cole. I'm bumming a ride with the Las Juntas crowd."

Knight's eyebrows jump to his hairline, and his eyes widen in disbelief. "You *are* fucking high. Get in the car, moron."

"They jumped us on the field," Vaughn clips as if it's a good explanation for his decision. The scent of weed and blood makes my head dizzy.

"And they'll hand you your asses without the football team

fighting on your side. Don't do shit before I come back. I just need to cart Princess Vagina back to her castle."

Vaughn raises his leg and readjusts a piece of masking tape he plastered against the bottom of his army boot that is completely torn.

"The fight tonight shouldn't have happened." He spits a clump of blood onto the concrete road.

"Please tell me Scully didn't break anything other than Daria's black heart. She looks like she's caught some feelings."

I punch Knight's leather seat from behind. I still can't breathe, but I'm grasping at every piece of information about Penn hungrily.

"His mom died this morning."

There's a beat of silence, in which I scream so loudly in my head, my ears ring. I look over at Knight, a guy who sees this scenario as something very real, and I'm not surprised to watch him freeze on the spot.

"That's why they started the brawl." Vaughn exhales. "When Daria was busy having a nuclear meltdown—great form, by the way"—Vaughn pins me with a look—"some guy ran onto the field and dragged Scully out of the dirt, screaming she overdosed this morning. Consequently, on his eighteenth birthday."

"Get the fuck out." Knight's jaw goes slack, and he punches the steering wheel so hard, the piercing shriek of the horn lingers in the sky for a few seconds.

Vaughn dips his head.

"His second birthday present was his stepdad kicking him out of the house. Las Juntas's players aren't gonna touch me. I'm just gonna stitch him up and make sure he's okay."

"I'll tag along," Knight says even though he knows it's dangerous. His first football game is in one week, and it's against the Las Juntas Bulldogs. They'll break his legs without even thinking about it twice. Of course, I can't tell him this.

Last year, the outgoing seniors of All Saints showed up at Las

Juntas High School in the middle of the night, took down their flag, replaced it with a pirate's flag, and smeared the pole with Vaseline for an end-of-school prank. Going there without his crew, even with Vaughn, is not only asking for trouble, it's begging for it. But that's the thing about Knight. Taking risks is a hobby of his.

"Just dropping Dar at home."

"Fine, whatever, I'll come with you guys," I huff. I know I can't face Penn, especially considering the circumstances. I'm probably the last person he wants to see because I will only remind him of what he's lost. And if my snotty friends hear I hung out with the Las Juntas crowd after spontaneously screaming like the world was ending tonight, they would have a field day.

Still, I want to see that he is all right. Personally, I guess.

"Shut up," both Vaughn and Knight say in unison.

Vaughn takes a step forward, appearing under the streetlamp. The tawny light illuminates the damage Penn inflicted on his face. Both his eyes are black, his lip and eyebrow have cuts, and there's swelling on his forehead that will only grow worse by tomorrow morning. He's never been beaten up so badly before.

"Don't bother, Mother Teresa. Dudebro's not gonna hang out for long," Vaughn says.

"Yeah?" Knight asks.

"Blythe Ortiz just coaxed him to go home with her afterward. Not sure how he can fuck in his state, but I guess that's for them to discover tonight."

Both guys chuckle darkly. *Blythe.* Why am I not surprised? She is *so* boy crazy. *Girl, Interrupted.* By dick. It doesn't usually faze me that Blythe is boy crazy since it actually makes me look better, but her touching Penn is just gross on so many levels because (A) he is clearly badly injured, and (B) he was my first kiss. Which in my weird mind means that no one from All Saints can touch him now.

"He's eighteen. He can fuck in any state—all fifty—even when he is physically in a coma," Knight deadpans. There's silence for a beat, and then he adds, "Gus is probably losing his shit. He put a lot of money on this fight, and technically, there's no winner." Knight strokes his chin.

"Gus needs a life and a neck. Not in that order. Guy's a douche, and I've met socks more sophisticated than his ass," Vaughn replies dryly. "He'll survive."

"You get in bed with him business-wise."

"I get in bed with anyone I can fuck over and have my way with business-wise," Vaughn says calmly.

I look down at my hands in my lap. Why do I feel so guilty? Vaughn bends over and pats my back like a big brother even though he is two years younger than me.

"Don't sulk. Scully is a tough motherfucker."

They don't know.

Not about Via, and not about Penn.

Not about my sea glass necklace, and not about the green Hulk living inside me.

I flip my hair and smile, but I'm not there. Not really. Even when Knight drives me home under the beautiful starless sky, the color of the night so pure, my eyes sting. The moon looks as lonely and seductive as ever, and Penn is somewhere underneath it, digesting his new reality.

Knight kills the engine and gestures his chin to the entrance of my house. A Tuscan-style mansion with eight bedrooms, it has a two-story foyer, a wine cellar, a ballet studio, and a pool that looks like it bleeds into the cliff of the mountain in our in a gated community called El Dorado. My dad is in investments, and my mom... well, she invested in bagging the right man, I guess.

Her former high school student. But that's a story for later.

Knight helps me to my door. He shoves his hand into my crocheted purse and fishes out my keys, kicks the door open, and punches in our security code.

"You look wasted, and I look inherently guilty. Please snap out of your bullshit meltdown before we hit the second floor," he drones, throwing my arm over his shoulder and dragging me up the stairs of the darkened foyer. There's a huge black-and-white picture of my mother arabesque-ing in ballerina attire, staring ahead, her elegance casting a regal vibe on the entire house.

It's not that late, and chances are, my parents are still awake. If not, Melody will wake up when the clock hits midnight. She always sets her alarm to make sure I don't break curfew.

I don't remember Knight tucking me in bed, but he does. I'm still wearing my dress and makeup. Time doesn't move. It just stands still in the room like heavy furniture.

Penn Scully is in trouble.

Big trouble. He just lost his mom and is about to be homeless. Just a few miles away, I'm tucked in my imported queen-size bed with designer Egyptian sheets wrapped around me and an entire aquarium wall filled with pink champagne staring back at me.

My actions are what got him into trouble.

If it weren't for me, he'd still have his sister around. Maybe his mom wouldn't have gotten addicted to crack or whatever. I squeeze my eyes shut and resist the urge to cry. He gave me the rarest thing in the world, and I gave him heartache. His mom died on his birthday. There's some relief in this pain I'm feeling. It reminds me that despite my bitchy ways, I'm still capable of hurting for someone else.

The sound of bare feet padding across the hallway attacks my ears. I recognize Mel's quiet pace and graceful movements. My door creaks open, and she tiptoes her way in. Normally, I pretend to be asleep to avoid conversation. I stopped calling her Mom and started calling her Mel shortly after Via disappeared, but I don't even remember why. We've been growing apart since, and talking to each other one-on-one is kind of torture. But right now, I don't know if I can pretend to be asleep.

Melody leans over and presses a kiss to my forehead, a gesture she has repeated every night since the day I was born. Lately, she's been hovering over my face an extra second to smell my breath for alcohol. I'm sober tonight, though I wish I wasn't.

"Good night, Lovebug. Did you have a good time at the movies?"

I momentarily forget the lie I told her before I left the house tonight.

I clear my throat, meaning to say yes, but the truth claws out like a scream.

"I saw Penn Scully."

Her body stiffens, then she sinks down to sit on the edge of my bed. She is trying to school her expression, but her lower lip quivers, and I see it even in the dark.

"How…how is he?"

"His mom died today."

I'm shocked at my own words. I haven't spoken about him…ever. No one knows what happened with Via and him. I never came clean. When Melody pressed me about it, I vehemently denied knowing anything. And I guess, in a sense, I convinced myself it didn't really happen. Until tonight.

She cups her mouth, looks down, and her shoulders begin to shudder. I scoot to a sitting position, pressing my back against my upholstered white satin headboard.

"It's his birthday," she says.

But of course, she remembers Via's birthday.

"He fought tonight."

She looks up at me. There's so much agony in those pupils.

"At Peet's?"

"The snake pit." I roll my eyes. "Yeah."

"Is he okay?" She doesn't even scold me for going there.

"I don't know. He's not exactly my crowd," I quip. I trust Vaughn not to walk away from Penn unless he's sure he's okay. *Physically* okay. Vaughn doesn't do feelings. And Blythe? Even if he shows signs of wanting to talk about it, he'll never make it. She'll sit on his face before Scully can tell her how he feels.

"What happened to his mom?" Mel asks.

"They said overdose." I fling my hair to one shoulder and start braiding it.

Her nostrils flare, but her mouth barely moves as she speaks. "That's horrible."

Isn't Scully supposed to be loaded? Rich people usually don't die from drugs. They go hug trees in fancy rehab centers in Palm Springs and come back thirty pounds heavier and thirty K poorer. Via was supposed to be swimming in it. I always thought Penn wore shitty clothes in the same way Vaughn does—to show the world he doesn't give a crap about money.

"Anyway, I just thought you should know since you were so close to Via."

Even after all these years, it still feels like death to say her name.

Melody stands and looks around my room, wanting to find something specific. Maybe she is looking for Penn. Picking up strays is not my forte. Luna, my neighbor, is the one who usually saves the injured birds, frogs, cats, stray dogs, and there was even a deer once. If someone were willing to smuggle Penn through a bedroom window, it'd be her. Knowing my luck, he'd end up falling in love with her too.

"Are you, like, going to talk to him or whatever?" I ask. My heart is beating superfast in my chest. Penn knows what I did. He could tell her, and she would hate me. She might never admit it, but she would. Hell, maybe she already does. When was the last time we talked? *Really* talked like this?

Mom halts at my threshold, clutching the doorframe, her head bowed down. "I'll do what I should have done when Via was around."

———

I wake up late the next morning with the feeling of an impending calamity scratching at my skin with its pointy claws. Jumping out of bed, I race downstairs to get a glass of water. When I pass my parents' bedroom door on the way back upstairs, I hear them whisper-shouting.

My parents are insanely in love, sometimes to the point of gross. Nothing's more embarrassing than having your folks hit second base on the bleachers while they cheer you on during a pep rally. More so when your father used to be a student at All Saints High, and your mom taught his senior English lit class.

I know whatever they're talking about is serious, so of course, I press my ear to their door without even considering giving them their privacy because—*hello*, I'm me.

"Just tell me why?" Mel growls.

"Because I was a teenage boy once, so I know firsthand how much I don't want one under my goddamn roof, especially with two teenage *girls* around."

"He'll behave."

"Like the way he behaved last night, busting Vaughn's face at the snake pit? Nah, I think I'm good. Vic gave me the rundown."

Vicious is Vaughn's dad and the deadliest mofo in the neighborhood. I crushed on him when I was five. Baron "Vicious" Spencer is still a hottie, so #SorryNotSorry.

I have no idea what they're talking about. Penn? Living here? Why?

"Jackie Chan Junior was hardly the victim here. Besides, you fought at his age too," Mom points out.

"*Exactly*, Mel. I wouldn't want teenage me anywhere near my daughters. Not in the same house, and frankly, not even on the same continent. This kid ought to have a family somewhere. Where's his sister? We'll buy him a plane ticket. Business class. I'll throw in private school tuition if you just get that idea out of your pretty head."

"We've been anonymously covering his football costs for years, Jaime. I've even gone as far as talking to his stepdad once and trying to open a line of communication. He doesn't need money. He needs love and people who care about him. If such people existed, he wouldn't be in this situation in the first place. I got off the phone with his stepdad a few minutes ago."

"Christ," Daddy mumbles.

"Guess what? The man is not even coherent, and Penn's things are already packed."

What in the name of the Holy Spirit and Kylie Jenner's Botox fairy is happening? I thought Penn was rich? Why would he need my parents to pay for his football? And why does it sound like Melody wants him to move in with us? I clutch my glass of water harder.

"If he touches Daria..." He doesn't need to complete the sentence. There's a baseball bat in the basement that he named *The Kissing Boot*. He said he'd use it to beat the asses of guys who tried to kiss Bailey and me.

"There's too much at stake. Besides, just because they're the same age doesn't mean they are going to sleep with each other. I've never met two people more different."

Silence. I know Mel won, but I'm not sure what it means. I think I just got myself into deep shit without even realizing what I was doing. Penn Scully can't move here because we'll kill each other before he walks through the door.

Who am I kidding? He'll be the one doing the killing.

"Nothing will happen," Mel repeats. "But we need to contact a family lawyer first thing tomorrow morning. I just got his file from Jim Levin, his counselor. He's no longer a minor, but there's still paperwork."

Bitch is not wasting any time pulling strings and making things happen. I bet she bought us all matching Christmas sweaters and is already planning to take the annual photo with her adopted hot child hugging his new sisters and a Labrador puppy on the family couch.

"I'll text Vic right now. Fucker probably has half a dozen on retainer with the number of enemies he's made in his extended family alone." Daddy sighs.

The glass slips from my hand, almost in slow motion, and I watch it crash right atop of my foot. I fight the scream wrestling out of my mouth as it crushes my bones, my foot softening the loud thud, and watch the water splash onto the carpet and the glass rolling off my toes.

I bite my lip so hard, the metallic taste of blood fills every corner of my mouth. Tears block my vision, and they help with keeping the scream at bay.

"Did you hear something?" Dad asks behind their door.

"It's probably nothing," Mel retorts.

Yup, I think. *That would be me.*

CHAPTER TWO
PENN

While you were worried about me
I fucked your friend from cheer.
She gave me a BJ and a beer.
I still hate you, make no mistake
And would love nothing more than to see your
pretty neck break.

I kick the small pile of cigarette butts aside and light a new one.

Technically, I was supposed to quit smoking by the beginning of senior year. Coach Higgins threatened to kill me if he found out I broke that promise. But technically, I will no longer be playing football or get to lead my team as captain, seeing as I have nowhere to live—not even a car—so school is definitely not a top priority right now. Getting a full-time job, on the other hand, is. Now it's just a matter of finding out which bridge I can crash under until I scrape together enough to pay for a motel.

Happy fucking birthday to me.

The thing about living on the wrong side of the tracks is that your friends live there too, and they all have a good excuse why they can't take you in. They're too poor, their places are too small, or their stepdads are also dicks. Boo-fucking-hoo. Still beats my current situation as I sit on a stair leading to Rhett's front porch with my duffel bag, in which he packed all my worldly possessions.

I shove my bag to the side. Light as a feather.

I let the lit cigarette dangle between my lips as I scroll through the contacts on my phone. Glass half-full: I'm so worried about where I'll sleep tonight, I don't even feel my swollen face, cut lip, most likely fractured rib, and growling stomach.

It's the little things in life and so forth.

Crashing at the Ortiz girl's place again tonight is a big, fat no. For one thing, her parents are coming back from their Caribbean vacation. For another, sleeping my way to a roof over my head is bullshit. Not the actual fucking part, obviously. Just the feeling like a whore portion.

I'm just about to hit the call button on Kannon's name—his parents have a backyard shed—when a brand-new Range Rover rolls to the curb and stops in front of me. I don't lift my head. It's probably Rhett's boss collecting drug money. I hear the driver's door open, and five seconds later, a woman in a floral sundress and mud-colored hair is standing above me, staring at me through huge sunglasses. The kind that makes chicks look like flies.

"Can I help you?" I squint up, billowing a cloud of smoke directly in her face just to be a little fuck. It's high time I justify the pet name Rhett gave me.

"Unlikely, but I can help *you*. Grab your things. You're coming with me." She takes her sunglasses off and looks at me as if she's been waiting for this moment her entire life or something.

I slant my head, gliding my eyes along her body. What the fuck is her deal? I probably ask it out loud because she actually answers.

"We met once. My name is Melody Followhill. I was your sister's ballet teacher. My daughter told me your mother passed away yesterday."

She then tells me that she is sorry for my loss. That she understands it seems out of left field, but she always loved my twin like she was her own kid, blah, blah, blah. Bottom line: she lost Via, and she doesn't want another Scully kid to fall through the cracks.

What a fucking saint. Mother Teresa—right behind you.

A lot of things are going through my head. The first one being I don't need her pity. The second one is that, technically, I *do*. The third one is I hate her daughter and taking anything from her family would feel a lot like selling my soul to the devil. The fourth is living under *no* roof is going to suck even more ass than sharing a house with Satan. Fighting shit is my MO right now. It's in my system. I trust adults just a little less than I trust a drunken, crystal meth-using gambler. When given an offer or opportunity, I always look for the minefields. This woman can't blaze into my life with her expensive ride and save my ass without expecting something.

"Mrs. Followhill, have your children ever gone missing at the mall or in a park?" I call her Mrs. Followhill because if I inherited one thing from my runaway crazy-ass grandma, it's good manners.

"Of course."

"How long did it take you to find them?"

She pauses before she answers because she knows where this is going. I lift a questioning eyebrow.

"Twenty-five minutes," she admits. "The worst half hour of my life."

"Then it suffices to say you didn't love my sister like she was your own. She's been missing for nearly four years now, and your ass showed up only two minutes ago, making grand announcements like a presidential candidate."

"Four years." She looks around her, drinking in the torn chain-link fences, cracked concrete, and boarded windows. "You still don't know where she is?"

After the truancy officer poked Mom, Rhett finally came up with a story about Via moving in with my dad. It's an interesting angle, considering no one knows where he is, least of all Via. Rhett went as far as faking a shit-ton of paperwork. Then he proceeded to beat my semi-unconscious mother for recklessly giving birth to kids she had no intention of raising. "As motherly as a stray cat," he spat in her face while tromping his way out the door. The fact was, Via disappeared with zero repercussions from the system, thanks to Mrs. Followhill's daughter. *And me.*

"Take a wild guess." I flash her a sardonic smile.

She squares her shoulders, narrowing her eyes at me. "All right. Get up, Penn."

"Nah, I'm good."

"You're anything but." She shoves her outreached hand in my face. "Stand up."

I laugh at that because I can. Because I'm eighteen years old and no one but a complete stranger wants to claim my ass. Because my mother died yesterday of an overdose (I'll give her one thing— perfect timing), yet I feel absolutely nothing. She hasn't been present in my life for as long as I can remember. Over the past two years, we've barely exchanged six sentences in total. Rhett didn't shed a tear. Just told me to pack my two and a half belongings and leave, adding that he hadn't screwed her in a year, and I should be grateful he let me stay beyond her expiration date.

"Penn, you need to come with me." Melody is snapping her fingers in my face now. I blanked. Guess that happens when you don't sleep for two nights straight.

"I do, huh?" I don't know why I'm smiling. I'm in so much shit even her manicured hand can't pull me out of it. "Remind me why?"

"The alternative is couch surfing and slipping at school. By the way, today is the first day of class. If everything were fine, you'd be there. And you're officially not the state's problem. Even if you do find temporary places to stay, you'll move around constantly, which will make it difficult to practice or even get a job. You will have no funds to sustain your football career—that is, if you move somewhere where they *have* a football team, and if they'll even let you try out for a position. Not to mention, according to your file, you're the team captain. Why lose your position? You're going to get drafted to a D1 college if you keep it up. Complete your senior year while staying with us, and we'll go our separate ways if that's what you want. But at least give yourself the chance to succeed. Don't turn this opportunity down because of your pride."

She knows a lot about my life, but it doesn't surprise me. Being a kid from around here, your file gets tossed around like beer pong.

"You and your sister both have more athletic talent in your pinkies than I've ever seen," she adds.

"So, what, I'm going to live at your place, and we're going to play fucking house for a year?" I crack my knuckles.

"We're not going to play anything. We *are* a family. And you *are* welcome into it."

"Put a lid on it, ma'am. You sound like a *This Is Us* episode."

I should stop. That much I know. I'm throwing away a golden opportunity. My stupid ego will make sure I end up without a scholarship *and* a roof, but I'm not ready to cave in yet. I have nothing against Melody Followhill. Her daughter, on the other hand, is a different story.

"We'll make it work." She offers me her hand again. I don't take it. *Again.*

She nudges her hand an inch closer to my face.

"Whatever your reservations are, we can work them out. I'd like to help you find your sister."

My sister is dead, I'm tempted to say, but hell if I need another dose of pity. It's only an assumption but an educated one. No way Via is alive and hasn't sent me a letter, or a text, or picked up the goddamn phone in four years.

"Good luck with that."

"I don't need luck. I have money."

I inspect her to see if she is for real. She doesn't make any apologies for being rich. I see where her daughter got the superiority complex. It stinks on Mrs. Followhill, but it positively reeks on her baby girl.

"Get your duffel bag," she commands.

When I stay put, she grabs it herself and heads to her Rover. After tossing it in her back seat, she throws the passenger door open.

"Fine. Stay here. You're not getting your things back. You officially own nothing."

I finally get up and get in, not looking back at Rhett's house. My hand hovers over the leather seats, not touching.

Fuck.

"You'll kick me out in an hour," I comment dryly.

"Try me, Scully."

I dig my fingernails into the leather seats, fascinated with how beautiful the imperfect indents of my nails look on them. When she starts the engine, I light a cigarette and roll the window down.

One last chance to change your mind, lady.

"Those cigarettes are going to kill you." She pushes her sunglasses up her nose and raises her chin. She's bold, this one.

"Good. The fuck are they waiting for?"

I don't know what I'm expecting. A lecture, a scowl. A punishment? Maybe some yelling. It's been a while since I've been parented.

But what I see in my periphery amuses me. A smile tugs at her lips.

"You have sass. You and my daughter, Daria, will get along just fine."

She has no idea how wrong she is, but she sure is about to find out.

CHAPTER THREE
DARIA

You poured misery into me
Let it simmer for a while
And now it is time for you to taste
What you've created.

I slide my journal on the edge of Principal Prichard's desk and step back. He doesn't raise his head from the documents he is reading, a frown stamped on his face. I rub my sweaty palms along my skirt. He licks his forefinger and flips a page in the brochure he's reading. It's a grown-up quirk that reminds me he is twenty years my senior.

That what we're doing is wrong.

I wrote my first ever entry in my little black book the day we did what we did to Via. The day I realized I wasn't just a mischievous kid, I was a mean girl. Since then, the notebook has become jam-packed with entries.

I take it with me everywhere, like a dark cloud over my sunshine hair, and at night, I sleep with it under my pillow. It harbors my not-so-Instagram-worthy moments. Things only Principal Prichard and I know. How I cut Esme's Disney-princess hair when she was asleep when we were fifteen at a sleepover. How I had my mom adopt the stray cat Luna wanted just to make her jealous.

How I ruined Via's life.

"Back so soon?" His tone is ruthlessly bored. It anchors me to the ground, reminding me of how little and unworthy I am.

Instead of answering, I turn around and lock his door. Behind my back, I hear the soft thud of his pen hitting the document and know he is setting his reading glasses down where the pages meet because I've seen this movie a thousand times before.

A chill runs down my spine.

Principal Prichard is attractive in the way powerful men usually are. In a symmetrical, clinical way. His hair is velvet black—almost bluish—and his nose is as sharp as a knife. A constant scowl knots his forehead, reminding me of Professor Snape, and although he is not particularly tall or muscular, he is slender and well-dressed enough to pull off the James Bond look.

Prichard and I, we go back. Our first encounter occurred a few days after Via disappeared, when I was still in middle school. Our counselor was on her honeymoon, so when I broke down in tears, my teacher directed me to the principal's office. Prichard was attentive and nice and *young*. He gave me tissues and water and a free pass from PE on cardio day.

I told him I made a terrible mistake and I didn't know how to tell my mom. When he asked me what happened, I handed him my journal and twiddled my thumbs as he read it. Confessing it aloud would have made it too real.

After he read my first entry, he put the notebook down.

"Do your parents punish you, Daria?"

"No," I said honestly. What did that have to do with Via? She was missing, and it was all because of me. I wanted to shout it from the rooftops and take it to my grave in the same breath. I was hoping he'd push me in the right direction.

"Do you have any house rules?" He drummed his fingers on his desk.

I guessed I couldn't puke in my sister's shoes, but nothing was written or anything. I blinked at him, confused.

"No."

"I think what you need more than anything else"—he stopped drumming, leaning forward—"is to be disciplined."

That's how our story began. *The Years of Daria and Principal Prichard.* When I moved to All Saints High, he moved with me. For him, it was a promotion. For me, it was a relief. Principal Prichard—dubbed Prince Preach at All Saints for his regal handsomeness—is the person I turn to for my atonements.

Every time I feel guilty, he makes me pay, and the pain goes away.

"Turn around and face me." His metallic voice rolls down my spine now.

I do.

"On your knees."

I lower myself.

"Bend your head and say it."

"I am Daria Followhill, and this is my church. You are my priest, and to you, I confess all my sins and atone for them."

After my visit to the principal's office, I splash cold water on my face in the bathroom and wonder what my chances are of looking like nothing happened.

Finding out I was assigned to the class my mother taught at All Saints High was the whole reason I ran to him in the first place. It creeps me out that I wouldn't exist if my parents hadn't met in this place. And it makes my skin crawl that everyone around me can practically imagine my parents getting it on over Miss Linde's desk.

I don't remember when I started nurturing the rumors about Principal Prichard and me, but I sure remember why.

"Aren't you the result of a sordid affair between a student and a teacher? Your dad knocked your mom up when he was a senior, and his mom forced him to marry her?"

A senior girl who looked like Regina George cornered me in the restrooms on the first day of my freshman year. She was armed with three other goons who looked like carbon copies of the least good-looking Kmart catalog model.

One of them shoved me against the wall.

"Bitch, I don't care who you think you are. Here, you're just an accident with a skirt, and if you're gonna walk these halls thinking you're all that, we'll make sure everyone knows it," she spat out.

I tilted my chin up, wiping the traces of her saliva from my face.

"My parents got married before I was conceived. My grandma actually hated the idea of my mom and dad being together. In fact, she still does, and we're not close with her. I only see her once a year even though we live in the same town. I'm telling you this not because I think you care, but because if you're going to be a bitch, better not be a dumb one. When talking shit, at least be factual. Not that it's going to help you. I came here to run this place, and guess what? You're already feeling threatened."

That earned me a slap in the face. I smiled, keeping my tears at bay. I got it—I was about to take their place. I was going to make the cheer team whether they liked it or not, because even though I was a crappy ballerina, I was a damn good dancer. I would date their boyfriends, wear their dresses better, and drive a fancier car. No one likes to come face to face with their 2.0 version. It's always fancier and includes all the upgrades.

"Better not get comfortable, Followhill. We're after your ass." The brunette spat phlegm onto my powder-pink lace-up heels.

I realized early on that I needed armor against my parents' reputation.

The only way I could protect myself from the fire was by creating a bigger blaze. If they thought I was untouchable, they'd fear me instead of taunt me. If they thought the hard-nosed principal had my back—or had me on my back, for that matter—I would not be messed with. So I nurtured the rumors, made them grow, gave them wings, and let them fly, like butterflies from a mason jar.

I'm smart, cunning, and understated. I don't actually tell anyone we're dating. I just keep going to Principal Prichard's office, and he always opens the door because whatever we are, he likes it.

He likes it a whole freaking lot.

Halfway through my journey down the hallway, I decide to cut myself some slack and ditch my last two periods. They're electives anyway. Fifteen minutes later, I park my cherry-red convertible BMW by the patio fountain in front of my house and head straight upstairs to the shower. I need to wash my hair and look presentable for dinner, during which I will feign shock when my parents tell me that Penn will be staying with us. If Mom can even convince him to live under the same roof as me. Then I'll corner the bastard and lay down the rules. Guilty or not, I run this show. Mom's Rover is nowhere in sight, which means the house is empty. Tiptoeing in, I confirm the coast is clear, then head to the bathroom. I dump my white miniskirt on the floor and let my baby-blue cropped shirt follow suit. My phone lights up on the marble counter.

Blythe:	Ditching school on the first day? #savage
Gus:	Nice of you to stand up for the Scully kid. Wanna slum it up with a hood rat? How about try one who's not TAKEN.
Esme:	Dude, your thighs look hella thick in that skirt. I know you're a base, but there's a limit. Abort mission or abort tacos. Your pick. 😏

The hot water soothes the past twenty-four hours as it hits my body from four different showerheads. I tilt my head back, close my eyes, and moan. I can handle Penn. I'm the goddamn queen of All Saints High, and he's just another random from Las Juntas. Whatever happened between us is water under the bridge.

The kind I can't let drown me.

I step out of the shower to stand on the bathroom rug. I left my pink towel on the floor by the counter next to the door yesterday. I tramp toward it, dripping water, as the door swings open.

"Bailey!" I gasp, but instead of meeting my baby sister's big blue eyes and tiny frame, Penn is standing in front of me, up close. His body fills the doorframe effortlessly, and he looks like a venomous kiss. Dark and sinful and irresistible. His jeans ride low on his hips, and a wallet chain hangs from his right pocket. His sleeveless black tank top has a hole where his heart is because, *of course*, he's an edgy asshole like Vaughn, and his arms are big, tan, and full of veins and muscle. His cuts are purple against his moss-hued eyes. And those greens are descending my body like a whip, potentially deadly, but for now, tender. I resist the urge to flinch, knowing the painful stroke is about to hit me. He drinks it all in.

My breasts.

My stomach.

My thighs.

And that private place between them that clenches hard against nothing right now.

A slow smirk tugs at his cracked, heart-shaped lips. I cover my necklace—of all things—more embarrassed about it than anything else.

"Oh my freaking Marx. Penn. Get the hell out!"

It's the first time I call him by his name. Officially, I'm not supposed to know it. His face is vacant. He is gripping the door handle, his knuckles ghostly white against his tan skin.

He picks up the pink towel, throwing it at me, and I catch it with shaky fingers, wrapping it firmly around my body and tucking the sea glass into it.

"Like what you see?" I flip my wet hair. My pride is beyond wounded. He just saw me completely naked and didn't even acknowledge me. All my guilt and good intentions wash away and are replaced with a weird desperation to show him that he's a peasant and I'm a queen.

"*Hate*," he corrects, rubbing his thumb over his lower lip. "I hate what I see and plan on seeing very little of it. You're Daria, I assume."

He is still not making a move to get out. This guy is unreal. I'm so mad, I could punch him in the face. Maybe I should. He won't hit me back. And it would hurt him like hell since he's already beaten to a pulp.

"Don't pretend we haven't met." I reach for my brush and comb my golden locks in front of the mirror. Might as well. Asshole's not going anywhere.

"We have, but we never exchanged names, just fluids," he barbs, "which begs the question: How the fuck do you know mine?"

"What fluids? You were too chicken to seal the deal," I purr, wondering if he really doesn't know my name. We're both pretty big deals at our schools.

I think about the sea glass necklace as I watch my face turning scarlet in the mirror. Am I an idiot for taking what he gave me, turning it into jewelry, and making it my talisman? The sea glass is a functioning organ of mine now. It reminds me that good people exist.

Only, I don't know if Penn is that good anymore.

I think I may have ruined him.

Watching him in the steamed mirror, I lean against the vanity. I can tell when a guy is checking me out, and he's not doing that. He's more like assessing the damage he wants to inflict on me. I know his hatred for me runs deep because when he talks to me, every word is a blade, causing a shiver to roll down my spine. Instead of ending in my toes, though, it explodes between my legs.

"This ain't shooting the shit, Daria. You stay out of my way; I'll stay out of yours."

"What are you doing here anyway?" I mumble. "Shouldn't you be at school? And don't tell me what to do. You're nothing but an unwelcome guest here." I snort out a laugh.

"I ditched, like you." He runs his eyes over me as if I'm nothing.

Air. "And agreed on my guest status. I'm a reluctant one, at best. But the offer was there, and I'd be stupid not to accept it. I see the way you look at me. Oh, Skull Eyes…" He throws the nickname in my face as though the past few years didn't happen. Then he takes a step toward me, his devious grin back in full force. "This round, I'm going to fucking destroy you."

I turn to him fully, dumbfounded. I'm clutching the edge of the marble sink with one hand, not sure how or when the tables turned. He's talking like he's the master of the manor and I'm a pawn at his mercy. I narrow my eyes, trying to crack his façade, but alas, it remains tough as steel. Penn Scully actually believes he owns me. *Me*. Daria Followhill. The most popular girl at All Saints High. I need to try to remind myself that his mother just died. That he is acting out. That this morning, he thought he was homeless.

"I don't want you transferring to my school," I hiss out. Melody would gladly file a transfer request, and Principal Prichard would salivate over the chance to snatch him up for our football team.

"That won't be a problem. You guys suck so much ass, you have shit breath."

"Still smells better than poverty. You're poor, right? Your sister was just bullshitting about being rich."

When someone hits me with a stick, I run over them with a tank. I'm so mean to him, I want to throw up. I hate this part of being me, the striking-harder-at-all-costs part.

"Just to make things clear"—I put the brush down, batting my lashes—"you're not my stepsibling, foster brother, or a part of the family. You're a stray dog, last of the litter, most unlikely to be adopted, and a charity case."

Penn takes a step toward me, and my heart is fighting its way out of my rib cage. The closer he gets, the more I realize that my heart might succeed. Penn's eyes remind me of a snake. Mesmerizing but inhuman altogether. They weren't like that before.

His scent messes with my head. I want to reach out and caress

his face. Kiss his wounds better. Beg for forgiveness. Curse him.
Push him away. Cry on his shoulder for what we've done. For how it
ended. For what we became afterward. Because I'm full of crap, and
he is totally empty.

We ruined ourselves the day of our kiss.

When Penn looks down at me, time stops. It feels like the world
is losing gravity, floating into a bottomless depth in space, when he
clasps my chin with his thumb and finger to lift my head. I can't
breathe. I'm not sure I want to either. My towel drops to the floor
with a thud even though I secured it over my chest, and I realize
that he tugged at it intentionally. I'm naked—my body, my soul, my
heart. All my walls are down. Somewhere in my head, a red alarm
blasts, and my inhibitions are arming themselves, ready to fight back.
I'm trying to decode his expression. He is amused, irritated, and…
playful? The mixture of emotions doesn't make sense.

"Mess with me, Followhill, and I will ruin you."

"Not if I ruin you first." I can't hide the lust in my tone.

A beat pulses between us.

"Actually, you're right. I do like what I see. Some of it, anyway."
His fingers slip around to the back of my neck, and my eyes flutter
shut. My brain is screaming at me to open them.

This is a hoax, the alarm screeches. *He hates you.*

"I definitely like what I see." His breath is sweet and hot. It
caresses the tip of my earlobe, and a shudder ripples through me. My
nipples pucker so hard, even the faintest brush of air makes me drip
between the legs. This could go in so many directions, and I have no
control over any of them.

His mouth crashes against mine, and I yelp into his open lips
just when his tongue invades me. He is swallowing me whole, and
I'm so frustrated with my sick attraction to him. I bite his bruised
lower lip and feel his blood gushing out, warm and coppery. My
hands clutch the fabric of his top, clawing to find the hole and fill it
with my greedy fingers. He grabs the back of my neck and clutches

like a lion taming his lioness as he deepens our kiss. There's nothing shy or experimental or promising about our second kiss. We're not the same kids. Not the same hopeful human beings. Our teeth clash, but we don't laugh it off or stop. At the same time, it feels like we've never moved from that spot next to the trash can. We're hungrier, and wiser, and angrier.

I've never been kissed this way before.

Not by him. Not by anyone.

His mouth disconnects from mine, and it takes me a few seconds to register what's happening.

"The rarest thing in the world should not be given to a basic bitch. I hope you didn't save me your firsts because I have no interest in taking them," he whispers into my ear, and my eyes snap open. Penn shoves something into his back pocket, then steps back. He turns toward the door, and before I have time to tell him to go screw himself or drop dead, he turns his head over his shoulder.

Those snake eyes, they speak to me.

They tell me that he doesn't want to be my friend.

That he is fully prepared to be my enemy.

"Nice seeing you again, *sis*." He slams the door in my face.

My hand jumps instinctively to my sea glass necklace, preparing to clutch it in shock.

It's gone.

Like all families, mine has a mind-numbing routine that rarely changes and includes me very sparsely.

When Melody picks up Bailey from school every day, they go straight to ballet, and Dad comes home from work around six. That means I have at least four more hours to avoid the jerk living under my roof, and I'm starving, thirsty, and constantly reaching out to play with the necklace before realizing it's not there anymore.

I pace my room, text Blythe and Esme, then decide to write an entry in my little black book.

Entry #1,298:

Sin: *Snuck into Penn's room when I heard the bastard taking a shower and stole his pencil. (Who uses pencils anymore? Is he five?) Swirled the eraser around my clit and masturbated with it. Put it back in his pencil bag.*
Reason: *Jerk walked in on me naked. On purpose. And I didn't hate it. At all.*

Sometime after exchanging texts with my friends, I crash in front of *Teen Mom*. I wake up to a gentle knock on my door, the colors from the TV dancing over my bedroom walls.

"Lovebug, dinner's almost ready," Mel singsongs from the other side. I fling an arm over my eyes. I don't want to face him. I especially don't want to face him after he saw me naked and kissed me and made my nipples hard and then told me he doesn't want anything to do with me.

"Coming," I yell. I change into supershort plaid shorts and a tank top. I'm going for the unaffected-by-your-bullshit look with a touch of just-because-we-kissed-doesn't-mean-I-want-you-loser.

Mel and Bailey are in the kitchen. Bailey is chopping vegetables, and my mother is marinating the chicken breasts. They're talking ballet. I ignore the sting that accompanies being an outsider and plop on a stool by the kitchen island. It's all cream-colored wood with dark brown granite counters. I pluck a cherry tomato from the salad bowl and pop it into my mouth.

"Hey, Bails, how was school?"

"Bumpin'. I have a new lab teacher, and she says I can use it after school under her supervision." My sister flashes her braces with a smile, each band a different color, like the LGBTQ+ flag. One day, she'll be a rose in full bloom, but for now, she is content being a wallflower. Her petals are already beginning to open, and I need to come to terms with that.

"How was yours?" she asks.

I think about Principal Prichard and my latest visit to his office. About my new, humiliating classroom.

About the text messages burning my cell phone.

"Amazeballs." I flash a white-toothed, straight smile. My eyes are already drifting. I try to find Penn around the open floor plan.

"Can you be a doll and take this to your dad? He's on the patio." Mel doesn't lift her head from the chicken.

I take the platter of marinated chicken from her hands and pad barefoot toward the patio, ignoring the heat spreading through my cheeks. My dad and Penn are standing over the grill, and I chuckle bitterly. She didn't even give me a heads-up that he was here. My dad uses the tongs to flip the steaks. Each of them is holding a bottle of beer, and they seem to share an easy conversation.

Dad is drinking beer with him? *Great.* Penn is only eighteen, but it doesn't surprise me. My parents sometimes let me sip wine at family dinners. They firmly believe that if you make teenagers feel responsible about booze, they won't go around getting shitfaced when they finally get their hands on alcohol. I never get drunk at parties. Sobriety equals a certain amount of boredom, which is necessary to make sure my game face remains intact.

I slide the glass door open and stop to watch them.

"I don't make a habit of trusting boys with busted knuckles around my daughters, but my wife loves to fix things, and since I'm a past project of hers, I thought it would be fair to pay it forward," my dad drawls.

Penn stares at him with guarded curiosity. "I appreciate your help, sir, but I don't need fixing. I ain't broken."

"You've been through a lot," Dad says, pressing his point. "It's okay not to have your shit together at eighteen."

"Don't worry about my shit," Penn retorts. "I'd appreciate if no one knows I live here. It's not my school district, and I'm the starting wide receiver at Las Juntas. My scholarship's on the line here."

"Graduating from a prestigious high school like All Saints would look better on your college application."

"It's too late to transfer. I'm captain of the rival team. There's no way I'd fit in at All Saints High. Besides, All Saints already has a wide receiver, even though he's a total prick," Penn says point-blank.

A giggle tickles at the back of my throat, but I swallow it down. They still don't know I'm here. I think.

"Point is, you live under my roof, you do not touch my daughters. Don't try me, boy. I have ties older than you. Word to the wise? These tongs"—Dad snaps them in Penn's face while the latter taps an unlit cigarette over his thigh—"they're good for more than just flipping steaks, kiddo."

"No offense, sir, but one of your daughters is entirely too young for me, and the other is entirely too Daria for me." Penn's voice is like black lace wrapping around my throat. I don't think my dad notices the dangerous tilt in his tenor, but I do. That's how I know that while my father is still oblivious to my presence, Penn isn't. Those words are meant for me to hear.

"What does that mean?" Dad growls.

"I think you know exactly what it means."

With that, Penn spins in place and gives me a close-lipped smirk. *Those eyes saw me naked. Those lips were on mine this afternoon. Then they told me to get lost.*

I remember Via was gorgeous, which bothered me, of course, but I don't remember her being *that* pretty. No guy has ever affected me like him. Ever. Even if I take all my encounters with hot boys and combine them, it still doesn't match the feel of just one measly look from Penn. He grew up from a dirty duckling to a dark swan.

"Chicken," Penn hisses, his lips maneuvering into a smile that is too calculated for a teenager. He tosses the unlit cigarette into a nearby trash can, his eyes still on mine. Where did he learn to be so sophisticated?

"Excuse me?" I arch a threatening eyebrow.

"Thanks for the chicken, *sis*." He walks over with the beer in his hand, snatching the tray of marinated chicken from me. He is taunting me with this sister BS. I bite my inner cheek because Dad's here, and his big thing is thinking before acting.

"No problem. Anything else I can do for you?" I smile sweetly.

"I think you've done *quite* enough," Penn says.

I look over at Dad's back, and his shoulders are shaking with laughter. I think he's relieved we're not flirting.

"I see you've already met." He stacks the steaks onto a plate.

"Oh, yeah," I retort. "Penn has seen quite a bit of me."

At dinner, we all sit at the table and eat as though the world is not ending. As if Penn is a legitimate part of our family. I push my food around. Mom and Dad introduce Penn as a family friend to Bailey and me, and I snort while she shakes his hand over the salads and crystal diamond water pitchers. Tasmanian rain, if you must know. Expensive and pretentious, just like us.

Penn is open and kind, even though he talks like a boy from the hood. His speech is lazy and confident and mesmerizing. He makes a point of ignoring me. His eyes and cheeks are still a nice shade of purple, but I can tell that in a few days, the bruises will fade and then his stunning immortal-god face will haunt me on a daily basis. No one talks about the unfortunate state of his body or why he is here until Bailey raises her head from her plate.

"What happened to your face?" She covers her mouth to hide her braces as she speaks.

"Bailey," Mom scolds at the same time Dad groans and shakes his head. Penn flashes her an easy smile. I stare at him, seeing what

I don't want to see. That when he's not dealing with me, he's not a douchebag.

"I punched a door." He throws a brussels sprout into his mouth, chewing.

"You did?" Bailey's eyes widen as they assess his knuckles.

"Swung right back and punched me harder."

"It looks awful." Mel states the freaking obvious, pushing a forkful of sautéed spinach into her mouth.

"You should see the door." Penn leans over to catch Bailey's gaze.

Then everyone but me bursts out laughing, and I can practically hear the crack of the ice as it breaks around the table. The only problem is, there are two icebergs. They're on one, and I'm drifting away on another, far away from them.

Penn clears his throat, running a hand through his hair. "I didn't have the best summer, and I needed an outlet. The door turned out to be…tougher than I thought, but it led me here."

I roll my eyes, stabbing a piece of chicken and dragging it in white sauce.

"So since we're addressing the subject," Mel says, carefully placing her utensils on her plate, "Daria, Bailey, Penn's been going through some dark moments recently. We thought it would be a good idea to have him here during his senior year before he goes off to college."

"*His* senior year? It's my senior year! And don't you mean *if* he goes to college?" I add, throwing all caution to the wind. He's been horrible to me, so why shouldn't I be horrible to him? I get that I hurt him. That we both did something terrible four years ago. But he didn't even give me a chance to apologize or explain. All eyes—other than Penn's—snap to my face. He digs into his steak, chewing on a juicy piece.

"Based on his grades and performance on the football field, I can assure you that Penn is on his way to Notre Dame on a scholarship." Melody sends me a tight, this-is-not-how-Followhills-conduct -themselves smile. She hates it when I'm Hulky and spiteful.

"What happened?" Bailey makes a face to Penn.

"My mom passed away," he explains.

Bailey shoots her gaze to me as though I'm the one who killed her. Consequently, I want to die.

"At any rate"—Dad's eyes narrow on me—"should you girls like to voice any concerns or issues, our door is always open."

Bailey looks over at Penn, then down at her lap.

"I always wanted a big brother. Is that what you'll be?"

I choke on my water, spitting some of it onto my plate. Is she freaking kidding me? She is thirteen. Who talks like that? Bailey. Bailey talks like that. She's goodness and sunshine wrapped in a pink bow. A straight-A student and her mommy's beloved ballerina. She and Luna volunteer to clean beaches and fold secondhand clothes for charities every summer break.

Penn slides into our lives effortlessly, and no one notices how uncomfortable it makes me feel. Or how he *still* hasn't acknowledged my existence since we sat down.

He takes a sip of his water. "Are you accepting applicants?"

I roll my eyes so hard, I'm afraid they'll end up on my plate.

His smile widens behind his glass.

"Job's yours." Bailey's eyes light up. "We could go bowling!"

"We could, but we won't because it's lame," Penn deadpans.

"Totally lame." She snickers, breathless.

"But I see you're a reader." He gestures with his chin to the stack of books piled on the coffee table in the living room. Bailey is a bookworm. She loves poetry. Another reason she is my personal 2.0 version.

"There's an open mic place in San Diego where people read their poems. It's pretty rad, and they serve a sick apple pie there. We could go. Your parents can come too."

Everyone grins as though they're starring in a toothpaste commercial. No one realizes he failed to extend the invitation to me. I slam my water glass on the table. I am ignored. Maybe I'm like the boy who cried wolf—so snappy and short all the time that when I actually have a reason to be pissed, no one gives a damn.

"This is the best," Bailey says at the same time Mel jumps into practicalities.

"You don't have a car, Penn. Since you'll need to commute to San Diego every day, you're not going to argue with me about this next thing."

Penn shoots her a look I don't think I'd ever be able to get away with. Part murderous, all infuriated. "Is this the part where you're getting me a car? Because I'm not a boy toy."

"Already did." Dad shrugs, popping a piece of steak into his mouth. "It's nothing fancy, and I forgot to extend my warning about not touching my daughters to my wife too—that toy boy-toy remark almost cost you your nose."

"*Fine.* Correction: I'm not a charity case." Penn stabs his steak so hard, the dead cow is almost groaning in pain.

"Are you sure about that?" I drone, swirling the water in my glass. "Because you look and dress like one."

"*Daria,*" Mel snaps.

Bailey shakes her head at me.

I hate this. I hate *him.* And I hate that I'm showing off my fake colors, the bitchy ones, in all their insecure glory, when he's around.

Penn pretends he didn't hear me and steals a brussels sprout from Bailey's plate.

"Thank Marx." She laughs. "I hate them. Do you know you have a hole in your shirt?"

I want to tell her that it's intentional. Symbolic. Because he always has one, no matter when and where I see him or what he's wearing. Instead, I count the pepper bits on my piece of chicken.

My sister and I aren't close.

"There's a story behind it," he says.

"A good story?" she asks.

"I don't have any other types of stories."

"Let me show you your new car, son," Dad says. *Son.*

I roll my eyes to keep from crying.

Marx, this is going to be a long freaking year.

CHAPTER FOUR
DARIA

You are beautiful like a song
Ugly like a scream
But beneath your pretty bones
You're lost from deep within.
I want to dig inside the fissures of your soul
Pull out all your secrets
Dump them at your feet
Then devour your expression
For your pain shall taste so sweet.

In the morning, I find a green apple with one discolored bite taken out of it on my desk when I wake up. It sits on my open history textbook, where a passage has been highlighted, the yellow marker beside it.

The Romans brought apples with them when they invaded Britain.

I want to rip down the walls in the house and scream until I faint. I settle, however, for skipping breakfast and going straight to school. Now, in the cafeteria, I'm mostly trying to breathe regularly and survive.

"Artists aren't team players. Only a true individualist can give birth to something of their own. You need to be both the egg and the sperm to create a masterpiece." Blythe stands on a cafeteria bench, delivering a theatrical speech. Across the room sits Vaughn, the unaware subject of her lecture. Sitting all by himself, he sketches his next statue on a pad.

"Shit, Blythe, you even make sex sound sad." Knight yawns.

Vaughn doesn't eat. Like, ever. I mean, he obviously does—otherwise, he wouldn't exist—but not in front of people. He doesn't seem to do a lot of stuff other people do to exist. I think that's what makes him legendary within these walls. He never goes into the restrooms at school. He doesn't participate in PE classes. If he hangs out with a girl, you only know about it *after* he breaks up with her because the crazy bitch vandalizes his locker or desk or mansion. That's the other thing—Vaughn can hang out with perfectly sane girls and turn them into bunny boilers. But the fact Vaughn refuses to choose a table and affiliate himself with a crowd? I think that's the cherry on his popularity cake. He can sit anywhere. It's like the world is his oyster, but he doesn't do seafood.

"What do you know about artists?" Gus snorts, tossing half his egg-and-tuna sandwich at Blythe. He's sitting on the table with his feet on the bench. It's gross and unnecessary, but I'm not in the mood for an argument.

Blythe catches the sandwich and plops down with a grin, tearing apart the plastic wrap.

"I know they're good with their hands. Something you're not."

She rips a bite off the sandwich and rolls her eyes. "Hmm, so good."

Esme curls her long, raven hair over her finger, popping her gum. "Not to be impolite, but you guys bore me to death. Cole, go tell Vaughn to come here."

Busy scanning the room for Luna, Knight's neck is still craned as he answers her. "Damn." He pats the pockets of his jeans, then checks the pockets of his golden Gucci jacket. "I can't find it."

"Can't find what?" Esme blinks.

"The memo that says I start taking orders from your sorry ass."

Everyone laughs. Even I have a smile on my face.

"C'mon, Knighty. We just want to hear about Vaughn's summer in Italy." Blythe tosses her hair and bats her eyelashes.

I swear, she would flirt with the priest officiating her funeral. Bitch is unreal.

"Please, girl. Miles from the chess club could take a trip to outer space and make a historical stop on the sun, and you still wouldn't give him a minute of your time." Esme laughs. She and Blythe are best friends, and she knows how much Blythe adores Vaughn Spencer.

"Yo, Daria," Gus hollers, and my head snaps from the salad I've been abusing with my plastic fork for the past ten minutes. "You're quiet."

And you're surprisingly observant for once in your miserable life.

"Miss Linde is all up in my grill." I shrug.

It's not even a lie. Bitch hates my guts. And I loathe sitting in her class, where my parents started screwing each other. I'd ask to move, but I would have to go through the guidance counselor, and she's already trying to corner me to investigate the Principal Prichard rumor. I don't want Prichard to get in trouble. Then I have Penn, public enemy number one, living under the same roof. This year was supposed to be my last hurrah before going off to college, and it started as a disaster.

"Do you want to make yourself useful?" Gus licks his lips. Did I mention he's gross? Oh. Right. Literally a second ago.

"To you?" I give him a slow once-over, stroking my chin. "Only if it involves a huge makeover followed by a nice feast of humble pie."

Gus is a beefy, blond, all-American dudebro with a superhero jaw and wide-set, generic blue eyes, making him look like a shaved alpaca. If this were a '90s movie, he would be the villain. Come to think about it, he already is. In addition to managing the betting ring at the snake pit, he also has a strict bed 'em and dump 'em policy that landed him in hot water with some of the parents here. And while I'm a porcupine—mean when provoked—he is a kangaroo. A straight-up bully with no direction or reason. I remember when my parents took us on a trip to Australia, and we were warned about driving at night in open areas because the kangaroos jumped onto the road to scare off vehicles. That's Gus—aggressive and stupid.

The only people he's nice to are Knight, his shining quarterback hero who saves most of our games, and Vaughn, the golden-egg-laying hen who shows up at the pit every weekend ready to be jumped by three gang members and an F-22 Raptor.

People snicker at my comment. The table is full of football players and cheerleaders. Knight finally spots Luna across the room and slides out of our bench.

"See you later, assholes. It's been real. Well, other than Esme's tits." He ambles away.

Esme's mouth goes slack, and she cups her boobs, clad in a colorful D&G dress, shifting her gaze from them to him.

Luna Rexroth refuses to sit with us. One time, when Knight was away, Gus made fun of her at the table for not talking. I didn't stop him, and I still feel bad about that. She's persona non grata and isn't worth fighting over, but she still didn't deserve his wrath.

"Useful how, Gus?" Esme munches on the tip of a carrot, shifting the conversation from her fake tits, her eighteenth birthday gift from her parents, back to me.

"Word is Penn Scully's paying us a visit after school to warn us off from pulling any shenanigans ahead of the game. Last year, All Saints killed the grass in Las Juntas's field, and the broke-ass pussies didn't have anywhere to play for weeks. I figured Daria can play Judge Judy since she wants to tap it."

My heart starts pounding so hard and fast, I feel it in my toes. Behind my eyeballs.

Marx, Marx, Marx.

"Scully?" I snort. "Hmm, no thanks."

"Is that why you screamed when Vaughn knocked his ass to the ground?" Gus cocks his head.

"He was piss drunk. I was just worried about Vaughn getting in trouble."

Gus runs his pale eyes over my face, his smirk unwavering. He leans forward and taps my nose with his finger. "I don't believe you."

"Good thing I don't exist to live up to your expectations." I open an invisible mirror, giving him my middle finger. More laughter. It might look as if I'm in my element, but I'm totally flustered underneath my cute sundress and lacy black pumps.

"Prove it today at three."

"Pass, jackass. I have cheer practice. Also, a life."

"The whole point of cheer is to help the football team," Esme argues, simply to defy me. She's still butt hurt about me getting cheer captain. But the thing about Esme is she fat-shames everyone into believing they can't consume anything more than Diet Coke. Nobody wants her to be in charge of the homecoming snack menu, let alone the cheer team.

"No can do, señor douchebag." I grab an apple from his tray and take a bite before I realize what I'm doing.

"Cheer practice is at three thirty. You'll make it." Blythe munches on her lower lip. Marx, I hope teenage girls grow out of the need to form alliances with the Boys Club.

"Fine. Whatever." I stand, grabbing my red plastic tray. Sauntering out of the cafeteria, I swallow the ball of tears in my throat. I don't want to face Penn. I know it's stupid because we live together now and it's inevitable, but I hate the look on his face when his eyes land on mine. He sees past my exterior and that scares me.

The rest of the school day is a dud even though I keep my head up and my smile extra glossy. It doesn't help that Blythe and I showed up in the same Reformation dress, and all I could think was that we also share the same taste in guys.

Only Penn was never in my bed.

He kissed me just to show me that he can. Then he ripped the sea glass necklace from my throat and told me he didn't want my firsts.

My heart clenches with every *tick, tick, tick* of the clock. It's like a ticking bomb, and when it hits three, the ring of the bell explodes in my ears. Gus waits outside my class, his elbow slumped against the doorframe, his ball cap backward. He pops his gum in people's ears as the pupils file out of class, and when I slip out, he peeks over my shoulder and flicks his nose with his finger, sniffing.

"Isn't that the classroom where your parents boned?"

How does everyone know that?

Because they all have parents who are alumni. People talk. People always talk.

"Let's just get this over with."

"Yes, ma'am." He pushes off the doorframe, and we both make our way toward the entrance and out the school gates. I try to tell myself that it is in Penn's and my best interest to act as if we don't know each other. This doesn't have to be a disaster. If anything, it's an opportunity to prove to Gus that nothing's going on between us. I would die before ever admitting to dating a Las Juntas rat.

As we approach the gates, I spot Penn leaning against his brand-new silver-blue Prius. I bite down on my lip to suppress a snicker. Dad got him the car from a fair-trade coffee-sipping environmentalist who thinks white sugar is akin to pure heroin. Penn's arms are knotted on his chest, and he is wearing a pair of Jax Teller Ray-Bans and a frown. His black shirt has a hole where the heart is, and his black skinny jeans highlight how tall and trim he is, especially for a wide receiver. Gus, in comparison, looks like a tank (and has about the same IQ as one).

Gus and I stop in front of Penn, far enough away to indicate this is not a social call on both ends. It feels like wielding a sword, and Gus hasn't seen Penn's yet, but it already has my blood on it from this morning when he promised to conquer my land and overthrow me.

"Howdy, asswipe." Gus thrusts his hand Penn's way for a fist bump.

"I see you brought some muscle," Penn says, ridiculing me. He leaves Gus's fist to hang in the air until it drops. "Is she going to bore me to death talking about hair straighteners? Is that your strategy?"

Gus looks back and forth between us, whistling long and low.

"Oh, shit. I thought you two were banging for sure when Daria showed an ounce of emotion when you got your ass kicked by a sophomore. This bitch's icy heart wouldn't melt in a desert."

"We are in the desert, idiot." I roll my eyes.

"Exactly!" Gus waggles his eyebrows. "How're things, Penn? How's your girl?"

Penn has a girl? That makes no sense. He kissed me yesterday. My heart starts beating way too fast.

"Not your business," he snaps.

"Let's get to the point. I have cheer practice." I wave my hand.

"I think the point is you don't belong in this conversation," Penn says in that lazy, unaffected way that drives me nuts. "Gate's that way. Use it." He motions to the school entrance.

Gus snickers, clapping Penn's shoulder.

Okay, that's it. Being a dick at home is somewhat acceptable, but in public? It's a declaration of war.

"I think I'll stay." It's my turn to cross my arms over my chest. "To translate your language to Gus. He doesn't speak fluent white trash."

"And you do?" Penn curves a devastatingly sophisticated eyebrow.

"Burn!" Gus fists the air, laughing. "Shit, you two hate each other. That's hot."

No joke.

Before I can think about the meaning of my words or their effect, they rush out of my mouth in a desperate plea to defend my honor.

"Fluent, actually. Your sister taught me." I smirk.

In my defense, I hate myself even before the words leave my mouth. After they do, it feels like my heart is a sieve and all the poison gushes out. I can't believe I just said that. I'm not even surprised when Penn's face morphs from bored to fuming. His nostrils flare, and he removes his shades, his eyes narrowed into hooded slits.

My hand flies to my mouth. Penn's expression turns volatile. It makes me think of the storms that rip through roofs and uproot trees.

"My, my, my…" Gus pops his gum, raising his ball cap and running his fingers through his blond hair. It's so shiny and straight, it looks like dunes of sand flying in the wind. "Penn Scully is making enemies in high places, but I can't say I'm surprised in the least. You were saying, Scully? I haven't got all day. Some of us need to practice. The first game of the season isn't one I want to lose." He winks.

"Forget it, Bauer." Penn shakes his head, pushing off his car. He's leaving. He is leaving angry. Because of me. He slides into his car, and it's all in slow motion.

I want to cry and scream, but I hit my quota of public meltdowns for this semester at the snake pit. Gus bangs his roof twice, parting ways with my new housemate with one last dig.

"Sick ride, dude. Did you steal it from a philanthropic divorcée?"

"Stole it from your ma, Gus. Although she likes a different type of ride, doesn't she?"

Gus goes red. I don't know why. I don't *care* why. They're both jerks.

I turn around and run back into the school. I can't stand here. I can't stay put. I can't *breathe*.

Gus is yelling behind me that I'm becoming a freak and I should stop hanging out with the Luna girl. Not that I ever do. Luna and Knight and Vaughn and Bailey and Lev are a tight-knit group that doesn't give a damn about what anyone thinks and has each other's backs—and then there's me. I give a whole bag of damns. It's ironic since I'm one of the most feared and loathed people in school.

I run to the girls' locker room across the football field. Since I'm late for practice, no one is there now. I swing the door open and lock myself inside a shower/changing stall. Collapsing against its wall, I drag my back along the ugly graffiti of slut-shaming words, some of them written by me, and rake my fingers down my face. Shit.

Why did I have to bring Via up? Why am I such a jerk? The Hulk pounded his fists against my chest when we were out there, telling me not to show weakness.

So why do I feel so weak?

I wipe my face, down a bottle of water, and unlock the door. When I step out, I rid myself of my dress, yank my locker open, take out my cheer uniform, and slam it shut. Behind the locker, a familiar face pops into my vision.

"Fight or flight?"

I jump back, slamming my spine against the lockers.

Penn.

"What the hell, Scully?"

He's in the girls' locker room at a school he doesn't even attend. He's got the word *trouble* written all over him, and if my dad ever finds out we were in here alone, he is going to hang him by the balls on All Saints' flagpole and let his broken legs flap in the wind.

Not to mention—he is seeing me close to naked. *Again.*

"Answer me."

"Fight. I always fight. So does your girlfriend know you slept with Blythe Ortiz and kissed me?" I smile sweetly, trying to look unaffected, but I immediately regret my question. I'm not supposed to know about Blythe, and I'm not supposed to care he kissed me.

Penn whistles, nodding. "Keeping tabs, Daria? I just kissed you to prove I could have you whenever I wanted you. But it doesn't matter what she knows or doesn't know because I *don't* want you. My turn to ask a question." He takes a step toward me, crowding me against the metal cabinets. The place is spacious, if not embarrassingly luxurious. The lockers are the color of our uniforms—blue and black—and our rich parents shelled out thousands for the fancy chrome sinks, glass showers, and upholstered navy benches.

Penn's gaze is so penetrating, my skin blossoms into goose bumps. As though he can see beneath my skin. I'm ugly behind the tan and makeup and mascara—all flesh and inner organs and blood vessels and hate. Marx, why am I so hateful?

"Are you actively trying to be a bitch, or does it just come naturally?"

A little bit of both, the Hulk inside me explains. *I'm naturally envious and petty, but being a bitch is a knee-jerk reaction when I feel threatened.*

Of course, I would die before giving him a real answer. I run my cold gaze over his healing face. Perfectly troubled and gorgeously flawed, like Johnny Depp in *What's Eating Gilbert Grape*. I'd flip my hair if he gave me room, but with his body flush against mine— much closer than he was when we were in my bathroom yesterday—if I move, I'll touch him. I want to touch him. Which is exactly why I won't.

"When it comes to you?" I run my eyes over his face. "I'm a natural, baby."

When he continues to ooze stoic boredom, I manufacture on a scoff. "You started it, okay? Gus thought we were peeps, so he wanted me to play mediator. But you couldn't stop throwing digs at me. Was I supposed to just stand there and take it?"

"Isn't that what All Saints cheerleaders are for?" He smirks.

"You're a jerk."

"And you're a liar. You ambushed my ass."

"Why would I ambush you?" I stomp, and my knee brushes his leg. His jeans are torn at the knees, and I caught a glimpse of the dusting of light hair on his tan legs when we were outside. I'm sure all of him is glorious, and it pisses me off that I don't have the entire mental picture of him naked. The same one *he* has of me.

"Because you're the cool kids' puppet? Because you think you're some bullshit queen bee who has to shove her nose into shit? Because I hate your—"

I crash my lips on his with a furious kiss that shuts him up. I know I'm a chickenshit and just don't want to hear the truth. What surprises me is that he relents. His hands cup my face, and his lips mold with mine. I don't understand any of this. I don't kiss boys I hardly know. I don't even kiss boys I *do* know. Kissing is a huge deal for me. Yet Penn is not exactly a stranger. It's as though I carried him the entire time he was gone in that sea glass necklace, and now that he took it from me, the only way to satisfy this craving is with his attention.

His stares. His wrath. His lips.

"My dad is going to kill you." I grin into his mouth, and his tongue wrestles its way between my lips again.

"You can't put cream in front of a starving cat and expect it to look the other way."

His breath is ragged, and his hands are big and calloused, rough and warm and familiar. His fingers trace my face and neck and hair, tugging it back to arch my neck, and he sucks on the spot beneath my jaw until I yelp as he marks me. Joy explodes in my chest. Penn's taste in my mouth is heaven. Sweet and dangerous, like a man. I taste cut grass and the California sunshine and a bit of sweat and toothpaste and heat. Our tongues are dancing together. I'm no longer sure if I'm sad or happy, but whatever I am, I'm feeling it. I'm living it. I'm alive.

His erection presses against my stomach, and I'm beginning to grind myself against it when reality trickles into my brain. I hear the whine of the door as it opens. At first, I think a teammate must've walked in on us, but when Penn plasters himself against me, covering my semi-naked body, and I find myself chasing his touch with my hips and lips, I realize he doesn't want to make out with me—he is *shielding* me.

I blink, desperately trying to sober up.

"…much explaining to do." A metallic voice seeps into the room like chemical warfare, causing my eyes to pop open.

Oh Marx.

When I twist my head, I see Principal Prichard standing in

the doorway, filling it with his intimidating frame. He is alone, but I'd rather the entire school watch me making out with Las Juntas Bulldogs captain than him. Penn steps in front of me and tilts his body fully toward Principal Prichard so I'm still covered. Instead of apologizing or explaining himself, he rummages in his back pocket for gum, unwraps it, and tosses it into his mouth. The wrapper falls to the floor.

I think he just unlocked a badass level I've only seen Vaughn and Knight ever reach.

"Principal Prichard." My mouth feels like it's full of cotton. He stares at my face behind Penn with raw anger that makes my cheeks burn. I shouldn't feel like a cheater—Prichard and I are not like that—but something about the scene feels wrong. Disloyal.

"Penn Scully." He clucks his tongue. "When I invited you to join our team, I meant the football one, not cheer, and I definitely did not count on you taking a tour in our facilities unannounced."

"Should've clarified." Penn pops his gum, running his fingers through his hair.

"Step away from Miss Followhill."

"Not before you look the other way," Penn shoots back.

To my shock, Principal Prichard averts his gaze to the lockers on the other side. Mr. Prichard doesn't do nice very well, so I need to fix this. Fast.

"This one's on me." I jump in front of Penn before he has the chance to escalate the situation any further. "I dragged him here. It was my idea."

They both stare at me, stunned. I don't mind taking the fall for this since my reputation is already toast with Principal Prichard, what with the way I let him use me. Plus, I genuinely feel crappy about what happened with Via.

I want to atone for what I did to Penn's sister. I'm not a monster.

"He's here because he wanted to come here. He has full motor control of his two legs," Mr. Prichard snaps.

"Three, if you count the important one, sir." Penn rubs his cheek, indifferent boredom dripping from his voice.

He is sticking it to Prichard. This punk is unreal.

"Actually, he is here because I lost a bet and needed to kiss a thug. We're done here anyway." I snort, slipping into my cheer skirt and cropped shirt. I don't dare lift my gaze to see their reaction. It's a lie, but it's one that would pacify Prichard and make him understand that Penn is not my boyfriend. That way, Penn won't get in trouble.

Prichard narrows his eyes at Penn.

"I don't appreciate you talking back to me, young man."

Penn rolls his eyes as though the man's dramatics have exasperated him.

"Penn," I whisper-shout. I clutch the fabric of his shirt next to the hole, and he shakes me off, still staring at my principal. He is fearless. That's when I realize I'm not only attracted to him. I envy him too.

"If I see you on my school grounds one more time, I'll inform the authorities." Principal Prichard turns around, his whole body rigid.

I chase after him on an impulse.

Penn grabs my wrist, pressing his thumb to my vein. His snake eyes ask me a question I haven't given anyone a straight answer to: *What the fuck?*

"I got what I needed from you." I wiggle free of his touch, yawning. "If you're here to clean the lockers, the mops are in the maintenance room across the field."

The walk to Principal Prichard's office is silent and long. When we reach his door, he tells me to forget about making it to cheer practice today.

"Esme can cover for you. She's quite clever when it comes to getting what she wants. Besides, we have some business to attend to."

He locks the door. My heart races.

A *click* never sounded so final in my life.

CHAPTER FIVE
PENN

You
Make me
Want to grow
Even though you act so small.
I want to put you in my pocket and save you
from yourself.

"Yo, Penn, heard your balls are softer than Tom Brady's. Maybe you could use them as stress relievers."

Some tool from All Saints High burps behind me, crushing an empty bottle of Gatorade in his fist and throwing it in my team's direction. We're standing in the tunnel leading to their football field because All Saints High has a fucking tunnel like it's the NFL. Their entire facility is top-notch and cost the parents a pretty penny. Yet the locker rooms for our use, the guest team, are closed due to flooding (read: Gus being his usual dickhead self). So we're in one tunnel. Together.

An All Saints player faints like a bitch—they mumble it's too hot in here, but I bet his lady corset is probably too fucking tight—and both our coaches hurry to get him to an ambulance and find a replacement.

It's the first game of the season, and it's a fucking shitshow before we even get on the field.

We haven't lost to All Saints High in five years. Let that shit sink in for a second.

Five. Fucking. Years.

Coach Higgins talked to the local news yesterday. He said if we concentrate, we have this in the bag. To our faces, though, Coach is anything but optimistic. He gives us less credit than he'd give a bunch of fainting goats in football uniforms. Which is total bullshit, seeing as we're number one in the state (ASH is number two—commence eye roll).

Coach also says I should keep my head cold and my legs warm and not vice versa. He knows ASH has mastered the form of trash talking, but other than Knight, their sophomore quarterback, their defense is nonexistent, and their plays are pretty predictable. Coming to Gus to mend shit wasn't my plan, but I did it because Higgins suggested we put an end to the rivalry off the field. Only I didn't count on Gus bringing Skull Eyes with him.

I haven't spoken to her since the kiss in the locker room yesterday.

We passed each other in the hallway, avoided eye contact at dinner, and then ignored each other while doing homework at the kitchen table, where Bailey broke a record of talking about absolutely nothing for two hours straight.

But Daria stood up for me against Prichard—something no one else has ever done—and at this point, I know she talks shit to cover her good deeds, so I was unfazed by her excuse for why it happened. She's a little pathetic, though, what with the way she thinks I have a girlfriend and still lets me have my way with her. Then again, rich, spoiled girls are self-indulgent. Why shouldn't I take advantage of that?

I watch Daria on the field, doing her number with the cheer squad. Her little blue-and-black outfit barely covers her tits and crotch, and I know I'm not the only one who notices. It's like looking at a scalloped picture, frayed at the edges. Everything blends in the background, and she stands out.

Las Juntas colors are red and white, so it's easy to see that there's less than zero attendance from our parents and friends on the bleachers. Todos Santos, on the other hand? Every second shop closes, hanging the same sign on the display windows:

Closed: Gone to the game
(You should too. Go Saints!)

Most people on our side of San Diego roll onto their busy night shifts on Friday nights. Hard work, however, is a concept most Todos Santos folks seem to be allergic to.

I look up into the bleachers and spot Jaime, Mel, and Bailey. Sitting next to their neighborhood friends, they're wearing All Saints High blue caps and burgundy shirts. The shirts are inside out, so nobody knows what's on the other side. But I do. I know because they're my shirts. With my number—22.

"*Sylvia and Penn, always come as a set of two.*"

The All Saints version is a little less endearing. They call me Double Deuce—*twice the shit.*

Last night, Mel took me aside and told me that she has people looking into Via's whereabouts. She asked me if we have any relatives she should check with. I told her I have a father and a grandmother who have been traveling from city to city for the past decade, trying to start a crazy Christian cult, an aunt in Iowa I've already checked with, and a half uncle in Ohio neither of us ever met.

The Followhills are not bad. My only issue is how they try courting my ass to a point they might blow my cover to the sky. They practically did everything to make people suspect I live with them other than flat-out tattooing the announcement on their foreheads. I mean, red shirts? For real?

Luckily, they just purchased uniforms and gear for my entire team for the season, so this could pass as them being their pretentious, charitable selves.

"What's Scully smiling about? Reminiscing about his time with his favorite dildo?" Gus stretches behind me, and Camilo shifts from foot to foot, his shoulder brushing mine. He wants to answer. I bet they fucking want that too.

What I'm smiling about is the fact Daria just did a pike and her abs and ass looked so fine while she did it, my dick almost broke free from my football pants and ran across the field to say hello.

"We can't afford the legal fees if we break their noses," I say loud enough for Gus to hear, pushing Camilo to the front of the tunnel. "Let them vent. We'll crush them on the field, just like Gus's friends crush his mama when they're drunk enough not to give a shit what they dip their dicks into."

"You sonofa…" But Gus never finishes the sentence. His team pulls him back when he tries to charge toward me. I stretch my arms out and laugh.

My players are bouncing and shifting next to me, ready to burst. The games with All Saints High are not only about points and stats and rankings. They're about pride and socioeconomic justice and revenge. Historically, the two high schools have been known to prank each other on the hardcore side before and after games. From us burning down their mascot costumes to them putting dish soap in our fountains because we're dirty, poor trash. We positively hate each other.

Josh, Malcolm, Kannon, Nelson, and the rest of my team have good chemistry on the field. I'm not gonna pull the whole "we're family" crap, but we're tight. Everyone's got a story on this side of the tracks, and we've all helped one another at some point during high school. Where we come from, there are two surefire ways to get rich: become a rapper or an athlete. None of us can sing for shit, so we might as well try for the other route together.

That's why I've felt guilty these past few weeks. None of my teammates know I've moved. Not even Kannon and Camilo.

"Pennywise," Knight hollers at me from the bowels of the tunnel.

I twist my head, my body still facing the field. I don't know what it is about him that makes me not hate him. He and Vaughn obviously know I moved in with the Followhills, and for some reason, I trust them with this information.

There's a certain irony about assholes—they usually don't give a shit. Knight and Vaughn are like that. They're not good guys by any stretch of the imagination, but unless you actively piss them off, they're not after your neck.

I jut my chin to him. We both wear war paint. But I swear, his looks like a makeup artist applied it. He grins.

"After the game. Party hard at Blythe's?" He moves his hand back and forth as though he's spanking an invisible girl.

I don't shit where I eat, and I don't mix with the All Saints crowd. Blythe was a one-off. An indulgence saved for a night in which I made Vaughn piss red and couldn't move my face. Besides, as Gus pointed out, I have a piece of tail—a girlfriend, if you will—and I should probably stop messing around with other girls in public.

"Pass."

"She asked about you."

"Maybe he gave her chlamydia, and she wants him to pay for the treatment." Colin, ASH's linebacker, hiccups, and everyone but Knight erupts in laughter.

"That's rich from someone whose face looks like genital herpes," I pipe out.

"Come at me, bro!" Colin bangs his chest with his fist.

"I would, but I don't hit chicks," I drawl.

When we get on the field, we "accidentally" tear through the *Go Saints!* sign made by the cheerleaders. Daria growls as I push through the fabric she is holding and shit all over her effort. The blinding bright lights and the fresh grass promise a big, green opportunity. The only one I've ever had. Rhett used to say that it's not coincidental that grass is the same color as money—top athletes swim in it.

It's the only semi-clever thing I've ever heard him say.

The game starts, and All Saints gets the ball. At first, I'm focused and loose. But by ten minutes in, I know something is off. That something is my defense. My useless, crappy, nonexistent defense. Seems like Josh, Kannon, Nelson, and the rest didn't bother showing up to the game. Physically, they're here, but they're dragging their feet, missing the ball, spacing out, and averting their gazes to the bleachers as though they're waiting for something bad to happen. I'm getting zero play time while Gus is going at it like a frat boy at a whorehouse. Coach Higgins is having a coronary on the sidelines and tries hard to balance his screaming so people won't think he's going to commit murder at halftime. He's making changes to both the offense and the defense, running some adjustments, but his orders fall on deaf ears. Even the kicker looks pissed, and Daria is on the sidelines, cheering on ASH the entire time.

When halftime finally rolls around, I tear off my helmet before we even get to the locker room as I'm trudging toward it. My teammates know better than to approach me. Once we get inside, I crash my helmet on a bench with a snarl.

"What in the actual fucking fuck is happening?" I yell at them, straining my vocal cords before Coach darts in.

"I don't know, but something's up." Camilo raises his helmet slightly to pinch one nostril and shoot snot through the other one on their locker room floor. Everyone grows eerily silent. Coach walks in, and the guys immediately look down at their feet. They know they suck. Fuck, UFOs from other planets can see how hard we suck.

"This is the worst I've ever seen you," he grumbles, quiet and stern, and I think it's because he doesn't want to have a heart attack. "Those people out there?" He points at the door. "You don't have their respect. You need to hustle. To bring 'em hell. Yet you're completely out of sync. You're lying there letting them screw you over. You need to wake up. Do you hear me?"

"Yes, Coach," we all say in unison, eyes on the floor.

"You need to compete, hit them, *destroy* them. Then everything else falls into place. Somebody needs to fix this for me. You need to play fast, play hard, and most importantly, play for each other. The offense is getting no play time because. Of. You. Those kids out there?" Higgins laughs, slamming his open palm on a locker. "They don't need this. This is fun for them. The shit they're gonna show their kids in a few years in fancy photo albums. They have trust funds and colleges secured for them. You? You depend on this. For your college applications. For your scholarships. Hell, for your *pride*."

I see the goose bumps raised on people's arms and hope like hell he managed to get through to them.

When we leave the locker room, bumping fists and barking, "Yes, Coach, yes, Coach, yes, Coach," I think we've got this.

I'm wrong.

———

The game ends with the scoreboard reading 38–14. We lose, and all fourteen points are due to touchdowns I scored. To say I'm crushed would be the understatement of the century. We're starting the season with a huge loss to a bunch of preppy douchebags we haven't lost to in five years. On my watch.

So this is what death feels like.

The coaches meet on the field to talk. Before the buses pull up to take us back to school, I take Coach Higgins aside and ask him if I can bum a ride with Knight Cole.

"Just wanna see what happened here," I lie.

"Sure. Sure, sure," Higgins says. He allows me this one-off because Camilo and I were the only functioning players on the field in red.

The Followhills descend the stands, and I snatch my duffel bag and meet them on the sidelines. The only reason I'm hanging out with them in public is I know no rich motherfucker would ever think the Followhills are stupid enough to take a hood rat under their roof. Most people see me and think of how I'd tarnish their daughters.

They'd be right too.

"Tough game." Baron Spencer runs his arctic eyes over my face. He is tall and good-looking in a Dracula sort of way. Pastier than a freshly painted wall. I know that he used to play for ASH at some point. I also know he wasn't any good, so I don't even bother smiling at him.

"No shit," I mutter, and now I have his attention.

"Shit indeed, but you were damn good." Another man with lighter hair and green eyes—Knight's dad, Dean, I suppose—nods. He was a football player too. They all were. Cocky bastards with their Photoshopped wives and impeccable clothes and padded bank accounts.

"I'm sorry. Were you watching another game? They dry-fucked our asses so hard I won't be able to sit down the entire semester." I wipe my forehead, my gaze darting toward the locker room.

Baron arches an eyebrow. Dean suppresses a closemouthed laugh.

"Doesn't matter how your team played. *You* were good, and that's worth something." Jaime tousles my hair and pulls me in for a hug. I don't know where this is coming from. Maybe I look as bad as I feel.

Knight saunters to us, freshly showered, in one of his over-the-top outfits. He is wearing some sort of a pilot's khaki jacket and oversized shades. He's the definition of a fashion victim. Somewhere in New York, a designer's snorting sixteen lines of coke Knight's daddy has paid for. Next to him is a girl with dark brown curls and big, gray eyes. You can tell she's not the typical All Saints princess. She is wearing jeans two sizes too big and an oversized *Lazy* hoodie. The opposite of her flashy boyfriend. She looks like a tough cookie, and he looks like a smashed birthday cake.

"This is Luna." Knight slants his chin to her, taking her hand in his and squeezing hard, pissing all over his territory. Daria groans next to me and I ignore her, reaching for a handshake.

Luna flashes me a lopsided grin. Her shake is firm, but her skin is velvety and warm. I can see why Knight likes her. I can see why Daria doesn't too.

"Penn," I say.

She doesn't say anything, just offers me a noncommittal half shrug. There's a lot of gaze shifting going on among everyone before Knight clears his throat, and says, "Luna's not big on talking."

"Good. Most people only have stupid things to say anyway."

Luna salutes me. Baron smirks at Jaime.

"Keeper." Baron jerks his finger in my direction.

Jaime nods. "He reminds me of your miserable asses when we were kids and helps with the yard work."

They all look at me, hoping to find some joy or gratitude on my face, but I'm mostly annoyed the fuckers are talking about my living there so openly. I spit phlegm onto the grass and check the time on my phone.

"So you're sure about Blythe's party?" Knight shoulder-bumps me.

After getting my ass kicked on the field? Yeah. Not about to come to an ASH party and become a human piñata. "Hard pass."

"All right. Good game."

Knight shakes my hand and pulls me into a bro-hug.

We make a quick stop at the house so Daria can shower too, then head to the pier. I analyze the game in my head the entire way there. Bailey is talking nonstop. The kid's cute, but man, she can talk your ears off. She was the one who decided we *must* celebrate my birthday—even if a week late—by getting ice cream at the best parlor on the Todos Santos promenade. I'm not big on ice cream, and I'm even less of a fan when it comes to celebrating birthdays since Via disappeared. Not that they were tolerable before, but at least we had the tradition of making each other shitty cards and stealing candy from the street vendors.

"Do you want to talk about the game?" Mel slides into the stream of Bailey's words as the latter explains to us how New Amsterdam became New York. Daria shifts in her seat beside Bailey, who is on the hump between us in Jaime's Tesla. Rich people love Teslas. They're clinical, impersonal, and futuristic. Anything to make them forget they take a shit and pick their nose like everyone else.

I grunt, giving her less than words but more than nothing.

"We're here for you," she pipes.

"Thanks for the pep talk. Where'd you get it, AA for Dummies?"

"I'm so sorry, Penn. I just blabbed and blabbed. Do you even want to hear more about history?" Bailey catches her lower lip in her braced teeth.

God, no.

"Sure. History's fine." I nudge her shoulder with mine, and she launches into another lengthy explanation about how the British claimed New Amsterdam. They were brutal, she explains, and Daria says that cruelty is underrated. Sometimes you "gotta do what you gotta do" to make your point. Then *Jaime* says that diplomacy is the best weapon and killing people with kindness leaves no evidence or legal consequences behind.

"Doesn't matter which way you conquer a place as long as you do," I hiss, producing an apple I brought from lunch from my duffel bag and tossing it in Daria's hands. She knows what I mean by it and groans.

When we get to Gelato Heaven, Mel claims that the type of ice cream you order says a lot about your personality. "It's a fact. I read it in *Cosmo*."

Daria rolls her eyes. I think it's a reflexive movement for her by now. Like breathing. "Old much, Melody?"

"Reading magazines is old now?" Mel's eyes widen, and she looks back and forth between her daughters, pretending to be scandalized. She is trying too hard, but Daria is still oblivious. It's like being on a first date with your all-time crush and trying too hard to impress. That's Daria and Mel. Constantly dancing awkwardly around each other.

"Might as well read hieroglyphics on Egyptian walls." Daria snorts.

Mel proceeds to ask the chick behind the glass counter for one scoop of low-fat vanilla ice cream in a cup.

Jaime shoves his fists into his front pockets and whistles.

"*Cosmo* is definitely wrong. Nothing vanilla about you, baby."

Daria makes a gagging sound, and this time, I'm in her camp. People behind us snicker, and I know she wants the floor to open and swallow her whole. My mama and Rhett, they would embarrass the shit outta me in countless creative ways, but I'll give them one thing—you could never accuse them of PDA.

Jaime tells the teenage girl behind the counter to choose any two scoops she thinks would complement each other for him.

Bails mulls over his choice. "Adventurous and trusting."

This family is so first-world and rich, I bet they shit potpourri.

Bailey orders one chocolate scoop and one strawberry in a cone.

"A conventional genius," Mel exclaims.

Kill me.

Daria shifts her gaze to me, then to the row of ice creams, and then to me again. We're both hyperaware of what the other one will order. I hate her ass, it's true, but that ain't gonna stop me from fucking her. It'll be poetic justice at its finest. She took my sister, so I'll take her vanity.

"Blue moon, green tea, and cheesecake, please. With sprinkles and a dash of caramel in a cone. And can I have a cherry on top?" Daria says.

"Sure can." The girl piles all this mess into a cone and turns to me. As do the Followhills.

"What's the most disgusting flavor you got?" I lean forward, parking my elbows on the glass.

The girl turns a nice shade of maroon, her eyes darting to the yellow-green pile on the far right.

"That'd be the key lime pie. People say it's so sour it makes them sick. But it's the owner's daughter's favorite, so we keep it."

"I'll take a scoop in a cone."

The girl gasps. "Are you sure?"

She melts into a puddle when I wink at her. Easy prey. My favorite snack.

I ask for her number. Straight up.

"I… Isn't she your girlfriend?" she stutters, her eyes shifting to Daria, seemingly for permission. I *tsk*.

"Foster sister and a real bitch."

"Penn!" Melody booms. "Oh my Marx!"

"Sorry, ma'am. Sorry, sir," I tell Jaime and cover Bailey's ears, muttering, "You didn't hear that."

The girl starts shooting out the number quickly. I pretend to program them into my phone while playing *Fortnite*. No chance of me ever calling her, but sticking it to Daria feels good. I'd throw Adriana in her face, but she is too good for those kiddie games. Besides, I'll save the best reveal for last.

We all settle at a round table on the parlor's balcony overlooking the beach. The sun is setting, the sky is pink and orange, and people saunter on the boardwalk hand in hand, the perfect postcard of SoCal. The sound of laughter and waves breaking on the shore and kids yelling fills the air. They recently added a Ferris wheel, mini golf, a carousel, and a roller coaster to attract more tourists. It made Todos Santos even more packed and touristy. I miss San Diego. Miss real ass people and real ass places and views that don't look like they've been filtered to death by some chick who thinks she's a professional photographer just because she has an Instagram account.

Melody complains about my slip of the tongue in the background, but I block her out. I take a lick of my ice cream.

"That's awful," I say flatly.

Daria takes the bait, just as I knew she would. "Shocker."

"Play nice." Mel stabs her plastic spoon in her ice cream, swirling it around methodically. Bailey is a lick-it-straight-from-the-cone type of girl. Daria probably won't touch hers. My guess is she doesn't do real feelings or refined sugar.

Who the fuck are you to talk? You're the Tin Man.

"Would you like mine?" Bailey volunteers.

Two sisters. Same genes. Same blood. Different hearts.

"Actually, Daria's looks good." I grin at my opponent.

Daria stares at me, her gigantic ice cream still in her hand, unlicked. She thrusts it in my direction.

"Jerk," she mutters under her breath.

"Marx, you are going to regret it when I ground you both for eternity." Mel sighs. Jaime chuckles. I noticed they replaced the word *God* with *Marx*. That's… I don't even know what the fuck that is. Quirky. Weird. Trying too fucking hard.

I take her ice cream and give it a good lick, handing her my key lime ice cream.

"Please," I say, forcing her to eye contact. "It would mean a lot to me if you *eat* it." I'm not talking about the ice cream, and we both know it.

"I'm on a diet," she snaps.

"Consider it my belated birthday gift." I cock my head, feigning virtue. There's loaded silence and a whole lotta staring. Then she sits back down, acutely aware of the fact her parents are watching. She takes a lick of the ice cream. Winces. Our eyes are still locked, and I wonder if she makes the same connection I'm making.

Us. Licking each other's ice creams.

She is tasting my sourness.

As I devour her sweetness.

"So what do you think happened on the field?" Jaime turns to me.

"They cheated," I say.

"You think?"

"I *know.*"

"Ever heard of being gracious in defeat?" Daria folds her legs on her chair. She is getting used to my ice cream. Doesn't even make a face anymore after each lick. I take a bite of her ice cream, swallowing it without tasting it. Her throat bobs with the meaning of what I want to do to her.

Part of me wants to chase her. To watch in slow motion as she collapses underneath me and I rip her to shreds. The other wants her to stand toe to toe with me so we can battle it out until we're both bloody and exhausted.

"Wise words, Daria. How about you live by them when someone you're jealous of gets something they don't deserve?"

"Kids," Mel warns for the third time. I like that Jaime and Mel don't put us on leashes and expect us to behave. Part of me suspects they brought me here to set her straight. She is a spoiled little princess who always gets her way. And me? I'm the exact opposite.

"I'll look into it." Jaime wipes the corners of his mouth with a paper napkin, slam-dunking the rest of his ice cream into the trash can. Not that he hasn't been nice to me so far, but he is also smart enough to remind me daily that if I touch Daria, he will kill me. ("Literally. And, yes, I *literally* mean the word *literally*.") I wish he knew his daughter was banging her principal. My tapping her ass would be a vast improvement. A public service, really. Jaime should thank me.

"I'll figure it out. Thanks," I say.

"You sure?"

"Positive."

"Has it ever occurred to you we might've played better? Just because Penn says something doesn't make it true," Daria says.

"It doesn't make it untrue either," Jaime points out.

"You should show more loyalty to All Saints, Dad. You're an alumnus. And you"—she turns to Mel for the first time this evening—"you were a teacher. *Before* you got fired for sleeping with your student." Daria licks the last of her ice cream and tries dumping it into the trash can like her dad. She misses, and it falls on the floor.

"Daria, you're being Hulky again." Jaime pins her with a look, like she knows what the hell that means.

"Why? Because I brought you and Melody up? It's okay to say gross things to her in public, but I can't point out that you've ruined my life by sending me to the same school—the same *class*, by the way, you hooked up in?" She juts her chin out, standing up.

"Don't excuse her behavior, Jaime. You invented the Hulk because you wanted to separate Daria from her bad behavior. The truth is, she needs to learn to rein in her anger when she's upset," Mel says, and this is going off-track, fast. I scan the Followhills individually, assessing the situation. Bailey's eyes are glued to her iPad, and she looks like she doesn't have a care in the world. The kid's used to this fucked-up dynamic. Daria's eyes are locked on her mom's.

"Mother." Daria plasters an arsenic smile on. "Do we have a problem here?"

Melody sits back and folds her arms over her sensible cardigan. "Why can't you be a little more like your sister?"

Daria's physical reaction to those words suggests she's been shot. She darts up from her chair, and it falls back from the momentum. Everyone around us snaps their heads to our table. Melody jumps up from her chair too.

"I didn't—"

"Don't." Daria lifts a finger. Her eyes are shining, but her face is stoic. She shakes her head. "Don't say you didn't mean it, Melody, because every fiber of you did. And maybe I should be more like Bailey. But you? You should be more of a *mom*."

She turns around and storms away, taking the three stairs to the sidewalk and running to the street. She flings herself toward the boardwalk, bursting into traffic, and when a car brakes and honks at her, she jams her fist on its hood.

"Fuck you! This is Todos Santos. Your daddy will buy you a new one," she screams.

My mind is telling me to sit this one out and let the shitshow unfold without my intervention. But my legs are assholes and so is my rusty conscience because they carry me down the stairs. Mel warns my back that when Daria's *Hulky*, she doesn't like to be interrupted. I think she needs some tough love and to be grounded until the next decade. She needs to be asked some hard questions. Questions like:

Are you fucking your principal?

Is your foster brother fondling you in the locker room?

Are your friends assholes who run betting rings in an illegal fight club?

What in the actual fuck is Hulky?

At the risk of sounding like a Dr. Phil wannabe, I keep this shit to myself. Jaime and Mel are still ten million times better than my parents. They care. Mel is just scared of her daughter, and Jaime... well, Jaime is a dude.

The light turns red, and I have to wait for cars to pass before I can cross the road. Unlike Daria, I don't have a good health insurance plan and can't go around slapping moving vehicles. I spot her sneaking into the dwindling line of the Ferris wheel and buying a ticket. She slips into a seat. My eyes flicker back to the traffic light. When it turns green, I sprint across the road. Since I left my wallet—which Jamie padded with a couple of hundred—at the house, I hop over the fence and slide into the seat next to her a second before she closes the metal bar and locks it. The guy operating the wheel has already pulled the handle, and the wheel starts moving. He shoots me a look and shakes his head. I don't mean to laugh in his face, but he should thank his lucky stars that Kannon and Camilo are not here with me. We'd have found a way to steal the entire Ferris wheel and sell its parts to travelers.

"What are you doing here?" Daria looks the other way, toward the ocean. She is holding the metal bar in a chokehold. The wheel moves slowly, and our car sways back and forth.

"Shit was getting real, so I decided to split." I take out my pack of cigarettes, and she knocks it out of my hands, letting it fall to the abyss of tourists underneath us.

Why *am* I here? Because I recognize that, although she's a brat, she's got a case. Daria isn't seen. Her mother barely talks to her, and when she does, it's to tell her to stop being horrible. She's normally left to her own devices, and other than a generic "How's school?" I've never heard her mom ask about her friends or dates or cheer. It's a vicious cycle because in order to get attention, Skull Eyes keeps on acting up.

You're only lonely if you're not there for yourself.

Some pearls of wisdom by the man himself, Dr. Phil.

"Cut the bullshit, Scully. What do you want?"

"A rematch, a greasy burger, and your cunt on my face. In that order exactly."

She scrunches her nose. "You're disgusting. I can't believe my parents took your side. We won because we kick ass, even if you guys didn't look bad."

"Don't worry, we'll meet you at the playoffs, by which time Gus will make the full transition from a dry vagina to the basic pussy he is."

Now she full-blown laughs, shaking her head. We're getting farther up, and people and places and palm trees are starting to look smaller. The lights dance across the horizon, and the ocean looks too blue and too infinite not to admire.

"Release the bar," I tell her out of nowhere.

"Why?" Her fingers are still curled firmly around it.

"Because I want to see if you trust me not to open the handle."

She stares at me with the same wild gaze that made me give her the sea glass four years ago. As though I'm the most fascinating creature in the world. I want to pocket that look and save it for the next time the world lets me down. Which should be in the next twenty minutes.

"But I *don't* trust you."

"Let's rectify that."

"Thanks, I'm good."

"Did you hear a question mark in my voice? It wasn't an offer."

She turns to me. "Tell me something real about yourself."

"Like what?" It's hard not to stare at her lips. She has great lips.

She's always had great lips. And the rest of her body is the kind of stuff that got Edgar Allan Poe and Pablo Neruda into writing poems about chicks. It saddens me that I can half understand how rich, gorgeous girls like Daria turn out the way they do. Too smug to feel, too bitchy to be tolerated. They are so much yet so little. They have everything, but they earned nothing by themselves. It's like winning the lottery and expecting to make wise investments on your own without any financial background.

"Why do you cut holes in your shirt?"

"Don't go for the jackpot before you win the fluffy teddy bear at the fair," I warn. "Ask me something else."

She rolls her eyes at me, sighing as though I exasperate her. "What kind of name is Penn?"

"Release the bar, and I'll tell you."

"How do I know you won't open it?"

"You don't."

Her face is so close, and I'm starting to realize why people love Ferris wheels. It feels like we're alone in the universe, isolated. She lets go of the bar, almost in slow motion, and tucks her hands between her bare thighs.

Don't look at her thighs, bastard. I can practically hear Jaime inside my head.

Why? Her thighs would make great ear warmers, I mentally answer back.

"Close your eyes."

She does. Just as she did when we were fourteen. I like that she is obedient when we're alone. I make a mental note not to abuse that power. Daria answers to no one and does whatever the hell she wants—except with me.

"Before drugs made my mom fall down the rabbit hole, she was this poetry chick with nerdy glasses and a library card. She met my dad at church when she was seventeen as a part of some Christian scouts program, and he knocked her up. Then a chain of really shitty things happened all at once. She was involved in a car accident that almost killed her and broke most of the bones in her body. My dad decided to leave with his mother and start a Christian cult. Mom got hooked on painkillers, then illegal drugs. I used to read poems to her when she was in the hospital, going in and out of there for one of her trillion surgeries. Anyway, her favorite poets are—*were*," I correct myself, remembering she is no longer alive, "Sylvia Plath and Alexander Penn. So she named us after them."

"Who's Alexander Penn?" Her cheeks flush.

She doesn't want me to think she's stupid. We are reaching the highest point.

"He was this Israeli Russian communist poet dude. Off the rails certifiable. He was desperately in love with this chick named Bella. She rejected him, so he tried to commit suicide and shot himself. Failed. She was so enchanted by his love and devotion, she decided to marry him."

"Just like Van Gogh. Only this girl said yes," Daria muses.

"Yeah."

"Kinda gross," she says.

"Yeah." I chuckle.

"Some fairy tales are screwed up," she adds. She can't shut up. She's nervous. Her eyes are still closed.

"All the good ones are, Skull Eyes," I say softly.

I unlatch the metal bar from its hook. She hears the click and sucks in a breath.

"What are you doing?" Her voice shudders.

"Tell me what's going on between you and Prichard." My voice hardens around the vowels.

Her eyes are still closed, not because she is still following my directions but because she is freaking out and would probably faint if she looks down.

"You're insane!" She squeezes her eyes shut.

"You bangin' the old man?" I ignore her psychological assessment.

"You said I could trust you!"

"No, I didn't. I asked if you did. For the record, you shouldn't trust me. Our loyalties lie with different schools and people. But I answered your question, so it's only fair you answer mine."

"Dream on, Scully."

I push the metal bar open. She can feel the breeze. I hold on to it, knowing I won't be able to pull it back if I don't, and that means I'm squatting, my ass in the air.

"Fine! Okay! Fine. No. We're not sleeping together."

I yawn loudly, so she can hear, dangling the handle from side to side. "Not buying it."

"We're not!" she screams desperately. People from other carts can probably hear her and see this. Giving a damn, however, is not on my agenda.

"Then what are you doing together? Playing Caribbean poker?"

"That's two questions," she bargains.

"Since when are you good at math, Followhill?"

I know Daria would have a lot of fun rubbing the truth in my face. She knows I would never rat her out to her parents. Not only because she holds my residence a secret, but I'm just not that type of asshole.

"What do you care, anyway? Gus said you have a girlfriend."

"Gus is an idiot."

"It doesn't make him a liar."

True, and I notice she doesn't ask me again about the girlfriend situation. Which is good, because she won't like the answer, and I'm not done with her ass, literally and figuratively. I close the metal bar. She hears the click and lets out a breath. She opens her eyes and stares at me. It's cool to see her like that. Vulnerable. Scared. She's not the head cheerleader right now, and I'm not the football captain of the rival team. We're just two teenagers who never stood a chance to be friends in this world, so we became what was expected of us. Enemies.

We reach the top.

"Ever been kissed on a Ferris wheel?" I ask.

"No."

All your firsts, baby.

I take that as an invitation, pressing my mouth to hers, RSVPing that shit without thinking about her parents down below, the complications of it, or the consequences. Without thinking this is taboo, and wrong, and twisted, and can surely come back to bite me in the ass.

She opens her mouth, groans into mine, and we kiss, and we kiss, and we kiss until nothing else exists. My hand slips to her neck and squeezes it, and when she protests in the form of biting my lip, I laugh and lick her entire fucking face. Then she laughs too.

"I thought you said you didn't want all my firsts."

"My mind changes according to my mood and how hot you look at that moment."

"How very stupid teenage jock of you," she murmurs against my lips.

"How very indeed."

Our cart is an invisible cloak until it starts to lower. Her parents will be able to make out our faces if they're standing underneath the wheel, waiting for us, which I'm sure they are because whether she realizes it or not, they give a shit.

We pull away together. Everything about us is a power game, and no one wants to be the side that got rejected.

My dick is hard and so is her expression. I think she's regretting it. I should be regretting it too. Not because of Jaime. Fuck Jaime. I never asked to crash at their house. But because of Adriana and Via.

But Via isn't here for me to feel guilty about or sorry to.

Via left me, just like the rest.

"I still don't like you." Her whisper caresses my face.

"Me neither," I say. About her. About me.

We spend the rest of the ride in silence. When we get out of the car, the operator is tapping his foot, waiting for his money.

Jaime slaps a twenty into his open palm, waving at us to join them. "Keep the change. You two good?" He looks back and forth between us.

Daria says no.

I say yes.

We say it at the same time.

We look each other, and she rolls her eyes. I smile because it's hard not to.

Melody complains about our level of cooperation when it comes to family functions.

On the drive home, Daria eats the entire apple I threw at her and tosses the core on my lap.

"Checkmate."

CHAPTER SIX
PENN

It was love at first sight
Hate at second
Lust at third
But four is my lucky number
So mine your ass shall be.

Time moves differently when you live a lie.

You swim against the stream, and every second feels like three hours and some change.

I park four blocks from school at buttfuck o'clock, an hour before practice starts. Mornings are for strength training, and afternoons are the real deal on the field.

Not only do I not live with Rhett anymore and dread the day he will get an unexpected visit or phone call from a school official, but I also have a brand-new Prius. The first time I have something semi-nice, and naturally, I don't get to flaunt it.

To make sure my friends don't ask Rhett about me when they see him at the gas station or supermarket, I tell them that he's losing his mind.

"Early dementia," I explain to anyone willing to listen. "The drugs really did a number on him."

Nobody questions it. But to give my alibi an extra shine, I have

Adriana—Addy, my girlfriend—tell everyone she spotted Rhett arguing heatedly with a jukebox at Lenny's, the diner where she works.

This is the first time I'll see my team since Friday's game. I needed the buffer time to digest what happened, and when the players begin to trickle into our chipped-wall locker room, I'm already there, hands on hips, with one leg flung over a bench. Our rusty lockers have so much graffiti, the color lies somewhere between gray and purple. The place always smells of dust, piss, and poverty.

Josh, Malcolm, Camilo, Kannon, Nelson, and the rest arrive before Coach Higgins. The fact he ain't here yet gives me pause. Coach is never late. Well, other than the time his wife went into labor. He was ten minutes late that day as he yelled at her on the phone. "Well, Meredith, it's our first baby. You're not gonna have her in the next hour. I'll be there as soon as I can."

On the same note, I don't know how his balls are still intact.

I close the door behind them and lean over the wall, crossing my arms. "Care to explain the fuckery that was Friday night?"

They all stare at the ground. Shit doesn't make any sense, and I've been trying to put it together all weekend. I know in my bones that my teammates are savages. All Saints is not a bad team, but they usually get ahead because enough money is thrown into their shit like a midranked NFL team. We have the talent, the motivation, the hunger.

"Cold feet," Kannon spits out, looking around him for moral support. He lands on the bench with a thud, tugging at the beanie that secures his hair and letting it fall to his shoulders. "All the trash talking and the pranks just got to us. It was the first game of the season and on their home field. The bleachers were all blue. It was just too much," he explains.

"Other teams will always try messing with our heads." I rub the back of my neck. "We can't let that shit get to us."

"Why?" Josh sneers. "Because you have a scholarship to a D1 college lined up and we all need to fall into place and make you look good? Shit happens. You missed the after-game hangout. Is that how you're gonna be every time we don't meet your majestic expectations?"

I stare at him, trying to keep my fists to myself. Josh is a linebacker. He is talented but with a fuse shorter than a hamster's dick. Possibly even Camilo's. Twice, he got into fights with players from the opposite team last year, and one of them ended with both players rolling under the bus that was supposed to take us home, kicking and screaming. I know he frequents the snake pit and that he's fought Vaughn a few times. I also know his dad doesn't want him to go to college. He's got an auto shop business to take over, so he ain't going anywhere. He was born in this neighborhood, and he'll die here too. Senior year is his last chance before he kisses the football dream goodbye.

"It's not about me." I bare my teeth, feeling white-hot anger climbing up my throat. Although I know part of it is. And so what if I want us to succeed? Every single motherfucker on this team will benefit if we win the league. There're enough scholarships to go around, especially when you're from my zip code. Just because Josh is too much of a pussy to stand up to his family and say no doesn't mean we need to look like shit.

"Leave it." Kannon stands, putting his hand on my shoulder. "We'll do better next time."

I shake him off, stepping toward Josh so we're nose to nose.

"Are we gonna have a problem this season, J?"

He bumps my chest with his, tilting his head sideways, a manic look glazing over his eyes. "Sure hope so, man. Can't pass up a chance to fuck you up."

If I head-butt him, I risk suspension. With my rich track record consisting of fighting people for food, cigarettes (done with that shit, BTW), and even football gear, I can't afford any slipups. I gave Coach my word I'd be on my best behavior this season, and he, in return, will give me a heads-up before the scouts arrive at our games or whenever a college asks to see my tapes. I assume head-butting a teammate would fall squarely in the realm of acting up.

"Keep talking like that, and I'll make sure you'll have to drink from a straw for the next few months." I shove my index finger into his face.

And that's when his fist swings at my face.

I duck and dodge it, then punch his lights out, acting purely on instinct. He drops like a brick. Malcolm and Nelson drag him toward the bench to try to set him up and assess the damage. Camilo punches a locker and curses. Then he turns around and pushes me against the wall, getting in my face.

"You lecturing me about being a hothead? Really, Scully?"

The door flies open, and Coach Higgins blazes through it in perfect shit timing. Also on instinct, Kannon throws himself over a passed-out Josh, covering the asshole, who is probably still seeing stars, but more importantly covering for *me*.

"Scully!" Higgins yells into the bowels of the locker room. His tan, round face is red, and his brown hair is everywhere. I hurry toward him, eager to push him out the door.

"'Sup, Coach?"

"Don't use that slang with me like I'm one of your homeboys," he spits out, and I bite down a smile. "Get your ass to my office."

I follow his chubby, short frame, wondering if Coach was a decent player before he started teaching. Then I wonder if he's feeling bitter about having to train a bunch of people who were born with the right height and build and talent. I'm guessing we're going to have a hard discussion about the game on Friday. He's going to bitch about it for a few minutes and then we'll move on. In the four years I've known Coach, he's seen me at my worst— underfed and underdressed, zombie-ing around on zero sleep when I needed to work part-time to make sure I had food in my stomach. He'll cut me some slack, as he always does, because he knows my life is in the toilet.

Tucked between the lab and the restrooms, his office is decorated in yellows and browns. He sits back behind his desk and says, "We have a problem."

I fall into the chair in front of him, releasing a yawn. "Chill, Coach. It's just one game. Besides, I—"

"Ain't nobody talking about the game." He slaps the table with his meaty palm, roaring, "I just got off the phone with Ryan Prichard, All Saints High's principal. He told me about your little incident in his locker room Thursday."

Dafuq? My mind reels with four thousand different questions. Why now? What happened? Has she dumped him? Did her parents find out? How does that fare for my sorry ass? I can't get suspended. *I. Can't. Get. Suspended.* Fuck all the Prichards and Joshes of the world.

"Spill it, boy." Coach laces his fingers together, cradling an invisible baby he's about to toss across the room. I've never seen him so red in my life. Then again, the principal of the most affluent school in California has never threatened him before.

"What, no beer and porn? I need to be in the right mood to talk about my sexcapades." I stretch my long legs. "I hooked up with a chick from there. I didn't touch shit. Other than the chick."

"Daria Followhill," he bites out, digging his fingers into his eye sockets in frustration.

"That her name?" I play dumb.

"You *know* her name, Scully."

Who the fuck doesn't?

"Is she too princess for me, Coach? Think I should aim a little lower?"

"I think wherever you aim, don't do it in her direction unless you want to find your football career dying a sudden, painful death. I struck a deal with Prichard, who seemed adamant about you not going anywhere near his school again unless in a professional capacity. I gave him my word that you will keep away from Miss Followhill, and he, in turn, will overlook the fact you were trespassing."

I live with her. I want to laugh in his face. But since volunteering this information is a no-go, I smirk. If he's expecting a thank-you or worse, any type of cooperation, he obviously hasn't been paying attention.

It's not that I don't want to go pro—I do. Hell, it's my best chance to get out of this shithole. It's that I don't listen to people like Prichard, who only care about themselves and their dicks. If I've learned one thing about this life, it's that you can't let the bad guys win.

And Prichard? He doesn't want me off Daria's back because he's concerned for her. He's doing it because he *wants* her.

"Scully, give me your word," Coach probes, his ten-month pregnant belly poking out of the edge of his red *Coach* shirt we got him for Christmas. "There's too much on the line, and there're a lot of pretty blonds out there. You'll be drowning in them at any self-respecting D1 college. Besides, think about Adriana."

I tip my head down, gesturing with my open arms.

"You have my word, Coach Higgins, that I won't get suspended."

He doesn't catch the semantics.

Because to him, I'm just a dumb kid, and she's just one blonde bimbo out of many.

———

I'm still clad in my gridiron football pants and varsity jacket when I kick the door to the Followhills' mansion open, holding my duffel bag, school backpack, and a huge-ass Amazon Prime box with something Bailey ordered. Probably more poetry books we'll burn through over the weekend. I don't wanna know what the Followhills' credit card bill looks like at the end of every month. Their daughters spend money like it's a competitive sport.

"Bailey, I swear to fucking God, you consume words just as much as you speak them, and that's somethin'," I groan. No answer back, so I guess the house is empty.

I dump the box in the foyer and walk over to the kitchen to fix myself a nutritious meal consisting of six slices of pizza and shove them into the microwave. While I wait for them to heat, I gulp down an entire carton of orange juice. It's crazy how quickly things change. When I moved here less than two weeks ago, everything in the fridge was so small and cute and mini.

Small cottage cheese. Tiny boutique personal bottles of juices. Individual string cheeses. Then *I* arrived. Melody got her Costco card two days later when she realized I'd eat the fucking counter if no one stopped me. Now everything here comes in bulk. There's enough meat in the freezer to reassemble an entire farm.

I lean a hip against the counter and hoover the pizza slices. That's my afternoon snack sorted. I wonder what Melody has in store for dinner. I have practice every day from three thirty to six o'clock, then I shower and do homework. I don't have time to play house with the Followhills, but one thing I never pass on is their fucking dinner. They sure love their fancy meals, and when Jaime is in a good mood—which is basically always—he slips me a Bud Light too.

Mrs. Followhill is a drill sergeant about being prompt. But since I moved in, Bailey said dinner on the nights Melody doesn't teach has changed from six thirty sharp to seven fifteen, when I get out of my shower. She's all right, I guess, for doing that. It's becoming increasingly difficult to resent her when she is trying so damn hard.

Harder than my own mother ever did, actually.

After I wash my plate, I go upstairs to dump my shit in my room, which used to be a guest room, but the Followhills have decorated it with Raiders merchandise, a flat-screen TV, an Xbox, and a guitar (more proof rich people love the whole show; I don't play the guitar). There's even a dark maroon pillow with my name and jersey number on it. Every day when I come home, I find more new personalized Penn shit. I already told Mel that if I catch her trying to put a diaper on me in the middle of the night, we're done.

I turn around, about to head to the shower, when I see Daria on my threshold in her barely there cheer outfit. The tiny, cropped, tight black-and-blue top and miniskirt should be illegal anywhere that's not a strip club or my bed.

Arching an eyebrow, I kick my shoes off, then throw my jacket on the floor. She folds her arms, leaning one shoulder against my doorframe. I know we're alone, because if we weren't, she wouldn't be standing here, openly ogling me. Jaime doesn't want us to be alone. Wouldn't be surprised if there are new cameras in the house too. My phone starts flashing with text messages. Adriana, having a sixth sense and wanting to remind me that she exists.

Addy: Miss you!
Addy: Come to Lenny's.
Addy: When am I going to see you?

"Do continue." Daria's gaze drops to my crotch, where it stays. "You were in the middle of something, weren't you?"

I grab the red pillow and throw it at her. She catches it and flings it back on my bed.

"Go play with your Barbies, Skull Eyes."

Her smile widens, and she blushes. It occurs to me that I might have a hard-on. I look down. Half-mast and firmly covered. So why is she practically red?

"You haven't called me Skull Eyes in forever."

"It's not a fucking pet name. Don't send our wedding invitations just yet."

"Mhm-hmm." She nods, biting down on a pink fingernail.

"How's your little boyfriend, Gus, doing? Still sucking ass for a living?"

"Penn Scully presents: When life gives you lemons, become a bitter jerk."

"One game," I stress. "You won one game. Life didn't give me lemons. It gave me a good opportunity to get even."

I need to make sure that Daria is a hobby, not an addiction. Adolescent hearts are trash and as loyal as a starving stray cat. They'll take anything. Even scraps. I don't want to feed my rusty tin heart junk. And Daria, she stomped on it hard enough for me to know she's not even a greasy burger. She's a Pop-Tart covered in cyanide.

I shoulder past her. She follows me into the hallway, and I'm trying to keep my heart rate reasonable, but the heart wants what it wants, and right now, apparently, it wants Pop-Tarts. The hair on my forearms stands on end, and my dick jerks in my pants. It wants a shot of cyanide too.

I stop when I'm in the bathroom and turn to her. "All right, show's over. Get the fuck out, Dar."

"Dar!" she squeaks. She really softened up to me after the Ferris wheel. The other option is that she is messing with my head to try to get me to fuck her and get in trouble.

Let's admit it, it's probably the latter. Daria doesn't have a heart, and she still hates me.

"Now I get two pet names. Should I get us friendship bracelets, *P*?"

"As long as they're pink. Yellow makes my knees look fat."

I'm bantering with her. I deserve every bullshit thing coming my way.

I hope Via's not really dead because her ghost would chase my ass all the way to hell for playing nice with Daria. But wherever Via is—she's not here. And I may hold a good old grudge against Daria, but my anger toward my sister is still fresh.

"What do you want?" I gather phlegm and spit it into the sink.

"You've seen me naked twice. I've seen you naked never. I think it's time we change that," she says. I stare at her for a full minute, in which none of the things that should cross my mind—my football scholarship, Prichard, her parents, Via, or my poor girlfriend, who had to endure the Blythe Ortiz rumor the first week of school—occupy me. The only thing I'm trying to figure out is if this is some kind of a prank because my dick might never recover from the disappointment if it is.

"Are you gonna tell your daddy I'm being inappropriate?" I

mock, pushing my lower lip out. I wouldn't put it past Daria to fuck my dick in order to fuck me over and throw me out.

"Are you gonna tell my daddy I lock myself up with my principal in his office three times a week doing Marx knows what?" she counters, pouting.

I see what she's doing. She's trying to tell me that we both have leverage on each other. She's giving me power, and I never turn power down.

"I ain't old and saggy. Would that be a problem?"

"Absolutely. Get the hell out of my bathroom." She laughs, but it's nervous.

I get rid of my shirt, exposing my torso. I have a prominent six-pack, cut, golden, and impressive, with that V that makes girls stupid and a trail of light brown hair arrowing from my navel and into my pants. I watch her watch me. I'm so hard my brain can barely function. All my blood is in my dick, and it's so engorged it might explode if she just looks in its direction.

So this is what it feels like to die of horniness. My obituary is going to be embarrassing if anyone bothers writing it.

"That's all nice and dandy, but what are your pants still doing on?" She licks her lips, pulling out the rubber band holding her hair in a ponytail and snapping it into the sink. She shakes her head, and her hair gets all puffy and sexy.

I pull my pants and briefs down in one go, then my socks, because very few things are more pathetic than naked men in socks. Then I stand, hard as a fucking stone. Both my cock and my expression.

She stands in front of me and says nothing for a long time. Then she takes a step toward me and lurches forward, almost touching me. My throat bobs with a suppressed groan, thinking she is going to touch me—thinking she might even touch *it*—but she turns the water on behind me and removes her top. It's nothing I haven't seen before, but I can't tear my eyes from her pink nipples, flat stomach, and the curve of her hips.

I swallow again. "Let me know what hole I should slide your tip into," I say. God. She is stripping. For me.

"Don't think you can afford me, Scully. I don't accept coins or coupons."

The tables have turned again, and I want to flip them up and rip the walls down to show her nothing has changed. I still hate her. I still just want to fuck her.

"We're taking a shower together, silly," she finally explains, shimmying out of her skirt. Her black cotton panties follow suit. "But you're not going to touch me. Because guess what. Even though you don't know how I feel about all my firsts, I do. And you don't deserve shower sex with me."

"You've never had sex in the shower?" Bullshit with a capital *B.* This chick has probably seen more cocks than a chicken farmer. Getting naked with me and not letting me touch her is payback. But it's a price that might cost me my balls.

"I plead the fifth," she purrs. Goddamn America.

"Fine."

"*Fine.*"

We both get into the shower. I'm aware her family might come home early from dance and work, but I still don't care. It's not that I don't like Mel, Jaime, and Bailey. I've just been let down by so many people in my life, so getting attached and giving a shit are not really a top priority to me.

Once inside, I grab the soap bar, lathering my body. She squeezes the hundred and five colorful bottles of whatever bathing oils she is using. I sniffed them all, and I'm not surprised she smells like a cake surrounded by every type of fucking flower known to mankind.

I watch her body moving, bending, straightening, *living,* and wonder why we're doing this. Nothing's gonna come out of it. It's pure, delicious torture. It makes my muscles and cock ache, and I wouldn't have it any other way.

The tormentor tormented by its prey.

"Had a good day at school?" She bats her eyelashes, a sugary-sweet smile gracing her lips. I think back to the conversation I had with Coach this afternoon about Prichard and my football career. Another guy would snitch on Prichard to her and let her deal with the mess. But (A) I don't take orders, especially from idiots in expensive suits, and (B) on the off-chance this puts her in a vulnerable position, I'm not going to have him press her back against the wall.

"I survived it." I flex my biceps when I rub soap off my shoulders to see if she'll check me out, and sure enough, she does. She averts her gaze quickly when I smirk.

"How 'bout you?" I ask.

"It was okay." She clears her throat.

"Daria"—I snap my fingers twice—"I'm right here. You can talk to my dick too, but he's more of an action man."

"You grew up from that scrawny kid," she says quietly, turning off the water behind me, and for a moment, our bodies are flush. Her stomach brushes my dick, but neither of us moves. We just stand there, dripping wet, with my dick poking her navel. Close but afar. Nervous but bold. I've never done this before with anyone. Got naked for the sake of being naked. I feel like I should take control of the situation, but then I'll have to shut her down, and as much as I feel shitty about doing this to Adriana, I can't not do it either.

Daria raises herself on her tiptoes and brushes her lips over my ear. I bend down the rest of the way to accommodate whatever it is she wants to tell me.

"Thank you for another first, Scully. I've never been naked with a man in a shower."

Before I know it, she's wrapped in her pink towel and sauntering out of the bathroom, leaving me in the shower with my hard dick pointing at the tiles on the wall.

I relock the door and rub one (fine, two) out before I can get out of there.

1–0 to the home team.

CHAPTER SEVEN
DARIA

You wear your lies
Like a tie.
Too beautiful to remove.
Too elegant to resist.
Too tight to breathe.

Boys are a sore subject for me.

First, let me say that the past few days have been trash, and I'm happy I get to unwind at the end of it. Throughout the entire week, Penn hasn't been home, both because of his football practices and business he has in San Diego. Maybe he is with his maybe girlfriend. I'd kill to get a straight answer about who and what she is to him, but I'm too proud to ask him, let alone ask around.

When Penn is home, he ignores my existence completely, locks himself in his room, and growls one-word responses when I need something concrete from him. He does seem to toss balls with Dad in the backyard whenever he gets a minute, as well as read with Bailey. Melody is trying to spend more time with me. She keeps asking me how school is, and I keep dodging. If she truly cared, she'd check. She hasn't checked in years.

I feel invisible. I always feel invisible. As though I blend in with the walls, and furniture, and the clear glass bowl on the counter where my parents keep apples shined by our housekeeper. Apples that I keep finding under my bed, in my backpack, in my shoes. Apples that invade my space, my room, my soul.

By the time Friday rolls around, I'm on edge. All Saints has a football game against Westmount, and we win but not by much. Blythe, who is a flyer and needs to be extra focused, is having a meltdown in the locker room but refuses to tell anyone what it's about. Esme does her makeup in front of the mirror and mumbles, "Bitch is probably pregnant with that hood rat's baby."

I excuse myself and go throw up in one of the toilet stalls.

"Maybe Dar is preggers too!" Blythe cries from the bathroom stall next to mine.

When I walk out, Esme approaches me and cocks her head with a *tsk*. "You look seriously bad, sweetie. Maybe you should sit this one out."

Maybe you should die.

High school is an aquarium full of sharks. People are always broiling with the need to burst free. Only the strong survive.

On Saturday, we decide to crash a music festival in the desert. I braid my hair and put flowers and golden stars in it, slipping into a pair of teeny-tiny white Daisy Dukes and a white crocheted bikini top. I tie a flannel shirt around my waist and finish the look with cute gray boots.

When I leave, my entire family and Penn are sitting at the breakfast table, shoving carb-ridden pancakes into their mouths.

"The only place you should be going wearing shorts that short is the ob-gyn for a checkup." My dad doesn't even lift his eyes from the *New York Times*. "Change."

"Daddy!" I exclaim. "The Lonely Man is like Coachella on steroids. I can't show up looking like a nun."

"If you want to show up *at all*, you'll put some clothes on," he replies.

I shove the Daisy Dukes into my backpack and change to boyfriend jeans, then run out the door and jump into Alisha's orange Corvette.

Esme and Blythe are retouching their makeup in the back seat.

"The guys are already there. Gus is apparently trashed, and Knight took off with a reality TV star." Alisha laughs, sliding her sunglasses on.

"I hate guys." I sigh.

And this brings me to my original point. I really, truly *hate* guys. Which is why that thing with Principal Prichard worked so well for me until Penn walked into my life and messed it up. People never bother to hit on me because no one wants to compete with the goddamn principal. What they don't know is that what Prichard and I have is different. Unconventional. But by blocking their way from asking me out and trying to hook up with me, I'm guarding my heart. It's not that I'm scared of having my heart broken. It's that I don't think any boy can truly like me. If my own parents barely tolerate me, then how can I expect a dude to fall in love with me for who I am?

That makes Penn a safe bet. I don't need to impress him because I know he already hates me. Plus, we have to keep this a secret. Whatever we have, it doesn't have a pulse, and a life, and a body. There isn't a beat or a rhythm to our forbidden encounters. They come and go. Like a flash in the dark.

Yeah, Penn is a safe bet. Other than the fact that everything about him feels dangerous to the core.

"Earth to Daria." Alisha snaps her glittery fingernails in my face when we arrive. We pour out of the car and go in. It's jam-packed at ten in the morning, so we meet the football team near the stage on dead grass, kicking beer cans out of our paths. Gus is wearing a deep-cut white muscle shirt, slamming his body against others in the mosh pit with a beer in his hand. Knight is nowhere to be seen—probably still with his hookup—and Colin and Will are dragging us by the arms to dance. I go through the motions the entire day, trying to pretend I belong in my own crowd. Feigning happiness is even more depressing than just being your gloomy self. Tears burn my eyeballs the whole time I'm dancing. By the time the sun sets, I feel so empty from all the partying, I'm surprised the wind doesn't blow me over to the other side of the state. Since I'm the designated sober driver, I slip into the driver's seat of Alisha's car and start it.

"Who am I dropping home first?"

"Home?" Esme laughs from the back seat, reapplying her gloss. "Followhill, stop being one hundred years old! Let's go to Lenny's."

Lenny's is a famous diner in San Diego. We usually go there after long nights out because it's open twenty-four hours, and it's more upmarket than IHOP. Blythe, Esme, and Alisha will never admit it, but they also like it because it's a great spot to pick up bikers, pretty fitness instructors on their way to make it big in LA, and other types of handsome, rugged men their parents would never let them hang out with otherwise. Consequently, I hate Lenny's. I always end up sitting in a red vinyl booth, drowning french fries in different sauces as I wait for my friends to come back from their hookups. I pretend to text Principal Prichard when I see them through the windows coming back and adjusting their skirts.

"Are you sure that's exactly what your ass needs right now? Fried food?" I'm officially turning into Esme. I'm fat-shaming people to get off the hook.

Alisha snickers beside me, gulping a bottle of Smartwater.

"Life's too short not to eat greasy food, then starve yourself for a week. Just drive to Lenny's, Dar. The guys are already on their way."

As soon as I set foot in Lenny's, I know I've stepped onto a minefield.

It looks like your typical American diner: black-and-white-checked floors, red-and-white vinyl booths, jukeboxes on every table, and walls crammed with pictures of the owner—you guessed it, Lenny—hugging legendary athletes and local celebrities. The menu flashes in pink-and-green neon letters above the silver bar. Packed, noisy, and carrying the mouthwatering scent of deep-fried onions and burgers, this place is heaven for our semi-drunken asses. We slip into the guys' booth, but I can't shake off the feeling that something terrible is about to happen.

Everyone orders a milkshake. Knight's hair is so tousled and his lips are so puffy it looks like a bear has assaulted him. Guys are so weird. They can love a girl to death but still mess with other people. The guys order an obscene amount of food. The girls get Cobb salads and french fries. I decide to stick to my vanilla and chocolate milkshake and grin when I think about what Penn would make of it if he saw my choice. Is it akin to ice cream? I would ask Mel if we were still on speaking terms.

Gus makes a police siren noise, sprinkling it with a burp.

"Yo. Loser alert at three o'clock."

We all twist our heads to the side and see the Las Juntas football crowd sitting in a booth opposite to ours. The only people I recognize are the big quarterback who seems tight with Penn, the handsome African American dude with the mohawk, and, of course, my housemate.

Penn is wearing a black shirt with a hole where the heart is and unintentionally baggy Levi's that're worn to death. His wallet chain is intact, and he is munching on an unlit cigarette he is never going to smoke. I know he quit; I overheard him telling Melody, who bought him patches and a book the size of my head called *How to Quit Smoking*, and he is talking to the waitress who is taking their order.

Her name tag says Adriana.

Adriana. Wasn't that the name of his so-called girlfriend, whose existence I'm trying to suppress?

"Are they still bitter about the loss?" Esme cackles, slurping her milkshake. Blythe is scrolling through the Instagram page of the Italian artist Vaughn went to study with over the summer, and I know why. There's a picture of Vaughn on there, sculpting. Vaughn doesn't have any other social media accounts and never will.

"Dunno, don't care." Gus snorts, and I know my instincts about the minefield were right. I don't want another altercation with Penn. A sad, distant status quo is better than igniting his hatred toward me. His flames of loathing eat at everything in my vicinity once they're directed at me.

"Scully seems over it. They don't call it the cave of wonders for nothing." Esme raises her phone and snaps a picture of Penn and Adriana laughing as she stands over him with the notepad. "Here, Blythe. I'm sending you a souvenir to the fact that you're pathetic." Esme laughs. "Are you still maybe pregnant?"

"Shut up, bitch."

Blythe goes eerily white. Marx, please don't let her be pregnant. It's like an ice pick in my chest, digging deep.

"Don't be sad, girl. You'll probably get a round on this stallion when he cleans your pool in oh, about five years or so." Alisha yawns, examining her pink-tipped fingernails.

Gus slurps his milkshake extra noisily. "What does Blythe have to do with Scully?"

Blythe flips her hair and pretends to laugh. I can see how badly she wants to cry, and it almost makes me feel sorry for her. "I may have taken him home after the fight. He was the next best thing after Vaughn."

The next best thing.

Gus throws his head back and hoots, slapping the table. "Penn Scully and Adriana are, like, damn serious. The golden couple of Las Juntas. Have been for about two years. Dude. They have a fucking *baby* together. Congrats, B. You were officially the other woman for half a minute."

Have a baby together.

I choke on my milkshake, spitting some of it back into the straw when no one's looking. Gus delivers the news with such casual confidence, and I know he truly believes every word. I look back at Penn and the waitress again. Leaning on his table, she whispers something into his ear, and he lifts his thumb and chucks her nose playfully. He hasn't noticed me—or if he has, he hasn't made eye contact yet—but it's too late to play nice. The Hulk inside me is growing by the nanosecond, and I know I'm about to burst.

He kissed me.

He touched me.

He took a shower with me.

I saw his dick. With my own eyes. My thigh even gave it a handshake.

So many things a guy with a girlfriend and a baby *shouldn't* do.

I glance at them again, and Adriana looks left and right before settling in Penn's lap. She has long, shiny, straight black hair and big blue eyes. She looks glamorous, her skin deeply tanned like honey. Maybe we're the same age, but I get a feeling she is just...*more*. The Hulk pierces through my ribs and stretches his fist across my chest. I'm so jealous I can't breathe. Looking away is a herculean task, but I manage. Somehow.

Gus drums the table and howls like a dog. "Yo, Addy," he yells.

Addy? He knows this bitch?

"Are you gonna make another baby with this loser in the middle of the diner, or are you gonna give us our food? No jizz in my burger, please. There's enough protein in the meat."

Everyone at our table laughs, and my gaze locks with Penn's. Adriana looks back and forth between us, and something floats over her face. A dark something I know all too well.

You have it too. A Hulk of your own.

"Who is she?" I read her lips as she ducks her head down to Penn, frowning.

"No one." I read his lips as he tucks a hair behind her ear. "Just a chick from ASH."

There's a stiff ball inside my throat, and I think it might be my heart.

Adriana stands up, flipping Gus the finger. They obviously know each other. Maybe the jocks frequent this place more than we do. I look away before I cry. I was so focused on Penn's hatred of me that I forgot I hate him too.

"So, Daria, how's Prichard?" Knight asks, loud and clear, throwing extra swagger into his cocky smile. It takes me one second, in which his eyes swiftly dart to Penn, then land back on mine, before I understand what he is doing. Getting back at my housemate for me. Saving my honor.

Do I really look like I need this win?

"A lady doesn't tell," I purr, flashing a smile and tossing back my flowered hair.

"I'd tap it." Blythe points at me with her straw, then sucks on its bottom tip. It is clear she has a dog in this fight. She needs to show that she gives no damns about him either. "I mean Prichard. Not you."

"Right?" I laugh. "I love that he's a real man. Not some boy with a chip on his shoulder."

I wonder if you can rot from within while still being alive. I'm pretty sure if they open me up now, all they'll see is green goo that the Hulk has left in its wake.

A girlfriend. Penn Scully has a girlfriend. And a baby.

He is such a filthy cheater.

Adriana sways her curvy hips to our table with two trays full of food. She starts distributing them, a chirp in her voice. "Cheeseburger with avocado and blue cheese?"

Colin raises his hand.

"Prime hot meat with extra spicy sauce?"

"You can just call me Knight, baby." Cole takes the hot plate from her and winks.

She actually blushes. Maybe she cheats on Scully too. Too bad Jerry Springer retired. They'd make perfect guests.

"Are you waiting for anything, sweetie?" She pops her gum in my general direction.

I flash a syrupy smile, crossing my arms on my chest.

Don't do it. Don't do it. Don't do it.

"Just for you to take your trailer-park ass away from me before I catch a disease."

Everyone sucks in a collective breath, and the room goes silent. So silent. Too silent. I'm panicking, but no one can see that. I'm still smirking. Knight places his hand on my shoulder as everyone starts glancing at each other, absorbing my words.

"Excuse me?" Adriana's voice prickles. Her pupils are so big I can see myself in them.

"You heard me. I'm not interested in eating somewhere the waitress is parking her ass on customers. I think you got it all mixed up. This is not your night shift at your local strip club, *sweetie*."

"Burn!" Colin cups his mouth with his fist and coughs.

"Daria," Knight warns. Normally, he'd drag my ass out and give me a piece of his mind. Not today. He and I both know he can't be that much of a hypocrite. If he saw someone hitting on Luna, he would rip them to shreds and dump whatever's left of them on the side of the road. I've seen him screw people up for less than looking at her. The only problem is, Penn is not my Luna. We don't have some long, elaborate, angsty childhood friendship that's dancing on the edge of more.

"Get the hell out of here." Adriana bares her teeth, and they are white, pearly, and a tad smaller than most people's. An imperfection I'm sure Penn admires. She is no longer chewing her gum. It's just hanging there, stuck to her bottom teeth. I yawn provocatively, staying put. Everyone is salivating over our exchange. Everyone other than her boyfriend, who just stares at me from across the diner with murder in his eyes.

Busted, jerk. I would tell her how good her boyfriend's tongue felt in my mouth if I didn't have my reputation to keep.

"I'm a paying customer. You're a cum dumpster. Who do you think should leave again?" I flip my hair.

She lifts her arm to take a swing at me. I think this will be the day I finally get slapped for being a bitch. But before she can follow through, Penn is standing behind her, holding her wrist in his hand. He lowers it slowly, his eyes hard on mine.

"Get your ass out of the booth, Followhill." He flips the menu on my cell phone, which I'm pretending to study with interest.

"Sorry, I don't take orders from lowlifes." I suck the milkshake out of my straw, batting my eyelashes. My nose is probably red from the sun, and my hair is wild and wavy from the braid I had today. His pupils dilate when he sees my messy, disheveled version.

Penn grabs me by the elbow and hauls me out of the booth. My skin rubs against the vinyl and creates a funny noise that makes me even angrier.

I shake him off. "I don't want to talk to you." I'd spit in his face, but I don't want to make a scene.

"Should have thought of that before you acted like a brat. Whoever follows us gets punched in the face. Guys. Girls. Wildlife. Don't fucking care." He hoists me over one shoulder and carries me out.

"Penn! Wait!" Adriana lets out a shriek.

I lift my head from his triangle back and watch Adriana jogging behind us before stopping, like she knows she shouldn't. Gus and Colin stand to interfere, but Knight yanks them both down by the back of their collars. *"Sit."*

"Are they, like, happening?" Esme whisper-shouts, her mouth agape.

Knight snorts and throws a french fry at her. "Nah. Just an old childhood beef."

He doesn't know anything—he's just covering for me—but he nailed it.

Penn throws the door to the diner open and stalks with me into the alleyway behind it, sandwiched between an auto shop and

Lenny's. He puts me down and takes a step back, like he, too, can't control himself. I lean against a huge *Smog Test* sign with coffee stains all over it and fold my arms.

He paces back and forth, waiting for me to say something. But I shouldn't be the one explaining myself.

"You need to apologize to Adriana," he says, his words clipped.

"You need to apologize to *me*," I say, still tucked firmly in the role of the cold-ass bitch. "You put your hands on me when you had a girlfriend. I'm not that kind of girl."

"You're definitely that kind of girl." He stops, staring at me through hooded eyes. A vicious smirk twists his lips as he sticks it to me. "You're the type of girl who would fuck a married man without batting an eyelash just to prove she can. You let me put my hands and tongue on you already knowing that I have a girlfriend, so don't play the fucking saint."

For the first time since I learned how to talk, I'm at a loss for words. I know he actually believes that. He will always think the worst of me. He is slowly morphing into my mother, losing faith in me too.

I turn around and stomp my way back into the diner to get my phone and order an Uber. He clasps my wrist and jerks me back. I twist toward him and slap him in the face. It's a knee-jerk reaction, and he doesn't see it coming. He stumbles back—not from the slap but from the shock. His eyes burn my face as they drink me in. There's a current dancing between us, and I'm afraid to move, knowing it could electrify me.

"I will never touch someone who isn't mine to touch. But you did. Don't turn this around on me, Scully. You screwed around behind your baby momma's back with the ice princess because *you* wanted to prove you could. But you know what? You are right about one thing. I'm selling myself short. Kissing you. Stripping for you. Humoring you. I'm done ghosting my wake-up calls."

With that, I try to dart back to Lenny's, but he scoops me up from the ground like I'm a toddler, and this time, my back crashes against the wall. He grabs my throat and squeezes, kissing me so hard my lips bruise. I ball my fists and rain them on his chest, ripping his holey shirt farther and dragging my fingernails across his exposed skin.

"I hate you," I cry. "Marx, I do. I hate you so much."

His hands meet the back of my knees, and he hoists me up. I knot my legs around his waist. He cups my face and squashes it as if he is milking this kiss out of me.

"Yet you're still fucking kissing me. With the girlfriend. And the baby. And the sister who will always be better than you. You're kissing your foster brother who hates you, Followhill. A whole fucking lot."

"Fuck you." My tears are unstoppable, raining down hard and fast. My body shudders violently as the sobs rip through me. We're swallowing each other's words and secrets and lies with our mouths. My body moves with his. He groans into my lips as though it's painful. As though he wants to pull away, but he *can't*.

He unbuckles his tattered rope belt and unzips his jeans, grabbing his cock through his briefs and grinding it over my slit through my Daisy Dukes.

"Eat me," I moan. "You don't deserve to enjoy this. I'm the one who should be taking everything in this situation."

He drops down to his knees and tugs my Daisy Dukes and panties aside, stretching the denim against my skin and causing me delicious pain. He throws one of my legs over his shoulder and presses his nose into my slit, inhaling deeply.

A feral growl rips from his throat, coming from somewhere deep and primal, and he bites my inner thigh.

"Blythe might be pregnant, so good luck paying child support for two children at eighteen, asshole." I groan. His tongue drags along my slit, then his mouth clamps on my clit, and he sucks on it hard. I moan. He grinds his straight teeth along my pussy, creating delicious friction. "Marx," I mutter.

He laughs a gruff, grown-up laugh that makes my bones quiver. I don't know why this eighteen-year-old feels like more of a man than my almost forty-year-old principal.

"Will you babysit?" he taunts me.

I grip his silky, light brown hair and pull hard, wanting to inflict pain. "It's not funny."

"She's not pregnant," he says between lazy strokes of his tongue, eating me so willingly and happily, I don't know what to do with myself anymore. He is driving me crazy. No one has ever gone down on me, and when I told him to, I was expecting him to laugh in my face and say no. I couldn't deny myself this either. All my friends get action at Lenny's. I wanted to too.

"So why is she having a meltdown?"

"Because she saw Vaughn before the game with Las Juntas fucking some other chick's mouth under the bleachers." After another flick of his tongue across my clit, he's back to sucking on it hard. My thighs begin to shake around his beautiful head.

"H-how do you know that?" My teeth are chattering. It feels too good to be legal. I want Penn to go down on me for the rest of our lives.

"Because *I* was doing something similar at the time under the same bleachers. You know, to get rid of all the stress."

Yeah. I know. With Adriana, most likely.

I throw my head back and squeeze my eyes shut as his lips clamp on my clit and suck hard while he rubs his chin over my opening. It's messy and hungry and beautiful. He squeezes my ass, and my body breaks into small spasms, a wave of heat blanketing me from head to toe.

My orgasm gallops through me like wild horses. I'm shaking all over. I've never come so hard in my life, and on someone's face, no less.

He sucks my clit between his lips one more time as I come down from the high before he rises to his feet. His whole face is glowing with my lust for him, his chin dripping my juices.

I want to tell him that he is an asshole, but his mouth crashes down on mine, and he demolishes me with a kiss, forcing me to taste my sweet, earthy musk. I hate myself so much for letting him do this to me over and over again when he has a girlfriend. It makes me sick to my stomach. I touch his chest through the hole in his shirt and tug at his lower lip until I suck all of it into my mouth. I take everything he is willing to give me and then steal some more moments, watching his gorgeous silhouette under the starlit sky.

"This is the last time," I promise. To him. To myself. It's not about Adriana; it's about me. I'll never be a cheater. And taking someone who doesn't belong to you knowingly—that's cheating.

He tears his lips away from mine and grins. "You really thought me going down on you is *you* winning?" he says, mocking, dragging his palm across his chin and sucking the rest of my juices from his finger.

I stare at him, stunned. What the hell happened to the fourteen-year-old kid who gave me a precious sea glass, the equivalent of a rare diamond?

"Oh, sweetheart, we'll be over when I say we're over."

CHAPTER EIGHT
DARIA

She's a work of art
And as such
There's nothing more devastating
Than watching her break.

"We can grab Starbucks on the way back home."

That's his peace offering after eating me out against a filthy auto-shop sign with his girlfriend not even one hundred feet away.

Penn offers the olive branch in his taciturn tone the morning after Lenny's, while I'm sitting at the kitchen island with my family, sipping coffee and messing on my phone. Since I haven't slept a wink, analyzing the entire timeline of our relationship, I decide to play along. This is what I've come up with so far:

1. Him having a girlfriend was speculation until yesterday, not a fact. When I asked, he dodged, and I never asked again. While it is true that my research should have been more thorough, he went home with Blythe so openly, I didn't think about it too much.

2. Yesterday, I was disoriented and shocked, which is why I let what happened happen. But it won't happen anymore. I can't

have an affair with the guy who lives under my roof and hates me for screwing up his possibly dead sister's life.

3. He may have taken all my important firsts so far, but he is not going to take the big V-card.

Penn grabs his varsity jacket and motions for Bailey to move it. They're going to the library together. They've been spending a *lot* of time together. I'm jealous of Bails. I'm jealous of Penn. But most of all, I'm jealous of the fact they are capable of forming a real relationship.

All eyes dart from newspapers and iPads and shiny magazines to us.

"No thanks, I'm going to Blythe's."

Her name makes both of us pause. Penn nods curtly, clearing his throat. Dad is looking back and forth between us, reading between the lines.

"Penn, don't pork Daria's friends," he drawls.

Melody gasps. "Jaime!"

"What? I'm not the one doing it!"

"Yes, sir." Penn plucks a donut from the open white box in the center of the table and takes a bite. "Happy not to touch anyone Daria is affiliated with. Her personality might be contagious."

I roll my eyes, knowing I am being watched, and that Dad—the only person on my team in this house—will flip his shit if he finds out Penn touched me.

"Hate you, *bro*." I smile sweetly.

"Indifferent to you, *sis*," Penn says midbite, ruffling my hair as he ambles out the door with Bails. It makes my heart flutter in my chest like a butterfly, but at the same time, I'm also sick to my stomach. Penn really is like a brother to Bailey.

A brother who also had his fingers and tongue in her older sister's privates.

I spend the day stalking Adriana on social media. She is gorgeous, and her baby daughter, Harper, is adorable. Harper is fair-skinned with green eyes, just like Penn. There are a ton of pictures of Addy and Harper together and two of them with Penn. He always looks at them like they're the apple of his eye.

Apples. He hasn't given me apples in a while. Does that mean he thinks he's already conquered me?

At night, another crisis ensues. Mel doesn't come to check on me for the first time since I was born. She doesn't tuck me in bed, kiss my forehead, and tell me she loves me. Probably because she doesn't.

Maybe she's given up on me after the ice-cream parlor stunt. Perhaps, she wants me to pack my stuff and move to college. I'm her glowing, shiny failure. Blackhearted and empty.

I tell myself that I don't care, but inside, my guts rip to shreds and bleed all over my stomach.

I take my little black book to my mother's in-house ballet studio. She turned a part of our basement into a well-lit workroom when we first moved here, and since then, she's spent a considerable amount of time here, mostly with Bailey. I can still hear the echo of their laughter crawling up the basement stairs every summer evening while I was holed up in my room, climbing the walls.

Mel never invited me here, so now I come here on my own, inviting myself.

The night I found out Via ran away, I stood in front of the floor-to-ceiling mirror in the studio wearing full ballet gear. I ran my gaze along my leotard-clad body, knowing I was too clumsy, too curvy, too *Daria* to be a ballerina. Melody found her joy in other girls. Girls more athletic, and disciplined, and regal. Girls like Via. I got jealous, and I started acting up. Instead of pulling me in and telling me that I was irreplaceable, Mel let me go.

So I drifted like a balloon in the sky, waiting for someone to anchor me back down, but no one ever did. It's been years since she stuck her nose in my life and figured out what was going on. Me and

Principal Prichard are doing things we shouldn't be doing. I have a journal where I confess all the horrible things I do to people. My friends are backstabbers who hate me, and I haven't laughed in my family's presence in over four years.

Four years.

Four unnoticed years.

A tear escapes my eye, rolling down my cheek. The door opens, and Penn walks in. He is quiet, somber. He is always quiet and somber. And present. I can feel his presence like the blood flowing in my body—vital and warm and full of my DNA. The problem with Penn is that he has a girlfriend, but he feels like mine when he's around, and that's dangerous.

"How did you know I was here?" I wipe the tear before he can see it.

He rubs the back of his neck. "I thought it was a wine cellar and was counting on some booze."

I roll my eyes, sniffing.

He plops down on the floor. Yanking me by the hem of my shirt, he motions for me to sit beside him, then he knocks his knee against mine. "Talk."

"With the enemy? No thank you."

I drink him in. The curl of his dark blond hair falling across his forehead. His sulking scowl. The love bites across his neck that I didn't do. I imagine Adriana nibbling and kissing and biting him, then stand, unable to calm myself down. I jog toward the door.

He gallops behind me, tugging me back to him.

"Talk, Daria. Fucking talk."

"Why!" I throw my hands in the air. "So you can hold it against me the first chance you get? So you can laugh at me with your friends? The prissy girl with the first-world problems? So you know how weak I am? Why should I talk to you? I'm nothing to you. I've always been your nothing. The bitch who drove your twin sister away. Don't pretend otherwise just because we shared a few sloppy, illicit kisses. Don't act like you give me a sliver of thought when I'm not in front of you. I'm not Adriana."

His lips curl in revulsion. I think I really pissed him off this time around.

He takes my face in both his hands and brings my nose to brush his.

"No," he hisses. "You're not Adriana. I agree."

He pulls back from me, digs in the back pocket of his low-hanging skinny jeans, and takes out a single house key with a blue plastic string tied around it. He throws it into my hands.

I catch it. My eyes widen. How did he…?

"Stole it from your pom-poms." He looks away, walking to the other side of the room, pacing like a tiger in a cage. This is big. Huge, maybe. He keeps me everywhere he goes.

I chase him across the dance room, planting a hand on his shoulder. He turns around. He looks ragged and heartbroken, and I think it's because of me. I *want* it to be because of me. What kind of person does that make me?

"What's eating you, Daria Followhill, queen bee, cheer captain, and the most popular girl in the county?"

My family.

My friends.

My secrets.

My insecurities.

My errors and mistakes and past.

And you. You bury me so deep in feelings I can't even explain.

"Melody stopped coming to my room. It used to be our thing. Every night since I was born, she would give me a kiss good night. I think she stopped loving me," I tell him, and when I do, I realize it's not a lie. It's a numbing notion inhabiting every cell in my body. My mother doesn't love me anymore.

I made someone programmed to adore me unconditionally forget all about me.

"She loves you." He slides the back of his hand against my throat, staring deep into my eyes. "But you hate yourself, so it doesn't matter."

I snort.

"I love myself. Look at me. I'm Daria Followhill." I motion to my body with my hands.

He shakes his head. He's not buying it.

Wordlessly, he pushes me toward the mirror in front of us. Standing behind me, he jerks my chin up so I have to look at myself. At us. He's over a head taller than me. Broad and muscular like a Greek god. His face is sharper, more symmetrical than mine. His charisma is blowing up this room, and I'm standing here, casing most of his body yet barely drawing any attention to mine.

"When I look in the mirror, I see an orphan. A football player. A student. A grieving brother. A guy whose dream is to attend Notre Dame so he can escape the shithole that's his life and break the poverty cycle. I know who I am. But who are *you*? Tell me what you see, Daria." His breath fans across my hair. "Help me get into this beautiful, awful head of yours."

My hand travels to my stomach, and I grab a thin tire of fat. "I'm too curvy."

My hand flies to my face, a finger rolling over my nose. "My nose is too small, and my eyes are too big. And my hair always looks hella dry."

"What else?" he asks. His hand travels to my pajama shorts and snakes into them, his fingers tracing my slit through my panties. "Confide in me, my hideous little monster."

I snort out a laugh, shaking my head. I want to tell him to stop. That he has a girlfriend and a child and I'm not like that. A Jerry Springer–style home-wrecker. But for the first time since yesterday, I feel seen.

"I'm the most jealous and petty person I know," I admit.

"That's because you live inside yourself." He kisses my neck, and I let him. I'm so weak and pathetic. "What else?"

"My soul is black, Penn. When I see competition, I smash it before it grows. I'm so vindictive."

"No, Daria, you are so human. That's what you are."

My toes leave the floor as he tugs my panties aside, his hand shoved deep inside my shorts, and he starts fingering me with two fingers, his thumb playing with my clit. I moan and roll my head over his chest, closing my eyes and letting myself drift somewhere only we exist. My ass grinds against his erection, and I love feeling how hot he is for me.

"Your insecurities are the hottest thing I've ever seen." He bites my earlobe softly, and when I open my eyes, I see that he is still staring at us in the mirror.

Of course he'd feast on my weaknesses. Why wouldn't he? It makes him stronger in our screwed-up relationship.

My knees give out, and my hips buck forward as he fingers me faster and deeper, then a door whines open upstairs, and heavy footfalls descend the basement stairs.

"Marx," I gasp, turning around and pushing Penn away. I look left and right helplessly, my eyes landing on the en suite bathroom of the studio. I shove him inside and slam the door behind him at the same time the studio door flies open and my dad steps in.

Shit, shit, shit.

I'm so busted. I pull my shirt down to cover a very prominent spot of lust on my shorts. My body shivers from the impending orgasm.

"Everything okay?" My dad frowns. "Went to get a glass of water and heard some talking."

"I'm alone!" I exclaim.

Real smooth, idiot.

I push my hair back, clearing my throat. "All alone, as you can see." My smile is so tight it might tear through my skin.

Dad jerks his chin toward the bathroom.

No. Please, no.

"Open the bathroom door, Daria."

"Dad…"

"*Now.*"

I walk over to the bathroom and open it, stepping aside. He is still by the door all the way across the room, but he has a good view of the majority of the bathroom.

"Open the bath curtain."

"Are you serious right now?"

"Don't stall. It's all fun and games until there's a boy in the house who wants to get into my little girl's pants."

I know it's foolish, but my heart is dancing in my chest at the reminder that he actually cares. Bracing myself and taking a deep breath, knowing he is about to see Penn, I open the curtain in one go. But Penn isn't there. I bite down on my lower lip to hide my shock, then turn around back to Dad and shrug.

"Accept my apologies, princess." He smirks. "And while you're at it, stay away from boys."

"Fine."

"I mean, forever."

"Go away, Dad."

"Go to bed. Daddy loves you."

As soon as he shuts the door, I reenter the bathroom, looking around frantically. There's no window, so where on earth is Penn?

"Down here, hideous little monster." I hear a chuckle.

He is fully clothed, lying in the bathtub, smiling up at me with that grin that can crack up the sky and pull the sun closer.

"Move," I growl, stepping in with him.

We lie there, him hugging me in the tub, until we drift asleep. There's no more talking or fingering or kissing. Just the two of us, soaked in something wrong that feels so right.

At half past four, his alarm goes off. We both fumble back to our rooms, and when we reach our doors, his closes with a hiss, not a slam. I smile to myself.

Small victories.

CHAPTER NINE
DARIA/PENN

I hate lying to your face
But I love watching what I can do to you
When my mouth says things
That undo you.

DARIA

The next day, I help my mother in the kitchen. She takes out a vegetable casserole from the oven at the same time I'm chopping a tomato for a salad.

"That looks like way too many vegetables and not enough meat. Right, Scully?" Dad walks through the front door and into the kitchen and plants a kiss on my forehead, then on Mel's lips. Bailey is excused from helping today because she has an exam tomorrow, and besides, Melody says her grueling ballet schedule has left her extra tired.

"Damn straight, sir." Penn waltzes into the house behind him, still in his football gear. I check the time on the grandfather clock across the room. Seven forty-five. Something kept him in San Diego for an extra hour after practice. Someone, maybe. Addy, *probably*.

Don't get jealous. You don't have the right to get jealous.

"Baby, we need to talk about Bailey's homeschooling and the

other thing." Melody kisses my dad on the lips, and entirely too much kissing is going on in this kitchen to keep my appetite healthy.

Hold on, what? Bailey is quitting school?

I shoot Melody a look.

"Oh, it's nothing." She waves away what must be my bitchiest expression to date. "We're just trying to make it easier for Bails now that she has six ballet classes a week."

So I was right after all. Melody *was* going to take Bailey and Via and move with them to London. I bet she is devastated that Bailey is hell-bent on staying in Todos Santos with the rest of the Totholes—children of the Hotholes.

"Do I have time for a quick shower? Didn't catch one at school," Penn asks.

I smirk to myself, my eyes still on the tomatoes. My mother is very strict about dinnertime unless we have a really good excuse, and we're already forty-five minutes late to the table. Banging your baby momma, in case Penn is wondering, is not a good excuse. Melody already moved it back once since he moved in, to accommodate his football schedule.

She won't move it back again.

"Sure," Mel chirps. "Bailey's not done with her homework anyway."

I stand there, slack mouthed, trying hard not to snap at her. She'd have never let me get away with something like this.

I dump all the vegetables inside the salad bowl in sharp movements.

"Here," I growl. "I'm going to watch *The Real Housewives of Dallas* until we eat."

"Or you can stay with me, and we can look at the new Chanel catalog," Melody suggests, cracking open a bottle of white wine.

"No thanks," I quip.

"Hey, maybe we could—"

"Nope." I plaster my most plastic smile, making a show of batting my eyelashes. "Please don't embarrass us both by trying again. Even if you offer me a shopping spree in Milan, the answer will still be no."

Twenty minutes later, we're eating dinner. Spirits are high. Bailey's excitement about her ballet classes is contagious. The girl is entirely too perfect compared to the huge bag of flaws that is moi.

"Also, they're going to take off my braces next week!" she announces, and she and Penn fist-bump across the table. I tell her I'm happy for her because I am, and then she says, "I know, right? Just in time for New York."

"New York?" I scrunch my nose, confused.

"Mom is taking me to New York!"

I drop my fork onto my plate. The room goes silent, and everyone is staring at me. I need to say something. Something positive. And I want to—I love Bailey, I do—but I can't. It's not even the Hulk that's pissed. Melody is right—it's *me.*

Bailey looks around nervously, and I hate that she is in the middle of this.

"It's an early birthday present. It…it was my idea," she stutters. "I…hmm. I wanted it to be a whole week, but Mom only agreed to four days."

My birthday is before hers, but I don't point that out. Now I know why Mel wanted us to look at a Chanel catalog. Funny, she failed to mention a trip to New York is *my* dream. I've been twice, but once was a layover and doesn't count.

"It's for a business meeting." Melody clears her throat, dabbing her napkin on the corners of her mouth. "And of course, I was going to ask you to come."

Dad changes the subject before I can reply. "I've been looking at colleges for you, Penn." He coughs into his fist. "Made a real dent in this project. I've got a list of at least six I want us to see."

"I've only gotten three invites so far from D1s." Penn shoves a forkful of casserole into his mouth, his eyes focused on his plate. I think he's pissed, and I don't know why. I'm the one who should be angry. I'm the one constantly ignored. "Coach told me to choose wisely because, at this point, it's a formality. Once they pay for your flight and accommodation, you're expected to accept it."

"No son of mine is going to the wrong college just because they're shelling out an economy class plane ticket," Jaime says.

"Guess it's a good thing I'm not your son because I can't be picky. *Sir.*"

I wonder how Adriana feels about her athlete boyfriend and the father of her child moving away. Maybe he plans to take them with him. I wouldn't be surprised.

"Your talent and good looks say differently," Dad says, bantering.

"Really, Dad? His good looks?" Bailey releases nervous laughter.

I wish my parents would stop calling Penn "son," so I wouldn't feel ultra-gross about kissing him and rubbing my thighs and stomach and the thing between them all over his cock through our clothes.

"You're like our son." Melody smiles across the table at Penn, who doesn't smile back.

"Which puts your number of children back to two after you dumped me," I mumble into my glass of water.

"Thank you, Daria," Mel bites out, cutting viciously into her casserole, her eyes sparkling. "We can always count on you to dampen the mood."

Penn frowns. I think he is starting to see that I'm not the only one to blame for this whole mess. He opens his mouth, but then my mother says, "Penn, sweetheart, we have something to discuss. Privately."

"Before or after you speak to Bailey about New York?" I inquire, tossing my napkin on the table and standing up. "And what about me? Do you need to talk to me about anything? Maybe about cheer? School? Who I'm hanging out with these days? College applications? Anything, Melody? Any-freaking-thing that's not Chanel?"

Silence.

"Whatever." I flip my hair. "Casserole's a dud anyway. Enjoy your carb-fest, losers." I plaster my fingers into an L shape on my forehead before retiring upstairs on a huff. I don't know why I'm leaving in such a hurry. No one is going to come after me. Melody used to before the thing with Via happened. Then she realized I was never going to confide in her about what was bothering me. Bailey tries to talk to me sometimes. It majorly sucks when that happens. Bails is so sweet, but she has zero life experience, and everything freaks her out. Dad…Dad will always be there for me, but I can't tell him anything about his precious wife. He loves her too much to see past the blinding glow she casts on him.

I slam the door, but the walls are thin, and I hear a chair scraping across the floor. It pains me that I know who it is without looking. Only one person in this house hasn't given up on me, and that's because he never believed in me in the first place.

"Leave it, Penn," I hear my mother say, and I can practically envision her taking a generous sip of her wine. "That's just Daria being Daria."

PENN

In the book *Survivor* by Chuck Palahniuk, there's a scene where the narrator realizes, after eating most of a lobster, that its heart is still beating. Living under the same roof with the Followhills is a little like that. You're being eaten and picked apart, but your pulse is still there.

Talk.

I frown at the unanswered message I sent her an hour and a half ago.

I'm lying in my perfect bed, in my perfect room, in this perfect gingerbread house, where everyone is so deeply flawed, they can't even stand each other. Who would have thought pristine, gorgeous Daria Followhill was the black sheep of her family?

The worst part wasn't that Mel ignored Daria's existence. It was that she was casual as fuck about it. As if her daughter was an annoying fly.

Mel is batshit scared of her daughter, who acts like anything *but* her daughter, and Jaime is tired of choosing sides. And Bailey is in the middle of this mess, gathering some bomb-ass material for her future therapist to work on.

Earlier this evening, when I washed the dishes and Jaime towel-dried them, he asked if I wanted to join his friends and their boys for a camping weekend. I told him I didn't think it was a good idea because Daria was already feeling fifty shades of messed up about Bailey and me monopolizing her parents' time. The funny thing is, I don't want their time. I just want their fridge. Bed's nice too, I suppose. Especially when their daughter's inside it.

"Since when do you care about Daria's feelings?" Jaime frowned at a plate he was drying, but he couldn't hide the delight in his voice.

"I don't," I confessed. "But your daughter's got ammo for miles on my ass. And as she is very trigger-happy, I don't want to be in her line of fire." This part was bull wrapped in a lot of shit.

Jaime stared at me skeptically. "Are you bullshitting a bullshitter, Scully? You don't care if you go to war with Daria. You don't even care if you go to war with Russia. You'd still show up. Probably in these jeans and your holey shirt, and maybe a cigarette."

"Daria could tell people I live here." I half shrugged. She wouldn't. I don't know how I know that, but I just do. She's not that much of an asshole unless explicitly provoked. Even then, she is more about the bark than the bite from what I've seen. She thinks she's the Antichrist when, in practice, she's more like Mary Magdalene. She'd watch Christ getting crucified without lifting a finger, but you better know she won't be happy about it. No, sir.

"And if she did? You don't need a scholarship," Jaime gritted out. "I'll pay for your education."

"Sir, I really appreciate your generous offer, but for the millionth time, I ain't about to take your hard-earned money."

"It's not that hard-earned, boy. The good thing about money is that when you have enough of it, it creates itself."

But it's not just my Southern upbringing or basic morals. It'd be weird to explain how my ass landed at Notre Dame all of a sudden. My friends would stab me in the balls if they found out I've been living in this sick crib and kept it from them.

"Besides, you're using it now," he countered.

"Because I have no choice. Well, I do, if you consider homelessness a choice."

We wrapped it up, and I went back to my room, waiting for Daria to initiate something. She didn't. When it became clear that she extended the cold war with her family to me, I shot her the unreturned message.

Talk is code for meeting in the basement. We can't risk saying anything else in case her parents decide to go through her texts.

Tired of sitting idly like some desperate loser, I kick my door open. It's past one thirty, and she may be asleep, but I'll take my chances.

I knock on her door. No answer.

I push it open. She is lying facedown on her bed with her blankets still tucked under the mattress. It's something the cleaners in this house do every day like it's a hotel. She reminds me of Via lying in the yellow grass the day Daria and I got rid of the letter.

Lights out. No one's home. Hopeless.

I think of ways to make her laugh. Of saying that her ass looks great from this angle (it does). Or maybe to tell her that it gets better (it doesn't).

Stopping over her bed, I splay my fingers on the small of her back and press. Hard. Sinking her into her plush mattress until she is drowning in satin fabric.

She groans. "Go away."

"And miss out on all this delicious teenage angst?" I murmur, mesmerized by how beautifully she fits under my palm. As though she was born to have my hands on her. "It's practically Netflix for free."

"I don't want to tell you anything."

"You don't have a lot of options."

"I have friends," she shoots.

"No. You don't," I say softly. "You have people you hang out with, and you'll never give them a truth. Not even a half-truth. Not even a fucking quarter. Now look at me."

She rolls to her back, and I suck in a breath. She's crying. She's been crying for hours probably. Her entire face is wet and swollen. I cup her head and pull her into me, sinking into her bed and cradling her. The door is open. The Followhills could wake up and walk in here at any moment. I hope they do. They need a wake-up call. A whole goddamn siren, more like.

"Talk."

"No." She laughs for the first time since I met her, wiping her tears quickly, only to make room for new ones. "I'm always the one who talks. You're the one who listens. I don't even know who I am talking *to*. Your walls are still up, but mine have been lowered enough for me to see that this relationship is one-sided."

She's right. I want to be her Trojan horse. To slip through her barriers undetected. But I never give her any part of me. I'm always the one to take.

"Pretend that I'm your friend."

"I don't have any friends, remember?"

"Sucks to be you." There's no menace in my voice.

She shrugs. "So why are you here?"

"Because it sucks to be me too."

Because it sucks less when we're together even though I should hate you.

I pull her into my embrace, and she pushes back. That only

makes me hold her tighter, and she stands no chance. A cheerleader against a wide receiver? You don't need a PhD in physiology to guess who wins.

"Say it," I growl into her ear. "Your family is bullshit right now. Your mom's all up your sister's ass, and your dad is torn. Make it real. Because the minute it gets real, you have to deal with it."

I speak fluent Dr. Phil because the only thing the woman who gave birth to me did for the past six years was lie on the couch watching his show and judging other people while getting high.

Shying away from your problems only makes them multiply. Kinda like cancer. Left to its own devices, it will spread to other organs in your body.

Daria is thrashing in my arms, desperate to push me away, her soft crying turning into heart-wrenching sobs. She is shaking against my chest, but her lips stay pursed.

She doesn't want to admit to the hood rat that life in the golden castle ain't perfect.

I envelop her. Even when Daria is growling like an injured animal in my ear. Even when the sea glass necklace, *her* sea glass necklace, burns a hole in my back pocket, right next to her pom-pom string, demanding to go back to its rightful owner. Even when a scream rips from her throat and I need to cover it with my palm. I hold her.

"Go to your girlfriend. She needs you more than I do."

She does. Addy and Harper need me desperately. But they're not who I want to be with.

"I bet this is your first time breaking." I wipe her tears away. "I used to break all the time. Under a bridge. Next to a bunch of homeless people. I used to scream at the river and punch concrete walls after Via disappeared."

She wanted something real and inconvenient, so she is getting it.

"I couldn't talk for days afterward. I once punched my own face to see if I could cry. The answer is no, by the way. And when my mom died? I went to the snake pit hoping Vaughn would kill me. I let him fuck me up just so I could feel something. Because, you see, I'm the Tin Man. I have no heart. Not since Via left. She was my entire world. Adriana and Harper, I take care of them, but it's not the same. My heart was rusty before she left, but after? After, it was gone. Is that real enough for you, Daria Followhill?"

She sniffs and gazes up at me. Her blue eyes are so spectacular, they look like two bowls full of diamonds. Skull Eyes' lips are trembling around the words she is still too proud to say. Her whole face is shiny with tears and snot. I press a soft kiss to the tip of her runny nose. She immediately sniffs. Like I give a fuck about a little snot.

"You're Saturn," she whispers. "Made of iron-nickel and surrounded by protective rings of ice and rock."

"How do you know that?" I smile, and I know the smile is warm. I know it's fucking up something in her chest, and even though I shouldn't, I *like* it. After all these years, I still want to ruin her. Then put her back together. Then do it again and again and a-fucking-gain.

"Bailey knows stuff about stuff. Sometimes I pick it up at the dinner table. Why were you home late today?" she asks.

Because I knew you'd be here.

"I saw Adriana," I lie.

I hug her tighter because she is squirming again, desperate to run away, and I can't let her.

And when she breaks within my arms, I glue her back, tuck her in bed, and kiss her forehead, not letting go until she is sound asleep.

CHAPTER TEN
DARIA

He wants to let her go
But can't seem to set her free
Because if she does end up returning
She'll see who he fell in love with and flee.

Lying on the giant flamingo float in our Roman-shaped swimming pool, I stare up at the sun through my sunglasses. The sun is a lot like hate—beautiful and lethal and essential for our survival. It can blind you, but it also keeps you going. Hate motivates much more than love. Love is content and peaceful. Happy people aren't driven. They simply…exist. Now, us, hateful people, we're something else. Hungry and desperate.

Hateful people make the best lovers.

The soft whoosh of the water underneath me tricks me into relaxing my muscles and giving in to nirvana. I blink at the tall palm trees, cloudless sky, and landscape of Todos Santos and wonder how someone with so much can feel so little.

I feel like a piece of the jigsaw, the one forgotten under the carpet that no one bothers to look for.

"Lovebug? Sweetie?" The double glass door slides open, and Mel walks out in one of her turquoise beach dresses and a giant straw hat. We're the same size.

Melody was smaller than me when she was my age. A true ballerina, her ribs stuck out, and you could see every fine muscle in her back. Every time she huffs and puffs in front of the mirror, complaining about not being a size zero anymore, she averts her eyes to me quickly and apologizes. "Not that size four is not small."

No, Mother. It's just not perfect. By your standards anyway.

I ignore her, still floating and staring at the sky.

She takes a seat on one of the 2K-apiece yellow-and-red Moroccan lounge chairs and sips from her skinny margarita. "We need to talk, Dar."

We actually don't. We haven't in years, and you didn't seem to mind.

"Are you going to ignore me forever?"

Not forever. Just until I can articulate to her how she is hurting me. By putting Bailey first. Dad first. Penn first. But telling her all those things conveys vulnerability, and the only thing I have going for me is that my mother thinks I'm strong. Penn is right—the minute you admit something, it becomes real.

"I have something to tell you, and I don't want you to get upset."

"Then why would you tell me in the first place?"

I stretch my arms and leisurely row my way to the edge of the pool with long strokes. I slide under the float and take the stairs leading to the deck, grab a towel, dry off, and slip on a skirt and cute tank top.

"You keep doing things that upset me, like hiding trips to New York and homeschooling plans for Bailey and adopting Penn." I shake off my long, wet hair. "But it's not preventing you from doing them anyway. Tell me, Mother, how many more secrets are you planning to keep from me?"

She slides her sunglasses down, and our eyes meet. Her greens sparkle with unshed tears.

"One," she whispers. "One more. How many secrets are you keeping from me, Daria?"

I think about Via's letter. About Prichard. About Penn. I shake my head. "I need to go."

"Daria…"

I pick up my phone and storm into the house, then grab my car keys and dart to the front door. She is on my heels, begging me to stop. But all I can think about is her and Bailey planning trips to New York and sitting together every day—all day—at home while I go to school, or college, or anywhere else that's out of their hair.

Penn is descending the stairs. Why is he always here when he doesn't have practice? Why doesn't he spend time with his daughter? He stops on the landing, his wide chest blocking my way, rattling with his soft, taunting laughter that usually sends hungry chills to my bones. He is wearing a black hoodie with a white skeleton hand giving you the middle finger—the hole is somewhere beneath it—and torn, black skinny jeans that hang too low on his ass. Unlaced sneakers. Rumpled locks. Pure perfection.

"Where to, Hurricane Daria?"

Tears glittering in my eyes, I push him off and duck sideways, slipping through the door. I jump into my car and start it. What is Mel planning now? Moving with Bailey to London? Sending me to an out-of-state college to get rid of me? Sell me to the mafia? I wouldn't put anything past her at this point. Before I know what's happening, Penn jumps into the passenger seat beside me. I slap the dashboard. "Fuck! Leave me alone."

Mel stumbles out the front door, scrambling. I don't understand why. She's been doing her best to stick it to me for months now.

"Hysteria doesn't suit you, Skull Eyes. Where are we going?"

"I don't know."

"My favorite destination."

"Why are you doing this?" I moan, pain slicing my voice so it's all cracked.

Mel gets to the car, rounds it, and slaps my window with her open palms.

I realize it's too late to kick Penn out.

"Daria!"

I kick the BMW into drive and watch her disappear in the side mirror. I'm driving past manicured neighborhoods and downtown Todos Santos. Rolling onto the highway and bolting between golden dunes. I drive until there is nowhere else to drive to. Belle and Sebastian are on the radio, asking me if I'm feeling sinister. I pretend Penn is not here, and he helps by not talking.

A white-and-blue gas station sign twinkles in the distance of yellow nothing. Neither of us acknowledges that it's my birthday today. That I didn't get a cake, or a card, or a hug. That my family thought they could skip this day just because they agreed to let me have a party in a few weeks. Every time my mother calls and the Bluetooth starts playing the *Jaws* sound effect—her personal ringtone, complete with a picture of her flashing a toothy smile—Penn sends it to voicemail.

"Pull in." Penn pops his gum.

"Why?"

"Beer."

"How exactly?" I roll my eyes.

He raises his ass from the seat and takes out his wallet, yanking out what looks like a fake ID.

"Ghetto," I cough into my fist.

He smirks, sliding the ID between my open thighs, swiping it across my slit like it's a credit card reader.

I suck in a breath. "What the hell do you think you're doing?"

"Showing you that I might be a punk, but you're the hideous little monster who is falling for him."

Pulling into the station, I shove him out of the car. I mull his stupid words over as I watch him through the 7-Eleven window. I'm not falling for him. I'm not. He saunters coolly to the register with a six-pack of Budweiser and potato chips. Then he asks for a pack of cigarettes even though he doesn't smoke anymore. When he slides back into the car, I ask why the cigarettes.

"An experiment." He throws a chip into his mouth and chews. "Pull out, birthday girl. I'll tell you where to drive."

Following his directions, I don't bother asking where we're going. The truth is, it doesn't really matter where he is taking us. He and Dad are the only people I would follow.

It turns out to be a park called Castle Hill. Tall trees swirl to the sky, rising through the wet soil and neon moss. It's surprisingly green for a place in SoCal, where everything is usually buttery. I park in front of a fallen tree trunk in the middle of the woods and watch Penn hop out holding two beers in his hand. I join him.

"This park is magic," he says. "It's where I come when I need to fucking breathe." He cracks a bottle open and hands it to me.

I shake my head. "I'm driving."

"One beer. I won't let you get tanked." He leans against the huge trunk. Tentatively, I take a long pull of the beer he offers me. It goes down cool and smooth in my throat. I groan, leaning against another trunk opposite from him. We stare at each other for a while before he takes out the cigarette pack, unwraps it with his mouth, spits the cellophane to the ground, and pulls one out with his teeth, lighting it up.

"Enjoying your cancer stick?" I grumble.

"Not as much as you're about to," he says flatly, handing me the cigarette. Something unspoken crosses between us, and I take it, awaiting further instructions. His legs are tangled at the ankles, and he looks completely indifferent. Like this is a presentation he's been giving for a few years now.

"Take a drag."

I do. I immediately start coughing. It tickles my throat and burns my lungs. I don't know how Knight and Vaughn smoke so much weed. I hate the way the smoke lingers inside my body.

Penn watches me like a hawk. "Now take a deeper drag. But this time, don't exhale. Keep it in."

He finishes his bottle of beer and throws it against a tree. It's a good throw, and the bottle shatters into tiny pieces. "Keep the damn thing in, Skull Eyes."

I do as I'm told, waiting for the point of all this. I take a hit and then wait. My throat closes in on the smoke, and I feel like I'm choking. My lungs are full of poison, and I want to throw up everything I'm holding in. My face flushes, and I don't know if I can hold it much longer.

He walks over to me, completely nonchalant, and crouches, locking his eyes with mine.

"Release."

I release the smoke and cough my lungs out. Oh my Marx. Why did I even do that? Because he was pretty and brooding and messed up, and he told me to?

Penn lifts my chin so that our eyes don't waver from one another. "This is what it feels like to hold rage inside. That shit's toxic for you. You're either going to have to face your mother, your friends, your principal, your fucking *life*, or prepare to feel like you're holding the smoke in your lungs for a very long time. Because, baby, it only gets worse from here on out. The older we get, the deeper the shit we're swimming in gets."

I look down so I don't cry. I've always been angry, but ever since Penn walked into my life and put a mirror in front of my face, I've been *furious*.

Who is Penn to tell me how to handle my issues? Just because he happens to be here when stuff gets messy doesn't mean that his grass is greener. He is far from perfect. In fact, if I remember correctly, he handled the loss of his mother by being a punk who fights at the snake pit, drinks, smokes, and talks trash to the entire world. Not to mention he has a girlfriend and a daughter he barely sees, opting to mess around with his shiny, new toy he came to live with.

"Wow. Inspiring words. Tell them to someone who cares." I trudge my way back to the car.

He grabs my wrist, jerking me back.

I turn around sharply, narrowing my eyes at him. "Getting me to smoke and drink, and now stopping me from going home? Not sure my parents are going to be on board with your behavior."

He cocks his head, scanning me. "Your parents won't give a shit if I fuck you on the dining room table while Bailey helps herself to another serving of pie."

I raise my hand and slap him. Hard. He throws his head back and laughs as if this is all a joke. As though he *wanted* me to hit him. Now both our cheeks are tinted pink. Mine from embarrassment, his from the slap.

"Shit. You actually think that." He shakes his head, grabbing another beer from the six-pack and cracking it open. "You think you're that unlovable."

"Stop," I say, plead, *beg*. I'm not sure he is wrong. "Please stop."

"So fucking gorgeous, so fucking popular, so goddamn *despised*," he continues. I advance toward him to slap him again because I don't know how else to shut him up. He puts down his beer to grab both my wrists and pins me against a tree, getting into my face and snarling. I stumble back from the tree, but he deliberately steps on my toes, and I fall butt-first onto a bed of crunchy auburn leaves. I lie on my back and stare at him, my tears clinging to my lashes for dear life.

He lowers himself on top of me, his knee pressed between my thighs, his gaze dripping anger and adoration I've never seen there before. He hates himself for being attracted to me. And he hates me for making everything so difficult for everyone. Him included.

Penn puts his hand on my throat and curls his fingers around it. My pulse quickens against his hot skin, and I fight the urge to let my eyelids fall shut.

"Why are they ignoring your birthday, Skull Eyes? Tell the truth."

It's painful to swallow. There's so much bitterness in my throat. The truth seems oceans away. I see it in the distance, but it's unreachable. So hard to put into words.

"I asked them to ignore it." I choke. "I made them promise."

I close my eyes, and I feel his breath on my face. We're all alone. Anything can happen. *Everything* can happen.

"Why?" he croaks.

"Because I can't take another disappointment."

Silence.

"I'm not going to have sex with you, Penn."

"Why's that?"

"You have a girlfriend."

"Maybe I don't."

"But you do."

"Actually, I don't."

"Huh?" I let out a nervous laugh, but it stops between his fingers pressed against my throat. "What do you mean?"

"Can't really get into it right now but think about it for a second. Am I with her? Do I go to her? Do you see us talking on the phone? Shooting the shit? Hanging out? Have I ever talked about her? Brought her over? Adriana is not my girlfriend."

So you just knocked her up. Sweet.

"Ever watch *Lady and the Tramp*?" He drags the tip of his nose along mine, trying to distract me from whatever's in my head.

"Y...yeah?"

"Remember the spaghetti scene?"

"I think so."

"Who was the one to pull away from the kiss, Lady or Tramp?"

I search my brain for the answer, but it's been years since I've watched it. Honestly, it wasn't one of my favorite movies. I always wondered what a royal bitch would find in a dirty stray. But I know now. Oh, I know very well why girls of pedigree love the mutts. They're forbidden. Exciting. And taming them is a challenge no silver-spooned princess can turn down.

"I think she pulled away," I say. "Lady."

"Ding, ding, ding. Ten points."

"What *is* the point?" I swallow as his knee digs between my thighs, pressing at my clit, spreading delicious pressure all over my sensitive area.

"You never pull away when I kiss you." He still holds my gaze.

"I don't?"

He shakes my head, looking down at me, his longish hair falling across his eye. "You want me," he says simply.

I snort. "Jesus, you are conceited."

He leans in until our noses touch again. His hand is still wrapped around my throat. He squeezes it lightly as his tongue brushes from the base of my chin all the way to my forehead, where he kisses my hairline.

"Tell me you don't want to fuck me as much as I want to fuck you, you screwed-up, messed-in-the-head, gorgeous girl with skulls in her eyes," he whispers hotly, his free hand traveling over my thigh, up my skirt, his calloused finger pads grazing my bikini line.

My throat bobs against his hand.

"Tell me you don't want me to push my finger into you and make you come."

"I don't want you to…" I start, but then his hand skims between my legs, and I shudder. My eyelids are at half-mast, and I can barely see what's happening. I spread my thighs wider for him. He said he doesn't have a girlfriend. Why should I hold back?

"Finish the sentence," he commands.

I look the other way, closing my eyes. It is humiliating to admit that I want him to do all those things to me, and he is not even my boyfriend. He's not even my *friend*. Penn slips his hand into my bikini and flicks my clit with his thumb, groaning when he touches it. He shifts a little on top of me to press his cock against my thigh. It's hot and hard even through his jeans.

I buck my hips to meet his touch, but he still doesn't kiss me. It's when I wince a second before an orgasm washes through me—my whole body a tense knot of muscles and red-hot pleasure—that he presses his thumb against my clit hard and slides his middle finger into me. And I'm wet. So wet. So embarrassingly wet for my foster brother. And now some time has passed, and I realize that it's what Penn has really become. A family member of a sort. I'm messing around with someone who's supposed to be my relative. Giving my virginity to someone I should feel brotherly feelings toward.

Marx help me.

His lips are on my ear now, his toffee-hued hair all over both our faces. Our foreheads are sticking together with warm sweat. We are heaving, in sync.

"Tell me not to kiss the shit out of you."

When I remain silent, his lips crash on mine. I'm still buzzing from the orgasm he gave me when he fingered me. He doesn't know that I'm a virgin. Not yet. But he is about to.

I pull away from him, breaking the kiss. "Tell me you don't want all my firsts," I challenge.

His jade eyes search mine for clues. I move my groin to meet his erection, and he squeezes his eyes shut.

"Tell me you don't want to take my virginity," I rasp.

His eyes snap open. I know that despite his initial shock, he believes me. So many guys didn't believe me when I told them I was a virgin, so I stopped telling people. There was no point in trying to convince my friends. They didn't want to listen.

I press my hips to his again, and we meet like a perfect puzzle.

His cheeks are so pink, his face is so beautiful, and I am so beyond screwed.

"Tell me that you don't," I whisper.

"But I do." His forehead crumples in anguish. "There's nothing I want more than every single thing you have to give."

Closing my eyes, I inhale as he reaches into his back pocket for a condom. It's not romantic. Or intimate. Or perfect. But it's us. Two dirty kids in a forest where no one can see or find us. Penn retrieves the condom and kicks his pants to his ankles. As he rolls the condom on, he asks me if I'm sure.

I smirk. "Are *you*? You have more on the line."

He stops, cupping my face in his hands. His eyes twinkle, but maybe I see what I want to see. I didn't mean to save him all my firsts. But it happened, and a part of me is glad that it did. Because he was the first boy to give me a gift. The first boy to kiss me. To want to become my friend, not because I was popular but because I was *me*.

He was the first boy who noticed the injured animal behind the camouflage of hostility and tried to give it water and shelter.

"Fuck the line."

The first thrust is like a sharp slice of a knife. My lungs squeeze the oxygen inside them. The discomfort subsides with the long, luxurious kisses that Penn rains on my mouth. On my cheeks, neck, and breasts. He stops every now and again, not wanting to come, to suck one of my nipples into his mouth and lick around it. He caresses my face and swipes stray locks of hair from my forehead. He is moving inside me as though he's done it a thousand times before, but he is also careful and gentle. The leaves beneath me crunch with every thrust as he pushes into me, and they tickle my back.

He growls, and it stirs something inside me. I wrap my arms around his shoulders, squeezing hard, wanting more of him against me, inside me, with me. I wish I could lock us in a bubble and never let go. I wish we didn't have to go back. That I didn't have to hate him, and that it wasn't so wrong to want this.

His thrusts become quicker and jerkier, and my eyes widen at that. I'm guessing he is going to come. I've never seen a guy come. *Another first.* The space between my thighs is sore, but the pain is lusciously sinful. I'm full of him and desire and want.

I only realize that I'm crying when he empties inside me. His jaw tightening, he is so beautiful, and I think that's a part of why the tears stream down my face. As soon as he realizes that I'm crying, his eyes narrow, and he kisses the tears away. He doesn't take a moment to recompose. He is still inside me when he licks them, one by one, chasing them.

"That bad, huh? I swear I leave more of an impression when they're half-drunk."

There's laughter through my tears now, and I swat at his chest.

I want him to tell me everything. Why he calls me Skull Eyes. Why he has a hole in all his shirts. What Adriana is to him. And for the first time, I think I might have the chance to find out all those things. Because the way he looks at me? He doesn't hate me. Not right now.

"Have you been with many girls?"

He pulls away from me, and it burns a little. We both look down, and there's a little blood on the condom. He tugs the condom slowly. We both watch in fascination as he knots the open end and tosses it behind the tree trunk.

"Not many. Less than five, more than three. I was your first?"

"Yeah."

"Say it. The entire sentence."

"Huh?"

"Penn Scully, you were my first."

"Penn Scully, you were my first." I roll my eyes and laugh.

He rises to his feet, zips up, and offers me his hand. I take it as reality slowly trickles into my brain. I let the Las Juntas football captain screw me in the woods. If anyone finds out, I'm officially dead. A sudden wave of fear washes over me.

"Tell me you still want to be my friend." I gnaw at my lower lip.

"I do. I *am*. I've always been your friend, Skull Eyes. Even four years ago."

"What makes you say that?"

He blinks at me, dead serious. "Because if I weren't your friend, I'd have fucked you over and made sure you paid for what you did."

I slip my hand under his black hoodie, over his shirt, searching for the hole I know I'm going to find. It's there but smaller. His heart is beating so hard against my palm. I know he is feeling this too.

I blow out imaginary candles and make a wish.

"You know what I feel like?" he asks.

"What?"

He can barely contain his wolfish, twisted grin. "An apple."

On the drive back home, Penn argues that I need to hear my mom out.

"She's neurotic as fuck, full of good intentions and bad execution, and she's shit-scared of you, but she loves you. It's nauseatingly clear."

"I'll think about it." And for the first time in a long time, I mean those words.

I know that Dad and Bailey would be grateful if we play nice with one another. I haven't felt this hopeful in years.

We pull up to my house, and Penn slams the passenger door and swaggers his way to the entrance. I follow. He stops at the door and turns around, pulling me to him by the waistline of my skirt.

"FYI, you smell like dirty forest sex."

"You smell like a cheap beer," I murmur as his lips find mine, drugging and perfect.

"You smell like my new, steady ride." His lips move against mine.

"You smell like a lot of really fun nights." I pretend to sniff his neck, armpits, face. My heart speeds without direction all over my chest. I push Adriana's memory aside. The other girls in Las Juntas. Blythe.

"You smell like you might be right." He smacks another wet kiss on my lips and pushes the door open.

My smile is so big, my cheeks hurt. We saunter in together but far enough away from each other not to arouse suspicion. Penn stops when we reach the living room, dropping his keys to the floor with a clink.

I sigh, picking them up and handing them to him.

"Marx, Penn! You're so clumsy." I laugh breathlessly. "You dropped your—"

"Via?" His voice is thin glass, waiting to be shattered.

I lift my eyes from his stupid keys to the stupid couch where my stupid family—Mel, Dad, and Bailey—are all sitting in one neat line, hands tucked between their thighs, and between them sits a grown-up version of Sylvia Scully. She's clad in a conservative black dress that ends at her ankles, and she wears a polite, robotic smile.

She stares at me, not Penn.

"*Surprise.*"

CHAPTER ELEVEN
PENN

You came back to me like a tempest
Beautiful and dazzling and destructive
Ripping everything in your wake
Including, but not limited to, my heart.
Be careful what you wish for.

For four years, I've dreamed of this moment.

In some of my dreams, I punch her square in the nose and tell her she's a cunt.

In others, I hug her close and fall to my knees, begging her to never leave me again.

In most, I tell her all the things I wanted to share with her while she was away. That Mom became worse after she disappeared, which means that maybe she gave a shit after all. That Rhett got beat up by a bunch of white supremacist drug dealers who tried to get into his territory several times and was hospitalized twice. That he is missing three teeth and half an ear now, adding playfully that his modeling days are over. That I hadn't lost my virginity to Adriana, like Via said I would, because "Adriana always looks at you like you're food, and the kind you don't leave leftovers of." That I made it as captain. That she was wrong about Kannon too. He didn't grow up to be an asshole and is actually surprisingly bearable for a human being.

But now that she is here, I just stand like an idiot and stare at her as though she took a dump on my football gear. I can't fucking breathe, and it feels like she is pressing on my sternum with her orthopedic shoes.

I'm taking inventory, for whatever the fuck reason, to make sure all the organs are still in place. Even sitting down, I can see that she is still a head and a half shorter than me, only we're both much taller. She is lithe and athletic, but her long, blond hair is now braided into an Amish bun, and she doesn't have any makeup or the nose ring that she had before. Her dress could belong to a nun.

This is not my Via.

She rounds the coffee table in small, gentle steps and goes for a hug. Stiffly, I feel her scrawny arms wrap around me. Finally, my brain tells my body to snap out of it, and I pat her back. I want to crush her with a suffocating hug, but I can't. She's a stranger. At least, she looks like one. I glance at Jaime and Mel, who are both standing up, their arms behind their backs.

Via is back.

They brought my sister back.

Melody, of course, is the first to cry. I swear, this bitch should've been born into a *One Tree Hill* episode. The drama is always high when she's in the room.

"Penn." Her lower lip wobbles. God, please. Don't let her film this shit and send it to *The Ellen DeGeneres Show.* "Via. You have so much to catch up on."

I know I'm in shock when my mind goes in a different direction. Instead of, you know, wanting to catch up with my sister and find out where the hell she's been all these years, I try to figure out why they didn't tell me before. Why they didn't give Daria the heads-up.

Shit, *Daria.*

Her juices are still on my pubes. I take a step back from my sister, who doesn't feel like my sister anymore, and twist my head to where I left Daria. She is still there, rooted to the floor, gaping at

Via in disbelief. Via meets her gaze and swallows. I'm waiting for my twin to talk so I can figure out who I'm dealing with. Because right now, she looks like a cardboard version. The blueprint before they poured personality, a soul, and character into her.

"Where in the good fuck have you been?" I curl my lips in revulsion.

Okay. Not the reaction everyone was expecting by the way Via flinched and Melody choked on her breath. But screw that. They weren't the ones deserted.

You made me the fucking Tin Man, Sis.

Via looks down at her untrendy tennis shoes, shined to perfection. She is twiddling her thumbs.

Who in the hell is this girl?

"With Dad…" Her voice is barely a whisper. It's so delicate and brittle, it breaks around the last letter. "And Grandma."

"I thought they were traveling around the country with their cult? Making the Midwest even more redneck."

The asshole who decided at some point in my childhood that my mother wasn't worth the trouble and we were in his way to achieving greatness. He, therefore, decided to be an itinerant preacher of some sort. Last I heard, he lived in a trailer from the eighties with my Southern grandmamma. Real fucking catch.

"They were." She is still looking down. "*Are.* After I ran away, I managed to find them in Mississippi. I called and called until he picked up, then I hitchhiked there."

"To Mississippi?"

She nods.

She is timid, shy, and doesn't look me in the eye. My real twin sister from four years ago would eat her for breakfast.

"Why don't we talk about it over a cup of tea?" Melody claps her hands, channeling her inner Queen Elizabeth. I don't want tea. I want to know everything. And I want to know why Via didn't pick up the phone to call me in four years.

"Why didn't you call?"

"Father said I couldn't." *Father*.

"You could have written. You knew my address."

"He said he'd throw me out if I made any attempt to reach out to you. I didn't have anywhere else to go. I couldn't go back to living with Rhett. I couldn't risk you writing me back. Please, Penn." She touches my arm, and I pull back instinctively. Bailey stands up from behind her and hugs my sister's shoulder. My sister turns around and sinks into Bailey's embrace. I'm so focused on what's happening, I barely register Melody yelping Daria's name and running after her up the stairs.

Daria bailed.

I don't even blame her.

I would probably kill my mom if she had pulled shit like this.

Lucky for me, she's already dead.

FUCK. TEA.

I put a hole in Mel's perfect wall, and now I'm dragging my twin sister by the arm. I fling her into my bedroom and slam the door. She's hysterical, shaking all over, and her eyes as wide as saucers. I don't care. I feel too much and nothing all at the same time. Everything I turned off four years ago is back in full swing, and I'm dealing with a grave issue—believing Via was dead was heartbreaking but comforting. Knowing she was alive and ignoring my existence, however, is pure hell.

"So you lived in their trailer?" I ask, no mingling to warm up the conversation.

She nods.

"Where'd y'all sleep?"

"Father took the mini bedroom. Grandmamma and I shared a mattress in the back room."

I see he is still a selfish asshole. At least one person in my family hasn't changed. "School?" I jerk my chin toward her. She shakes her head.

"Technically, I was homeschooled, but…" She worries her lip, clearing her throat. "I have a lot to catch up on."

"We'll give you all the tutoring you need!" Melody cries from behind my door. *Motherfucker.*

"Ma'am!" I punch the door with my fist. "A fucking moment and some chill would be nice right about now."

"Yes. I'm sorry. I'm leaving now…oh, and no cussing!" she barks, and I hear murmuring between her and Jaime. Jaime, who looked pissed off on the couch, didn't even have time to register what Daria and I looked like when we entered the living room.

"I missed y—" Via starts, but I cut her off.

"Where are you going to sleep?"

"Mel is giving me the room next to the studio in the basement. It's already furnished as a guest room."

"Nice."

Like a puppy kicked in the ribs, she curls up on the edge of my bed with her hands on her lap. I'm guessing the past four years were very sheltered for her. I put my hands on my waist, and the scent of Daria is everywhere. On my skin and clothes and fingers and inside my mouth.

"You still cut holes in your shirts?" A small, sad smile that tells me she is not sure who I am either tugs at her lips.

I hitch one shoulder up. She knows the score. Knows when the hole will finally close.

"There's not one thing about you that I recognize," I tell her frankly.

"I'm still the same Via."

"My Via wouldn't leave me."

"Your Via didn't have a choice."

"There's always a fucking choice." I smash my fist against the wall. *Again.*

Via jumps back. She knows this conversation is going in ways she doesn't want it to go, so she stands up and plasters her hands over my chest.

"I'm here now. I know I've been the worst sister the past few years, but the beauty of our situation is that we don't have a choice. We have to be there for one another because neither of us has anyone else. Mom's dead. Dad and Grandmamma will never accept me again. Not with you, anyway. They think Mama and Rhett ruined you. And maybe not at all. So you have to forgive me."

Shaking my head, I start pacing the room, knowing damn well that my burning knuckles need some ice on them before the skin breaks and everything hurts like a thousand bitches. Since I still can't figure out how to approach her, I move on to practicalities.

"So you're going to stay here with us?"

Like the Followhills and I are a unit or some shit.

She shrugs. "Mrs. Followhill thinks it's in everyone's best interest."

Other than her daughter's.

"Gonna go to school?" I fold my arms across my chest.

"Yes."

"Well, I leave early every morning to Las Juntas for strength training, so your 2.0 version better be an early riser."

"I…" She looks around the empty room, biting on her lower lip. "I'm actually going to attend All Saints High. It's closer than Las Juntas, and they have an extensive tutoring program."

"Daria goes to ASH," I deadpan. In my mind, this is the end of the discussion. They can't go to the same school. I doubt they'll survive living under the same roof for longer than three hours.

Via picks imaginary lint from her nun dress. "Mrs. Followhill said Daria can give me a ride. I won't be in her way." Her tone is soft, coy. "I just want to graduate. I'm probably at junior level, if that. I'll have to talk to their counselor and take a bunch of tests."

I look away, breathing through my nostrils. Finally, something I can understand and decode—pain for my sister, for the screwed-up situation she's in.

"No one can know that I'm here," I warn her. "Coach Higgins still thinks that I live with Rhett. I can't move school districts and stay with the football team."

She nods. "I would never tell on you, Penn. You can trust me."

I snort. First of all, I can't. And second of all, she sounds twelve.

I walk to the door, throwing it open and cocking my head. I can't see her face right now. There's too much going on inside my head and chest.

"Out."

Her steps are slow and cautious as she marches out, stopping at the threshold.

"Look, I just want my brother back. I swear. I'm not here to cause any trouble. Can you try? Please?" She presses her palms together in front of her.

"Are you serious about this?"

"God, Penn." She closes her eyes and shakes her head. "You're the only thing that makes sense in my life anymore. Yes."

I walk over to my desk, open a drawer, and produce a Swiss Army knife. I drag it along my open palm, thumb to little finger, then hold my bloodied hand up in invitation.

She hesitates only for a second before opening her small palm.

"Cut yourself." I throw her the knife. Via has always been scared shitless of blood and needles and fucking everything. I mean, she was scared of flies. But blood makes her woozy.

She swallows, gawking at my hand, the knife, then my hand again.

"*Bleed* for me," I hiss.

Like I bled for you. Every sleepless night. Each excruciating day.

I watch her body rocking with silent sobs as she pierces the skin of her palm and cuts herself open. Our blood is dripping between us on the lush cream carpet of the Followhills' mansion as we shake on the promise that we'll never betray each other again.

"I'll take you living here to my grave," she chokes out.

Later that night, I lie on my bed, staring at the dried-up blood in my palm.

Then my mind travels to the blood on the condom when I pulled out of Daria earlier.

How I made a blood oath with two different girls today.

With two perfect enemies.

One who celebrated a shitty birthday, the other experiencing a glorious rebirth.

One thing's for sure—one of them will be betrayed.

CHAPTER TWELVE
DARIA

You're tearing confessions from my mouth
Reactions from my flesh
Fights from my fists
Blood from my heart
With your eyes alone.
Sometimes I want to break the wall I built
between us
Let you in
And watch you destroy me.

I count the beauty spots on my thigh.

I study all six of them with my forehead pressed against the steering wheel while I wait for Via to come out. I agreed to drive her to school and drop her off at the counselor's office, then show her around. I think I mostly said yes out of shock. The reality of Mel bringing her here and Penn knowing about it and keeping it from me, and Dad and Bailey just accepting this whole circus is starting to nibble at my sanity.

There's no way Penn had no idea, and there is no way Via just appeared out of thin air, showed up at our house, and decided to stick around.

I picked out a cute navy summer dress with a little red bow

on the collar, then paired it with my cutest Jimmy Choo sandals. Dutch braided my hair. Sat at the dining table with everyone. Drank OJ. Ignored the bagels. Ignored Mel. *Was* ignored by Penn, Via, and Bailey, who talked about a new TV show that premieres tonight. Via didn't know about it because she didn't have a TV back in Mississippi. Penn sneaked glances my way, but I pretended not to notice, staring hard at the orange liquid in my glass. The only person I talked to was Dad.

"You look beautiful, Dar."

I mock-toasted him with my glass of juice.

"You know you're my favorite, yeah?" He leaned forward, chucking my chin.

I knew what he was doing, and I appreciated it. I even believed him. "I know."

Dad is the only reason I'm playing nice. After Melody's hundredth attempt to talk to me, he came into my room. He explained they didn't tell me earlier because Via didn't show signs of wanting to stay with us, and they didn't want to put more strain on my relationship with Mel. I only half listened up to the point he confessed that for the past couple of weeks, he and Mel had been fighting over whether they should tell me. It's the first time he admitted to not being in full agreement with my mother.

"I'll deal with Mel," he promised softly. "But for now, Via is here and so is Penn. Make your life easier—get along with them."

"I hate her." I meant Mel. But let's admit it—I also referred to Via.

Dad locked his jaw, his throat bobbing with a swallow. Any other day, he'd tell me off and make a big fuss about how Mel lived and breathed for us.

"Stay strong, baby. We're Followhills. We literally follow hills. Always on top. Show me what you're made of."

"I'm made of the green goo of the Hulk."

"You're made of fucking gold, Daria. And soul. So much soul."

And here I am, staring at my thighs and trying not to cry.

Someone smacks my window, and I roll it down without even checking who it is. Knight, Vaughn, and Luna stare back at me.

"It looked like you were having an intense moment with your pussy." Knight snaps the shoulder straps of his Louis Vuitton Supreme backpack with his thumbs, popping his gum. "Just wondered if your vagina makes more sense than you do."

"I wasn't talking to my vagina." I narrow my eyes at him, wiping at them in case there's a mist.

Knight laughs. "I swear to God, Followhill. You're fun-sized, but that's the only thing fun about your ass."

Vaughn parks his elbows on my open window and shoves his entire head inside. "Word is Penn's sister's in town."

"How do you know?"

"Bailey told Lev, who told Knight, who told…" Vaughn looks skyward and frowns, mockingly doing the math with his fingers. "The entire Northern Hemisphere."

"Spencer's exaggerating, as per usual." Knight hooks his arm over Luna's shoulder, planting a kiss on her forehead. "I only told the team. And just because she's Penn's sister, and I wanted to cement the fact that she lives here, but he is still with his piece of crap stepdad. Get everyone's story straight."

"Why are you protecting Penn?" I frown. Knight is about as charitable as a used diaper. He blinks at me, his expression genuine.

"Because no one else does."

Luna takes a step toward me and slants her head sideways. She doesn't speak actual words, but this is her way of asking if I'm okay. I roll my eyes.

"I'm fine, Luna. I can handle it."

"Anyway." Vaughn spits on the ground, grabbing his helmet and sauntering over to his bike. "Watch your back. Your name's hot, what with all the Prichard rumors. Don't let this chick get her hands on the juicy stuff."

My blood runs cold in my veins all of a sudden. *Shit*. I haven't even thought of that. But my black book stays with me. At all times. It's in my backpack now.

Three minutes later, I start the car and open a text message to Daddy to tell Mel to tell Via to get her ass in the car before I get my first tardy slip for the school year. Call me Petty McPetterson, but after the latest string of treacheries, addressing Melody directly is off the table. Just before I hit send, the passenger door opens and Via slides in. She is wearing one of my favorite outfits. A gray floral print maxi dress from Neiman Marcus. A far cry from the potato sack she wore yesterday.

Awaiting explanation, I eye her, long and thoroughly.

You will not lose your shit, Daria. Especially as her twin brother just deflowered you and hinted at you going steady.

"Oh, this?" She runs a hand over the dress. "Melody told me to pick anything I wanted."

I'm surprised she can cram so much venom into one sentence. That ought to be some kind of Guinness World Record. I run a hand over my braid.

"Next time, pick something you can pull off. Ready to roll?"

She scans my body, and I instinctively suck my stomach in. She is still much skinnier and taller than me.

"You obviously are."

I will kill you dead, bitch. You're going to be as relevant as the Spice Girls in my school.

I kick my car and brain into drive. Via has not changed in the past four years. She is not sweet or shy and timid. She is just pretending to be those things to get in my parents', sister's, and her brother's good graces. Now I have to figure out what her angle is and how far her real persona is from her fake one. Luckily, I have a lot of experience when it comes to fakeness. My personality is basically one hundred percent recyclable plastic. The only person who can still scrape a bit of authenticity from me is her brother.

"Did you and Penn have a good time catching up?" I signal right with my blinker as we zoom past Tudor mansions and sprawling Spanish villas.

"The best." She flicks the overhead mirror open, fluffing her hair, and I catch a glimpse of her palm. It's been cut open, and there's a line of dry blood.

My gut clenches.

"He is *so* protective and loving." She digs inside my old backpack, taking out a makeup kit that looks familiar. Because it is also *mine*. I bite my inner cheek.

"How sweet," I say distractedly, wanting to throw up as panic washes over me. I gave him my virginity. Hell, I gave him much more. She is vindictive and mad and hungry for attention and love. She has every reason to want to ruin me.

She can't know about the Royal Academy letter.

"It'd be good to hang out with him, you know? And with Kannon and Camilo and Adriana. Oh my God. She's probably so gorgeous nowadays. Penn always had it hard for her."

I smile, breathing through my nose. Her taunt is spot-on, but I doubt she knows about her brother and me. Penn is more secretive than the CIA. He'd never volunteer any information about us.

Or would he?

He hid his sister's arrival from me, so maybe he is hiding more stuff.

"You can always check on her. Your glamorous BFF works at Lenny's." I pop my gum. "And could use laying off the foundation and purple eyeshadow."

Each word feels like a knife gliding on my tongue. Already in troubled water with my mother, neck deep into my arrangement with Principal Prichard, and drowning while trying to keep my status as queen bee, I can't afford to open any more fronts. But Via is practically begging for a battle, so it's my duty to show her the weapon under my cowboy jacket, so to speak.

"Aww, someone sounds jealous."

"Just personally offended by her lack of style." I smirk.

"Yeah. You seem easily offended. Like yesterday, when you ran to your room when you saw my face. Some things don't change, *Lovebug*."

She claps the overhead mirror shut and pins me with a glare.

I pull into a parking spot in front of All Saints High and unbuckle the seat belt, twisting my whole body to face her.

"We don't have to be enemies, Sylvia. I know you're trying to rock the whole Goody-Two-shoes vibe with my family, but it's not who you are, and it's not who you have to be to fit in my family. We had our differences in the past, but we were fourteen and competing for the same spot. That spot is yours now if you want it. I have no interest in ballet anymore. We're only going to have one senior year. Why not make it our best?"

She leans toward me, a sly smile gracing her lips. I forget to breathe as I wait for her words. Forget that the Scullys were born with smiles that can very well kill or at least drastically wound when they're aimed directly at you without sunglasses. They're *that* beautiful.

"Four years ago, you flaunted all you have in my face while I had nothing. Now, I'm going to take every single thing that belongs to you and make a show everyone in town is going to have fun watching while doing it. I want it all, Daria. Your dedicated mom, sweet sister, loyal dad, and popular friends. If you have a boyfriend, I'll take him too. And fuck him better." She grins.

I want to LOL in her face when I think about the one and only guy I've slept with. Then I feel like throwing up. Marx. What have I done? This complicates things so much.

"Oh, and good luck convincing them that I'm a bitch. My brother and me, we have one thing in common: we play a really good game." She throws her door open.

With one leg flung out the door, she releases her hair clip and drags its sharp teeth along the delicate chiffon dress she is wearing, right around the fabric bunching at her cleavage, ripping my garment in the process to show off more skin. "After all, I spent the past four years being *good*."

I escort Via to our counselor, feeling as though I'm on death row. On our way there, we pass Colin Stimatzky in the hallway. He gives Via a once-over, sucking his teeth in appreciation. She is fresh meat. The kind that makes your mouth water. She knocks herself against his arm deliberately, like in a bad teenage flick, then turns around and giggles. When she introduces herself, sparks fly. I can practically feel them biting at my skin. I drop her off at the counselor's office and dash to my class before the bell rings, refusing to contemplate what it all means.

Daria Followhill is no longer the prettiest girl at school.

Sylvia Scully is.

Consequently, Sylvia Scully is going to pay for that little declaration of war.

I spend the first half of the day obsessing over Via's words and munching on my fingernails, thinking about this unfortunate turn of events. She's back, and now her brother is ignoring me. Her brother, whom I gave my virginity to. Her brother, who obviously knew she was coming but still took what did not belong to him. At lunch, I force myself to play nice like Dad asked me, so when I hit her hard— and I will hit both her and Penn like a wrecking ball—no one will see it coming, and no one will blame me.

This time, when I strike, no one will suspect it.

I text Via (Dad programmed her new number in my phone) to ask her where she is. She replies that she's in the art room, and I put two and two together. She's with a senior class. At least for now. I meet her at the door.

"I'll introduce you to the ton. You'll be all the rage." I loop my arm in hers, pretending to ignore her parting words to me, in which she promised to strip me of everything I care about.

"The ton?" She huffs, pulling away and putting some space between us.

"Yeah. You know, like, fashionable society. Sorry. I'm kind of big on historical romances." I play humble. I haven't voluntarily read a book in a decade. Most of my friends use this term all the time, but I like making her feel dumb.

"No, I'm the one who is sorry." Her lips twitch in annoyance. "I wasn't allowed to read anything but the Bible for the past four years. I'll have to play catchup."

Great. Now I feel shitty again for having her go through this. What is it about the Scullys that puts me through the emotional wringer?

We walk toward the cafeteria, and Esme, Blythe, Alisha, and the football team join us, following us from their lockers. I make quick introductions, then we settle at our table, and I shove Blythe out of her usual spot and pat it.

"You can sit with me," I tell Via.

"That's some reverse psychology *Mean Girls* shit right there." Knight points at me with a piece of carrot and pops it into his mouth.

Via gazes at him from under her lashes, all doe-eyed and ready to charm his pants off. "And you are?"

"Not interested," he deadpans.

I smile inwardly, bursting with happiness. Knight is loyal to a fault. Vaughn too. Rumor has it when she smiled at him in the hallway earlier, he breezed past her and drawled, "You haven't earned the right to talk to me yet. Try again in two months."

It's just the people inside my own house who are warming up to the foe.

Gus is late, as usual. When he arrives, the first thing I notice is that he halts in place a few feet from the table, his knuckles white from his firm grip on his tray. He blinks at Via, shock and worry lacing his glare.

I sneak a peek at Via. She stares at Gus like she's come face-to-face with a ghost.

"Gus Bauer."

"Sylvia Scully. But everyone calls me Via."

"Via." He tastes her name in his mouth. And for a moment, he stares at her as though she is holding half the sky.

He takes a seat, his eyes never wavering from hers. He's doing a crappy job of playing it cool. My heart sinks further down to my toes. The easiest way to climb the social ladder at All Saints High is to date a first-string football player. If she dates Gus, my prom queen title can basically rest in peace. I won't be attending its funeral, though, because Via would be there—collecting my crown.

"Where do you live?" he asks. Not a weird question to ask a new kid, I guess. Only in Via's case, it seems as if he is accusing her of something. I look around and realize that nobody else notices this exchange. Maybe because everyone is talking about Vaughn's new mystery girl who enjoys sucking him off in public places.

"El Dorado. I live with the Followhills," she answers, her tone polite and docile. She has the faintest Southern twang, and I know it's fake because she didn't have it when we were in the car. This time, she covers her mouth with her hand when she talks, and I'm guessing it's because she has a missing tooth. She's been reinventing herself for the past few hours. The question is—why?

"Huh." He opens his yogurt and licks the lid, tossing it onto the tray. "Are you an only child?"

Alarm bells start ringing in my head. This time, Knight and I exchange looks.

Gus knows.

Regardless of Penn's betrayal, I'd never blow his cover. His whole football career depends on this little lie. And Knight is right—he deserves a break.

Via doesn't flinch. "I have a twin brother. He lived here the whole time I was in Mississippi with my dad."

"And where does your brother live now?" Gus tilts his chin down, no longer mesmerized by Via's good looks. He's now completely focused on finding out more about Penn.

"My stepdad's."

"Hmm." He frowns, feigning confusion. "Why not together?"

"My stepdad and I don't get along. He is why I left. But the Followhills are another story. I adore Daria." She flashes me a smile, rubbing my back, and I think I'm going to be sick. "And I've always been Mrs. Followhill's favorite ballerina," she stresses, sticking it to me. "I'm hoping to pick up where I left off."

"So no cheerleading for you?" Esme gazes at Via down her nose. She is the only one at the table who is not completely on board with Via joining us. I wonder if she'll change her mind once she figures out Via is after my neck too.

I know what Esme is trying to do. She is trying to make Via come off as a snob. Someone who considers cheer to be beneath her. I want to laugh in her face. The Scullys are too smart to fall for this type of *Riverdale* nonsense.

Via straightens her spine.

"Oh, I would *love* to join! I wish I had come in time for tryouts. As it is, Mrs. Followhill says there's a lot of work ahead of us, so maybe cheer is not in the cards for me. But I know she can push me to the top."

Yes, I think bitterly. *It's me she is content with leaving at the bottom.*

By the time the school day is over, Via is everyone's new favorite person. People like the fact she is pretty and an athlete but also polite, Southern, and eager to please. The girls give me these looks when I pass them in the hallway as if it's game over for me. As though no one would be able to look at me anymore without comparing us, since we live together. That I will always be on the losing end.

When Via and I get into my car, I take out my phone, and there's a text message waiting for me from Penn.

Talk.

I try to tuck it back into my bag, but Via catches it and lifts an eyebrow.

"I hope it's not what I think it is," she says dryly, taking out her (no, *my*) makeup bag and reapplying her lipstick.

"And what would that be?" I snap, starting to lose my patience.

"If you think you have a shot with my brother, for as long as I have a breath in me, you're going to be proven otherwise, *Lovebug*."

CHAPTER THIRTEEN
DARIA

I wish I could rewrite you out of my life
But all your pages are highlighted
Dog-eared and thumbed to death.
I can no longer read you
But you are still my favorite poem.

That evening, my two public enemies both raise the white flag.

The first one is Mel, who summons all of us to the garage after dinner and after taking Via to the dentist to fix that missing tooth of hers. In the garage is a vehicle clothed in bright pink parked next to Dad's Tesla. I'm standing with my arms folded. My face suggests a hostile terrorist organization has kidnapped me when Melody, with her fake enthusiasm and mental pom-poms, unveils the vehicle and presents it with her arms outstretched like Vanna White on *The Wheel of Fortune*. It's a bright pink Hummer.

"I know we said no presents and no celebrations—you only wanted a party—but I just couldn't help myself." Melody squeals and claps her hands. Via and Bailey gush right along with her. Dad and Penn are silent next to me. After the female excitement dies down, and the garage goes silent, I react.

"Wow." I walk around it, deliberate and placid. "That is horri-fyingly *ugly*."

I raise my eyes to meet hers, and I'm smirking. I'm smirking because, as it turns out, she doesn't know me after all. If she thinks she can buy her way into my heart with fancy things, she obviously misread me. Sure, I like my designer collection of dresses, shoes, and bags, and I have expensive tastes—maybe not as expensive as Knight's but definitely more upmarket than Vaughn's and Luna's—but I don't *need* it. Materialistic things don't excite me. I like them because they're there and available. Because they're a calorie-free treat.

Melody's smile collapses like a straw house in the wind, and she blinks back at me. I think she is about to cry but find it hard to care. She brought my nightmare into my house without even warning me. She made it so perfectly clear that she is not half as impressed with me as she is with my sister.

"I think it's amazing, Mom." Bailey rushes to console our mother, hugging her tight. "Don't worry. It'll grow on Daria."

Via looks around and tentatively joins Mel and Bailey, rubbing Mel's back the same way she did mine this afternoon.

"Yes, Mrs. Followhill. I'm sure she is just shocked."

"I'm not shocked. I'm a little offended she'd think I'd voluntarily drive this thing. It looks like a giant clitoris."

Penn bursts out laughing, and Dad reluctantly joins him even though he tries to cover his mouth with his fist. They elbow each other to stop, but it does nothing more than throw them into a rowdier version of hysterics.

Bailey's eyes widen, and Via somehow manages to fake a blush. Great. I'm uniting them against me. Via must be thrilled. She is probably inwardly dancing the cha-cha.

Mel looks up at me, her eyes glistening. She pays no attention to Via and Bailey, who are fussing around her, but it's too late. The damage has been done.

"What do you want from me, Daria?" she asks, so quiet I can barely hear her.

"Nothing."

Everything.

"What can I do to make you happy? To get to you?" The plea in her voice is so shrill, it's tearing me apart. And for a moment, I actually believe her. Until I remember she put me in a school where she screwed her student, brought me a brooding, angry, hot foster brother, then his even angrier, batshit crazy sister, who is my enemy, then ignored and belittled my existence for four years to a point where, at times, I wondered if I was even real anymore.

"Is my party still on for this weekend?" I pretend not to catch the true meaning of her words. I can't break down in front of all those people.

"Yes, but that's not what I—"

"Thanks, Mel! Good luck selling this thing. Don't they say that a vehicle loses half its worth the minute it rolls off the lot?"

I bounce out of the garage, leaving them behind. I close the door to my room, shoving back the bitterness at not being able to go downstairs to the studio and cry myself to sleep privately because Via's got the entire place to herself. I fling myself onto my bed, grab my phone, and message Principal Prichard, who is saved under "Prince" on my phone. I have a feeling I'm going back to triweekly meetings with him at this rate.

I need to see you. I'm desperate.

I've never seen him off school grounds, but I don't know who else to turn to. My friends are fake, Knight and Vaughn will give me the third degree, dragging Dad into this will only put more strain on his relationship with Mel, and Bailey is amazing, but she is too young and too sweet to understand all those dark feelings swirling inside me.

Tomorrow.
I can't wait until tomorrow.

He types.

You made me wait long enough the past couple of weeks.
Tomorrow.

My head falls against my pillows, and I close my eyes, sighing. Shit. I was in la-la land, consumed with everything Penn Scully, and was able to dodge Principal Prichard's many advances. He knew better than to hunt me down in a way that would be too obvious.

When I hear my door pushed open, I'm expecting Melody or Dad. Maybe Bailey with her naive Hallmark words of wisdom. But Penn stands in my doorway with his elbow braced against the doorframe. His white V-neck rides up and shows off his incredible V, leading like an arrow to his groin.

"Are you going to ignore me for the rest of your life?"

I blink at the ceiling, desperate not to let my traitorous eyes slip to his face. I'm already suffering from PPSD—Post-Penn Scully Disorder. "That's the plan."

"Always knew you were a pussy. Nice to get valid proof."

Eat shit, Scully. I'll give you a second serving too.

"I thought we established I had a pussy the other day."

"There she is. Hideous, little, sarcastic monster that you are."

"Why are you here, hood rat?" I huff.

"To talk it out." He steps into my room and closes the door behind him. I glance at him, just to make sure I didn't imagine the click. A smile kisses my scowling lips.

"My dad is going to kill you if he finds out you closed the door."

"Best of luck to your dad trying to catch my ass," he shoots back, unblinking. I right myself and press my back against the headboard. I allow myself an ounce of optimism. Maybe he cares.

"Why didn't you tell me about Via?"

"Didn't know."

He is still standing all the way across the room, and I don't know if I'm grateful for the space or want him to drown me in a suffocating hug that would steal my breath and give me life all at the same time.

"You expect me to believe that?"

"What you do with this information is up to you. I had no idea Via was coming back. Your mom mentioned she was trying to find her a few times, but honestly, she didn't appear too optimistic either."

"Well, thanks for deflowering me, then ignoring me while you figured the situation out."

"You're welcome," he says, then looks away at my door, blinking. He lets out a ragged breath, moving his fingers through his hair. "Look, it's all pretty fucked up. Emotions are running high. I wanted to take a step back and figure shit out."

"And did you?" The dark chuckle I'm producing actually tastes bitter in my throat.

"Not by a long shot."

I break, tears falling down my cheeks. I wipe my nose with the sleeve of my pale pink cardigan. Penn makes his way to me, jerking me up to my feet and wrapping his arms around me. I drown in him. In his touch. In his body. In his soul.

"Marx, Penn. I thought you were using me."

"Whoa." He pretends to pull away for a fraction of a second. "Who said that I'm not?"

I nuzzle my nose into the hole in his shirt where his heart is and laugh.

He takes a step back so he can cup my cheeks. Our eyes meet, and my heart accelerates.

"I'm not even sure how I feel about her being here. It's like being born with a limp and given a second pair of legs. Supposed to feel good but it's an actual shitshow. I already learned how to live without, you know?"

I know.

I want so badly to tell him that she is just pretending to be good and nice.

That she threatened to take everything away from me earlier today. The words burn on my tongue, begging to come out. A few months ago, I'd have spilled it all out without batting an eyelash. But I've seen all the damage it has caused Penn to be alone. I can't do this to him. I can't ruin his chance at reconnecting with his sister, no matter how much I despise her.

"I know." I pull him back into our hug because I miss him already. I miss him even when he's here. There's not enough of him to satisfy me, and maybe I'm dragging my feet about college because life post-Penn doesn't even register right now. "Give it time. It'll get better."

And just like that, muscle memory kicks in. My lips find his, and we are kissing. Deep and long and passionate. He groans into my mouth and takes my face in his rough hands, backing us both up to the bed. My knees hit the bed frame, and we both dive onto the mattress, breathless chuckles escaping our lungs. He is straddling me, kissing my neck and chin.

"Fuck. I missed your lips."

"I missed your ass." I squeeze his ass, biting his lower lip.

"You're a solid hobby, Skull Eyes. Just remember that it's nothing more, and the minute you get attached, that's around the time I'll probably cut you off."

"See if I care, baby. You're just a phase. Maybe my future surgeon husband will fix up your broken leg if you ever make it to the NFL."

He chuckles, kissing his way to my chest and unbuttoning my cardigan. "Maybe he'll chop it off altogether when I taunt him about how much fun I had inside his wife."

"More fun than you had with Adriana?" I pull away, inspecting his eyes.

"Lima or my classmate?"

The one your sister said you're in love with.

"The latter. As if Adriana Lima would give your ass the time of day."

"Are you jealous?"

"Are you avoiding the question?"

He drags his teeth down my neck and sinks them into my collarbone. I know he is piercing my skin, marking me for everyone to see and know. The sheer relief washing over me suggests that one of the reasons I felt like I was holding a seven-ton weight of angst on my shoulders the past few days was because I couldn't be with Penn. And while I'm his hobby, he is turning out to be my...*everything*. My solace. My good part. My favorite thing about life.

"Adriana is not a factor here. She's a permanent fixture in my life that has nothing to do with you. You..." He fists the collar of my cardigan and jerks me to his face. "You're the best temporary treat I've had in a while."

"Don't believe you for a second." My lips tremble around the words. I have to convince myself that it's not true.

He dips his head down, smirking at me.

"It would be a pleasure to prove to you just how little you mean to me."

Our lips are about to lock again when there's a frantic knock on my door. Penn peels himself off my body, releasing a frustrated groan. Even though he doesn't give a damn if we get caught, he knows I do. He runs his fingers through his hair, smoothing it back, and shoves a hand into his faded Levi's to rearrange his hard-on.

"Yes?" I ask, a little too chirpily, considering the mood I left the garage in. I clear my throat, readjusting my tone. "What?"

"Daria?" Via's nervous, fake voice bleeds from the other side of the door. "It's me. Sylvia. I know I'm probably the last person you want to talk to, but I'd really like to make you feel better."

I immediately know that Via saw Penn sneaking into my room and is trying to ruin the moment. It makes perfect sense. She told me herself that I can't have her twin brother. And to make matters worse, us locking the door just confirmed that we are, in fact, hiding something. I can't say no to her. Not with Penn here. She is allegedly trying to reach out to me. He can't know the truth.

Penn and I exchange looks. There's hope in his eyes, and it's crushing me because Via is setting me up for destruction. He is starting to get used to the upgraded version of his sister. He may have known her as a cunning, tongue-in-cheek, driven teenager, but now she is all sunshine and good intentions. He is falling for her when he should be falling for me—in very different ways, but it's happening, nonetheless.

I decide to play her game. If she is going to pretend, then so will I.

"I…" I look around frantically, but looking for what, exactly? I can't hide her brother anywhere. He is a wide receiver the size of an industrial fridge. My closet is too crowded and full of stuff, and the space under my low bed is tiny. "Let me put something on and unlock the door," I say as I run to the window and open it for Penn to get out. He is still standing in the middle of the room in all his height and muscled glory. I'm not even sure he could fit through my window, let alone slip through it undetected.

"For real?" He arches an eyebrow. "I can barely fit through fucking doors, Skull Eyes."

"Well, it's either that or being pushed under my bed or into my closet. Your pick of a high school movie cliché." I wiggle my eyebrows.

He smirks, pulling me by the hem of my shirt and kissing me leisurely, with tongue and all, as though his sister is not waiting on the other side of the door.

Penn squashes my butt, pulling me close to his erection and rubbing my body up and down against it, manhandling me in one hand without even breaking a sweat.

"You playing nice with Via doesn't go unnoticed."

I cup his dick between us, clutching a little, not enough to hurt but enough to tease the hell out of him. He licks his lips and raises his head skyward, squeezing his eyes shut.

"It costs me all my patience and goodwill."

"I'll pay you back with my tongue and dick."

He steals one last kiss before he fumbles out the window, his laughter rolling on my skin. He is not even pretending to hide himself. Hide *us*. If he is open about us to Via, then that means he is not ashamed of me. That he is not one hundred percent in her camp.

I open the door, allowing Via to walk into my domain. I've decided I am going to be so nice she'll want to throw up rainbows and unicorns by the time I'm done with her. If I don't give her any ammo on me, she'll eventually get tired of trying.

Via doesn't take a moment to appreciate my pink champagne aquarium wall and fancy room—but why would she? She's already been here, digging through my clothes. She closes the door and throws herself onto my bed as if it belongs to her. She inhales a deep breath, smiling from the throne of my satin pillows and vintage teddy bears.

"Smells like my brother in here."

Does that turn you on, perv?

I sit on the edge of the bed, knowing somehow she is privy to the fact he's already left. She doesn't have the balls to stand up to Penn. I don't think anyone does.

"You know, you could take the Hummer." I examine my perfect french manicure. "Mel is probably not going to return it, so it'll go to waste."

I want my mother to choke on her prejudice against me, thinking I'll be awful to Via. And if I can kill Via with kindness in the process, well, that's just a big fat bonus.

"Ech." She sticks her tongue out. "That thing was fucking disgusting. No thank you. I don't know how you deal with that woman. She is so submissive. It was a huge turnoff back then, but it's a total nuisance nowadays."

My mouth goes slack. Did she actually just talk about my mother like that? The woman who invested more in her than in her own daughter? The woman who fought tooth and nail to bring Via back? Who housed Via? Who freaking jeopardized her relationship with my father and me—both of us guarded by nature—just to save Via?

My expression probably gives away my shock and disgust because Via explains herself.

"I vanished four years ago. She only found me, like, a month ago. And not a minute before she took Penn under her wing. Where has she been all this time?"

I saw Mel mourn Via. It was half the reason I kept mum about what Penn and I did that day. I knew she'd never forgive me. She'd hate my guts and mentally disown me if she knew. I'm not Mel's biggest fan right now, but even I know that this is bullshit.

"She tried really hard to find you when you disappeared," I say in what I hope to hell is an even tone. "She is not your mother."

"Thank God. Imagine if I'd have inherited her thighs, like you." She springs off my bed and saunters toward the aquarium. She taps it with her finger, watching the bubbles rising from the oxygen tank below. "Ever wonder what would happen if you put a hammer into this thing?"

"No," I snap.

"Hmm." A faraway smile curves on her lips before she returns her attention to me, twisting her head in my direction. "As I said before, you can't date my brother. Correction—you can't even fuck my brother. You're just a piece of ass for him, and even though you have zero self-respect, I'm here to tell you that even *you* can do better. Adriana would never let it happen, and she is the girl he'll eventually marry and take to college with him. She gave birth to his kid, for crying out loud. Stop embarrassing yourself and finish this stupid thing with him. Today."

"What did they feed you in Mississippi? Acid and delusions?" I examine my nails, trying to come off as blasé. "What if I liked to be used? What if he's only a piece of ass for me too?"

She stares at me in bewilderment as if I just revealed a piece of information that is completely new to her.

"I can make your life a living hell."

"Go ahead." I gesture to her with my hand. *You already are.* "Be my guest."

"Is this war, Daria?" A spark of madness ignites in her eyes. I've seen this flash before, the day Penn suggested we should be friends all those years ago. The adrenaline zing. This is how you know a Scully is excited.

I pretend to yawn. "If you want it to be? I'll bring my tanks; you'll bring your sticks."

"Paper tanks." She smiles sweetly, and for some reason, her gaze on my face makes me feel naked. At some sort of disadvantage. "Glittery paper tanks I can crumple in my fist. It's on, Followhill."

———

Penn leaves three hours before my birthday party starts.

An hour after Bailey and my parents left to stay at a Malibu hotel for the night, to be exact. They cleared out of the house until Sunday morning so I can throw the mother of all bashes. Before Penn moved in, I was notorious for my parties.

Before he left, Penn and I stood at the door, making out, groping, and kissing for long minutes before Via descended the stairs. Penn groaned, tearing his mouth from mine with a pained frown. Shame she didn't catch it. At this point, I wanted her to see that we were still on. I recently told Knight and Vaughn about us—I had to tell someone, and Marx knows I can't trust Esme and the cheer crew—and they both told me that I'm crazy for doing my foster brother even though I haven't explicitly mentioned sex.

Principal Prichard, on the other hand, has been avoiding me on principle all week since those text messages. I think he is testing me. Or maybe he wants me to crawl back to him. Things have been awkward since he caught Penn and me in the locker room. I know I need to face the music, but I have so many war fronts, I can't even begin to tackle the Prichard problem.

Now that my party is in full swing, I can sit back and relax for the first time in what seems like a lifetime. I watch people cannonball into my pool, lit in a million different lights, from my spot on the couch overlooking my backyard. I'm tucked next to Esme and Blythe. Knight, Colin, and Vaughn are sitting on recliners around us. Gus is nowhere to be seen, and I'm guessing Via is somewhere, sucking the souls out of random babies while pretending to be their unassuming nanny. Mel was so excited that Via "agreed" to stick around for the party.

"I'm so glad you're making friends, Via."

Yeah. *My* friends. And not by freaking accident, Mother.

"Where is Gus?" I ask as I sip from my champagne. I put a handful of my junior minions in the kitchen on bartender duty, and they've been serving us champagne and imported beer all evening. Not that they care. They get to mingle with high school royalty and be seen. Not to mention, they got a Followhill invite, which is practically a winning lottery ticket in this town.

The thing about parties at All Saints High? If they're good, with a lot of alcohol, sex, and good music, you usually don't know about them unless you're in.

Next year, they'll pass it forward and act just like me. For tonight, though, they will bask in my afterglow but only from afar.

"He's been working on the new chick for like two hours or something." Colin takes a sip of his beer, nudging Knight's thigh for him to pass him the joint.

"Via?" My mouth goes dry. I hope they are not hooking up. Penn absolutely hates Gus and vice versa.

"Yeah, her." Colin yawns, pointing at me with the beer. "I hope she knows he is called Texas Gus for a reason."

"Gus is called Texas Gus?" Blythe wrinkles her nose.

Esme reddens next to me, downing her drink in one go.

"Correct." Knight passes Colin the joint he just meticulously rolled using my mascara wand. "He once gave a certain girl pink eye by shooting his hot sauce in a strategic direction."

Blythe snorts. "So embarrassing. Who was it?"

Esme pretends to text on her phone, but her fingers are not moving.

Knight smirks, averting his gaze to her. "Guess it was someone who wasn't worth fucking."

"Excuse me," I singsong (like my mom, I realize after I do), slipping from the couch to go look for Via and Gus. "Killing in the Name" by Rage Against the Machine is blasting through the speakers as I make my way across the packed living room, crammed with teenagers drinking, dancing, and making out against the walls and furniture. I hear laughter from upstairs, as people jump from Bailey's window right onto the trampoline outside, and make my way to the second floor, holding the banister as my vision sways. I'm drunker than I thought I was, zigzagging my way upstairs. I start throwing doors open, my pulse picking up as I do. Penn's is locked, but I knew it would be. I saw him packing everything that might've hinted at his presence into trash bags and tossing it straight into Vaughn's pool house earlier today. He's not taking any chances. I haven't been bringing any friends to my house ever since he moved here, and I'm guessing he knows it's a sacrifice. What I don't tell him is that I do it gladly. What I never voice is how freaking proud I am of him going through all of this without complaining.

When I reach my room and open it, I find Via writhing in my bed with Gus on top of her. Their mouths are fused, and he is running his fingers up and down her bare leg. She is wearing a dress I don't recognize. Mel must've taken her shopping between the time she broke my heart and the time she crushed it with her fist, just to make sure that it's extra dead.

"Texas Gus," I purr, and Gus's eyes shoot up from Via, but he is still on top of her. "Take a hike. I need to have a word with Mississippi Sylvia."

"Nah, Followhill. I think I'm comfortable right"—he thrusts his jeans-clad crotch onto Via's groin, and she is laughing evilly—"fucking"—he leans down to bite her nose—"here."

I elevate my phone to my face and start typing with a cheerful bravado I don't feel.

"I guess I'll report it back to your QB1. You know my daddy always puts him in charge, making sure everyone's on their best behavior when I throw parties."

"Bitch." Gus nips at Via's lips one more time before he jumps to his feet, grabbing his varsity jacket from my lilac bed bench and storming past me, his shoulder brushing mine.

I continue standing at the door. I'm not even going to touch the subject of them making out on my bed with a ten-foot pole. It makes me want to throw up in my mouth, and I'm mad about it, but not as mad as I am about her sleeping with the enemy—quite freaking literally.

Via huffs and gets up, about to leave, but this time, I'm the one to close the door behind me and push her back onto my bed. "Sit."

"Give me one good reason to." She makes a move to stand again.

"It's about your brother, and if you care about him at all—which you haven't shown any signs of doing in the past four years—you will listen."

I settle next to her on my bed. We're both staring at our feet. I feel tipsy and frustrated with the past few days. Just when I thought I was making real progress with Penn and Mel, Via came back and screwed up everything.

"What's going on with you and Gus?" I demand.

"As if I'll ever tell you anything." She sulks. I peek at her from my peripheral vision, and her eyes are brimming with tears. It must be so hard for her to see all this and know it wasn't a part of her youth. That it never would be. She can't get her high school years back.

"Have you ever been kissed before Gus?" I trail my linen with the tip of my finger, trying another tactic but also genuinely curious.

She snort-laughs through her tears. "Get to the point, Daria. We're not friends, and this is not a heart-to-heart."

"Okay." I take a deep breath. "I just want you to know the whole picture before you date Gus or even mess around with him. He and your brother have an open beef. I heard there was mad trash talk the day the Saints beat the Bulldogs on the football field when the season started. Penn came over to our school a few days before that to try to patch things up with Gus, but it didn't work. Penn thinks Gus cheated somehow in order to win," I explain, manically trying to convey to her the level of hate these two share. "And every single time I see them in the same vicinity, Gus is trying to throw Penn off-balance."

Via takes a deep breath and closes her eyes.

"I feel like Penn gave up on me the moment I ran away and that nothing I can do will ever narrow the abyss between us," she admits.

I perk up, looking at her cautiously. This sounds a lot like an admission. And an admission is better than an attack, which is what I've been getting since the day she came to live with us. "How so?" My voice is so small and encouraging, barely a whisper.

"Penn is being weird with me. Not exactly hostile but...distant. I feel like I've let him down so much by leaving. As if I had a choice. I thought Rhett was going to kill me at some point. And Penn, no matter how much he loved me and was there for me, he was still only a child himself. He couldn't protect me. I realize that I'm the only one to blame—"

"No, you aren't." I cut her off. "Rhett is to blame. Your late mom is to blame. Your school and the system and, to an extent, even my mother for not noticing. But not you."

"*Penn* isn't to blame," she stresses. "And he is the one who got hurt the most."

Now I have my own admission. The truth is clogging my throat, and the alcohol begs for me to let it loose. It's a confession. A difficult one. But one that would make her let go of her inhibitions and guilt, and maybe start building a strong bridge to cross that gulf.

"Penn and I are also to blame," I admit quietly.

"What?" Her eyes shoot to me. "What in the hell are you talking about? You didn't know each other back when that happened."

I tell her everything about that day. Rehashing the entire thing from the moment I stood at the door and prayed not to see her to the moment Penn gave me my first kiss. And all the horrible things in between. The letter. How he tore it. The glee I felt when he did. How I wrote about it in my little black book that same evening. How the book got thick.

"He tore it, but he didn't know. He didn't know, Via. He didn't know," I keep repeating.

After I'm done, I feel out of breath. As though I just ran a marathon. I shift my entire body on the bed so I can look at her better. She is shaking, and tears stream down her face. I realize my mother never told her that she got into the Royal Academy. And why would she? It's cruel, bittersweet news. I try to hug her, but she shoots up to her feet. I do too.

"There wasn't one day in my life I didn't think about the letter, and about you, and about what a horrible person I am," I confess, tears blurring my vision. It's true. Even when I hated her, I hated myself more for what I did. I still do. This was when Mom became Mel. When my downfall started. "Please, believe me."

The slap comes out of nowhere. Sharp as a knife and full of heat. I feel her palm on my cheek long after she withdraws it and instinctively raise my hand to rub it.

You just got slapped. My brain is screaming at the rest of my body, an echo ringing between my ears. *Ad infinitum.*

"And that makes it okay?" Her entire face twists. "You and my brother ruined my life. Rhett was an abusive jerk. Mama was unresponsive and passed out eighty percent of the time, and your mom was pushing me away because you couldn't handle us being close and she didn't want to upset you," she tells me, and I choke on my breath. I didn't know that. I didn't know Via and Mom weren't super close. "I would have never left had I known I got in! I would have made it through, Daria."

"I know." I'm sobbing, bracing my hands on my knees and shaking my head. The tears burn where she slapped me, but drunk and armorless, I acknowledge that I deserved it. "*God*, I know."

My shoulders are shaking as the sobs flow through me. I advance toward her, planning...I don't know, even to go down on my knees if I have to, but she backs up again. Her legs hit my nightstand, and she picks up the first thing she can get her hands on—a golden alarm clock Luna brought me from her family trip to Switzerland a few years ago—and aims it at me.

"Stay away from me, Daria. I mean it."

"Please don't think any less about your brother. That wasn't my intention at all. I just wanted you to know that everyone was to blame for what happened four years ago. But now you're back, and we can make up for that time."

"You can't make up for that time!"

She is screaming at the top of her lungs, hunching her body from the effort to produce such a profound yell. We're lucky the music is deafeningly loud outside. "Tainted Love" by Soft Cell is playing, and I can't help but agree with the sentiment.

Love is so contaminated. It tarnishes all that is beautiful and corrupts the soul. Love is so much uglier than hate because when you hate, you're not confused. When you're in love, you're dumb.

"You can't turn back time. I was miserable and abused in Mississippi, only in a different way."

"So why did you give my mother trouble about coming back?" I'm trying to gain control over my voice, my muscles, my heart. "Why did you want to stay there when Mel begged you to come back?"

"Because I hated you too much!" She throws her arms in the air. "Because I knew I was going to get a front-row seat to the perfect life of Daria Followhill. Because a part of me knew you would seduce Penn. Because that's what you do, Daria. You take everything that I have and make it yours."

"Funny." I sniff, my mouth filling with bitterness. "I feel the same about you."

Via shakes her head. She dashes out my door, and I run after her. I push past people and bark at them to move out of the way. I probably look possessed, and everyone is glancing over their shoulder to watch Queen Daria running after her new foster sister. But I can't let her walk away from this conversation. Not like this. Not when nothing has been sorted. Panic rushes through my veins like a river. The more I try with her, the harder she pushes me away.

Eventually, I lose her in the crowd and get swept away by Alisha, who wants to raid Mel's closet and see what fashion week garments she has ordered this season. I comply on autopilot.

The princess's castle is falling apart.

And I know that, soon enough, doomsday will arrive.

But I just smile and wave, as princesses do.

Even—and especially—when they crumple.

CHAPTER FOURTEEN
PENN

You think you are so fake
But you're the realest thing I've ever seen.
Painful to watch.
Beautiful to see.
Shattering to touch.

Curiosity killed the cat, and it was about to land my ass in equally deep shit too.

I knew coming back home before I got a text clearance that the party was over was a special brand of stupid, but my dumbass self is here anyway.

The party is in full force when I park the Prius all the way on the other side of the neighborhood, a mega creep move if I ever made one. I make my way to the Followhills' mansion by foot, wearing a ball cap to stay under the radar, approaching it with hands tucked deep inside my pockets.

"Yo. Little shit." I hear someone chuckle behind me and—because intelligence is not my friend tonight—decide it's a good idea to turn around. It's Dean Cole, Knight's dad. He is sitting on the front porch of his colonial—a weird architectural design for SoCal, but apparently, his wife is from Virginia and he is crazy about her so he designed her the perfect Southern-style house from scratch—sipping whiskey.

"You think it's a good idea to go in there?" He jerks his chin toward the Followhills' mansion.

I spit my gum out and kick it all the way to the Spencers' lawn. "Nope."

"Just checking." He laughs.

"What are you doing up?" I eye him curiously. Is he snitching for the Followhills?

I can hear feminine coughing from his house. He winces, tossing his whiskey back and finishes it with a gulp.

"Missus is feeling under the weather. She's about to join me outside for some fresh air."

I have nothing to say to that, so I just nod.

"You can crash here tonight," he offers.

"Nah. I have some unfinished business with your spawn's friends." I bite off a callus from my palm and spit the dead skin on the ground.

Maybe I just want to be near Daria and Via. Make sure they haven't killed each other yet. I turn to leave.

"Do you love her?" Dean Cole's voice makes me stop dead in place.

I don't know how he knows.

I don't know if that means Jaime and Mel know too.

And I have no idea why my face feels so hot.

All I *do* know is that now's not the time to think about this question.

I shake my head, chuckling. "It's just harmless fun."

"Harmless for who?" he calls as I resume my way to the Followhills'.

For me, I want to say. *The Tin Man.*

"Are you gonna tell Jaime and Mel?" I turn around as I continue walking backward.

He refills his glass with a bottle on the arm of his recliner, his eyes on the liquid.

"And miss out on the moment he finds out and kicks your ass? I think I'll let your sloppy ass do the job for me. But save me a front-row seat when that happens."

"Deal."

I slip behind the pool house, a good few feet from Gus and the All Saints football team.

In my defense, I didn't come here with the intention of playing Sherlock and eavesdropping. The task rolled into my lap the minute I slipped through the backyard. I was about to cross the lawn and find my sister, to make sure she wasn't overwhelmed, when I heard Gus's voice. Now, I can't stop listening.

"...if we don't make it to State, Coach's going to cold-blooded kill us. Principal Prichard is going to burn whatever's left of our bodies, and the mayor is going to kick us out of town." I hear their running back moaning into his beer. "And, Gus, dude, I know we've been lucky, but you've seen our form at practice. We, like, suck."

Gus laughs. I peek behind the pool house and watch him boomerang a loaded ashtray into the pool.

"Just because you suck doesn't mean everyone else here does."

"Alexa." Knight Cole billows smoke after sucking on his joint, turning to the virtual assistant sitting next to him on a table between pool loungers. "Tell Gus that he is not fooling anyone. That we've been so bad the last couple of games we won by very little, even though the other teams weren't on the field, and that we're about to run out of luck and need to start talking to Coach about making some serious changes if we want to get to State."

"Relax, Cole." Gus puffs his chest. He rearranges his ball cap on his head. The one that looks like it stinks. "I have it all under control. Shit, that rhymes! I'm hella creative when I'm high."

"How do you mean?" Knight asks seriously. I detect some alarm in his voice, and Knight doesn't get his feathers ruffled easily. I know Gus is off guard, drunk, and high, and if he is going to say something that would put him in deep shit, it's going to be right here, right now. I suck in a breath, my skin bursting out in goose bumps. Gus opens his mouth, and the first words come out, but then I hear a loud whine directed at Gus.

"There you are! I've been looking for you." Via throws her arms around his neck and purrs.

Her voice is bubbly, bright, and as per usual, all fucking wrong. I close my hand into a fist, using every ounce of self-control in me to make sure I don't slam it against the concrete wall I'm leaning against. Via blabs about trivial shit—apparently, they're folding out and everyone's leaving, so if the guys want another beer, now's the time to get it. She just ruined my chances of hearing an admission from the horse's mouth.

So much for reconnecting, rebuilding, and all that crap.

People are starting to file out of the house. A neighbor threatened to call the police, but they gave Daria thirty minutes to get her shit together before they sent the boys in blue. Something tells me that Dean's doing me a solid. I know if I stay behind the pool house, people are bound to notice me when they round the house and head to their cars, so I slip into the pool house to hide.

Inside, it's more like a guesthouse with an open-plan living room and a kitchenette, turquoise marble over dark oak throughout. There is also a bedroom with a glass wall. You can see into the bedroom from any spot in the living room. Not that I currently have to. As soon as I reach the switch to turn on the light, I stop. The moans bleeding into my ears tell me I just walked in on a very private moment in the see-through bedroom.

Chuckling, I turn around, about to open the door and head back, when a small body bumps into mine. I look down and see Daria.

Her eyes widen, and her mouth falls open.

"What's your ass doing on this side of the house?" I demand, continuing my hat trick of stupidity/creep behavior for the evening. She lives here. I'm the one who was supposed to stay away tonight. But Daria is always a tad disoriented when we see each other, something that brings my ego and cock much delight.

"We keep the ice here, and some loser punched a wall trying to win a bet." She rolls her eyes, in full-blown cheerleader mode.

I grab her by the collar of her dress and pull her into the pool house, shutting the door behind us.

"I—" she begins, and I bite her lower lip like a savage. Hard and out of nowhere.

"Shhh," I snarl. "We've got company, my hideous little monster."

Still engulfed in complete darkness, I turn her body around and rest my chin on top of her head, pointing at the glass wall of the bedroom. We can only see their silhouettes, but their positions are clear. There's a guy bracing his arm against the wall, thrusting himself into the mouth of a chick beneath him. He is fucking her mouth ruthlessly, one hand bracketing her head. A whimper escapes Daria's throat, and my cock jerks in my jeans. It's been too long since I've been inside her.

"Ever went down on anyone?" I lean down, my lips feathering over her shoulder blade. I grab her by the waist and pull her back into my body, my hard cock pressing against her back through our clothes. Damn height difference. I don't know why I ask this. Getting an honest answer I'm not fond of might send me on a rampage. A criminal record is the last thing my ass needs, but if I find out Principal Prichard has been getting blowies from Daria, I just might slice him up into tiny pieces and fry him up for breakfast.

Hey, athletes can never get enough lean protein.

She inhales sharply but doesn't answer.

My fingers travel along her inner thigh from behind, my teeth grazing her ear as I travel upward, toward her panties, then tug them aside.

"Answer me."

She gasps when I pinch her clit, so I do it again. I'm so hard I'm about to burst all over her dress, something I'm sure my preppy princess wouldn't appreciate. Her head rolls back on my shoulder when I start fucking her with my index and middle finger, swirling her clit with my thumb. My other hand is working her nipple through her dress.

"All my firsts," she chokes out brokenly. "You stole all of them."

"*That's my girl.* Look at them," I hiss, my voice so husky and gruff, I barely recognize it. "Take notes, Skull Eyes. This'll be us tomorrow."

She refocuses on the couple in front of us going at it. His thrusts become jerkier and faster, and he groans. Daria cups my dick from behind and squeezes, and I close my eyes.

Don't come. Don't come. Don't come.

Outside, people breeze past the pool house. They're talking and laughing and yelling and living their mediocre, average existence. The place is clearing out, but there are still some assholes milling around, refusing to leave. Including the couple in front of us, who are not about to appreciate the audience when they're done milking an orgasm from this guy's dick.

"Coming," the dude jeers, his voice laced with venomous boredom.

I can practically envision Daria's eyes widen when she hears his familiar tenor and have to work her extra fast to keep her in the pre-orgasm zone.

It's Vaughn.

"Not on my face this time," the girl purrs, giggling with her mouth full of him.

Daria groans. "*Esme.*"

I quickly move my spare hand from her chest to cover her mouth in case she's in the mood for a confrontation.

Personally, I don't give two shits about who they are. I just know they made my balls tighten, and now I need an outlet. Vaughn pulls out of Esme's mouth and tugs her hair, tilting her head up and coming all over her neck and tits through her dress. I swear at this moment, I nearly shove my whole fist into Daria, and she comes so hard, she yells my name, biting my palm where there's still a cut from my blood oath with Via.

Count on Daria to kill any good intention I have with my flakey, fake sister.

Esme snaps her head toward us while Vaughn is still pumping his jizz lazily into the crack between her tits, and without thinking, I grab Daria's hand and sneak her out before they can see our faces. My hand is dripping blood between us on her manicured lawn.

"Crap." She runs across her backyard with me. Her heels are digging into the moist earth, slowing her down, and I tug on her hand, not in the mood for ASH assholes to see the Las Juntas rat crashing their precious party.

"What if they saw us?" she wheezes.

"They're the ones caught with his dick in Esme's mouth. Let them figure it out." I round her house and bend her under the kitchen window that's facing a wrought-iron gate and high bushes. No one can see us here.

"Where have you been tonight?" The accusation in her voice is harsh. I was visiting Adriana and Harper, but it's Daria's birthday party, and I'm not about to shit all over her night. I pull her between my thighs, cupping her ass.

"Missed me?" I use my thumb to wipe my blood along her lower lip.

She licks it without hesitation, her eyes on me. "Answer my question, Penn."

"I got you a birthday present."

"A blood oath with your sister?" Her gaze drops to my hand.

A perceptive little thing, she is. I don't think people give Daria the credit she deserves. She could've found Bin Laden in a week had she been given enough Red Bull and good internet service. I'm still not sure how I feel about Via. I don't buy her good-girl charade, and the more time that passes, the more I realize maybe I loved her just because someone had to. Because our mother didn't. When Via was being her real self, I could at least relate to her anger. I felt it too. This *Brady Bunch* version, though? Straight-up made of cardboard and fake glitter.

"Turn around." I change the subject.

"That seems to be your favorite view of me." Daria sighs but still spins in place. She is wrong. I can look at her face all fucking day. I wish it were a legit job so I could make money doing it. I would put in all the extra hours and become a billionaire within a year.

(The math doesn't add up, by the way, so don't try to do it.)

I collect her blond locks and let them fall over her right shoulder, then kiss her nape. I produce the sea glass necklace from my pocket and put it on her.

She gasps when the orange sea glass hits her delicate rib cage, and her chest caves.

Daria twists back to me with tears in her eyes. I can't bear her vulnerability because it seems real, and I can't think of her as real. Even if she is genuine, this can never work out. Even if I don't give a damn about what Jaime and Mel think, Daria does, although she would die denying it. And her parents will never be okay with us being together. Not to mention the hell Via is going to give me. But before all of this can even materialize, there is also the Adriana and Principal Prichard mess to sort out, and nothing promises me that Daria won't get cold feet about telling her precious rich friends she's dating the token charity case.

Every single time I'd take her out, I'd pay for the bill with her daddy's allowance. I won't be getting any money of my own before I play college football, and when I do, who knows where Daria will be? We've never talked about it. I'll go wherever I'm offered a full scholarship.

The world is wide-open for her. She can go to the East Coast, or Midwest, or fucking Europe.

My world, however, is narrow pathed and dingy. I don't believe in fairy tales. I think Shakespeare got it right. When two people try to go against the grain, they get fucked up. End of story.

"Skull Eyes," I whisper.

She links her arms around my neck and rises on her toes to kiss me. "I felt so lonely without it," she whispers into my mouth.

"It felt so lonely without you," I admit.

"Are we still talking about the necklace?"

We both laugh, but it dies down quickly. Our lips find each other as if they were programmed to do so. We kiss for so long my lips burn and crack at the edges. There's a desperation in that kiss that wasn't there before. It feels like goodbye, and I don't like how it tastes. I pull away, wanting a redo. I also want to tell her to stop seeing Prichard. That it's time to cut all the background noise. I still don't know what to do with Adriana, or with Daria's parents, or with my fucking life, but I've always been good at figuring shit out as I go along.

The minute I open my mouth, a scream of horror explodes from my right. Both Daria and I whip our heads, and it's Via, standing in front of us, cupping her mouth.

My twin sister pivots on her heel and runs away, and I go after her. It's an instinct more than anything because last time she did it, Rhett stopped me.

This time, nothing will.

I tackle Via to the grass by the pool, and we both slide on the damp blades. She squirms underneath me, yelping. Wet and freshly cut grass, and Friday night lights are where I thrive. I rise from her, pulling at her arm to get her to stand and holding her elbow as I drag her all the way into the house. She protests between sobs, and I have a feeling she is too deranged to think clearly right now.

Once I enter the empty house—that's in an advanced stage of trashed—I direct her to her room downstairs. I'm momentarily disoriented by all the pink Melody put in there. Someone needs to sit her ass down and tell her not everything feminine and teenager-y needs to look like a pussy. I throw Via over a beanbag and square my shoulders.

"Look," I say with a calm I don't feel. "It is what it is."

Even I acknowledge the lameness of the explanation. Not that it makes it any less true. If she is freaked out about Daria and me exchanging juices, she's about to get a whole lot more uncomfortable.

"Are you dating her?" Her eyes are sparkling red. Her whole face is a mess.

I knead my forehead, giving it some genuine thought. "Your guess is as good as mine."

"What about Adriana and the baby?"

"They have nothing to do with this." I pause. "Wait, how do you know about Harper?"

I guess it makes sense that she does, but I'm still mad she found out like this. I'm mad that we didn't get the chance to discuss it, that we're not who we're supposed to be to one another.

She looks down, pouting. Then it hits me. She wrote to Addy. She kept in touch with Addy. This shit is unreal. I knew Via was mad at me, whether she admits it or not, but then something dawns on me. Something that gives my Tin Man, half-functioning heart a reason to break.

She didn't come back for me.

"Does Adriana know?" she asks between sniffs.

My story with Addy goes back to age five. We grew up in the same neighborhood. Via and I used to sneak into her house every time the smell of her mom's pozole and Spanish rice was too much for us. We begged for food, and Addy's mother took mercy on us. And I returned it with a very unwelcome favor in the form of knocking Adriana up. At least, that's the version I'm sticking to.

"She knows," I drawl. After what happened at Lenny's, Adriana started asking questions. She's used to my messing around with other chicks, but it was never serious and never got to a point where anyone has threatened her place.

Needless to say, Adriana was not pleased. I think a part of her is hoping that I'll take her and Harper with me wherever I go for college. But I've only ever promised to provide for them, not to stick around.

Via flings herself over the bed and presses her arm to her eyes. She is crying again. "I can't believe you fell for her, Penn."

This is the third time this evening I'm being poked about my feelings toward Skull Eyes. No wall in this mansion is safe from my fist.

"You can't see her anymore." Via wipes at her tears.

I stare at her pitifully. "It's not for you to decide."

"No." She shakes her head frantically, standing up. "You don't understand. You can't. I will never forgive the betrayal."

"*What* betrayal?"

"The letter of acceptance you both destroyed."

Sonofabitch. How does she know?

"That's right." She tilts her chin up. "Daria decided to throw it in my face tonight. She thought it'd be fun to see me agonized over it. Penn, how could you like someone like that? I know she's pretty, but she's horrible. She did awful things to me and other people. She tore us apart."

I suck in my teeth as the world tilts sideways. I'm losing grip of my shit. Sometimes I wish I'd been born an eagle or a wolf or a fucking wombat. Anything not to deal with people.

"Break up with her."

"Via," I warn. I don't take orders from anyone. Not even Coach.

"It's an ultimatum." Her voice turns steady and metallic.

"That's a big word for someone who currently means so little to me." It's my turn to cut deep.

Her face twists in agony to my confession.

"Oh." I cock an eyebrow. "You thought I was still the same asshole you left behind?"

She is quivering like a leaf now. She rushes over to me and grabs my shoulders. I don't know why I hate it even more than I've hated everything about her ever since she came back. The original Via was a lot of things, but she wasn't tacky. She was real. Real petty. Real vindictive. Real hungry. But real all the same.

"You don't understand!" She stomps. "It's either her or me."

"I don't do ultimatums," I announce emotionlessly. "Make me choose, and you won't like the results."

"If you don't break up with her, I am moving back with Dad. It's been horrible there, but at least I feel like I have some sort of family. They mean well, even if their way of life is all wrong. I can't be here, among strangers, with a brother who is in love with my archenemy, the girl who ruined my future. Why should I stick around for a guy who helped Daria Followhill get rid of my acceptance letter to the Royal Academy? That's why I left, Penn. Now watch as I hitchhike back to Mississippi. Just pray I won't be raped and beaten to death this time around. And before you ask if I mean it, please remember, I did it four years ago, when I was much younger and even more helpless."

My blood runs cold in my veins. We both know I will never forgive myself if Via leaves again. Her past four years have been hell, and we weren't there for each other. Yes, she returned a little kooky, and preachy, and way too nice and proper for my liking, but she is still my twin sister. We shared a womb for nine months, and all the problems life threw at us after that. Her absence hasn't changed that. A girl with eyes like the endless ocean and hair like golden beaches doesn't change that.

Then Via puts the last nail in the coffin.

"If you don't break up with her, I'll tell her mother, friends, and everyone she cares about what she did to me. We both know they love her but don't like her one bit. All they need is a little push to make Daria become a reject, and I'm more than happy to shove. It will be a spectacular fall. But if you do as I say, her secret's safe with me."

I turn around and stalk out before I do something stupid.

Stopping at the threshold of her room, my back still to her, I drop a counterstrike. Call it friendly fire, but a soldier doesn't go down without taking an enemy with him.

"You don't want me with Followhill? Stay the fuck away from Gus."

CHAPTER FIFTEEN
DARIA

If I could hate you
Like you hate yourself
I wouldn't be eaten alive
By guilt
Desire
And lust.

I wake up with a blossoming hangover that presses against my eyelids like cold metal. Reaching for my face, I graze my hand over the necklace Penn gave me back. A grin spreads on my face before I remember Via slapping me. My admission to her. How Penn ran after her. My mouth goes dry.

She could tell Mel.

She could tell Penn.

She could tell the whole school.

Shitballs.

Melody, Dad, and Bailey are already downstairs. The scents of fresh cleaning products from the crew that came in last night to take care of the mess we left and bacon, eggs, and honey buns waft through the crack of my door. I feel for my phone on my nightstand and check it, frantic.

There are the usual group messages from my friends, then another message from Penn.

Meet me in Vaughn's pool house at noon.

My heart paces back and forth, trying to decode this invitation, shaking its imaginary head. I try to calm it to a reasonable pulse. Penn probably wants to do what Vaughn did in *my* pool house at my party, and we can't do that here with my parents around. He doesn't sound mad. He sounds like good ole, dry Penn.

I type back.

See you there. xoxo

During breakfast, Melody tries to convince me to go with Bailey and her to New York. I say no. When that turns unfruitful, she explains that Via will be joining them. I should've seen it coming from miles away, but my answer remains a big fat no. If anything, I'm glad to get some downtime with just Dad and Penn. Other than Bailey, they're the only people I can stand.

At a quarter to noon, I sneak into Vaughn's pool house on the Spencers' estate. I'm not sure how Penn is planning to get in. I guess through Vaughn. I have all of the Spencers' security codes. They have ours too.

Once inside, I decide to defrost Penn's Tin Man heart.

I strip down to my panties and bra—matching black lace items from Agent Provocateur that go well with the black velvet sofa I'm lying on—and mess with my phone as I wait.

Penn enters the pool house five minutes later, looking ragged and ruffled. There's sweat on his brow, and he is wearing his sneakers, basketball shorts, and no shirt at all. It's obvious he's been running. From what or who, I don't know. His torso is bronze, cut, and muscled to a fault. I would lick the sweat off his body drop by drop if he'd let me. His eyes, however, are rimmed with black circles. It looks like he hasn't slept a wink.

"Whoa." We exhale at the same time when we take each other in. But it's his face that falls as soon as he sees me half-naked.

I sit upright, covering my bra with my arms. Penn saunters to my clothes in the corner of the room and kicks them toward me.

"Put some clothes on, Daria. You're embarrassing yourself."

Daria? What happened to Skull Eyes? I actually grew attached to the stupid pet name. I frantically pull my Daisy Dukes over my legs, getting dressed without eye contact. This isn't a booty call. But I do agree that it's freaking embarrassing.

"What the hell, Penn?"

"Nothing. I got what I wanted from you, and you got what you wanted from me. Time to cut the bullshit." He delivers the news with no hint of emotion in his voice. My knee-jerk reaction is to tell him it's a good idea. *Great.* That I wanted to break it off a long time ago. That he is trash. That his sister is a two-faced bitch. But that's the old Daria. The one who pretends she doesn't care about losing things.

The new Daria? She doesn't want to lose him.

"Where is this coming from?" I slip into my shoes, covering myself up more and more, only to feel more naked.

He shrugs in my periphery. "I'm bored of you, and it ain't worth the risk. Your parents are going to kick our asses if they find out. Besides, you have Prichard, and I have Adriana." He scratches his barely existent stubble with the back of his hand. "Game over."

"It's not like that," I say hurriedly. If I have to tell him what's going on with Prichard, I will. I'm not proud of it, but pride is a very slippery slope where love is involved. Marx. *Love.* I don't use the L word lightly. I don't go around telling people I love pizza or chocolate or *Riverdale.* I *like* those things. Love, I save for the important stuff.

But I am hopelessly, tragically in love with Penn Scully.

That's why I can't really hate his sister. Not entirely, anyway. She is an extension of him, and he has my heart.

"Let me explain." I rush toward him, placing a hand on his damp chest. It squeezes on instinct, and he swats my touch away.

"No explanation necessary. Just wanted to give you the bottom line somewhere private, you know, because you're so prone to crying like a little wuss."

My mouth goes dry, and my breaths become shallow and fast. My heart is all over the place, elbowing its way out of its cage. It wants out, and it wants Penn. Me? I just want to make him understand Principal Prichard and I are not what he thinks. But this came out of nowhere, and at an odd time…

Via.

Via did this. Via killed this for me. Again. My blood is boiling in my veins. I know he is being mean and unfair to me, but in my desperation to explain myself, I don't see that.

"But, Penn, Principal Prichard and I—"

He cuts me off harshly. "You deaf? I said I don't care. It's not about Prichard."

"Then tell me what—"

"Because of Harper, okay?" he snaps, kicking the velvet sofa. "I'm never going to leave Addy. Much less for your spoiled ass. She's coming with me to college. Grow some self-respect and give it a rest."

He turns around and stalks out, slamming the door in his wake. I suck my lower lip into my mouth, trying not to cry and fulfill his rude prediction. Pacing the room, I grab the back of my neck and pull at it, raking my fingers over my neck until the skin breaks.

Penn has a daughter.

He said he and Addy are not what I thought they were to him, but he lied to get what he wanted from me.

He got into my house and pants and then my heart, feeding me whatever bullshit line he thought I wanted to hear.

The door opens, and I twist, expecting to see Penn on the other side. Praying that he came here to tell me it was all a stupid prank gone wrong.

It's Vaughn.

When he sees my eyes brimming with tears, he looks away as if I'm not decent. Feelings make him wince.

"Did you know?" I whisper.

He waltzes deeper into the room, clad in black, a teenage Lucifer out for misery and blood.

"That he was going to break up with me," I explain. "That he was playing me?"

"No and no. All I knew was that you needed some privacy. Something you weren't very good at giving me last night." He arches a meaningful eyebrow.

Bitter laughter clogs my throat. "About that. Are you screwing around with my best flyer?"

"When time permits."

"Are you falling for my best flyer?" Esme doesn't deserve a guy like Vaughn.

"I'll fall in love with a pet rock first."

"Don't diss pet rocks. They'll never die on you." I sniffle.

He pulls me into a hug. A rarity I know not to take for granted when it comes to Vaughn. I bury my face in his chest and let myself crumble, feeling my bones shaking inside my body.

"You'll be all right, Followhill."

For the first time in a long time, I don't believe this.

CHAPTER SIXTEEN
PENN

There is nothing more poetically inspiring
Than loving the right person
At the wrong place
At the wrong time.

After practice, I visit Adriana at Lenny's. I don't want to be anywhere near the Followhills. I can't look Daria in the face and dealing with my sister is out of the question. They both hover in the hallways like ghosts. Silent, pale, lifeless. Melody is on the verge of being committed. Speaking of Mel, she shoots me a text when Addy is serving me steak and green beans, clutching my bicep and telling me, "You work so hard. You're so buff. If you ever need to unwind with someone…"

> Melody: This house has rules, and I am tired of all the teenagers inside it breaking them. You are to be at home by seven every day for dinner. If you don't have it in you to let me know you are late, you can always pack a bag and live with the Coles.

I flip the phone over. She is finally getting a backbone. Good for her. Not that I will ever reply to this shit, but still. Addy slips toward me, rubbing my arm.

"What's going on, hon? You look like hell. Was the interview okay?"

All Saints High Saints and the Las Juntas Bulldogs both made it to the playoffs. The entire town of Todos Santos is ecstatic. They interviewed Gus and me for the local news channels today. Both our coaches were there to make sure no fists were thrown.

"It went fine," I say.

"What is it, then?"

I can't tell her I broke up with Daria because that would give her ideas. I shake my head and stand. It's time to face the Mel music anyway. I grab my varsity jacket and kiss the top of Adriana's head. She holds on to the collar of my shirt and pulls me in, kissing my mouth. I groan and not with pleasure. She is erasing my last kiss with Daria.

Listen to yourself. You sound like a fucking maniac.

"Give me a chance," Addy whispers against my frozen lips. "I can make it good for you. She doesn't know you. I do. I know exactly what you need."

"Did Via talk to you?" I ask conversationally.

Addy nods. "Don't hate her, Penn. She just wants to see us happy. With Harper. Together."

Later, Jaime and I arrive at the house at the same time. We meet at the front door. He is wearing a suit and a somber expression, but he tosses a stack of letters into my hands. Jaime has stepped up and, in recent weeks, began stopping by Rhett's on his way back from work to unlock the mailbox with one of Bailey's bobby pins and get my letters of interest.

I catch them in the air and start browsing through them, tucking my chin down so he can't see my face. I haven't slept well in a while.

Jaime walks over to me and slaps my back. "Keep going," he tells me.

Oklahoma. Texas. UCLA. Ohio State. I'm waiting for that drum in my chest that signals excitement. Those are the D1's I've been waiting for all along. My eyes pause on Notre Dame's symbol. My dream college. The one thing I worked for.

I feel nothing.

Jaime shakes my shoulder. "Hey. What's with you?"

"Nothing," I mumble, shoving the letters into my backpack. We'll go through them tonight as we've done every night recently. It's not like I can spend time with Daria anymore, and I'd rather get beaten to death with phone books by evangelistic widows than actually talk to my sister after the fuckery she pulled.

"Look at me," Jaime orders.

I look up, blinking at him. He is not his wife. He is full of confidence and self-assurance. I don't screw with him.

"What's wrong?" He frowns.

"Nothing," I say again.

"Is this about Via?"

I shrug. As far as I can tell, he is silently tolerating my sister's presence here. He is close enough with Daria to know how much it kills her to see my sister here.

"Is it about my daughter?"

"Which one?" I raise an eyebrow.

"The legal one, bastard."

I smile. I don't lie to him because I can't. Because he deserves fucking better than that.

"We should get in. Your wife's gonna be pissed."

"My wife is already pissed. She has two girls she can't control living under her roof, and she loves them both too much to give them tough love. Believe it or not, Penn, I'm on your side. That's why I'm going to give you a valuable tip. Right here. Right now. Are you listening?"

I blink at him, waiting for it.

"Choose your sister."

"Sir?"

"Choose her. Don't choose Daria. You'll end up giving her less than she deserves. And my daughter deserves everything. Not half of it. Not a quarter. And definitely not messy. Let her go. Unless, of course…" He pauses, cocking his head to examine my expression.

I don't breathe. "Unless?"

"You love Daria. Then I do not allow you, under any fucking circumstances, to break both your hearts because Sylvia still holds a grudge."

"Do you know what colleges Daria is looking into?" I swallow.

He throws his head back and laughs before shaking his head. I guess we're all too transparent for our own good. Jaime yanks the door open and walks in.

"So screwed, Scully. So goddamn screwed."

CHAPTER SEVENTEEN
DARIA

You kill me with your eyes.
Burn me with your smile.
Bury me with your indifference.

I join Mom, Bailey, and Via in New York.

Mostly to put some distance between Penn and me. When I send Mel a text informing her it's a go, she replies with a string of emojis, but this time refrains from begging me to go with her for coffee or inviting me on a shopping spree.

She's been getting chiller lately. But it's too little, too late for me to appreciate her change in attitude.

I strategize my time at home as though my life depends on it. Because it does. My heart can't take much more than it already has in recent weeks.

In the mornings, I keep my nose buried in my phone. During dinner, I let Bailey and Via do most of the talking and cling to my conversations with Dad. Sometimes I hear Via in the hallway, begging Penn to open the door.

He never does.

When we get to the hotel in New York, Via and Bailey kick off their matching ballet flats and jump on one of the two queen-size beds. The room is relatively small for what we usually get, and I know it's not because Melody was trying to save money.

"You'll sleep with me, Lovebug. You don't mind, do you?"

I pretend not to hear her. I have a feeling I'm about to add to my little black book this weekend. Principal Prichard will be delighted. Especially when I show up at his office, ready to atone for my sins.

I'm numb and only speak when I'm directly spoken to, which is not often. Mel takes us to an Italian joint for dinner. Bailey and I order pasta and a panini each, and Melody and Via share a salad.

"Remember how I used to eat the protein bars you got me every class, Mrs. Followhill?" Via pretends to wipe a stray tear. "I didn't even know they had, like, a thousand calories in them."

"You needed those bars." Mel leans across the table, catching one of Via's crocodile tears with her thumb.

I look away as if I've been slapped.

"What I needed was someone like you. I'm grateful you're in my life," Via murmurs. Now it's Bailey's turn to smile at her softly. I look down at my sparkling water. This, from the same bitch who called my mother unbearable when she was in my room. But I can't call her out. Not when she knows about what I did to her four years ago.

"Girls." Melody sucks in a breath. "I need to tell you why we're really here."

Mel explains that the New York Ballet wants to open a branch in Los Angeles, and they're considering her for the cofounder role. There are tears hanging on her lower lashes as she delivers the news. My heart hurts because normally—a year ago—even though we weren't super close, she would have told me about it before she confided in anyone else.

"You've got this, Mrs. Followhill." Via fist-pumps the air.

"Please, call me Mel."

"*Mel.*"

"I believe in you, Mom," Bailey cheers.

Melody turns to me.

I pick up my slice of panini and take a small bite, looking around me. When all eyes are still on me, I say the only thing that pops in my head. "Those energy bars were disgusting."

———————

At night, I toss and turn. Mel is trying to sleep next to me. Every time she reaches to rub my back and soothe me, I coil into myself. I keep wondering how we got here, and if there's a way to go back to how we were the night I saw Penn at the snake pit. When Melody and I were civil. When we still communicated.

In the morning, Via wakes up with blisters on her feet the size of bricks.

"It's all the walking." She breaks into a heart-wrenching sob. "Daddy and Nana never took me anywhere in Mississippi. I guess I forgot what it feels like to walk any type of real distance."

Make. It. Stop.

"We'll go to Duane Reade." Mel pacifies her, rubbing *her* back now. No objections here.

"We can buy you sneakers at the Nike store!" Bailey adds.

They fuss around her, assuring her that her mammoth pus balloons will be a thing of the past by nighttime.

"Just wait here," Mel says, eyeing both of us carefully. "Bailey and I will be right back."

"Oh, I wouldn't send you to run my errands. I'm coming!" Via cries out dramatically.

Of course, she is. Spending a second with me would be the end of the world.

They dash out the door, and I notice Mel's phone is still on the nightstand beside our bed. I initiate a conversation for the first time in months. It seems like a big deal to me because I've been so reluctant to talk to her. I've been avoiding it like the plague for what seems like months.

"Hey, Melody," I holler at them as they run the length of the hallway toward the elevators, trying to catch one that's sliding closed. "You—"

"Not now, Daria!" She shares a laugh with the girls, disappearing between the closing doors of the elevator.

Daria.

She is Melody, and I am Daria.

Mom and *Lovebug* are officially dead.

I turn around and exhale. I check my phone. No new messages. Penn forgot about me, and maybe it's the way it should be. I handed him my icy heart only for him to thaw, heat, burn, and then stab. He doesn't deserve me, and I don't deserve to be saddled with the title homewrecker.

I drag my feet to the bathroom and start a bath before noticing Mel's phone is lighting up with a new message.

Hello, Melody. Grace here. I was wondering if we could reschedule our meeting from tomorrow at 2pm to today at 2pm? Our HR director has to leave town this evening and won't be able to go through the fine print with you.

I stare at the words. My hands are shaking, and each breath feels like I'm gulping lava into my lungs. All the anger and frustration I've been feeling for the past few months bubble inside my chest.

First, she took Penn in.

Then she decided to homeschool Bailey.

Then she took Via in.

Then Penn broke my heart.

And Via stole both her and Bailey from me.

I know I'm only here because Mel couldn't *not* invite me. A sense of overwhelming vindictiveness washes over me. I try to tell myself not to do it when my fingers float of their own accord over her phone screen.

Actually, I appreciate the opportunity, but I decided we will
not be a good fit after all.

I shoot the message across to Grace.

I regret it immediately, but confessing what I did is only going
to make it worse. Mel already hates me. She doesn't need any more
excuses to want to disown me.

I am so very sorry to hear. Please let us know if that ever
changes.

What have I done?

What have I done?

I delete the entire chain of messages and block and erase Grace
from my mother's contacts, then put the phone exactly where she
left it before she went out with the girls.

Burying myself under the blankets of the queen-size bed, I don't
come up for air.

CHAPTER EIGHTEEN
DARIA

Behind every untrusting girl is a boy who
made her that way.

Mel looking frantically for her phone.

Mel searching for Grace's number in it.

Mel sniffing, whispering shit, shit, shit *as the pieces fall together.*
She is not getting this job. She is not fulfilling her dream.

My fingers quiver around the pen as I stare at my last entry in my journal and the memories of the exact moment she found out slam into me. By the time she reached Grace, the position had already been filled by the runner-up for the job.

When I started the little black book, I never thought I'd reach the level of evilness I did with Via again. But not only did I repeat the grave mistake of preventing someone from an opportunity of a lifetime because of my jealousy, but I did it to my own mother.

I roll on my bed and stare at the ceiling. Recently, especially since Penn and I started hanging out, I've been thinking of breaking things off with Principal Prichard. I don't need him anymore. Now, it burns in me to see him tomorrow and share this with him.

I pad downstairs to get a glass of water. It's probably close to midnight. All the lights in the house are out, and the only audible sounds are the thermostat humming and the coffee machine, which bubbles water automatically.

I grab a glass of water and make my way back to my room when the front door pushes open. I turn around on instinct. Stumbling in is a banged-up looking Penn. His face is bruised, cut, and downright purple. He limps toward the kitchen, dragging his left leg, his shoulders crashing into walls, a Greek statue, and a massive plant. He is obviously shitfaced on top of being injured.

I open my mouth to ask him if he was at the snake pit, then clamp it shut when I remind myself that it's not my business. His baby mama can take care of him. He made it perfectly clear. If anything, I should stop humiliating myself by caring for the boy who so ruthlessly played me. Who took my virginity while promising himself to another girl. At least this time he wore a condom.

Perhaps you're not a worthy longtime mistake to make.

I turn around and start climbing the stairs.

"*Scullys,*" he croaks. I keep my pace steady. Up, up, up to my room. I can do it. If I don't turn around. If I don't get lost in his light eyes and dark soul. "Skull…Eyes," he amends.

A hand jerks at the hem of my shirt, and he yanks me the two stairs down, back to the landing. He pins me to the wall in an alcove between the kitchen and the living room in one ruthless shove. I wince when I smell the alcohol and coppery blood on his breath.

His eye is swollen, and his lower lip drips blood onto his shoes. Drunken Penn is a sight I didn't think I'd see on a school night. He usually wakes up at the same time, rain or shine, for his morning strength training, always looking like a million bucks in a tattered ten-buck outfit.

"What do you want?" I hiss. I feel so breakable in his arms.

"A kiss."

I push on his chest. He is not making any sense. "Drop dead, Scully." It actually looks like he might. I turn back around toward the stairs.

He tugs my wrist again. His eyes are pleading, his eyebrows pulled together. He looks...pathetic, and the old Daria would take great pleasure in basking in this sight. But the new one wants to die knowing he hurts. Even worse than that, that he is *hurting*. That Via reentering his life was not everything he hoped it to be.

"Clean yourself up," I say quietly. "Or you'll get seriously infected."

"Help me?" he croaks, his voice throaty, laced with pain.

"Why don't you ask your girlfriend to do it?"

"Because she lives two towns over."

"Wrong answer."

"Because I don't want her help. I want yours."

I close my eyes. I tell myself that I'm just helping him clean up, not getting in bed with him. I don't think I've ever seen Penn so messed up. Physically—maybe. He's a physical player. But emotionally... For the first time since I've met him, I see him feel. The walls are soaked with his emotions, the air dense with them.

I make my way to the cabinet above the sink and take out a first-aid kit, motioning with my head for him to come closer. He hops onto the kitchen island and gulps me in as I wash his face with a warm cloth I'm pretty sure our cleaners use to wipe the tiles. Then I clean up his bruises with antiseptic wipes and put a Band-Aid on a gash on his forehead that probably needs some stitches. I don't ask him what happened. He tells me anyway.

"I fought three guys at the snake pit."

"That's dumb," I whisper.

"Simultaneously."

"That's *seriously* dumb."

He tries to chuckle, but it splits the cut on his lip again.

"There." I take a step back. "Bet you're feeling brand-new."

"How was New York?" he asks.

I can't even think about that city without wanting to throw up. I wonder if I'll ever be able to set foot in it again. "Don't."

"Don't what?"

"Don't pretend we're friends." I close the first-aid kit, push it back into the cabinet, and make my way upstairs to finish my entry.

When I get to my bed, the little black book is not there anymore.

CHAPTER NINETEEN
DARIA

Listen to the chaos
Brewing in your head.
This, my pretty, reckless lover
Is how our story ends.

The next day, I'm a dead girl walking.

When I see Via in the hallway, I pass her wordlessly. I'm scared that if I say something, I might go apeshit, and my situation is very delicate. I've lost so much in the past few weeks, and I don't trust myself to react anymore.

I'm passive. Timid. Scared.

Exactly as she wanted me. Precisely what she pretends to be.

Cheer practice is the only thing I have left, so when I put my uniform on in the locker room, I try to take a deep breath and enjoy the nothingness around me. Everyone is waiting for me outside. It's time to shine. To be the old me. Whoever that may be.

I gather my hair into a ponytail, turning around to make my way to the door at the same time it bangs shut. I look up and see Esme leaning against it, arms folded. She is wearing her skimpy cheer outfit and a triumphant smile.

"Can I tell you a secret?" Her voice is sugary sweet, and my hackles immediately rise.

I tilt my chin upward. "Sure. I'm getting good at keeping them."

She pushes off the door and saunters deeper into the room until we are face-to-face.

"I always knew you would be your own downfall. You were so pretty and perfect, with your shiny hair and long lashes. So conceited and entitled with your crazy lineage, ex-teacher mom and Hothole father. Sometimes, at night, I had to cry myself to sleep, convincing myself that you would fall because it didn't look like you ever would. And let's admit it." She chuckles. "The cheer captain title always belonged to me. I'm the better dancer. I'm a better leader, better mediator, the better human being."

I stand straighter. She is talking about me in the past tense, and I don't like that. I elevate my nose, reminding her who's the boss. Though, truth be told, I haven't felt in control for a really long time. "You can't strip my title, Esme. That's not how things work, no matter how much you want them to."

"That's where you're wrong." She puts two fingers to her mouth and whistles. The door opens and in trickles the cheer team in all their glory, complete with their uniforms. And at the end of the perfect line is Sylvia Scully, wearing a uniform she must've stolen. From me.

I see red.

I take a step back, twisting my mouth.

Esme takes a step toward me, cleaning invisible lint from my crop top. "You've been spacey, out of focus, and MIA when we needed you. Not to mention, poor Via told us about what you did to her four years ago with the letter." She pouts.

Shooting an accusing glance at Via, I see that she not only meets my gaze, but she smiles too. She got a new pixie haircut, stylish and expensive, and new stud earrings to go with it. She is already reinventing herself, and no one is stopping her from ruining my life.

Melody is compensating for our lack of connection by showering Via and Bailey with everything I won't accept from her anymore, and for whatever reason, Penn is firmly in her camp. The only person I still matter to is Dad, but even I know he is isolating himself in his quest to be there for me.

"You won't get away with this." I bare my teeth to Esme, getting in her face.

"What'll you do?" She cocks her head at me, smiling.

For one thing, tell Blythe, your BFF, that you've been sleeping with Vaughn. Then, I'll tell Vaughn to drop you, and make no mistake, the boy doesn't have a modicum of emotion in his body. He will do so without even mourning the lost blowjobs.

But I can't say this. At least publicly. The acts of the Hulk are to be done in secret.

"I'm guessing it's settled, then?" I ask, twisting my head toward the rest of the team.

They all look down, backs against the lockers in a row. Everyone other than Via. I laugh hysterically, shaking my head and waving at them dismissively.

"You guys are pathetic. You hate Esme."

No response.

"Good luck living off Diet Coke and air for the next semester."

I'm losing it, and I'm losing my place in the world, fast. The worst part is, I can't even fight for what's mine. Not when Via holds my journal. Dangling my life, future, and reputation above my head.

"Did you even mean it when you voted for me? Do you mean anything you do anymore? How fake can you be?"

Blythe takes a sharp breath, shaking her head. A tear escapes her eye, and I know Esme's pushed her, but I still hate her for not growing a spine. Looking around at their faces—grave, guilty, uncomfortable—I don't even know what to think anymore.

Everything I have is crumbling.

Everything I've worked for is perishing.

Via promised she'd end me, and so far, she's kept her word.

I stalk outside, back to the school, before the tears fall. Maybe

Penn is right. Maybe I cry all the time and make scenes. But here's a scene I'd never forget:

The day Via and Esme took my cheer captain badge, which I earned fair and square, is the day I found out I wasn't the only girl born with a green Hulk inside her. They have one too. And it just burst through their bones and skin and chased me away.

My stomach lurches.

At least I managed to put mine on a leash.

"And lookie who we have here."

Gus slams my open blue locker with a bang when I get my books out and gives me a playful shove. The hallway is empty. I'm ten minutes late because I'm running on no sleep, two cups of coffee, and anxiety. And there are cameras around, but he's the football captain, so he can get away with murder. Probably literally.

I don't move to pick up the scattered textbooks that fell when he ambushed me.

"Sure it's a good idea for you to skip classes? You're not the sharpest tool in the shed as it is." I feign disinterest and nonchalance, but I'm not feeling it anymore. I'm so drained, I'm surprised I'm still standing.

"Too funny, Followhill. I wonder…" He gets in my face, tilting his head with a manic smile on his lips. "Would you still be so funny when I show you what I have?"

He raises his arm, and it's my little black book.

My mouth goes dry. I'm going to faint. Shit. Via really did it this time.

I plaster my back to the lockers and try to breathe, but the oxygen doesn't hit my lungs. I think I'm having a panic attack. A real one.

"You look a little pale, Queen Daria. Where are your minions to bronze your face back into fake perfection?" He laughs boisterously.

"What do you want?" I grit out. I already know whatever it is, I'm going to give it to him. No one can get their hands on my diary. The prospect of people knowing what I did to my classmates or with Principal Prichard is paralyzing, but the real kicker is Mel. If she finds out I killed both her dream and Via's, I will lose her forever.

I would lose my everything.

Gus taps his chin, tilting his head skyward, my journal still held high in the air above his head. I glare at it, willing it to fly across the narrow space between us into my hand like in a Harry Potter book.

"Let's see. What do I want? Oh, I know! I want for Las Juntas to throw the playoff game and give me what I deserve—a victory."

To that, I actually laugh. It's a hysterical laugh, but it bubbles from my throat all the same. I drag a hand over my collarbone and neck, wiping away cold sweat.

"Shouldn't you be asking for something I can actually give you?"

"You're fucking the captain. It's in the journal. Surely, you have power over him."

I wince. "It happened once, and he doesn't care about me." It's a brutal admission, but he has to know I can't make this happen.

He rolls his eyes at me. "Popped your cherry, huh? Lucky bastard. Anyway, you asked for the price, and I gave it to you. It's your problem now. Not mine."

"I can't do that," I croak. I'm losing grip of my indifference. My mask is falling. I can't give him what I don't have. "He'll never do anything for me. He's with Adriana."

"For all I care, threaten to tell Adriana he's been fucking you all along to make him do it. Whatever it takes to make his team shitty come Friday. Otherwise..." He waves my journal around as if it doesn't harbor all my secrets and insecurities and vulnerability. As if the Hulk doesn't live there. "This shit is going to be printed out—every single page of it—into thousands of copies and stuck on every single locker and inch of the bathroom, art room, lab, and locker rooms. I'll post it on every social media site, and I'll make sure you can never escape it, no matter how fucking far you go. And don't even try to pull the parents' angle, Followhill, because the entire school would kill you for ruining the state championship for us."

He turns around and stalks down the empty hall. I chase him, choking on my own saliva. I'm too stunned to produce tears. My life as I know it is about to be over. I trip over my own legs, grasping his backpack so I don't hit the ground. He turns around sharply, growling.

"Hands off, Followhill."

"You can't do this to me." My knees hit the floor. How fitting. From this angle, I can finally see the view for what it is. All my mistakes, the people I chose to affiliate myself with—the jocks, the fakers, the popular kids—are ricocheting back at me. Gus holds my future, my reputation, between his sausage fingers.

"Please," I say, stripping off my remaining pride. "I beg you. I will do anything else. Tell me what to do. I can't get to Penn. No one can get to Penn."

Penn is the Tin Man.

Gus smiles politely, grabbing the collar of my dress and yanking me up to my feet.

"I actually think you're a very resourceful girl, Daria. Figure it out. Or I will bury you."

———

"We need to talk."

These are the words I could have imagined myself telling my mother, my future boyfriends, my friends, my family...*not* my principal. Yet here I am standing in front of Principal Prichard, telling him just that. I just threw up my nonexistent breakfast into a toilet bowl and cried my eyes out, and I probably look like just as much of a mess from the outside as I am on the inside.

When I walked in, I closed the door without his explicit order to do so, the first sign that something was off. Normally, I submit to him, awaiting specific instructions. That's how it's been since my first entry. The Via entry. When I walked into his office in middle school, I expected him to call my parents, set off a chain reaction, and fix my error. Fix *me*.

Instead, he tipped a jar of M&M's he kept on his desk over the edge, his eyes never wavering from mine. Colorful chocolate pieces rained down the floor, rolling at my feet like marbles.

"Pick them all up, Miss Followhill. On your knees, as I read your sins to you."

It became our ritual.

Over the years, he barked at me to rearrange the shelves in his office, clean his carpets, shine his shoes, and more recently, after Penn entered the picture, he'd strike the inside of my hands with a ruler. Where the red welts could be explained away by my grueling cheer workouts.

He always read my sins slowly behind his locked door, pausing melodramatically when he got to the juicy parts.

Most sinners say Hail Marys.

I atone for my sins in strokes of his ruler.

I deserve it. I deserve the pain. I distribute so much of it to others, I can't even blame Principal Prichard for putting me through all of this.

Principal Prichard says our sessions are about discipline. Putting me back on the straight and narrow. But honestly, we both know I'm not getting any better, and the more the years pass, the deeper the misery in which I drown.

I always figured we were both just two fucked-up people doing screwed-up things because no one else around us would understand. It wasn't until Penn that I realized Principal Prichard was possessive toward me. And that lust feels better than the striking. It feels glorious when experienced right.

Since then, Prichard's tasks have become more radical and meticulous. The strikes of the ruler harsher.

"I beg your pardon?" He doesn't look up from the paperwork he is signing. It has the Saints logo, so I know it's football related. Everything seems football related these days. Rumor is Gus is on Xanax and has been hitting the bottle to deal with the stress.

I sit down on the chair opposite to him. His eyes snap from the pages. "Were you invited to sit down, Miss Followhill?"

"We have a problem." My lips wobble. I reach out, putting his pen down for him.

His eyes narrow into slits, zeroing in on my hand. "Quite right. Get your sin book out."

That's what he calls it. It always drives me mad. As if he's above sinning.

I take a deep breath and release it all at once. Here goes nothing. "I don't have it."

"What do you mean, you don't have it?" His jaw flexes.

"Sylvia Scully stole it from my room last night. She lives with me now, as you know. Gus has it, and he is threatening to go public with it unless I convince Penn Scully to throw the playoff game."

They probably planned it together and laughed all the way throughout. And me? I was stupid enough to buy into Penn's distraction. I helped him clean himself up while she was upstairs, stealing my most valuable possession. The one thing that could destroy me.

Principal Prichard's lips twitch. With dark circles under my eyes and the tiny red bursts of blood inside them, I'm sure I'm not the same pretty girl who lured him into this arrangement. I didn't put on makeup this morning, and my hair is a tangled mess.

"I wrote about you in the book," I add matter-of-factly to remind him how grave our situation is. Prichard is featured in my journal many times. I squeeze my eyes shut and blush when I remember all the things I shared there.

Entry number one hundred twenty-two chronicles how one time, when I went into his office and he wasn't there, I rubbed myself against his executive chair. When he arrived, he made me lick the traces of myself from said chair. It's the most sexual thing we've ever done, and it did not involve touching each other, but it's enough to bring both of us down.

His jaw tick, tick, ticks, and I know he is losing his patience with me. We're both in deep trouble now. Which is why I'm here. We need to stop Gus.

"He will not publish anything related to me," Principal Prichard informs me, the picture of calm.

I blink, flabbergasted. "How do you know this?"

"I'm smarter than a cheerleader, for one thing. And so is he."

I sit back, staring at a spot behind him, wide-eyed.

"I don't know. Maybe I am stupid," I bite out, "but so is Gus, and trust me, he will compromise your perverted ass."

"Really!" he thunders, standing up and tossing the entire contents of his desk aside. I jump back in my chair. I've never seen him so angry before.

"What am I supposed to do? Threaten Miss Scully and Mr. Bauer? Just because you decided to spread your legs for the boy from the wrong side of the tracks even though I warned you not to?"

It's my turn to stand, my hands balled into fists beside my body as anger rolls off me, threatening to spill over.

"We're in this together, and we have to think of something."

"No. *You*'ll think of something. This doesn't sound like a me problem. It's a classic *you* problem."

"Even if you get Gus to agree not to print out your pages, I'll tell the world," I warn.

He smirks darkly. "And? No one will believe you. You're just another lost, spoiled brat who is hot for the principal. Don't forget what happened here. You paraded your tits and bent over. I never had sex with you. I never touched you, skin-to-skin. I never even kissed you. It was. All. On. You."

I'm floored. It feels like someone's pulled the rug out from under my feet. But I'm working on autopilot because I can't let him get away with this.

"Are you taking your chances, Ryan?" *Ryan.* I never call him by his first name. Only now, I have very little respect for him.

He runs a frustrated hand through his hair. "Leave, Miss Followhill, and do not come back unless it is with the recovered book to get punished until your behind turns blue."

"As if I'll ever get anywhere near you again." I throw my head back and laugh with humor I don't feel. "You were always jealous of Penn, who, by the way"—I pop my finger into my mouth and pull it out with a sound—"is a *fantastic* lay."

"Daria…" Prichard's never called me by my first name, either.

"He was *so* good when he took my virginity. Not too long after you found us in the locker room, actually."

"Stop it right now." He rounds his desk toward me. Slowly. Predatorily.

"Of course, by then I was fully prepped for the—"

"Stop!" He produces his ruler from under his desk, pointing it at me. My smile broadens. I'm free-falling off a cliff with a faulty parachute. Might as well enjoy the ride.

"Having him inside me as I writhed and moaned and orgasmed so hard I nearly fainted—"

In one swift movement, he throws me against the wall, my stomach hitting the cold surface. He pushes my dress up and strikes me with the ruler so hard I'm seeing stars.

"Don't!" I yell. "Don't you dare touch me, you asshole. We're done, Ryan."

He tugs my hair and whispers into my ear, "We're done when I say we're done, *Daria.*"

Strike, strike, strike.

My ass cheeks are burning and so are my eyes. I'm too stunned to move, to run away, choking on the bile coating my throat.

My principal, my priest, the man who held all my secrets, who I thought I could trust, just whipped my ass with a ruler against my will. Not once. Not twice. About a dozen times, in a frenzy like I've never seen before.

When he stops, it seems as though the world is rocking back and forth on turbulent water. Seasick, I slide off the wall, my mouth hanging open, but I don't really know what to say. Principal Prichard is not going to help me.

My war with Via and Gus is not only going to be fought alone, but I just found out they have a very powerful ally.

When I hear him take a step back, I turn around to face him.

What happened to you in that church?

I watch him through a curtain of tears, waiting for the apology. For the begging. For the remorse. Not just for what happened right now—I don't think I even fully comprehend it—but for the past four years. I look down, and he is hard.

So hard.

So very hard.

How did I miss this? The proper, abused Catholic boy turned out to be an improper, abusing man. My butt feels so hot and sore, I doubt I'll be able to sit on it anytime soon. My legs are shaking, and my heart aches dully in my chest.

I lost everything in the span of a semester. I didn't get the boy, or the happy ending, or the perfect family, or even to keep my status as queen bee or the cheer captain badge.

"You are my worst mistake," I whisper to him.

He smiles devilishly. "And you, my darling, are my favorite sin."

CHAPTER TWENTY
DARIA

The weight of my love for you
Buried me so deep
I can no longer sleep
Or eat
Or meet
My own eyes in the mirror.

When the first domino falls and my reality collapses in quick fashion, everything hovers in the air, motionless for a fraction of a second. That's the moment I suck in a breath, bracing myself for the hit.

It's where I am right now. Sore and wounded and scared. I've experienced the most tragic thing to ever happen to me—sexual and physical abuse—but somehow know the worst is yet to come.

I examine the red welts on my behind in the bathroom mirror at home, blinking back tears. They mar me with shame and horror and fear.

He touched me against my will.

He hit me against my will.

I played with fire and got so burned, it left a mark. Dozens of them.

The sad thing is, it doesn't hurt half as much as seeing Penn in the hallways does.

I apply some aloe to the welts and slip into knee-length pajamas, going commando. Wearing any type of fabric against my bruised skin hurts too much. My phone chimes with a new text message, and I hesitate before picking it up.

It's Prichard.

Meet me at Castle Hill Park at seven. The bench under the cherry tree.

Ryan Prichard doesn't apologize or make excuses. He is dangerous, a loose cannon, and even though I've made up my mind about never seeing him again, there's a good chance he came to his senses. Realizing Gus and Via can screw both of us over, he is probably planning to make it right. I know he thinks I'm too scared to tell my parents, but why take the risk? I type back.

So you can abuse me some more? No thanks.

He replies within seconds.

So we can sort out this thing and move forward with our relationship.

I'm about to let out a hysterical laugh when a fist crashes the door from the outside.

"You've been in there for an hour," Via whines. "Save some hot water for the rest of us, princess."

Of course, she feels comfortable talking to me like this when we're home alone. I lift my pajamas, chance one last look at my butt in the mirror, and unlock the door, my hand still on the handle. I stare at her, waiting for an apology. An acknowledgment of what she did. Any. Freaking. Sign. Of. Humanity.

Nothing. Blank. *Gurnisht.*

Via arches a blond eyebrow, folding her arms over her chest.

She is wearing a gorgeous floral minidress Melody probably bought her. Perhaps in New York. Possibly while I grieved the death of my family as I knew it.

"You look like shit. Have you been crying?" She snorts, shouldering past me to get into the bathroom.

I shake my head. "You're so screwed." My voice is quiet. Eerily calm.

It's the only thing I can think of saying right now. Maybe the only thing that matters at all. Because my life may be over, but so is hers. The difference is that I know my fate, and she doesn't.

"What are you talking about?" She unleashes her hair from its elastic in front of the mirror, grabbing the makeup bag and getting pretty, no doubt, for Gus.

"What do you think Gus wanted from me when you gave him my journal?" I ask, parking a hip over the cabinet. She takes a step back. I take a step toward her. Her back hits the shower glass, and this is where I keep her boxed in.

I'm not going to hurt her. Not physically, anyway. Maybe not at all, seeing as I am desperately in love with her brother, and he wants her happy. But she doesn't know that. She doesn't know what it means to love until everything hurts, and you shed your dignity and pride for someone else.

"Gus wants Penn to throw the game."

Via's eyes widen. It's news to her, and that actually makes me release a little sigh of relief. Her wanting to screw me over is a given. Her getting back at Penn, however? I can't stomach the idea.

"He wants to ruin your brother," I say, my hand traveling from the glass to her chin, tilting it up, so we stare each other in the eye, something we should've done weeks ago. *Years* ago. "And you just handed him the weapon with which he'll do it."

She swats my hand away. "*Bullshit.*"

"Yup." I grab her face, willing her to look into my eyes again. "Penn is broken, frustrated, lost, because of *you.*"

"You can't tell him." Via swallows, pushing me.

I stumble backward, laughing. That's what she cares about right now? She sounds like the old me.

Via paces back and forth, raking her fingers down her face, leaving pink streaks in their wake.

"He can't know. He can't know," she repeats.

I turn around, making my way to my room. I need to start getting dressed if I want to make it to the park in time. Prichard chose the same place where Penn took my virginity, which is something he knows, of course, because he's read my journal. We've met a few times after Penn entered the picture, though our sessions were few and far between. I tried not to think about them, to push them to the back of my mind. And for the most part, I succeeded.

Via follows me, yanking my pajamas and spinning me on my heel.

"What do I do!" she screams.

I stop. I smile. Enjoy the view.

"You know, Via? For the longest time, I envied you. For years, actually. Ever since you showed up at my mother's studio. Not because you were pretty or allegedly rich or any of those things. But because you were talented. You were better than me, and well, I guess I couldn't accept that. So imagine my delight and surprise when you returned, and I found out that you weren't better than me after all. Sure, you might have been the better dancer, but everything else about you is rotten. You are selfish and ugly and even more insecure than I am. You're vindictive and small and afraid. You will never be happy, Via. Ever. And that's the best revenge one could ask for."

I arrive at the bench fifteen minutes late.

Panting and sweating, I spot Ryan seated on the bench, wearing gray sweatpants, a North Face jacket, sunglasses, and a ball cap. He obviously doesn't want people to recognize him. I take him in for long moments from afar, trying to adjust the image I have of him in my mind—sharply suited and ready for war—to this unexpected, destructive time bomb.

"Sit," he commands, still staring at a spot across the park from where he sits. I stumble to him, my heart pumping in my chest. I take a seat on the other end of the bench, as far away from him as possible, stifling a groan. My ass hurts so bad it is hard to breathe. But I won't show him any more of my misery. I'm done giving him what he wants. I pray for this nightmare to be over, and right now, I need to concentrate on minimizing the damage and making sure the journal isn't leaked.

I don't ask him why I'm here. I don't demand an apology. In fact, I keep the very little, very shitty cards I have close to my chest.

"Look at the bench across from us under the oak tree," he says, his words clipped.

I follow his gaze. A hill and scattered trees veil us from the other side, but because we're at a higher point, we can see through them and have a direct view to the bench on the other side of the gardens.

My breath catches. Penn and Adriana are sitting together, huddled close. Harper is between them, cooing in Adriana's lap. Penn props himself down, kissing Harper's nose and pretending to bite her cheek. The toddler giggles, waving her little, chubby fists in his face, begging to be picked up.

Adriana grins and hands Harper to Penn. Penn smiles down at Adriana and laughs. I can feel his laughter in my empty chest as I break into a thousand minuscule pieces. So tiny are the parts of my broken heart, they feel like dust and ash rattling in my chest.

I want to look away, but I'm chained to the moment. *Their* moment. To this perfect picture of family bliss that I tried to stomp all over. My family is crumbling, and I tried to kill another one in my quest to have this boy.

But this boy is in love with another girl—the mother of his child.

I'm the mistake. A blip in his existence. A plaything to pass the time with. This? This is real. Penn Scully is not mine. He never pretended to be.

Everything I've given up—my time, my heart, my vanity—was in vain.

"This is the reason you turned your life upside down. For a guy who is deeply in love with his high school sweetheart. Who *fathered* her innocent baby." Ryan's voice prickles with an edge. "There are times in life when evil takes over our soul, and it is our job to seek the purity and solace in those who care about us. You came to me wounded, corrupted, and without direction, Daria, and I did what I had to do. You needed that spanking today. Needed this wake-up call. You have to allow Penn Scully a fair chance to build his family. Come back to me, sweetheart. To us. It is time to let go."

"You're not going to help me retrieve the journal," I whisper, realization dawning on me.

"Of course I will. After all, I am your savior."

You're my demise.

"How did you know they'd be here?" My lips tremble, and I sniff. I'm keeping the tears at bay and getting good at doing it.

"Bauer," he says simply. "I'm the puppet master, Daria. I play you all, keeping your strings tight and short. Gus would never defy me. Now, we can do it the right way and make Penn see that he needs to throw the game. I'll recover your journal—I will even get Gus to hand it back to me personally. Or we can do it the wrong way, where the journal comes out and we're done."

"Done?" I blink. He still thinks there's an "us." Unbelievable.

He slides the length of the bench between us and cups my cheek. I want to bite his hand off.

"Adultery is the greatest sin of all, but I am willing to forgive you. You are, after all, terribly young and impressionable."

So many things slam into me at once. This psycho actually thinks I cheated on him. And he is in on it with Gus. He is so desperate for our school to win, to justify the insane amount of money spent on the Saints, that he is actually making pacts with a teenage bully.

"Why do you think I have a hold on Penn? You said it yourself. He's in love with someone else." I turn to him. Ripping my gaze from Penn and Adriana is like taking off a Band-Aid. I can hear her laughter bouncing off the trees. It's everywhere, and I can't escape it. Her happiness is my misery.

"Because"—he turns to me—"you'll tell the whole world he lives with you if he doesn't. You will blackmail him, my darling."

My mouth falls open. The consequences are clear.

He'll lose his captain badge.

Get kicked off his football team.

And his friends and peers would hate him for living on the right side of the tracks without fessing up about it.

"Sylvia told Gus about her brother's little secret," he explains calmly. "Teenage hearts are highly traitorous, but it worked to my advantage in the end. See, after your stint in the girls' locker room, I sent the message across to lover boy that he was not to put his hands on you anymore. Now, after it is obvious that he has, I have no choice but to retaliate. And what's more beautiful than killing his future and having him suspended from the team?"

Every hair on my body stands on end.

Via betrayed Penn. She destroyed his acceptance letter, so to speak. She never wanted to come back to start over. She came back to get even.

"Tell me you understand, that you will comply, and that this matter is sorted, Miss Followhill." He stands up, parking his hands on his waist. His crotch is in my face, and I feel the need to throw up again.

I have an epiphany at that moment. I know what I need to do to save everyone.

Penn.

Adriana.

Harper.

Bailey.

Most of all, myself.

I nod, my heart hardening as I come to terms with what I have to do.

"Crystal clear, Principal Prichard."

I crawl to my room with what little energy I have left. Every bone in my body is sore. My muscles are stiff, and my butt burns with each step I take.

The house is quiet. Bailey and Melody are at ballet. Dad's at work. Penn…is probably at practice or still with Adriana and Harper. I don't even have it in me to feel relieved that Via isn't here. I haven't seen the hideous pink Jeep she ended up accepting (*"Mel, it's the best thing that ever happened to me! So, so beautiful, thank you!"*), and there's no sign of anyone else in the house.

Pushing my door open, the sour scent of alcohol and wine fills my nostrils, and I stumble back, my spine hitting the opposite wall.

As the door creaks ajar, I get a better view of my room and see the reason for the odor. My bare toes are soaked and sticky on the floor.

My champagne aquarium wall is shattered. The hammer Via used is still hanging in the middle of the glass, from which the pink champagne filters down, making a hissing sound of a freshly opened beer bottle.

I stagger inside, supporting myself on random furniture. I'm trying to open my eyes all the way, but the skin around them is too swollen and tender. As I enter deeper into my room, I notice a piece of cream-colored paper stuck to a wet piece of glass that's still standing in the aquarium. I recognize the note instantly. It was torn from my journal. I pluck it out.

Tell them it was an accident
Or your mom will find out you killed her dream too.

My eyes roll inside their sockets, and my knees give out. Everything turns black, just like the book where I keep all my secrets, and there is no light at the end of my tunnel.

CHAPTER TWENTY-ONE
MELODY

Love is so much like death.
Certain.
Absolute.
And out of our control.

The future is always blissfully Photoshopped.

We're always a few pounds lighter, a few brain cells smarter, and soaked with life experience and healthy logic.

The sad reality is, you never grow up to be who you'd imagined yourself as.

Through adolescence and my twenties, I thought I'd be the best mother in the world. Motherhood was the endgame, the goal, the quest. I was so acutely aware of the mistakes my own parents had made with me, and I vowed to be perfect.

From the outside, parenting looked almost easy. Whoever said it doesn't come with a guidebook was wrong. There were dozens of thick, helpful books—all of which I read while pregnant with Daria—and a few principles I thought were vital for success:

1. Don't raise your voice to your kid.
2. Don't lose your shit (see: number one).
3. Give them space.

4. Trust them.
5. Encourage their independence.
6. Shower them with love and gratitude, and they will grow up to be good humans.

I was bullied into becoming a ballerina by parents who wanted their daughter to be everything my mother couldn't afford to be. So when Daria came along, and I saw from a very young age that she was spirited, rebellious, and full of the same anger her father harbored—raw fierceness that couldn't be contained—I didn't push her to follow my footsteps. Ballet, after all, is harsh and demanding. I always made sure she knew she wasn't expected to be like me. But it seemed like the more choice I gave her, the harder she tried to prove me wrong.

I wonder where it all went wrong while folding the kids' clothes in the laundry room. Doing the laundry is not a task I need to do with the amount of help I get around the house, but it's a telling job when you raise teenagers.

I can see, smell, and find all their secrets.

I found Daria's pom-pom string in Penn's back pocket. Penn's mouthguard in the pocket of Daria's cardigan. There is still a resistant bubblegum-pink lipstick stain that refuses to leave one of Penn's shirts. A lipstick I know belongs to my daughter. Bailey's clothes are always full of mud—she rolls with Lev, our neighbor, on the hills of El Dorado. Via is the only one who is careful not to show where she's been. She is, therefore, the kid I know who hides the most.

She thinks she is fooling us. But the fact of the matter is, I let her get away with her behavior because she's been through so much.

I stop when I get to Daria's pajama dress. It is sticky and heavier than the rest of the clothes as though it's not completely dried. I turn it around and sniff—a mother always sniffs her kids' clothes—and it smells like aloe.

Why would she put aloe all over her behind?

Clutching the fabric in my fist, I leave the laundry room to ask her just that.

Over the past few months, I've been begging for crumbs of her attention, knowing somewhere deep inside me that I don't deserve them. I've failed her one too many times. She always seemed so strong and opinionated, and I made the gravest mistake a parent could. I treated her like an equal.

But Daria is not my equal. She is my daughter. My very sensitive daughter. She's been hurting beyond belief recently. I've done nothing to rectify this situation, only escalating it by bringing in more factors that drove us apart.

I make my way toward her room and stop when I hear my husband's voice behind her door. "Of course, you can tell me, Dar. You know there's no judgment inside these walls."

Frozen, my jaw slacks. A part of me, the logical part, tells me to turn around and walk away. She is confiding in Jaime, not me. But another part—the mother in me—refuses to let go. I resent my own husband for having a superior connection with her. I resent the entire world, including Bailey, and Via, and Penn, and our friends, for coming between Daria and me.

"Principal Prichard hit me."

The air leaves my lungs, and I stumble backward. Silence. My husband recovers after what seems to be like a full minute.

"Tell me everything, please." His voice is barely restrained.

She does. My daughter spends the next ten minutes chronicling her last, scarring, infuriating four years. She doesn't leave anything out. Not the fact she destroyed Via's letter—something I knew but never confronted her about—not how she started writing in the journal, and not how Prichard used it against her. She breaks down when she confesses to deleting Grace's messages in New York. Not that I needed to hear it from her to know it to be true. I figured it out when I finally found Grace's number and called her. By that point, I could hardly blame Daria. I was a no-show for the past six months of her life. Too busy saving Via and Penn and giving Bailey everything she needs. The way I saw it, until the New York incident—my own wake-up call, if you will—I was staying out of her way, just as she had asked me to do repeatedly.

Daria always seemed so distant and independent, as if she had it all figured out. How could I have been so stupid?

Daria acts like eighteen-year-old Mel: dazed, confused, and hurt.

In New York, when Bailey and Via fawned over me and Daria awarded me with long yawns, I did what I always do when I get frustrated with her: I built up an ice wall from the same variety she raised every time I came knocking on the doors of her heart.

I shouldn't have built more walls.

I should've broken them down.

Smashed them and stormed in and given her everything she needed so she wouldn't have to search for them in an abusive educator who took advantage of her.

I hear my daughter crying in her room and muster the courage to tiptoe and peek through the slit in the door. They are so quiet and content and wrecked together. My beautiful, perfect husband sits on the edge of my daughter's bed, hugging her close to his chest and kissing the crown of her blond head. She is falling apart in his arms, and my heart hurts so much I can't even breathe.

I should be hugging you.

I should be comforting you.

Collapsing against the wall, I suck in air. Sourness rises in my throat, and I swallow it down, but it keeps coming up, wanting to spill over. I want to purge whatever's inside me on the floor. All the frustration and hate and animosity toward the person I gave birth to. This has been going on for far too long. I need my baby back.

"Daddy?"

"Yes, the love of my life?"

The love of his life. I know he means it. Jaime would die just to put a smile on his mini-me's face.

"I can't stay here, you know. I'm not going to let Penn throw the game, and I won't be able to show my face at school after the journal goes public."

"It'll never come to that. I will hit Gus up tonight."

"No." I hear Daria sniff and know she is shaking her head. She's made up her mind. "It's too late. My reputation is shit. If the truth comes out, people will know I killed All Saints High's chance at taking the championship, and Gus and Via will spin it against me. Besides..." She takes another deep breath.

I know why. I know because I fold their clothes and tuck their secrets into their closets every day.

"I need to put some distance between the Scullys and me."

"Is that right?"

"I'm so sorry, Daddy. I know you didn't want this to happen. And I know I let you down a gazillion times. By letting the Hulk win. By being jealous. By being mean. By not being the best version of myself I could have been. By falling in love with a person I had no right to fall in love with."

"Shh," he murmurs into her hair, cradling her. They are moving back and forth to a soundless lullaby, cocooned inside a world I'm no longer a part of.

"You are the perfect version of yourself, kiddo. The real deal. We're the same, you and me." He kisses her nose, then the tears from her eyes. "When I was your age, I was frustrated and confused. I always had the best intentions, but my actions came out all wrong. As for falling in love with the wrong person..." He chuckles, shaking his head.

A ghost of a smile finds my lips.

Don't say it, Jaime.

"I'm a lot of things, but a hypocrite is not one of them. I fell in love with my high school teacher. And guess what? We still made it work. Don't let people tell you who to fall in love with, and don't think just because the past few years have been shit, the rest of your life will follow suit. Look at your old man. I got my happy ending. You will too."

She mulls his words over, munching on her lip. "I need to get away."

"From your problems? Not a good idea."

"No, from the people I've hurt. There's a lot of healing to be done. I need to start fresh, where I'll have a chance to reinvent myself. To be who I know I can be, Daddy."

He says nothing and everything at the same time. His eyes tell her it is hers. The fresh start. He would never deny her anything. Not even if it means leaving us.

I want to hit him. Scream at him. Hug him for keeping our daughter's mental state above water all this time when I couldn't. Another bone-crushing hug passes between them. Daria is having the most defining moment of her adolescence without me.

That's my punishment for my mistakes. That's the price I have to pay.

"Do you think Mel would let me leave next semester?" She tears away from their hug, blinking up at him.

Mel. Oh, how I hate my name on her lips. *It's Mom,* I want to scream most days.

Jaime grabs her cheeks and draws her in to kiss her forehead. "I think she loves you too much to deny you anything—including breaking her heart."

My fingers tremble around the steering wheel as I zip toward Ryan Prichard's house.

Fifteen years ago, after things calmed down and Jaime and I came back to Todos Santos, I decided to volunteer at All Saints High. Form a connection with the other teachers and clean up my reputation for my kids' sake. I figured if I wanted to stay in this town, I needed to prove that I'm not some deranged cradle snatcher.

Connections. It only took one phone call for me to find out where the bastard lives.

I'm not in the right headspace for confrontation, but I have no doubt I'll be pulling it off because it's not about me. It's about my daughter. Neither Jaime nor the kids know where I went. I ordered a pizza and stormed out the door without explanation, leaving a trail of freshly done laundry in my wake. Daria was upstairs, oblivious to her mother's meltdown a few feet away. I'm glad she didn't witness me at my worst when I found out what he did to her. The last thing I want is for her to feel ashamed or humiliated about what he did to her.

I cut the engine in front of a Tudor-style house on the outskirts of Todos Santos and pop my knuckles, inhaling a ragged breath.

Do not kill the bastard. Your kids still need you, and you'll be of very little help to them if you're in jail.

Easier said than done. When I slam the driver's door and dart toward his front entrance, not one bone in my body can resist going apeshit on his garden, and house, and face.

You touched my fucking daughter.

I forgot to add: even though I tell the kids to keep it clean, I curse in my head—*a lot.*

For the sake of appropriateness, and for my plan to succeed, I fix my ballet-teacher smile on my face before I knock on his red door. My relationship with my daughter may be beyond repair, but no one can hurt her like this and get away with it, regardless of the fact she may not fully accept me ever again.

He opens the door dressed in pale gray cigar pants, a crisp white shirt, and a frown that collapses into a wince the minute he sees my face. Was he expecting my daughter? I can't ask even though I want to.

"Mrs. Followhill. This is quite unexpected."

"Is it, though, Ryan?" I tilt my head, wearing a smile I'm pretty sure is downright nuts. "Let's think about it for a second. Is my visit really a surprise?"

He does the whole charade. The scowl. The blinks. The grave shake of his head.

"I'm not sure I know what you're referring to." His voice is calm, but his left eye is twitching. I'm already under his skin, and I haven't even gotten to the good stuff yet.

"I'm referring to the fact that today, I spent twenty minutes trying to figure out what the sticky, persistent stain on my daughter's pajamas was before realizing that it was aloe. Aloe she put on her butt to ease the pain of you ruthlessly beating her with a ruler."

I deliver the news flatly, knowing if I let my emotions slip, I'll mess it up. I can't mess it up. Not when Daria is involved. I'm done letting her down.

"That's quite the accusation, Mrs. Followhill, and I must say, I don't know what you're talking about," he says, but the blood has drained from his face, and he is clutching the edge of his door as though his life depends on it. I take a step toward him, tilting my chin up so we look each other in the eye.

"Should I refresh your memory? Because I have full access to my daughter's phone, contacts, and text messages, and I believe one of us has been very reckless while messaging my Daria."

This is both a blunt lie and an educated guess. While I would never entertain the idea of breaching Daria's privacy this way, I still remember my own affair with her father. The lust. The wildness of the situation. The feral need to keep in touch after school hours. He is probably saved under an alias, and maybe he calls her from a separate phone, but there is no way they don't have a connection outside of school.

He shifts from foot to foot, moving his hand over his face when he realizes I might have hard evidence against him.

"Mrs. Followhill, please do not patronize me in that department. You were in my position. These kids," he says, referring to my husband as a *kid*, "are of legal age, with raging hormones and wicked plans. You, of all people, know lines get blurred."

"One," I say, "Daria was not of legal age when she was fourteen and first came to you. Jaime was legal long before I touched him, so don't compare. And two"—I point at him accusingly—"I never hurt any of my students. Do you realize how much trouble you're in, Mr. Prichard? I don't think you do."

Another manipulative twist of my knife. I'm talking to him as though he's already admitted to it.

"Regretfully, I feel like this matter should be settled through my lawy—"

"My, oh my, how this will ruin your perfect track record. Continuous abuse…" I *tsk* dramatically. "Exploiting a minor, inappropriate physical conduct—"

"She needed it! She WANTED it!" he screams in my face, throwing a sudden fist into the door. It swings back from the impact, and he slaps it again with his open palm, crying out like an injured animal.

"Your daughter begged for it! Other than the last time, it was always with her consent. She encouraged me. Lured me in. A seductive little siren, a Lolita with big, blue eyes. You've already let her down, and I was there to pick up the pieces and guide her through this world. I stepped up when *you* stepped down." It is his turn to point at me, spitting in my face with every word that comes out of his mouth.

"I care for her. I worry about her. I moved schools for her. You think I like dealing with teenagers? With an entitled, untalented football team? You're wrong. I did this for your daughter. I stayed single—for your daughter. I live in this awful, plastic town—for your daughter. Don't you come knocking on my door lecturing me about morals. Daria feels half-orphaned because of you. I just became who she needed me to be. The only person in her life to care for her enough to give her the discipline she craved. And the spanking?" He stops, out of breath. His chest rises and falls. He is manic. On the edge of falling apart. He wipes sweat from his brow. "When I was young, I got spanked, a lot. It corrected my ways when I strayed from God's word. And look at me now." He gestures toward his body with his hand. "In one piece."

For now, bastard.

I take a step back, steadying my breath. His words cut me like a knife, but what I'm about to do is going to split him in half. I clutch the pearls on my neck, pushing the buttoned-up pale baby blue shirt down to reveal a little recording device clipped to the shoulder strap of my bra. Would this hold up in court? Who the hell knows? All I know is that Prichard is not dumb enough to find out.

"My bad, Mr. Prichard, this makes everything you did okay. I just hope the authorities will find your version of things sufficient as well."

His eyes drop to the recording device, and I know this is my in. I have all the evidence in the world to bring him down now. A blatant admission. But I don't want the messy way out. I don't want to drag my daughter through court. I want his quiet, silent defeat. Even though nothing brings me more pain than to know he is about to get away with this.

There can't be a trial.

This can't go public.

Daria has suffered enough.

"Name your price," he growls, his eyes darkening.

"Quite simply: your job, your location, and your word. I don't want you anywhere near kids or teenagers again, Mr. Prichard, and you're about to sign on it."

CHAPTER TWENTY-TWO
PENN

I want to be your everything.
Other than one thing.
Your past.

I thrust the vodka bottle into my glove compartment and wipe my mouth with the back of my hand.

Great. I'm turning into fucking Rhett. I've been avoiding the Followhill mansion since breaking shit off with Daria except for the times I needed to sleep, shit, and shower, and even though I'm jumping through hoops trying not to bump into Daria and Via, every time I do, it feels like they cut me down the middle, dragging my two halves in opposite directions.

Throwing the driver's door open, I zigzag my way toward the snake pit. It's too early for the fights, but people are already milling on the bleachers, passing beers, vapes, and cigarettes. I find Gus underneath said bleachers, reading through statistics of fighters, which he writes down with a Sharpie on a clipboard. He licks his finger and flips a page when I approach him, not even looking up.

"Scully."

"Are we gonna make up and out, or are you going to tell me why the fuck you invited me here?" I hiccup, bracing myself on the side of the blue bleacher we are standing underneath.

Yesterday, Adriana called me and asked if we could meet at the park. Stressed that it was urgent. I said yes because I thought it had something to do with my stepdad. He's a notorious shit-stirrer in my old neighborhood. In the background, I heard Gus talking, almost whispering, but I chalked it up to maybe her serving him at Lenny's. Only when I parted ways with Addy and Harper at the park, in which she told me Harper might be running a fever (she wasn't) did I remember that Addy had taken time off work to focus on school last week.

Now I'm interested to know just how deep Gus thrust himself into my life without my knowledge. Because if he's playing Addy and messed around with my sister, who knows what else he touched without permission?

Not Daria, for his fucking sake.

"Aw." Gus tosses his clipboard to the ground, adjusting his ball cap backward because, apparently, he just doesn't look douchey enough. "Someone's being a bad sport."

"Spit it out," I snarl.

"I just wanted to talk." He lifts his hands in surrender.

"I have nothing to say to you, other than your team sucks, but actions speak louder than words, so I'll just remind you of that on the field next week."

"About that." Gus taps his mouth with his finger, making a show of it. "I see your little girlfriend didn't bring you up to speed on our latest convo."

I rub my jaw. "Adriana tries to forget you exist. She hates you like the rest of us."

"Nah. The one you actually give a shit about."

Daria.

My jaw clenches, and I'm ready to fuck his face up if he so much as breathes in her direction. She's going through enough—partly because of my miserable ass—and doesn't need him on her case.

"Leave her out of our beef, or you'll have a much bigger problem than getting your ass kicked next Friday." My voice turns to steel, and any traces of the booze leave my system. I'm wide-awake and sober now.

"Too late, lover boy. I got my hands on her journal. Fascinating shit." He whistles, fanning his face. "This thing'll blow up the school when it comes out. Spanked and humiliated by her principal in his office like in a bad porn flick, dicked by you in a forest, and basically shitting all over your sister's and her mom's dreams. Daria's been good at being a bad girl these past four years."

Principal Prichard spanked her? The words burn on my skin, and all I see is red. He touched her. No, worse—he hurt her. Under my fucking watch.

Anger clogs up my veins and settles in my stomach. I am on the verge of detonating under the bleachers all over Gus.

Taking a step toward him, I wrap my fingers around his throat. I can choke him to death in cold blood right now and not even regret it tomorrow morning. The thought scares me because it is real. I was livid when I found out he was messing around with my sister, but apparently, the two parts Via and Daria split me in aren't that even after all. Daria's chunk is bigger. I care about her more.

"If this shit comes out..." Gus tries to swallow without success, producing a sound that's between a cackle and a gag.

My hold on his meaty neck is so firm, I can see his blue veins popping out from between my fingers. His eyes turn red as his blood vessels begin to burst.

"What do you think is going to happen if you fuck me up, Scully? That's right. Whoever keeps the journal for me is going to print it out and give it to anyone who's willing to read it. And trust me—people'll line up for your girlfriend's shit."

"What do you want?" Spit flies out of my mouth. I'm losing it. I'm losing her. The air begins to pulse, and the world is a living thing, swaying and swinging, trying to trip me.

"Lose the game, bro. I told her the only way she is getting

this bitch back without any repercussions is if your ass lets us win. Everyone knows you've been approached by all the big ones. Just take a step aside and let others have a piece of the pie."

"I still have my teammates. They're the ones who deserve the pie," I grit out.

Not everyone has been contacted yet with potential scholarship offers. Kannon hasn't. Camilo has scouts eyeing him but has yet to receive a concrete offer. Neither has Nelson. By throwing the game, I'm throwing their futures too.

Not to mention Coach Higgins.

Not to mention my goddamn morals.

"They don't have your back, so I don't see why you should have theirs." Gus pushes my chest, and I realize I've released my hold on him without even meaning to. The red marks on his neck are going to be purple tomorrow morning.

"Don't talk to me in riddles. If you have something to say, say it."

He picks up the clipboard and slaps the plastic above him three times. I hear people standing up and circling the bleachers, and less than a minute later, I am standing in front of his entire football squad, sans Knight Cole. His posse is here, arms folded, chests puffed, ready to bring Gus's point home.

"Throw the game." Gus jerks his chin up. "Save your princess. She'd do the same for you."

I stare at him through a mist of rage that's blinding me.

I get in his face, sneering too.

"Mark my words, Bauer. I'm going to fuck you over so hard and raw, no college will want to touch you with a ten-foot pole."

Via stole Daria's diary.

Via is *still* banging Gus.

Via also most likely told him where I live.

On my way back home, as I was struggling to pull my shit together so as not to get into a fatal car accident while the adrenaline coursed through my bloodstream, I figured out why Gus hasn't thrown my sister into his mix of blackmail even though she handed him the ammo against me on a silver platter.

Gus protects Via.

Via protects Gus.

Nobody protects Daria.

I storm into the Followhills' living room without so much as registering their faces. The only thing I see is my sister's head peeking up from her homework on the kitchen island. I bunch the fabric of the back of her dress and hurl her outside to the backyard. Bailey lifts her head up from her homework and starts protesting before seeing the look on my face.

"Penn, what are you—?"

"Shut up."

Surprisingly, it does shut her up. Maybe the look on my face is warning enough that I'm not above locking her in the utility room if she doesn't cooperate.

"Oh my God! You've lost your mind! What are you doing? Let me go!" Via alternates between yelling and begging. "Penn! Wait! I can explain!"

"You can, but I'm done listening to your shit," I say tonelessly.

My twin is still cawing like a raven when I use the back of her collar to toss her into the deep end of the pool. I watch as she stumbles on the edge, sinks like a brick, then rises to the surface. She shakes off the water, hair plastered to her face. I stand on the edge, watching her. Waiting to feel something more than disdain and discovering I feel *nothing* at all.

"What the fuck is wrong with you?" She punches the water, shrieking.

I throw my head back and laugh. "Dropping the F-bomb now, are we? Took you long enough to take off that cheap-ass mask of yours, Sylvia, but now that you have, I'll give you one thing. I can see your real face now, and it's pretty ugly."

She wipes her face and starts swimming toward the stairs. "So I'm Sylvia now, huh?"

"Feel lucky that you are anything at all. I told you not to touch her. We had a deal. A *blood oath*."

The day I told Daria to go look for dick elsewhere, I walked into Vaughn's pool house thinking I was doing her a favor by temporarily breaking her heart. Smug fucker that I was, it never occurred to me that I'd be breaking mine too.

I can't eat. I can't sleep. I don't even think about getting my dick wet, let alone allow the harem of cheerleaders and groupies to do the honor. I can't breathe without thinking about the girl across the hall. I function solely for the purpose of proving to myself that I still can, and I can't even look my sister in the eye without wanting to make it black around the edges.

Via climbs out of the pool looking like Samara Morgan from *The Ring* at the same time Jaime slides the glass door open, popping his head out.

"What the hell is going on?" His voice is an impatient growl.

"Nothing." I wave a flippant hand. "We need to sort some shit out is all."

Jaime glances at my sister with frost that wasn't there before. Mel might have the patience of a thousand nuns, but Jaime knows what's up, and he is Team Daria all the way.

Via nods at the same time she shivers her way to a lounger. "Thank you, Mr. Followhill. I'm okay."

Jaime closes the door behind him.

I walk toward her, casting a shadow over her figure, and kick her shin lightly. "Answer me."

"She ruined everything," she huffs, her lips twisting in abhorrence. If she thinks she is getting off the hook by crying, she is gravely fucking mistaken and officially doesn't know the Tin Man she created the minute she left. "I hate her so much. And I swear I didn't know about Gus asking you to lose the game. You have to believe me, Penn. I just wanted to get back at her for throwing my letter out."

"*I* threw the letter out," I yell in her face, stubbing a finger on my chest where the hole is. A hole that had been shrinking for weeks but has now become bigger than ever since Via came back. I ripped my shirts the day I broke things off with Daria, cutting the holes so big, you can now see half my chest. "I'm to blame just as much as she is."

"I hated you too." She darts up, pushing me and taking a step forward. "Is that what you want to hear? Because it's the truth. Even before I knew you ruined my letter, I hated you. I hated you for looking at her with starry eyes every time you waited on the corner to pick me up after ballet class. I saw you falling in love with her before you even realized what your stupid ass was doing. And she was the enemy. You fell for my downfall."

Clamping my mouth shut, I rub the back of my neck. All this time, I thought Daria was a bitch for doing what she did to Via. I never stopped to consider that my sister gave her a run for her money even back then. Via always covered for her shortcomings by being mean. These two were awful to each other, and Daria just happened to stumble upon something big she could ruin for Via.

If Via had found an identical letter, she would have destroyed it too.

"I'm done with you." I turn around, walking away. I hear her wild footsteps gaining on me. She's tugging at my sleeve, falling to her knees in front of me, and I'm forced to stop.

"Penn, please."

"You're with him," I say, not ask. She doesn't deny it. Just keeps on saying *please, please, please*. I'm not even sure what she is asking for, but if it's my forgiveness, she is officially high.

"I'm with him because I need someone. I need an ally," she admits.

I laugh because it doesn't matter anymore. I kick off her arms, which are hugging my shins. "Who do you think was my ally, Sylvia?"

"Daria is my enemy," she moans.

"Gus is mine," I retort.

I won this battle and lost the entire fucking war. It's like crawling back home defeated and finding your home burned to ashes once you enter the gates of your fallen kingdom.

I take a few more steps, then stop at the threshold and pivot to her. "My only regret is trying to pacify your sorry ass and breaking things off with Daria. I loved you when no one else did. I grieved for you. I thought you were dead and tortured myself, blamed myself. But my actions were never intended to hurt you. I made a mistake. You did all this on purpose. So now *I'm* leaving you, just as you left me. Only I'm four years too late."

When my mother was still into poetry (and life in general, I guess), she used to read us passages every night. There was one that really stuck with me for years afterward. Not the entire thing—that shit sucked as a whole. Just the one sentence.

Love is humbling.

Those three words boggled my mind. What could be humbling about love? Love is celebratory. It is victorious. It is the exact opposite of humbling. Even back then, I understood the definition of the word *love* but not the meaning of it. Now, as I stand in front of Daria's closed door for the first time in weeks, after not exchanging a word, or a kiss, or a fucking glance with her all this time, I am truly, devastatingly, shoot-me-in-the-fucking-face humbled.

I knock on the door before deciding it's a stupid-ass move. A real man would barge in and hoist her up over his shoulder. The man I was at Lenny's, when I still had confidence, I could have her.

But that was before I caved to my sister's wishes.

Back when I really was a real man.

Fuck. This is hard.

"Come in." Her voice is throaty and callous and distant.

I push her door open and step in. Closing it, I keep my back to her so I don't have to see her face and what's on it.

"Talk?" I ask, still staring at the door. Since when do I use question marks? Since I fucking lost the right to tell her what's up.

Say yes.

Say yes.

Say yes.

She says nothing instead.

I wait. And wait. And wait. I deserve this. All of it. My phone pings, and I take it out of my pocket.

Talk.

A tired smile finds its way to my lips. We're still us, and there's some comfort in that. When you don't talk to someone you see every day, you start to wonder if they blocked out your existence. But Daria remembers. The Ferris wheel and ballet studio and the woods. The pool house with Vaughn and the locker room in All Saints High.

I text her back, my back still to her.

I'm sorry.

She replies.

So am I.

I text back.

Gus has your journal. He asked me to throw the game unless I want it printed out.

She types back.

Gus is a coward. And good luck to that idiot trying to work
a copier.

Chuckling, I shake my head. Daria and Sylvia as I've never seen
them before. One sacrifices herself for me, the other sacrificing me
for herself.

Can I turn around?

She answers.

I don't know if it's a good idea.

Breathe, motherfucker. Breathe.

I need to see your face when I type this next thing.

Two minutes pass before she relents.

Okay.

Turning around, I drink her in. She is sitting on her bed, wearing
an oversize nightdress. Her hair is braided the way I like it and flung
over her right shoulder. My heart is staggering like the drunken
town fool right out of the brothel and into the arms of the Disney
princess that are no longer stretched open. And I'm stupid because
I let her go, but maybe I'm smart too, because I realized my mistake.
I just hope it's not too late.
I look down, my thumbs flying over my phone screen.

Look at me.

I watch her reading the text. Her face screws up and tenses in agony. She doesn't look up.

I try again.

I'm throwing the game and retrieving your diary. I'm sorry it took me so long to get my head out of my ass. It was dark back there. Hard to see right from wrong. I was my sister's keeper for so long, I never once wondered if she was worth keeping.

She still won't look at me. Tears roll down her cheeks. I suck at this. I don't know much about girls. I know even less about girls I like. And apparently, I know next to nothing about girls I love.

Love. Four letters can't cover what I feel for Daria Followhill. They seem too trivial, too small, too overused.

Via made me choose between you two. Said she'd run away back to Mississippi if I made the wrong choice.

Her fingers are placid, hovering over her screen. She is not saying, or typing, or doing anything. And love *is* humbling, I know now because I want to punch myself in the face for being the smug bastard who assumed he'd just walk out of this shit unscathed. This Tin Man didn't ask for a heart—but got one anyway.

I love you, Daria Followhill, and I think you love me too. In fact, I think we fell at the same time. You, like rain, in drizzles, over the weeks. Me, like the fucking sky above my head, all at once, crashing without the faintest chance of stopping.

Her fingers are moving. I'm mesmerized. She types, looks up, and meets my gaze through the screen of her tears, then puts her phone down.

"It's too late."

Rushing toward her, I fall to my knees, wrapping her waist in my arms and burying my head in her thighs. She doesn't move.

"Skull Eyes?"

"Don't lose the game. The journal will eventually get out. It's *already* out of our control. You shouldn't deprive yourself and your teammates of this win."

"Fuck the game. What about you? What about *us*?"

What about the fact I just ripped my fucking heart out and dumped it at your feet, waiting for you to pick it up, and you kicked it across your room? Huh?

I look up.

She bites her inner cheek. Her nose is pink, and her eyes are glittering, and I realize I no longer enjoy her suffering. It's ripping me apart.

"I told you I love you," I remind her quietly as though she wasn't here two seconds ago.

"If this is how you love…" She shakes her head. "Then I don't want your love, Penn Scully." I open my mouth to say something, but she beats me to it. "Besides, you have Adriana and Harper to take care of."

"Adriana and Harper are complicated." I rear my head back about to spit some real shit.

"I've known Adriana ever since I was a kid. Adriana developed a crush on me, but I never reciprocated. I was stuck in the girls-are-disgusting stage when she started noticing boys. That didn't stop her from frequenting my house almost every day. I warned her so many times not to, especially as the years passed and things got worse at home. Mom was out of it, and Rhett became more violent. One day, just before sophomore year, she came over while I was at practice. Rhett opened the door and told her I should be in any minute, so she waited. He raped her."

I watch Daria's eyes widen, then she swallows hard, so I continue.

"She got out of there, shocked and ashamed. She didn't want anyone to know. Three months later, she found out she was pregnant. It was too late to do anything about it." I clear my throat.

I remember all the times Adriana agonized over not wanting Harper before she was born. How bad I felt for her. How *guilty*.

"Mostly, she was scared that Rhett would tell someone. Boast or brag about it. Most people would try to hide it, but Rhett is a fucking tool and not the sharpest in the shed. Not to mention he flirts with sanity sparsely. So Addy and I made up a story to protect both her and Harper and gave Harper a semi-legitimate background. We told everyone I was the dad because I didn't have a good reputation to lose—I already came from an impressive lineage of fuckups. I didn't mind telling people that Addy was my girlfriend. It kept the teeny-boppers at arm's length. Plus, I never really wanted to date anyone."

Until you.

"That's how things have gone for the past three years. And for the most part, everything ran smoothly. When I hooked up with girls like Blythe, Adriana turned a blind eye. And I hooked up with girls all the time, since I wouldn't touch Adriana. But the minute you stepped into the picture, things got messy—and real."

"I'm so sorry for Adriana." Daria squeezes my shoulder.

"She is crazy about Harper now, so don't worry about it."

"I saw you at the park. Castle Hill." Daria drops her hand from my shoulder. My mind pivots back to two days ago. Addy calling me. Urgent meeting. Gus in the background.

Ding, ding, ding.

My jaw locks. Everyone's a fucking traitor. The only person who hasn't betrayed me so far is, ironically, Daria herself.

"I…" I start, and she presses her finger on my lips. I kiss her finger.

"Trade secrets?" She grins, but it's a sad, tired grin.

"Sure." I press my forehead to her thighs, breathing her in. "Make it count."

She tells me what happened with Principal Prichard. How they went on like this for four years. Then about her last visit to his office that ended with her being so sore she still can't sit properly.

"He was the one who brought me to the park to watch you and Adriana. I think he wanted me to give up on you."

"Did you?"

She stands up, lifts the hem of her nightdress, and turns around.

Purple, black, and faded yellow welts cover her ass cheeks and the back of her thighs. I clamp my mouth shut so I don't fucking wince. The rage of an entire army is lodged inside my body, and for the first time in my life, I worry about my lack of control over what I might do to Ryan Prichard. I've always been a hothead but never as deranged as I am now. The hatred I have toward Bauer and Prichard is too all-consuming for me to leave this house for the next decade.

"Oh," she says with a wince as she sits down again. "And I told Dad about the entire thing and so, by default, spilled the secret that we were sort of together for a second."

Sort of.

Were.

For a second.

"That's fine," I murmur, not sure where we go from here. So much has been said, and I'm still on my knees, and she is still not showing any signs of the warm, responsive Daria who I pushed away one time too many, reminding her that she was not enough. That she will never be enough.

I stand. She does the same. Our bodies sway in the same direction, never touching.

"If you care about me at all, win the game."

"Why?"

Kudos to her for doing the right thing, but fuck, this is extreme, even for Mother Teresa.

She inhales, bracing herself for what she's about to say next.

"Because I'm boarding a plane next Saturday and finishing my senior year somewhere else."

My mouth goes dry, and I shake my head slowly. She takes a step closer and folds my shirt under her palm so that the hole in my chest looks like it's closing in when, in reality, it opens up like a shark's jaw.

"Everything I touch is tainted, Penn. Everything I want turns to ash. I spent the entire semester trying to be yours, but you've never once claimed my heart. I'm sending you to Adriana's arms, not because I don't care but because I do. So much. Maybe too much. Because I screwed up so many relationships, the only way for us to heal is if I take myself out of the equation."

You are the fucking equation, I want to yell in her face. *The riddle and the answer and the numbers within it. You're math. You make sense.*

"Don't go," I croak. I sound like a wuss. I don't even recognize this voice. I want a refund on my vocal cords. They suck.

She takes a step back. I try another tactic.

"Where are you going?"

She shrugs, flinging herself onto her bed, disappearing into the soft mattress like it's a cloud.

"Come the fuck on, Daria. Give me something to work with."

She smiles at the ceiling, drifting away from reality.

"You don't know how the weekend is going to pan out." I make another point.

"But I do," she says softly. "That's the thing about sins. They stack up and blow in your face. You can't be my shield."

I can be your anything. Fucking try me.

I turn around. Tug at my hair until my scalp burns. Curse under my breath. The thing about nightmares is that you never know which one your worst is until you live through it. Via and I pushed Daria out of this place. Out of her own home.

Maybe it's because I can't move toward the door, can't end this shit, or generally suck at being human, but after a while, Daria stands up again and escorts me out.

So this is what it feels like to die. Cool. Good to know.

She rises on her toes. I don't bend down to meet her halfway, knowing a kiss could very much end me at this point. She settles for pressing her lips against my throat.

"Me too," she whispers as she shoves me out the door.

I look back, my face a huge question mark.

"You were never a drizzle, Penn Scully. When I fell for you, you came beating down, and I felt you everywhere. You were hail."

CHAPTER TWENTY-THREE
PENN/JAIME

Why didn't you tell me we were in love?
Why did you wait for me to find out
When you broke my heart?

PENN

I show up on Cam's doorstep the same night looking like death and probably not smelling much better.

Kannon is peeking behind him, as well as Cam's sister, brother, mother...his entire neighborhood, basically, stares back at me like I'm fucking ET, complete with the bike and white knitted throw. Naturally, I'd have an audience on the worst day of my life. Karma has a sick sense of humor like that.

"I haven't been living with Rhett for a while now." I jump straight to the bottom line, pleasantries be damned.

"We know." Cam opens the door wider, stepping sideways so I can enter. "Everyone knows, Penn. You think no one tried to drop by? Leave a message? Even your hookups were wondering where you were. No one said anything because we figured you had your reasons. Where were you?"

"The Followhills," I say. "Via's there now. She's back."

"And how do you feel about it?" Kannon asks.

"Shit." I smile tiredly.

Everyone nods. Cam's sister jerks me by the hole in my shirt.

"Little punk, you really got in over your head."

The week is unadulterated torture. I don't even bother showing up to the Followhills' for food and sleep. I sleep on Camilo's couch, ghosting a worried Mel and a furious Jaime. I'm waiting for the other shoe to drop, probably on my ass, when Jaime finally confronts me about touching his daughter. But so far, he seems more irritated than cross.

Jaime: You can't avoid this forever.

Watch me.

Jaime: You realize I'll see you at the game, right, Einstein?

Good point, but I'm eighteen. I don't think further than what's going to happen in the next ten minutes.

Jaime: Daria's been asking about you.

Of course, I'm dumb enough to take the bait.

You BS-ing me, sir?

Jaime: Yes. But you need to come home if you want to see
      her before she gets on that plane.

What I don't tell him is that I can no longer see planes in the sky without being filled with hatred toward those fuckers. Every jet is a personal offense against me. Whenever Via tries to call, I send her to voicemail. When she shows up at Camilo's with her horrid

Hummer, I slam the door in her face, regretting it didn't hit her ass in the process.

Since we're heading toward the end of the season, Huggins is giving me shit for hitting it too hard and not backing off. I have so much pent-up rage in me, I could give the biblical Samson a run for his money. Coach Higgins is trying to make sure that by the time we get on the field Friday night, we're so hungry and ready, failure is not an option.

Gus has been sending sporadic text messages with question marks. I don't know how much Via has told him, but I do not negotiate with terrorists. On Thursday, a mass message goes out from Colin, Gus's goon, that there's a spontaneous gathering at the snake pit for special pre-playoff fights.

I lock the football team in the locker room as soon as I get it.

"If I hear any of you miserable fucks have been fighting, I'll raise hell, you hear me?"

Everyone nods. Everyone but an angry Camilo. "They've been talking trash about us all season."

"So what? They're just words," Kannon replies.

"Words are *everything*," Camilo responds. "They called me a fucking beaner."

I shake my head. "Your future is everything. Don't throw it away because Gus is trying to get under your skin."

Later that day, I decide to show my face at the Followhill household, knowing I can no longer prolong what could be my last one-on-one with Daria before she moves away. I'm still at the don't-go negotiation stage although I should probably try to focus on getting her to tell me *where* she is going. Not that I will have much success in that department either, by the looks of it. In the movies, the bullshit ends once the guy reaches the realization that he loves the girl and makes some grand announcement.

In our story, it's just one twist out of many.

I park in front of the house, use my key, and stroll inside. I'm downplaying the fact I haven't been here in days. I find Bailey and Via sitting on the sofa with books in their hands. Daria is on the other side of the room, filling out a document—an application?—and Mel is next to her, staring at the pages Daria is filling out like they are actively trying to stab her. Everyone hears the door close behind me, but Jaime is the one who descends the stairs and volunteers to deal with the clusterfuck also known as my arrival.

He clucks his tongue, shaking his head. Doing the whole theatrics. Via stands up and disappears to the basement. Without seeing them communicating, I can tell Via is no longer Mel and Jaime's precious project. It's obvious they barely tolerate her after what she did to their daughter, and rightly so.

Daria excuses herself. She takes her application with her. I want to scream at her that she's the only reason I came back in the first place.

"Sit at the island," Jaime instructs me. I do.

Mel stands up and gets a pitcher of lemonade. I look down at my hands. I wonder if things could've gone differently. I wonder if they still can.

Jaime takes a seat in front of me and releases a breath.

"You think being a no-show is making things better around here?"

"I think thinking is not my best virtue when it comes to the people in this house. The more I try to make shit better, the more it blows up in my face," I answer honestly.

"How's the training going?"

"It's going," I say, my words clipped.

"Are we going to address the fact you shoved your tongue into my daughter's mouth?"

Among other places, sir.

I raise my eyes to his, showing him that I'm not weaseling out of this conversation. "Look, I know you warned me, and I know

I ignored it, but for what it's worth, it meant something. To me, anyway. Can't speak for your daughter, who is currently packing her bags and moving away."

Cheap shot, but I can't be the bigger person right now. I can barely be human. He should cut me some slack; it was his spawn who made me this way.

Jaime's gaze shoots to Mel, who flicks her hand across the back of my head on her way to the island. She looks terrible. Skinnier than her usual malnourished self.

"You've had your time to sulk about it. You're coming home after the game." She sets a glass of lemonade and a plate with grilled cheese in front of me.

Like I'd miss my last night with Daria for the world.

"Can I talk to her?" I apparently ask the grilled cheese because that's what I'm looking at right now.

"You need to talk to your sister first." Mel splits the sandwich in half and distributes it between Jaime and me.

"Not happening in this lifetime."

"Mel, can you give us a moment?" Jaime asks, his eyes still hard on me.

She stands up and waves her hand as she saunters upstairs. "Boys will be boys."

When she is out of earshot, Jaime snaps his fingers to get my attention. "Ever heard about the game Defy?"

I elevate an eyebrow. I'm not in the right mental state to think about anything that's not Daria or the game tomorrow. It'll be a pretty shit move to lose to save Daria's skin, but I will fuck over the entire world to protect her.

"The All Saints High tradition? Yeah. Why?" That shit died before I was even in middle school. They stopped playing it over a decade ago.

He stands up, tucking his phone into his back pocket. "I'm pulling the game out of retirement one last time."

I sit back and laugh. "You don't have to defy me. You can just kick my ass. I'd probably do the same."

"Not your ass. I can't resent your puppy love, even though thinking about your busted knuckles on my daughter's skin makes me want to punch you."

"Who are you fighting, then?" I ask, but then it comes to me. Clear as day.

Of course.

"Ryan Prichard," we say in unison.

"He quit last week. Packing up and getting ready to bolt before we get to him," Jaime explains.

"When is this happening?" I ask.

"Today."

"I'm coming with."

JAIME

Heavy is the fist that belongs to a father who just learned his precious daughter has been mentally abused since age fourteen by her school principal.

Heavier is the fist of a man who learned about it *after* his daughter has been through hell and back this year.

I'm a take-no-prisoners type of man.

When I aim, it's for the kill.

Prichard's got a house on the outskirts of Todos Santos. The only light from the distance is the one of his Alfa Romeo. Otherwise, it's pitch-black as we turn onto the dirt road, me leading the way in my Tesla and Vicious's Mercedes following closely. Trent Rexroth, my high school friend, is next to me, and Penn Scully—bless his broken fucking heart—is in the back seat, looking ruthlessly determined, with dead eyes like the rest of us. Vicious and Dean signal us with the lights to stop.

I throw the vehicle into park and twist around. "You wait here."

"No fucking way. He hurt her," Penn spits out, his hands already balled into fists. Ryan losing his job is not enough for me. Not by a long shot. I want him to lose everything else too, including his ability to sit down for the next couple of years.

"You can get into trouble," I warn him, but my heart's not in it. If someone hurt Mel, I'd probably kill them too.

"Oh, and you can't?"

Trent's shoulders shake with a conceited laugh next to me.

"Why?" Penn challenges.

"Prichard's got too much to lose. He can't touch us."

"Can anyone?" Penn wonders aloud, just as Trent's door opens from the other side. Dean whistles for him to get outside, swinging my baseball bat and parking it over his shoulder.

"Maybe God," I answer curtly.

"Even that's debatable." Dean snickers. "God, I missed the days of good ole shenanigans. Out, Rexroth. Lover boy." He whistles to Penn. "Make sure you're good and quiet unless you want your football dream to get flushed down the toilet."

Prichard, who is oblivious to our parked vehicles a mere few feet from him because our lights are off, comes out of his house, flinging two suitcases into the trunk of his running car. I get out of the car and round it with Vicious, Dean, and Trent following close by.

Every muscle and bone in my body is lit, hot with adrenaline as I tap his shoulder from behind. His body turns rigid, hard like stone. He turns around, and his face whitens, his car lights illuminating the fear on his ugly-ass face.

"Good evening, Mr. Prichard." I smile like the fucking royalty I am in this town. Too important to touch, too golden to lose control.

Dean swings the baseball bat behind me as though he is warming up.

Prichard is shaking his head violently.

"Oh no. No, no, no. I've already talked to your wife. We settled things. We—"

"You didn't settle anything with me," I bite out. Mel told me what she did after she did it, and although I wanted to kill her, I could understand where she was coming from too. "Us letting you off the hook is only because we don't want Daria to suffer." I erase the distance between us, smiling devilishly. My eyes are dead. My muscles loose. "Now it's time to pay."

Vicious slaps the trunk of the Alfa Romeo shut at the same time I push Ryan on the back of his car, bending him over in one rough movement. Dean hands me the baseball bat, chuckling.

"And if we find out you went to another godforsaken town and tried to rekindle your career…" Dean pushes down Prichard's pants and briefs in one go, exposing the milky-white ass of a middle-aged man. Bright as the goddamn moon.

"Help! Help! Help!" Prichard is bawling like a baby.

Even through his pussy cries, I can hear the leaves crunching under Penn's shoes as he advances toward us. He can't keep himself out of this. Good. I wouldn't let an asshole who could sit by and let something like this happen to Daria touch her.

Penn is by my side now, shoulder to shoulder. I don't say shit because Prichard can't know he's here. He's not as protected as we are.

"Heeeelp," Prichard drawls, his face still slammed against the cold surface of his trunk, his cheek smeared all over it.

"Shut up," I bite out metallically, ripping his sports jacket from his body and balling it in my fist. I shove it into his mouth until he gags and chokes on it.

Vicious plasters his hand over Prichard's back and looks at me, smiling serenely.

"Say a few Hail Marys, you sick *son of a bitch*. Maybe it'll slow down your perverted ass on its way to hell."

I strike Ryan with the baseball bat across the ass, using every ounce of power and muscle in my body. The hit is so hard, the sound rings in our ears and we take a few seconds to let it die down.

The second hit is even stronger, as though I found my footing. I think about everything my daughter has been through these past six months.

About her mother, whom I love more than life itself, who insists on saving everything that's broken, and in doing so, had a hand in breaking our daughter.

I think about how I can't stand to look at the eighteen-year-old girl who lives with me because she tarnished my princess.

I think about her twin brother, who is too in love with my daughter to give her up, whether he knows it or not.

On my third strike, Ryan spits out his jacket, yelping to the sky like a lone wolf.

After eighteen strikes, one for every birthday my daughter has celebrated, I pass the bat to Vicious, but it's Penn who puts his hand on my arm and takes it without asking for permission.

I shake my head, motioning for him not to say a word. It's too dangerous.

He opens his mouth, talking to Ryan Prichard but staring at me.

"Thank your lucky stars that I'm not alone because if we were, you'd be dead by now," the boy says with no trace of emotion in his voice.

"Penn? Penn Scully?" Prichard chokes.

Penn swings the bat, hitting him so hard I actually wince. Prichard faints on his trunk.

By the time we drive back home, Prichard is bleeding and can't make out shapes, let alone faces. Before we leave, we tuck a copy of Mel's recording into his jacket's pocket to make sure he knows not to mess with us. Especially with Penn.

Prichard will take this, like what he did to Daria, to his grave.

PENN

"Just gonna grab my shit from Camilo." I fling my backpack over my shoulder and let Mel kiss my cheek. It's almost midnight, and it looks like we're going to eat in the middle of the night, but that's because the Followhills all understood why Jaime and I had to leave to take care of business before Prichard skipped town.

Mel is chopping vegetables as lasagna bakes in the oven, giving me her stay-safe pleading eyes. Forever the multitasker. Bailey is beside her, squeezing lemons into iced tea. Via is outside, sitting on a lounger by the pool, hugging her knees together. The undercurrent in the house has changed. Via is no longer the prized, newly found miracle. She was dragged down to the status of a mortal.

"Do you need help?" Mel wipes at her nose with her sleeve while cutting onions. "Packing, I mean."

"Only if Daria is offering."

I've officially lost my privilege to go up the stairs and ask her myself. Jaime throws me threatening looks when I even *look* at the stairs leading up to the second floor, and Daria doesn't seem to be coming downstairs anytime before her flight. I wonder if he realizes I'll have to go up there when I go to bed tonight.

"Jaime can help you."

"He can carry his half-empty duffel bag on his own." Jaime is flipping channels, obviously not done holding a grudge.

"I'll be back before dinner." I grab my keys and snatch a garlic bread roll on my way to the car. Out of habit, or maybe because I'm not done quite torturing myself, I twist my head to see if Daria is watching me through the window. No dice. Her bedroom light is off through the curtain. Mentally, she checked out of here long before she's getting on the plane.

As I drive to Camilo's, I try to call him to make sure he knows I'm stopping by.

He is not answering, and I'm growing irritated. I gave him a direct order to get his ass as far as possible from the snake pit. If I manage to keep my fists to myself when Gus shits systematically on everything I know and love, so can he.

I park in front of Camilo's door, knowing I can't knock on it at midnight. Then I hear a baby crying and a woman mumbling in annoyance and know I won't be waking up anyone. I knock. His sister opens with her toddler on her hip. I push past her to retrieve my duffel bag by the couch.

"Where's your dumbass brother?" I ask.

"Hell if I know. Maybe that place all the cool kids go to."

"The snake pit?"

"That what it's called?" She laughs, opening the microwave in the kitchen to grab a bottle and shove it into the baby's mouth. "Make sure you protect that pretty face of yours, Scully. Cheekbones like that, you can knock your rich girl up and live off her parents' money."

When I drive to the snake pit, my nerves hit an all-time high. Camilo is both hotheaded and easily swayed into doing stupid shit. I know that because for a while, doing stupid shit was our favorite pastime. I kill the engine outside the deserted football field and race toward the chain-link gate. Screams and curses pop in the air like gunshots. There's a cloud of anger and sweat rising from behind the bleachers, and as I hop the chain-link fence and get in, I see why.

It's a goddamn war zone.

There's a mass fight, and everyone is in it—including Knight, Vaughn, Colin, Will, Josh, Malcolm, and Nelson. Both the Bulldogs and the Saints are in it to win it. Underneath all of them on the dry, brown earth is Camilo, lying on the ground.

I track toward him, shoving people off him as the crowd thickens. Players stomp and kick each other, paying him no attention. Camilo doesn't move.

"Dafuq happened to you?" I lower myself on one knee. I'm afraid to touch him because I'm not sure of his injuries.

"Broken...I think it's broken." He barely finishes, looking down at his leg.

I follow his line of sight and see it clearly, even through his jeans. His leg is bent unnaturally. Cartoonlike. His fibula is all distorted. It looks bad.

"We need to get you to the hospital," I say.

"No shit, Sherlock." He laughs, his voice dry and crisp. He's been lying like this for a while, I gather. I call an ambulance while Gus sneaks away from the bleachers, hollering in his wake, "Clear out, clear out, Scully invited the pigs."

Everyone's sprinting past us now, leaving dust in their wake. Guys push and yell and plea. They boo at me as if I give a fuck. Knight grabs the end of my shirt and yanks me up. I shake him off.

"I'm staying with Cam."

Vaughn stops next to him, eyeballing me hard. "You have a game tomorrow," he reminds me.

"Would you have left Knight?"

Both Knight and I look at him. He claps his best friend's shoulder. "His funeral. Let's go."

I turn back to Cam. "What happened?"

But I think I already know. Gus didn't think I'd throw the game, so he sent someone to make sure my quarterback wouldn't be able to play. It was a calculated, cold move to get rid of Camilo and eliminate our chances of winning.

"Colin went straight for it. Tackled me and jammed his foot to the side of my knee. Knight and Vaughn came two minutes too late and shoved him off me."

By the casual way he tells me this, I understand that it still hasn't sunk in.

No football.

No scholarship.

No future.

"You're going to be fine," I lie, elevating his upper body.

He laughs.

"I'm not an idiot, Scully. I know what's up. You were right. Is that what you want to hear? Because you were."

My team just lost one of its greatest players.

For nothing.

CHAPTER TWENTY-FOUR
DARIA/PENN

Falling in love is similar to déjà vu.
It's finding a home in a stranger.
When I met you four and a half years ago, I
saw who you were.
I just had to figure out who I was.
So I gave you something to make sure I could
seek you out again.
And maybe, so you'd fall in love with whoever
I was too

DARIA

I keep my head down as the cheer team storms onto the field, waving their pom-poms in the air. Dad calls it a huge victory that I'm here. I call it asking for more trouble.

The huge, plastic smiles on the girls' faces say it all. I'm out. Via's in. Our blue-and-black uniform clings to her lithe body like a second skin. She dazzles so brightly, Esme positioned her as far as possible from the center. Far away from *her*. I feel naked without my pom-poms. I long to feel them in my hands but know it's too late for me. My cheer days are over, at least in high school.

Mel pretends to rummage through her bag, but I know she just can't look at Via. Surprisingly, it doesn't make me feel good. Or at all. I'm a taco. A crisp, empty shell.

Melody doesn't leave my side even though I refuse her love, care, and silent apologies. Bailey visits my room every morning with a tray containing a glass of OJ, a piece of toast with egg whites, and a cute inspirational quote she prints out from Pinterest, and Dad sweetens my nights by coming in and giving me a good-night kiss to keep me going. He always peppers it with reminiscing about a good memory to remind me that good times are still to come.

Remember when Knight drew a rocket on your forehead when you were kids, and I almost murdered him thinking it was something else?

Remember when Vaughn walked around on the beach with a live jellyfish in his hand and declared it as his new pet?

Remember when Luna thought you were a princess because of your hair?

It is an unspoken truth that Melody can no longer give me good-night kisses.

Daddy says it's a good thing. That when things get destroyed, you can build a better version of them from scratch. But building takes strength and courage, and I don't have either right now.

Esme is doing a toe touch, and Via follows by pulling a perfect herkie. Mel clasps my skinny jean–clad thigh. I'm wearing a yellow top, no longer affiliated with either team. Things have been crazy since Principal Prichard stepped down abruptly, citing a morbidly sick relative he had to take care of on the East Coast. Word around town is I quit the cheer team because I'm nursing a broken heart. While it's true, everyone thinks it's Principal Prichard I am pining after.

No one suspects the boy who is about to get on the field today is the one who smashed my heart into dust, and now it's drifting in the air, evaporating from me. No one knows what I've been through ever since that boy admitted his love to me, and I couldn't take him back, no matter how much I want to. Being sorry for breaking something doesn't make it whole again.

"Don't look at them," Mel whispers, squeezing my thigh. "They aren't worth it."

"Let go of my leg, Melody."

She does. Dad is clapping when both teams get on the field even though I know he wants to snap Gus's spine. Las Juntas is sporting a brand-new quarterback, who looks like a whopping one hundred pounds of bones, and people actually snicker from the bleachers. I feel bad for the kid. And I used to be the mean girl who'd be the first to point out that he isn't built like a brick wall.

The game starts, and as soon as Penn goes on the field, it is clear he is shitting all over the game. Blatantly so. He doesn't even do it gradually. My heart lurches in my chest as Penn pretends to struggle with dropped passes, dragging his feet from side to side. He is immobile and doesn't catch the ball even when it hits him in the chest. *Literally.*

He is lagging on the field, heavy and dense, the opposite of the talented player he is. His teammates yell in frustration, one of them kicking a mountain of mud. On the sidelines, his coach is on the verge of a heart attack, but Penn pretends not to listen. Tucked in his own universe, he keeps missing balls, looking the other way in confusion when he gets an opportunity, and stopping every few minutes to lean down on his knees as if he is out of breath.

Midgame, Penn's coach summons them, probably coming up with a new strategy, and Penn nods and looks attentive and determined. But then when he gets back on the field again, he is looking even worse.

Then there's Knight. Dean is almost spitting out a lung screaming next to Dad in the stands. Wondering aloud why on earth his quarterback son just missed a chance at a touchdown by throwing the ball to the sideline.

"What the heck is going on?" Dean kicks the bleacher seat in front of him, and an overweight, fiftysomething father turns around and looks at him sharply.

"Your son plays like shit."

"Least he doesn't smell like it," Dean retorts.

"I think I know what's happening," Dad murmurs wryly. "And you can be damn proud, Cole."

"And why is that? En-fucking-lighten me, Jaime."

Because Knight refuses to win the game. Penn is trying to kill Las Juntas's chance to win so he can save me, but Knight doesn't let him because he knows he deserves it.

Knight is privy to another thing too: he knows I'm done here.

I'm leaving town tomorrow. I have nothing to win and nothing to lose. Which is exactly why I find myself standing up and descending the bleachers. I don't know what I'm doing. All I *do* know is I'm definitely going to draw attention to myself, something I vowed not to do since I got kicked off the cheer team and Principal Prichard bailed, leaving a trail of scandalous rumors about us in his wake. I run down the stairs, hop over the fence, plant myself on the sidelines next to All Saints High's coach. With my toes on the grass and my heels on the concrete, I cup my hands around my mouth.

"Penn Scully, if you're half the man I know you are, you will show up on this field," I scream.

All eyes dart to me. Penn, who is already running slow, stops completely, tearing his helmet off and dumping it on the field, his hard eyes colliding with mine.

"Number twenty-two!" The referee throws the yellow penalty flag for unsportsmanlike conduct. "Your team loses fifteen yards."

"Scully!" his coach barks. "I will bench you."

"Be my fucking guest." Penn's lips curl in amusement, our eye contact never breaking.

I feel naked and raw and judged. The world continues spinning, and the game carries on. The Bulldogs went over on downs, and now Knight has it. Las Juntas are on the defense, but Penn is still glued to his spot, mesmerized by the pleas in my eyes. The cheerleaders stop dancing on the sidelines and throw me a pitying look. I know what they think.

It finally happened. Bitch has lost her mind.

I smile, free-falling into being someone different. Someone imperfect. Someone *real*. Unchaining myself from what people think of me, of how they see me, of what they will say after the game.

"I want you to bury these assholes in the ground." My lungs burn as I scream the words, a deranged smile threatening to cut my cheeks in half, but I'm not even remotely happy. I'm going against my team—against the Saints, whom I cheered on for four years. I can hear footfalls coming. Two of All Saints High's teachers who act as security—Miss Linde and Mr. Hathaway—take me by my wrists and usher me away from the field. Daddy jumps over the fence, lithe and athletic like one of the football players, and tears Mr. Hathaway's hand from me.

"Touch my daughter against her will one more time, and I will bury you with legal shit until your retirement day."

"Twenty-two!" I hear a whistle, and Penn's coach is practically storming onto the field, but our eyes never waver. "Twenty-goddamn-two! Put your damn helmet *on*, boy!"

"Penn!" I cry out.

He is breaking approximately five thousand rules by talking to me in the middle of the game, and now everyone stops. Gus kicks the grass, cursing. He puts his hands on his hips and shakes his head. Dad's arms wrap around my waist, dragging me away from the field and back up to the bleachers.

"Can you do something for me?" I scream at Penn. My legs are not moving, but I'm laughing manically. Penn nods. "Make them eat dirt!"

The whole crowd boos at me as Daddy grabs Melody and Bailey, and we all make a hurried exit before I get burned at the stake. Dad hooks his arm around my shoulder as we stumble out of the gates, drawing me close and kissing my head.

"My crazy, out-of-this-world daughter. And you thought you were anything less than fierce."

PENN

People are apples. Good apples. Bad apples. Too ripe or too raw. Hard or soft. Sweet or sour. And in every apple, there's a core. A heart. Something that makes them uniquely themselves.

My mother once told me that she wasn't worried for Via because my core is security. I'm the protector. I sheltered Via when no one else wanted to, and now, when Daria is begging me to take what is mine—this win, this game, the championship—and my teammates are spitting out sweat and blood to try to make it happen, and Knight Cole gets pasted to save my skin, I can't do it.

Protecting Via was a duty. Protecting Daria is an honor.

I pretend to trip on my own feet yet again after Daria and her family leave the stadium. The cheers and catcalls turn to boos and cusses. Then it's halftime. In other words: time for Coach to rip me a new one. We get off the field with a stellar lead—28 to 14, but it's nothing I can't screw up if I try even harder.

"Scully!" Coach Higgins roars so loud, his voice bounces off the huge projectors. "Get your ass over here right now!" He points at the ground.

I swagger toward him as slowly as humanly possible, tearing the helmet off my head and brushing past him as I continue to the locker room. He tugs at the back of my jersey and pulls me back to him. Everyone else drifts through the tunnel and into the lockers, and he motions for them to continue as he plasters me against the tunnel wall, snarling.

"Are you losing my game on purpose, son?"

Any other guy would take what Daria so generously offered and show up to the game the next half and kick ass. Not me. I don't care what Daria wants, and I don't care that she won't be there on Monday to see the pages of her journal plastered on every locker and square inch of the school. She doesn't deserve this shit.

"Sir, I lost focus. For that, I apologize." I tell him whatever he needs to hear to keep me on the field.

"Because of the pretty blond?" he spits out.

"Because of an asshole blond guy," I correct, jerking my chin toward Gus, who is making his way to ASH's locker room. "Fucker has been shoving Josh's pads into his throat. Dude still tapes quarters to his knuckles like it's the fucking nineties." I let out a bitter cough of laughter.

"Language!" he yells. "And I don't care what you feel toward Bauer. If you let him get to you, you will never get drafted. You will never make it big. You will never be NFL ready. Just another poor boy with a lot of potential and no brains who is throwing a game because someone said something about his girlfriend. You think she's gonna stick around after the jock glory wears off? When y'all go to college? You think she's worth your future? Your team's future? My future?"

Yes. Yes. Yes. Yes. And yes.

I shake my head, shouldering past him. He chases me down the tunnel, his voice carrying the echo of the cave-like place. "Answer me, son!"

I storm to the locker room. I'm done explaining myself. Especially to the man who told me to stay away from my girlfriend so that Prichard could abuse her.

Ex-girlfriend. Fuck.

Lowering myself to a bench and releasing my breath, I watch as Coach Higgins enters the room and slams his fist into a locker, making a huge dent. When he withdraws his hand, his knuckles are bruised and bloody.

"Every single one of you rowdy idiots is like my own kid.

Someone needs to step forward and tell me what happened to your captain, or I'm benching the hell out of him and making sure every single phone call I get from colleges about any of y'all will be met with the same response: He is not good enough. He is not ready. Don't give him the scholarship. In other words, if you don't rat out Penn and tell me what his problem is, you go down with him, understood?"

"Yes, sir!" everyone answers in unison.

I chew on my mouthguard and stare at the floor. Maybe they know. Maybe they'll rat me out, and that'll be the end of my career. All I know is that I've never been more sure of anything my entire life as I am sure of this—I'm not bringing Daria down, with or without her blessing.

"So," Higgins screams, "what happened to Penn Scully?"

"Nothing, sir!"

"What happened?" he screams.

"*Nothing*, sir!" they all bark at the same time.

I should feel proud. Touched. Something. Anything. I don't. I fucking don't. It's too late.

"I will ruin your goddamn football careers, boys!" He punches the lockers again. And again. And again.

"Penn Scully is our captain, sir."

For the first time in weeks, I smile.

I have Daria's back.

And my team's got mine.

CHAPTER TWENTY-FIVE
PENN/DARIA

Loving you is like
Listening to a song
For the first time
And somehow knowing all the lyrics.

PENN

The game ends with 42–17 after much hard work from me trying to lose. Our scrawny quarterback ended up having an arm like Brett Favre, and the defense played their hearts out and forced fumbles that they recovered. Las Juntas Bulldogs win anyway. Kannon gets the game ball for being MVP, but we both know who deserves it.

I leave before the after-game prayer. Stalking toward the locker room, I take a quick shower, throw my duffel bag over my shoulder, and burst into All Saints' unlocked showers. Most of the players are inside, lathered in soap, sporting bruises on their foreheads and chests. Gus is sitting on a bench, a towel wrapped around his waist, holding his head in his hands. He is still dry as a bone.

Kicking his shin with my toes, I snap my fingers before him. He looks up. He looks like death. His eyes bloodshot, his cheeks sunken. People are whining about my being there as though I came in with a ruler to compare our dicks. I ignore the protests and requests to see myself the hell out.

"Your girlfriend's dead." He smirks darkly.

"Meet me at the pit tonight, Bauer. And this time, you're not in charge of the fucking paperwork. You're fighting. With me."

Daria asked that no one know she was leaving. She preferred it that way, not trusting Gus with the information. But I don't put it past my sister to tell him, and I have to make sure he doesn't get to Daria tonight.

"Give me one good reason to do anything you ask, you fucking lowlife. I have every right to—"

I punch him in the face, knocking him back. He falls backward, and Colin—*I'm not done with you, either, Colin*—manages to catch him before his head hits the floor.

"You'll come because I know where you live, and if you make me come to you, I will, and without witnesses, you will fare so much worse. You too, Stimatzky." I look up to meet Colin's gaze. "I have a *bone* to pick with you."

I storm out, hearing Knight yell, "I knew it," and lockers slamming in the distance.

Not all the All Saints High team are fuckers. But their captain is.

War is a universal language. Christian, Jew, Buddhist, or a Muslim. Beautiful or ugly. Rich or poor.

They're about to find out that it is especially vicious when you're the underdog.

———

"I need to tell you something, bro." Kannon bounces his knee fast and furious while we drive back from the hospital and toward the snake pit. We had to make a stop at Cam's bedside to give him the MVP ball, signed by all of us, and while we were at it, we took him some greasy-ass food he'd never be able to get from the gross cafeteria.

"Spit it out." I roll my window down and spit out phlegm. My mind's not on the fight I'm about to walk into. My mind is back in the Followhill mansion, where Daria is packing her bags to fly fuck knows where. Jaime and Mel are going to drive her to the airport tomorrow, and they already made it clear that this is one family function the Scullys are not invited to.

Daria was a rock star today, telling me to save my own ass because hers was already on fire. But when she stood there and yelled at me, her hair up and her neck exposed, the only thing I could focus on was the fact the sea glass necklace was no longer there.

I punch the steering wheel.

"Whoa. What's wrong with you?" Kannon asks.

Everything. Every-fucking-thing is wrong with me. "Just say what you gotta say, K."

"First, I want to know what was up on that field, Penn."

"Nothing. And if you don't say what you have to say right now, I'm throwing you out of the car," I inform him matter-of-factly, without missing a beat.

"Well, shit, I was kind of hoping you'd be in a better mood but better late than never, I guess. So remember the first game of the season? Against the Saints?"

"How could anyone forget?" I throw the car into park in front of the snake pit. The lights are already on, and there's more commotion than usual. In fact, it looks like my entire school is heading toward it. All Saints High too. Dozens of kids are marching through the gates that have been busted open somehow, and a cold sweat finds its way to the back of my neck.

"We threw the game," Kannon says.

I twist my head toward him. "Repeat that."

"We threw the game." He looks down at his hands. "The whole team did. Well, other than you and Camilo. Gus didn't even think to approach you. We figured we looked so good, we could handle losing one game. Gus paid us five hundred bucks each. You know how it is, bro. Turning down money is not in the cards for most of us. Whether it's for gear, shoes, or to help our folks with the rent… or, hell, you know? Just to eat at Lenny's and live. Even those of us who didn't need the money didn't wanna ruin it for those who did."

"You sold the game?" I can feel the tics in my eyelids. Never a good fucking sign.

He groans, throwing his head against his headrest. "We took State, man, and not thanks to you, so don't give me this shit."

Wordlessly, I step out of the vehicle and round it, opening Kannon's door and throwing him out on the ground. I'm now oblivious to the growing crowd streaming into the snake pit. The only thing I can see is his face when he realizes he shouldn't have confided in me.

I straighten him up against the car and squat down to his eye level.

"You try to throw any other games this season?" I park my elbows on my knees, squinting.

He shakes his head. "But I know Gus bought pretty much all of ASH's games."

"With what money?"

"The betting ring. He makes money there, then uses it to pay off players from other teams."

"That's thousands of dollars."

"Vaughn loves to fight, and people love to think others have a fucking chance against him." Kannon shrugs.

"What happened tonight, then?"

Kannon shakes his head. "He came to Josh the other night— Josh is the one who's been listening to him since he has nothing to lose, and all. Gus tried to up his price. A thousand a head. And… until yesterday, people were going to do it. I wasn't going to anymore, bro, I swear, but I couldn't snitch on the others. Hell, people need this money for medicine for their parents and diapers for their baby siblings, and I'm no snitch."

"What changed?"

"When they did what they did to Camilo…when he didn't want to take part in this…I guess that's when we officially lost our shit and decided enough was enough. It just didn't sit right with us anymore. Him screwing around with your twin and trying to ruin your team."

Anger bubbles in my blood, and I grab the collar of his shirt and raise my fist, about to put a hole in his face, when he looks me in the eye, dead calm, and says, "You have bigger fish to fry than me, brother."

"What do you mean?"

"Look behind you."

I twist my head and see the pink Hummer my sister has been using, parked across from where we are. I watch Via pouring out of it, hand in hand with none other than Daria herself. My fist drops as I gravitate toward them, my legs carrying me there without even meaning to, mesmerized.

"…I'm so glad we had a chance to start fresh. The entire cheer team would like to apologize. I know you're moving away, but we wanted to straighten things out before you do. You know, not to leave things awkward," Via explains to Daria, who looks like a ghost. About five pounds lighter than when the school year started, her eyes dead. She is still gorgeous, put together, and looks like a model, but her heart's not in it anymore. Into flaunting her beauty like she earned it somehow. I recognize Via's lilt of fakeness. It's the one she often used when she was still her old self.

I race across the parking lot, determined to protect Daria from whatever my sister has in store for her.

Praying I'm not too late.

DARIA

The minute I step into the snake pit, I chuckle at my own stupid mistake.

This is not a last-ditch effort to try to make me stay. It's not even a peace offering. I came here because Via begged me to stop the fight between Gus and Penn.

"Penn's future is on the line. If you truly love him like you say you do, you'll come and tell him not to fight Gus."

It's a trap. I should have known the minute Via knocked on my bedroom door. She seemed too hysterical. Too nervous. But her reasons for seeking a ceasefire were too logical to overlook. Teary-eyed, she explained that she was tired of the hateful looks her brother gave her. I truly thought she wanted to cover her ass and get my blessing before I move away.

I forgot one important thing—Via cares more about ruining me than saving herself.

It's in her DNA and has been for years now. She already knows what it feels like to lose everything because it happened to her when she was fourteen. Because of me. She'll never be the prima ballerina she could have been. She knows that too. Too much time without proper training has passed. My mother can hole her up in the ballet studio fifteen hours a day, but youth shapes art, and she's been artless for so long, her craft has wilted.

Her dream is an empty shell. The pearl that's supposed to be inside is nowhere to be found. That's why she keeps ripping into what's mine. She knows we both lost, but I have the means to still live a comfortable life. She's screwed. Maybe forever.

My eyes swallow the scene unfolding in front of me. The world moves in slow motion as hundreds—no, thousands—of flyers rain down on the dead field. They volley on the bleachers and brown, muddy ground and are speared to the chain-link fence and handed over between people who are whispering and laughing. The cheer team stands on the top row of the bleachers, and all the cheerleaders are throwing them around, with Esme laughing so loud, I swear they can hear her in Japan. One of the pages sticks to my shin as dozens of its friends fly past me, and I bend down and pick it up.

The paper was printed so hurriedly, there are smudges of ink from people touching it before it had time to dry.

Entry #842:

Sin: *Opened a fake dating profile on a website I knew Miss Linde was a member of and had virtual sex with her. Screenshot everything and sent it to her ex-boyfriend.*
Reason: *She gave me two Cs just because she is jealous of Principal Prichard and me but too scared to rat us out.*

Entry #843:

Sin: *Ordered Esme full-fat lattes from Starbucks every Thursday for an entire semester when it was my turn to do the coffee round before practice in hopes she'll gain weight.*
Reason: *Bitch always fat-shames everyone.*

Entry #844:

Sin: *Frenched Colin Stimatzky and let him cop a feel.*
Reason: *Wanted to get rid of my obsessive thoughts about Penn Scully AKA hole-in-a-shirt boy (UGH IT'S BEEN THREE YEARS, BITCH, GET OVER THE LOSER).*

I'm on the verge of puking when I notice Penn darting around the place, plucking the papers from people's hands with murder in his eyes. Every person in his way immediately drops their paper, but the damage has already been done. Everyone is standing in the center of the field or sitting on a bleacher and reading about my sordid deeds. People point, joke about me, and whisper about me. I am officially the laughingstock of the county, and nothing will change that. Ever.

I turn around, about to run away, when Via catches my wrist and tugs me back. She pretends to hug me, but I can feel her smile on the shell of my ear when she talks.

"It was a bad play on your part to ask your family not to tell anyone that you're leaving. Totally drove me to tell Gus we needed to kick our plan into high gear. Now we're even, Daria. Now, when I take everything away from you like you did from me, I can move on with my life. Now, you've finally tasted what it feels like to be thoroughly ruined."

I squirm away, digging my feet into the ground and trying to escape, when Penn's hand—warm and big—grasps my other wrist. Via releases me immediately.

I want to kick him away and yell at him for preventing me from escaping, but I'm defenseless against his touch. I break down on his chest, and his arms wrap around me, shielding me from the rest of the world. The tears are falling, and his chest rumbles, telling me that he is breaking too. And somehow, at this moment, it's enough. The world is against us—everyone knows about every single awful thing I ever did—and still...

Penn turns around to his sister, still holding me in his arms. "You can run, but you can't fucking hide, Sylvia. And when I catch you—and I *will* catch you—you will regret the day I was born, five minutes before you, because I'm going to make ruining your life a full-time job, and I'll be putting in some extra hours too."

It takes a lot for me to elevate my head from his chest to peek at Via's expression when her brother officially disowns her. His voice is so low and threatening, shudders move down my spine. Via looks pale and panicked in front of him. Her lips are colorless; her entire body limp. She obviously wasn't expecting Penn to be so mad. She expected him to have her back again. To make excuses for her. To protect her as he does—*did*, at least—unconditionally.

"Penn, I—"

"Shut the fuck up," he commands, stalking to the other side of the field with me in tow. He's holding my hand now. I don't know why I'm letting him. We're not together and never will be. Not because he chose his sister, but because he chose to break not only our fling but also my heart. He went with the worst route possible. Hurting me on purpose. And I'm officially done with people who don't choose me or see me.

Penn stops in front of Gus. I make myself look at the guy because this is my reality, and I need to face it. The entire football team, sans Knight, and the cheer squad surround Gus. His chin is up, and he's wearing his varsity jacket and a vacant scowl. When he laughs, vodka breath fans across my face even though we're a few feet away.

"Look what the cat dragged in."

"Someone who's about to put a stop to your pussy ways." Penn fishes out his Zippo from his jeans, spinning it between his finger and thumb. Before I realize what's happening, Via is standing behind Penn with tears streaming down her face. His teammate—Kannon, I think his name was—is next to us too. And the Josh guy. And the Malcolm guy. And the Nelson guy...

"Via," Gus barks. "Get your sweet ass over here."

Via shakes her head slowly behind me, looking at the ground that's now wet with her tears.

"*Now!*" Gus stomps his foot.

Penn takes a step toward Gus. Then another one. They are chest to chest now, and both teams are on edge, glaring at them impatiently, begging for a fight. I look around and see Adriana a few feet away from me. She shifts from foot to foot, clearly nervous about a rematch between us. I give her a tired smile and motion her with my hand to come a little closer. When she does, I grab her hand on instinct and squeeze it as hard as I can in my frail state.

"I'm sorry," I whisper. "So sorry. I shouldn't have said those things to you. I was blinded by jealousy and desperate to keep something that wasn't even mine to begin with."

My popularity. Penn.

"I'm sorry too." She looks the other way, her chin trembling. "I shouldn't have held on to him with everything that I had. He was never mine to hold."

I feel something brush over my arm where Penn stood just a second ago. It's Knight. And next to Knight stands Vaughn.

"Cole?" Gus twists his lips, glowering. "What the fuck?"

Knight clasps a hand on my shoulder, hitching a shoulder up while lighting a joint.

"The fuck is, you don't *fuck* with my family and integrity and assume you get out of it in one piece. Or, you know, at all."

Penn pushes Gus's chest, and the latter tumbles into Colin's arms.

"You've been spending the past four years taking bets in this place, never once getting your hands dirty. I think it's time to remedy that. But first, let's address the fact you are such a bitch, you resorted to trying to ruin Daria's life because yours sucks ass. You spilled all her secrets. Throwing rocks when your house is made of glass." Penn *tsks*, shaking his head. "When your house is made of *nothing*, actually. Bad call, Bauer. Terrible."

Penn proceeds to circle Gus dispassionately, separating him from the rest of his crew. After the All Saints players see that Knight and Vaughn are with us, they take a few steps back. Not yet jumping ship but visibly more wary about giving their team captain a glowing, full endorsement.

"You like secrets, assholes? Here's a juicy one to keep you entertained. Gus's mom is a whore. A real, get-paid-for-sex whore." Penn lets loose a wicked smile, and Gus actually flinches in place, looking away. My mouth goes slack. *What?*

"Been sitting on this piece of info for four years now, never stooping to his level while he played filthy and tried shooting his mouth off. But now that he touched the only thing sacred to me, he is about to find out that even the sturdiest trunks can snap. Ever wondered why Bauer never throws parties at his crib? Why he never gives out his address? Yeah. That's because he attends All Saints High on a scholarship. Sleeps in his fucking car. He'd sleep in his house, but it's pretty busy there with horny fucks coming in and out every hour of the day and night. Oh shit, I failed to mention—Gussy here is a neighbor of mine. A boy from the wrong side of the tracks, just like yours truly. That's why he started the betting ring. That's why he's been paying off people to rig his games. He is just as desperate for a scholarship as I am. With one significant difference—one of us has talent and a future. The other just killed every chance of escaping here tonight."

"Ohhhh," the Las Juntas crowd, which I'm standing in the middle of, taunts, turning their thumbs down in a boo motion toward Bauer. Gus is bright red now, and despite everything, I feel sorry for him. For me. For all of us, really. Vanity cost us every single thing we achieved for ourselves. Our athletic career. Friends. Family. Our love interests.

Gus looks up, recovering quickly.

"Strangers might be screwing my ma. But you, Scully? Your worst enemy is screwing your *sister*. In every position under the sun."

"Not my sister anymore." Penn spits on the ground as he continues to circle him, still toying with his Zippo. "My sister was angry." He raises his eyes to Via and smiles bitterly. "But she wasn't *soulless*."

I wish he'd stop saying things like that. I wish he'd stop playing with his Zippo.

If in the first act you have a pistol hanging on the wall, then in the following one, it should be fired.

"Penn." Via runs toward him, but she stops halfway when his body freezes and his jaw hardens into a rigid square. "Please. You don't understand. Hear me out. I'm sorry, okay? You want a secret? You want dirt? I'll give you filth that'll make Daria very happy. Four years ago, when I ran away, I was heartbroken over quitting ballet and leaving you. But I was also heartbroken over leaving Gus. We *loved* each other," Via cries out, pushing Gus's chest as she turns to face her brother. "I thought he was the love of my life. Stupid,

I know, but I was so young. We went to the same middle school together. He was my first crush, my first kiss, my first time sneaking out and jumping on rooftops together, defying death. When I came back, I desperately wanted everything I once had back. Getting back together with Gus was a no-brainer. I never realized how much he'd changed in the time we weren't together, and he went to an all-rich high school and wanted to fit in. And I guess I changed too. I was so focused on ruining things for Daria, I did it at the expense of gaining a family, and a friend, and my brother back." Her shoulders slump, and for the first time since I met her all those years ago, Via turns around to look at me, and she doesn't look like she hates me. She looks tired. Destroyed. She looks exactly how I feel.

"We all have embarrassing secrets. Every single one of us. We're just happy it's not our diary on display. My secret? I've always envied you, Daria Followhill, and I tried to hurt you as much as you hurt me. With the only difference that you only did one bad thing to me. I did a lot of nasty things, and now I'm more isolated than I've ever been before. Even in Mississippi. Revenge tastes like shit. I wish I had known that before I put everything on the line to get it."

Colin steps forward. He runs his fingers through his hair, exhaling sharply.

"Gus told me to go for your quarterback's leg," he says. "That's my secret. I'm sorry. I fucked up. I haven't slept in two days. Haven't eaten either, which might explain why we were so crappy back there on the field. The truth is, my brother got drafted to the NFL, but I'm a subpar player. My parents don't even bother coming to our games. I wanted this championship so badly. I just wanted them to see *me* for once in my miserable life."

Esme steps forward. It feels like a huge purge of feelings, secrets, and sins. The snake pit has never been more crowded...or poisonous. Yet the antidote to all the venom is honesty.

Esme huffs, taking off her high heels and throwing them across the field, leaving her barefoot.

"Shit. Ugh. I hate these!" she exclaims, laughing. "God, I hate heels. And those miniskirts." She wiggles her butt as she tries pulling her very short skirt down her thighs.

Blythe is beside her, eyeing her with a look I decode as fear.

"My secret? Ha. Where do I even begin? My mom told me I was fat when I was, like, probably five or something, and I pretty much haven't eaten a carb since. Not that she cares anymore. She's on husband number three right now and too busy traveling the world with him. I hate anyone and everyone with a semi-functioning family and therefore loathed Daria before she even opened her mouth. Then she started talking smack about her mom—who bakes cupcakes for us when we had pool parties at her house and used to braid Daria's hair before school and send her with home-cooked food until this semester—and I had a really good reason to hate her. I want everyone to feel the pain I feel. All. The. Time. Maybe that's why I've been fucking Vaughn Spencer since the beginning of the semester. Sorry, Bly—"

The slap comes before she can even complete the sentence. Blythe growls in her face and rushes toward me, flinging her arms over my shoulders. I freeze.

"I'm so sorry, Daria. Esme never should've gotten your title. I'm sorry I took her side. My secret is that I'm insecure, probably too insecure, to stand up against bullies. To tell people how I feel about them." She sniffs, chancing a glance at Vaughn. "I don't know. I sometimes feel like I'm too afraid to *live*."

Esme looks up at me hesitantly, and I shake my head while drawing Blythe into a deeper hug. I feel bad for both girls, but that doesn't mean I can forgive so quickly.

"I...uhm..." Adriana takes a step forward, wiping her sweaty palms on the back of her jeans. "I'm probably going to regret this as soon as it leaves my mouth, but I care too much about Penn not to say this when I have the balls to do it. Harper is not his, okay? I can't say more than that, but Penn's been sticking around because he is good, and responsible, and my best friend. Not because he should've or had any responsibility to. I outstayed my welcome in his life, even when it was so painfully clear that his heart wanted something I could never give him." She looks up at him and chuckles to herself. "I'm sorry, Scully. I hope it's not too late for you guys."

He gives her a slight nod without looking at me.

"Hey, guys, I have a confession too." Knight steps forward, rubbing the back of his neck. "My dick is not six inches long. It is actually a full seven and a half inches. When flaccid. It's really uncomfortable, and my junk gets hit practically anytime anyone goes for my legs on the field. It's been really hard for me. All puns intended."

Everyone other than Gus bursts out laughing. Gus just keeps on standing and looking like his life is over. And I guess now that the truth about the rigged games is out, it kind of is.

"You forgot to give us a secret, Bauer." Penn folds his arms on his chest.

"That makes the two of us." Gus tilts his chin up.

"Tell you what, you go first, and if it's good enough, we'll strike a deal, and you'll get out of here without a broken nose. That is if Daria gives me permission not to kill you." Penn looks over at me, and I nod.

Gus blows out air. "You want a secret? One that'd save my skin? All right." He looks over at Via, regret in his eyes. She sees it too, and coils into herself, preparing for the blow.

"When I was born, my mama put me on the steps of our local church. The pastor knew her from around the neighborhood, so instead of doing the right thing and handing me over to the police, he gave me back to her. I guess she was too embarrassed not to take me back. He said he and the church would help us, but of course, the fucker never did. Your, er, stepdad, Rhett..." He coughs. Starts walking around in circles. Marx, no wonder we were all so terrible to each other. "He came to see us often. He used to talk about Penn like he was the next Jerry Rice. That's what got me into football in the first place. Said Penn's gonna make it big and buy his entire family mansions, and I wanted it too. I started pursuing Via because I wanted to be close to Penn, but Penn was never close to anyone other than Cam and Kannon. Years passed. We all went our separate ways. And when Penn came to the snake pit months ago, drunk off his ass…" He trails off. "I gave him my best fighter, Vaughn, because I was hoping—praying, maybe—that he'd kill him. I didn't want the competition. I need a scholarship, goddammit. Need out of this shithole before I become the help to the same people I grew up with in middle school."

There's a beat of silence as his words soak into everyone's brains.

"Your turn, Scully." Knight grins beside me, squeezing my shoulder.

Penn turns around to look at me, so everyone else does too. Even though I should be embarrassed because of everything that went down and because practically everyone here knows all of my secrets, I'm surprisingly calm.

"I owe you two truths. One, I'll give you now, Skull Eyes. But the other…" He takes a deep breath. "The other you'll get if you decide to stick around. If Lady ends up with Tramp."

He walks over to me and lifts my chin up with his finger. I stop breathing. Everyone circles us in a backdrop of faces and blurred figures. He's the only thing I see, and maybe it's always been this way. Maybe I needed to look for him when I still could and demand he took all my firsts as if I owed them to him.

"The truth about the holes in my shirts is as follows: My last recollection of Stan, my dad, was when he left us. I was five, and I'd been climbing on the tree in our backyard, trying to create a makeshift tree house. I was fucking obsessed with tree houses. And forts. And sand castles. Looking back, I probably just wanted a real home, something I didn't have. My dad didn't want to spoil us, so he refused to help me build one. Anyway, I ended up falling on my ass, but on the way down, my shirt got caught on a branch, and a huge hole opened right where my heart is. It was a close call, for sure. My mother was already halfway addicted, so she just told me to be more careful next time. My dad's mom, though, went berserk. Ioanna Scully is every shade of insane in the coloring book. The kind of religion that believes in curses and spells. She said I was an unruly boy, and I called her an old hag because that's what my mom called her. Of course, I didn't realize Mom was saying those things behind her back for a reason. At any rate, Ioanna cast a spell on me. She said my heart would be broken until I found the one. That I was going to walk around with holes in my shirts to symbolize what I don't have until I experience true love. But until then, I would be miserable. Naturally, I thought it to be bullshit. But then weird things started happening to me every time I didn't wear the holed shirt. One time, I almost got run over. The other, the money I stole from my mom mysteriously disappeared from my pocket. A dog bit me, my bikes got stolen…so I started cutting holes in all my shirts as a safety measure. I had no choice. I got a lot of mouthfuls from my dad about it, obviously, but it worked."

"What about when you play football?" I ask, mostly oblivious to our audience. I can't believe he shared it with me. With both our schools, actually. Penn has always been so private. It's a struggle to get him to admit what hour it is.

"I always have a holed shirt underneath my jersey."

"And why do you sometimes have big holes and small holes? What does that mean?"

"My holes were the same size for a while. Until shortly before Via came back. Then I started cutting them smaller. That's because…" He tilts his head and smiles at me, but it's a sad smile, one that breaks my heart. "Well, now we're treading into secret number two, and you'll only get this if you're going to stay. So, are you? Going to stay, Daria? Fight or flight?"

Fight. Always fight.

That was what I told him the last time he asked, but there's an ocean between that Daria and the one I am today. And I won't be able to truly explore who I am unless I take a step back. He and Via will never be able to heal while I'm still in the picture.

I take a deep breath, pressing my index to his lips on a smile. "Thank you for sharing this with me."

"Dar…"

I raise myself on my tiptoes and kiss his lips. It's a chaste, nervous kiss, but it tells him what I think he needs to know. That he is forgiven. That I hope he forgives me. And that it is time to move on.

"So? What's happening now?" Gus asks behind us.

Penn closes his eyes and shakes his head, forcing himself to turn around and face Bauer.

"We won the championship. You have your ass to save and a scholarship to start praying for. I call a ceasefire on a few conditions," Penn says with his hand on his hip.

Gus tilts his chin down.

"First things first, from this moment onward, you do not initiate any communication with Daria and Via, dead or fucking alive. I don't care if it's good or bad, you get out of their lives forever."

Via bursts into tears beside us again. I think they're happy tears. I think she's relieved he cares enough to warn Gus off.

"Fine. I won't," Gus growls. "How do I know if everyone else here is going to keep silent?"

Colin steps forward. "We don't let anyone leave without giving us a secret. That way, we all have leverage on each other, and nobody wants to get screwed over."

"That's the dumbest, most brilliant idea I've ever heard." Knight nods. "Unless, of course, my giant dick confession doesn't count."

Vaughn flicks Knight's head and rolls his eyes. Colin and Nelson run off to the chain-link gate, closing it so no one can slip out without giving away a secret.

Adriana, Esme, Blythe, and Via gather around me. Via is the first one to pick up one of the printed pages of my diary and ball it in her fist.

"Let's clean this up in the meantime."

Penn grabs her hand, removing it from the page.

"No," he says. "The snake pit needs to die."

On the drive back to my house, it's just Via and me.

The snake pit is in flames behind us, eighteen gallons of gasoline later. The idea was Penn's, but it was Vaughn who backed him up and cited fire as the best way to burn things to the ground so that it's nearly impossible to rebuild them.

Via taps the steering wheel and looks around her, clearing her throat and trying to figure out what to say. I'm too tired to talk. Sitting there for four hours hearing about other people's admissions—how they killed their neighbor's dogs, made out with their stepdads, cheated on tests, stole valuables from their friends, and so forth—left me even more drained than I previously was. But Gus is off the hook, and so is Penn. Las Juntas won, and All Saints will have to deal with whatever consequences occur. It's just sad that there were so many casualties in the process.

"Wanna grab something to eat?" Via asks me. Being nice to me is new to her and vice versa. I haven't eaten in days, but I can't even entertain the thought.

"No thanks. I'm just tired."

"Yeah, me too."

Silence. More tapping on the steering wheel. I look out the window, and it's pitch-black as we enter El Dorado, the gated community where I live. Lived, anyway. I won't be staying here for longer than the next few hours. My next chapter will begin tomorrow morning, and Daddy will help me settle in for my first week in my new town.

"So what do you think Jaime and Mel are going to do to me?" She chews on her bottom lip, still looking at the road.

I smirk at her worry. "Probably nothing. Melody loves you, and Dad loves her, so your ass is covered."

"She loves you too, you know." She parks in front of the mansion, and I get out before we share a moment. I'm not ready for moments with Via. I just want to survive the next few hours without more hiccups than necessary.

I push aside the fact that Penn's car is already here and try not to think about it. Going into his room to say goodbye will only make things harder for both of us. Once upon a time, we may have had a chance to get our happily ever after, but in this fairy tale turned nightmare, we both did too many awful things for the prince to claim his princess.

We walk into the house, and the minute Via pushes the door open, Melody pushes *her* out of the way, borderline violently, and launches toward me in a suffocating hug.

"Marx, where have you been, Lovebug? I've been calling and calling. I wanted to spend tonight together."

I blink at her differently, taking a step sideways to dodge her hysterical behavior. Kids will be kids, and we all did shitty things. But Melody is an adult. More than that, she's my *mother*—and I'm still not done being mad at her.

"I'm fine," I say.

"Did Via take you somewhere against your will?" Mel twists her head and stares at Sylvia accusingly. Well, well. That's a change of tune. Too little, too late comes to mind, though. None of this makes any difference anymore.

Via turns ghostly white, her eyes widening at me. Technically, that's exactly what she did. But I've met my drama quota for the next three decades, thank you very much.

"No. Everyone was hanging at the pit, and I bummed a ride with her. It's, like, one in the morning. I'm going upstairs to sleep."

With that lukewarm endorsement of Via, I go up the stairs and into my room.

In bed, I stare at the brand-new drywall in front of me and blink away the tears. After the aquarium got shattered, they replaced it with a sturdy, ugly thing to replace the beautiful, fragile one. The story of my life, I guess. I am finally digesting everything that's happened to me in the past six months, and the overwhelming notion of loneliness grips my body.

I'm moving away from my family. My parents. From Bailey. I'm turning my back on Vaughn and on Knight without saying goodbye because I know they won't let me go. They'll promise to protect me and fight my battles at school, and a part of me still wants that to happen.

But I can't.

I have to make it on my own.

The door creaks open, and I close my eyes and smile. He closes the door behind him and leans against it—things I hear rather than see—and my heart swells in my chest.

"My dad's gonna kill you if he finds out," I whisper.

"Still worth it," he retorts, taking my taunt as permission to saunter deeper into my room. My bed dips, and when his body presses against mine, I'm shocked to find out he is naked except for his briefs. My eyes snap open and I suck in a breath.

"Whoa," I say. My hands shoot out to trace his collarbone, chest, washboard abs, and his V without even meaning to. Then they trail his bulging triceps, his tennis-balls of biceps, and all the delicious veins wrapped around them. Every inch of bronzed skin. "Escalation, Scully."

"Skull Eyes." His lips are already locked on mine when he speaks, and he is moving smoothly, thrusting his briefs against my clothed groin, even though I'm still in my jeans. "It's done. So much dirt has been spilled tonight, yours is a drop in an ocean of sins. Don't get on that plane tomorrow. Don't fucking do this to us."

Rather than answer him with my words, I answer him by thrusting my groin back against his erection. He moans and unbuttons my jeans, yanking them along with my panties down my legs and balling the fabrics, throwing them over his shoulder. He then spreads my thighs and dips two fingers into me, curling them and taking them out, sucking on them hungrily.

"I've loved you in secret, and I've loved you openly in front of both our worlds, and if you think I'll stop loving you if you put an ocean between us, you're dead wrong."

I cry out and arch my back when his fingers reenter my body, chasing his touch as he fingers me mercilessly. My legs quiver around his arm, and I'm about to come when he stops and lowers himself down, throwing my legs over his broad shoulders. He sweeps his tongue up and down the length of my entrance, flicking against my clit every time he does.

"Oh, Penn. Marx, Penn."

"Marx." He laughs into me, thrusting his tongue deeper, penetrating me before licking me faster. "My favorite fucking word."

He licks between my legs until no more air is left in my lungs. The desire is so sharp, the pleasure so profound, I stop breathing and brace myself for the storm that is the brewing orgasm inside me. When it finally crashes down on me, greater than any physical feeling I've ever experienced, he rises on his forearms and enters me in one go, filling me to the brim. I arch farther, clutching his back. He shuts up my moans with a dirty kiss that tastes and smells like me.

"Your dad killing me might be inevitable, but there's no need to make it happen prematurely."

I laugh as he starts moving inside me without a condom or a care in the world. I'm on the pill, but he doesn't know that. I'm having crazy thoughts. Like maybe he is doing this on purpose. Like maybe he wants to chain me down to this place. Like maybe I should stay. And it makes my heart laugh through the tears because it's too late.

We move seductively, kissing and biting and breathing each

other in. I can taste the goodbye on my tongue, and it's bittersweet. Wonderfully tragic.

I caress his face, his jaw, his lips. *I will miss you.*

I study every inch of his beautiful face. *I will never forget you.*

His hands roam and mine caress. *This was so much more than first love. It was first hate too.*

And when he empties inside me, I don't even mention what we did was irresponsible and wrong. I know he is doing it to keep me in his messed-up, desperate way. So I just kiss him long and deep and hard.

"I'm staying the night," he tells me, hugging me close to his chest. Our hearts are beating in unison. I squeeze his hands under mine.

"My dad really is going to kill you." I chuckle, bumping my shoulder into his. "Come on. I'll see you in the morning."

"Promise?" he asks.

"Promise," I lie.

CHAPTER TWENTY-SIX
PENN

I breathe your name
Hoping to fill my lungs
With more than just air.

The ER doctor unwraps my hand from all the ice packs and observes the red-blue thing that's swollen to five times its usual fucking size.

"How'd it happen?" The middle-aged, white-haired man scrunches his nose. *I know, asshole. It looks nasty, but you ain't a sight for sore eyes, either.*

Via flinches at the question because she already knows the answer.

How did it happen? Let's see. This morning, I woke up with my dick still smelling like the girl I love. Instead of going to the bathroom to brush my teeth and take a piss, I launched straight into her room to wake her up with an orgasm and my face between her legs, only to find out she wasn't there anymore.

The stack of suitcases by her door was gone, and so was the girl herself. The only things she left behind were her new and ugly drywall, the sea glass necklace I gave her, and a rusty, tin heart turned human, which she manages to somehow, against all the odds, break a thousand fucking times, over and over again, to a point where I'm still not sure how it is beating.

"He was… He got angry. Lost his cool and punched a wall."

"A concrete wall?" the doctor asks.

Is he a *wallanitarian* or something? Why does he give a fuck about the *wall?*

Via nods. I still hate her, but no one else was in the house to drive me to the ER. I sure as hell couldn't drive myself with the state of my hand, and now it's pretty clear that I've broken a few fingers by the way they hang off my hand. Perfect timing. A day after the last game of the season.

The doctor is talking, explaining to me what happens next. I sit on the white bed in the white room in a hospital that looks more like a fancy hotel and don't even pretend to listen. My thoughts drift to the house I'm going back to. A house that is going to feel so empty without her.

Twelve hours later, we're discharged, and my hand looks like it's gloved and ready for boxing. When we pull in front of the Followhills' mansion, I don't want to go inside. But I don't want to be that pussy-ass, broken guy who can't deal with the fact his girl just doesn't want him anymore.

The minute we get in, Melody runs toward us. Her face looks like what my wrapped hand did a few hours ago. Red and swollen.

"Where've you been?" She charges at both of us. She's obviously back from the airport, which means it's done.

Good, Skull Eyes. Fucking perfect. Watch me rip out all my shirts and walk around shirtless for the remainder of my life.

I'm so tired of the lies and the secrets that I straight-up walk past her and open the fridge, taking out a pitcher of iced tea with my healthy hand.

"When I found out your daughter left, even though she promised me she wouldn't, I got a little creative as far as how anger management goes. In other news, you probably need some work done on your garage wall."

"Penn." She gallops toward me, shaking her head. Via is retreating to her room, still staring at us, wide-eyed. She knows better than to assume I'll fess up to any emotion while she's around. That shit between us will be much harder to fix than the wall.

As soon as Via's not around, Mel hugs me. I let her, solely because she is partly Daria in DNA and I'm a glutton for punishment. I can still smell her daughter on her clothes, which doesn't make any sense. Knowing Daria, she didn't hug her mother goodbye today.

"Where is she, Mel?"

She shakes her head in the crook of her neck.

"She doesn't want anyone to know. I'm sorry. She wouldn't even let me come with her to help her settle in."

"But she let Jaime?" I ask.

She is nodding now.

"Did you get your closure?" I want her to say no. I want her to tell me that I'm not the only one here feeling like every breath is a fucking nail jammed straight into my lungs. If this is what love feels like, it's complete bullshit. I want my money back because Shakespeare was right all along. True love truly sucks ass.

"No." She bursts into tears. "She barely even told me goodbye. Did you?"

"Not by a fucking long shot."

The next few weeks are pure torture. The days crawl, time slithers on the walls of a house that's not empty but not alive either. Somehow, all those days add up to a month without Daria. A month in which Jaime comes back, acts like nothing is wrong, and every time he gets a call and it's from her, he closes the door to his bedroom behind him while shooting me a don't-even-think-about-it look.

Regretfully, I'm starting to fucking lose it. After caving in to modern society, I open Instagram and Twitter accounts only to find out that Daria is officially not active on any of them. She hasn't deleted her Instagram, but she doesn't post there anymore, so the old pictures of her with her cheer team and friends keep me going. I stare at them for hours every day as I do constructive, emotionally healthy things, like figuring out what time zone she is in by making a sheet with all the hours she calls Jaime and Mel.

Yes. About a month after she went away, Daria caved in and started speaking to Mel too. Bailey always talks as though she's been keeping in touch with her too, so I guess it's just the Scullys Daria wants out of her life, and I can't even fucking blame her. We stormed into her life and ruined it completely in less than six months. If there were an Olympic medal event for being the biggest cunts, Via and I would have been the pride of this nation.

If my calculations are correct, Daria is still somewhere in the United States. She calls very early in the mornings or in the early evenings, which gives me East Coast vibes, but it might be Midwest too. Heck, maybe she just likes to get up super fucking early and she is around the block. No one knows. No one will tell me. And I'd be climbing the fucking walls if I hadn't fractured four of the five fingers on my left hand.

One evening, Jaime sits me down and tells me that we're going to Notre Dame to check out the facilities, flirt, and say yes. He booked us both first-class tickets and all. I guess that means he is over the fact I had my tongue and dick in his daughter's privates. Ain't he a fucking champ.

"I don't want any illicit behavior while we're on campus. I catch you smoking, drinking, or fucking—simultaneously or individual-ly—I swear you'll be finding a different sponsor to subsidize your next four years because it's not going to be me." He waves his finger in my face.

I push the brochures across the coffee table and nod.

"Clear, sir."

"Jesus." He flings himself back on the couch, throwing an arm over his face. "You're about as lively as a puppy that's been run over by every truck in the state. At least try to pretend that you're here."

"I'm here, sir."

"But you're not present."

What do I say to that? This bitch is Hare Krishna now?

"And stop calling me 'sir.' You're like a son to me."

"I wish you'd stop saying that, sir, since I feel very strongly about your daughter and not in a sisterly way."

He exhales, levels up, and slaps the coffee table to grab my attention. I'm still the same lax, drooped-over-the-couch motherfucker I was a second ago. Life just seems to have an aftertaste of nothing when Daria is not around, and whoever said time heals was given LSD or something. Because it wasn't time that healed them. The more time that passes, the more I want to rip my own fucking skin from my body and let my heart pack a suitcase and go looking for her. It doesn't escape me that I was crushed about Via but never had the balls to actually go and find her. With Daria, it's a different story. The Followhills can beg all they want. Come graduation, I'm packing my bag, breaking the piggy bank, and going to look for her.

"Penn," he warns.

I throw an actual pen—the one I've been using the past ten minutes to write all the shit about our bullshit trip down—and stand. "Just give me her number. I won't call. I'll text."

"You're just making it harder. If you truly have feelings for her, you will let her have her way and not contact her, not go against her wishes while she's trying to heal."

"Like you did with Mel, right?" I chuckle bitterly, shaking my head. I make a beeline to my room, but he stands and raises his voice to me. For the first time ever.

"Penn Scully."

I turn around, slow-clapping him. "Whoa. Escalation. You just used my full name. Not all of it, of course. You don't know my middle name. You're not my *real* dad, after all."

I'm just being a double douche with a side of jerk. I don't have a middle name. My mother never fucking bothered. And the truth is, even if I had one, my biological dad wouldn't know it. If he knows the color of my eyes, then I'm the pope.

"Stop feeling so goddamn sorry for yourself, Penn. She's the one who has to handle life away from her house, her parents, everything she knows, and start from scratch." Jaime's voice booms.

"How *is* she doing?" I throw the question I've been asking for an entire month at him once again. "And please spare me the bullshit answer of 'she's handling it.' Daria doesn't handle things. She either slays or she crumples. She has no middle ground, and we both know it."

And fuck, did I love it when she slayed and played with me. She was a sweet torture I'd go through all over again, even knowing how it's going to end. She doesn't want me. She made it perfectly clear.

"She's dealing with it." Jaime grins devilishly, sticking it to me, and his eyes are mad, sparkling bright blue. Like Daria's when she's in her element. "Now, are you going to get your head out of your ass and soldier through this like a man, or are you going to fall apart like a boy?"

"Only if you do something for me."

"I think I've done quite enough for you, boy." He throws his head back and laughs. But I'm dead serious. When he sees that, he stops laughing and rolls his eyes. Again—like Daria. It's only now when I look for stuff to remind me of her that I'm beginning to see how alike she is to her parents. How can she possibly think she is an awful person when she is made of two people who took in totally vindictive, awful teenage strays when no one else would?

"You don't want me to see her? Talk to her? Know where she is? Fine. But I want you to give her this." I grab my backpack and take out a leather journal, identical to the one Daria had. It wasn't by coincidence that we have the same journal. Melody gave it to Via the day she gave Daria hers, four and a half years ago. I think—though I'll never ask to confirm—she wanted both girls to reach the same realization and try to bridge shit together. Much good it did Melody. Via bailed, and Daria went off the freaking rails. I don't know why I kept the untouched journal. It just seemed like a waste to throw away something that seemed expensive, being leather bound and all. I started writing in it only four years later, the night my mother died and I saw Daria for the first time in years.

Writing so I could remember.

Writing so I could let go and forget.

"What is this?" Jaime frowns at the journal. I think he thinks it's the original one Daria had. But that shit burned to the ground with the snake pit.

"Some stuff I wrote for her. Don't read it."

"You know I will." He laughs.

"Whatever, asshole," I groan. "So will you?"

"Will I what?"

"Send it to her!" I roar. He is playing with me, and I fucking hate it.

Jaime looks up at the ceiling and pretends to think about it. "If you start acting like a human being and not like a zombie, maybe."

We shake on it, and for the first time since I've met him, my shake is harder than his.

CHAPTER TWENTY-SEVEN
DARIA

How sweet must it be
To look into your eyes again and see
If I'm killing you like you're ruining me.

My apartment is beautiful.

Off-campus, it is new, large, and spacious. When I first came here with Dad, it looked pretty bland, but then Melody sent out an interior designer, Tiffanie, and things kind of picked up. I grew to like the place, even if it's completely new to me.

It's been three months since I came here. Two since Dad came for a visit to give me Penn's journal personally. I am not one for self-control. I immediately read the whole thing, then did it again, and again, and again.

A million times, I wanted to pick up the phone, call him, and tell him to come to me.

A trillion times, I simply wanted to purchase a ticket and go back to Todos Santos to his still-open arms.

But every single time, I slammed that idea, knowing that now was not the time for us to be together and that we needed to stay focused. I'm attending high school here, and Melody or Dad flies out here once every two weeks to spend the weekend with me. I'm slowly learning to get used to calling Mel Mom again, but baby steps.

I don't feel particularly alone here. It's a college town, and all my neighbors are twenty-one or below. There are Rich and Welcott, and Beth and Fiona, who I seem to be getting along with really well. Beth and Fiona have Mel on speed dial and vice versa. They get their grocery shopping for free, and in exchange for that, they promised to snitch me out if I throw a party or bring a boy to the apartment. As if. Like I ever would.

Melody says things are getting better at home, and I'm not surprised. Someone needed to step back and let us all heal, and that someone had to be me. I'm not bitter to be making this sacrifice. I want Penn to have a strong relationship with his sister. Knight, Vaughn, and Luna text my new cell phone almost every day. So far Knight's reported that Vaughn dumped Esme after her confession, Blythe somehow managed to kick her off the cheer team and became captain, and Colin made sure his father went to visit Camilo at the hospital, and they are going to pay for his first year of college. Vaughn said Gus got thrown off the football team for using steroids trying to get bigger and more desirable for scouts and decided to drop out of school. No one knows where he is, and quite frankly, no one really cares. Via has parted ways with the cheer squad after everything that went down, and apparently, she is hanging out with the freaks and geeks of senior year. It made me laugh, and I could hardly even believe it. Luna, who is not big on gossip, texts me that Bailey misses me and talks about me all the time. She sends me fun facts about where I live to try to get me more amped up about the place.

Luna: Word is you have the best popcorn in the States. Make sure to get white popcorn and pop it in the Whirley Pop I'm shipping you.

Luna: Garfield the cat lives there. Give him a squeeze from me.

Luna: Sent you two tickets to the circus via snail mail. GO! It's supposed to be awesome.

Luna: Also sent you a coupon for that breaded pork tenderloin place you have to try. Try it and let me know, okay?

Bitch is vegetarian and knows I'd die before using coupons (I think she is the only person in Todos Santos who even knows what they are), but I appreciate the effort, so I always text her back. I think I'm finally getting over the fact she is magic and I'm real, but maybe being real is no less magical.

I put on my coat, scarf, and beanie and take the keys from the ugly bowl by the door. I got it in a souvenir store. It's shaped like a golden football helmet. I walk out into the crisp winter day, watching my boots crush semi-dirty snow that's wilting on the sidewalks. The sky is gray, the trees are white, and the campus is quietly getting back to its post-Christmas routine. I know I'm not thinking any of this through, and that I should turn around before I see them. *If* I even see them. But I can't help myself. Wanting to see Penn burns in me so bad, I can't even feel the cold that's kept me tucked in my apartment for much of the past few weeks. I'm shivering with adrenaline, and my stomach churns as I swallow down my nerves.

I stand behind the statue of Jesus in front of the campus and watch Penn and Dad on the steps of the beautiful building.

Penn is taller than Dad. I don't think I've ever noticed that. Broader too. And my dad is a big guy. They look like they're arguing. Penn shakes his head, pacing back and forth. He is saying no, but I'm not sure what to. My father is trying to reason with him—they are almost playing a slow-motion catch—but Penn refuses to relent and descends the stairs fast.

I want to run to him and ask him if everything is okay, but I don't have the guts.

I want to follow him and see if he breaks down and if he needs me, but I'm too scared.

Instead, I take out my phone and text Dad.

Is Penn okay?

He is nowhere in sight now, and I'm getting worried. Edgy. I hate this.

Dad: You can go to him and see for yourself.

I can, but I won't.

Because I know that no matter how hard it is right now, we were toxic while we were together.

Instead, I turn around and walk back home. Clutching my coat tight, I wrap it more firmly around my chest so the wind won't slip in.

After all, I have a hole in my shirt the size of Penn's heart.

The day after, I sit on my cold patio and read Penn's journal. The pages are wrinkled and yellow, and the spine is almost completely ruined. I need duplicates before I destroy this one. But I'm not ready to replace the real thing with a copy. I flip through the pages, noting the change in his attitude and feelings from his first entry, right after the fight with Vaughn at the snake pit, to the last entries when we were both ripped apart by our feelings. I reread my favorite poem from him.

You're tearing confessions from my mouth
Reactions from my flesh
Fights from my fists
Blood from my heart
With your eyes alone.
Sometimes I want to break the wall I built
between us
Let you in
And watch you destroy me.

I smile at his bravery. Penn never much cared about getting hurt. Even when he was the Tin Man, even when his heart was just a faint beat, merely surviving and not doing much else, he always gave me a run for my money. It is stupid, if not completely awful, that I'm too scared to love him.

Too terrified to get hurt.

More than anything, I'm too unsure of myself to know I wouldn't screw it up.

I hear low growls from the balcony and tip my head forward, peeking down. I live on the main street right in front of quaint, super-pastoral shops. I watch as Penn and Dad come out of a Starbucks. They look like they're fighting.

Only this time, I can hear them. Unlike the old Daria, I stop and think if I should. If they'd want me to. I stand and—I don't know with what strength—begin to make my way back into my living room when I hear that the conversation is about me.

"You're going to throw away everything, Penn? Really? We had a deal. You said if I gave her the journal, you'd pretend to still be in the game for this. Still make an effort in this thing called life. Well, she got the journal, all right? Move the hell on. Apply yourself and fulfill your part of the deal."

"I'm not enrolling. I want to go find her," Penn says dryly. "And we can do it the hard, roundabout, not-gonna-talk-to-each-other-again way, or my way, in which you leave me the fuck alone. I said thank you. A thousand times. I'm not going to take a fucking schol-arship and let this thing go away. It's not going away. Trust me."

My heart is in my throat. Penn is about to give up his scholar-ship to try to find me? That's crazy talk. I pace on my balcony, just a few feet away from them, though they can't see me from this sharp angle, and rub my face with my hands.

What to do? What to say?

"You will ruin your life for a girl who doesn't want you anymore," Dad says, and it's like a shot in the back for me. Because I want him.

I want Penn more than I want my next breath. I just don't know if I'm good enough for him, and I can't risk hurting him one more time. But it seems as if he's already hurting just as much as I am.

Penn chuckles darkly. "Well, then. The only difference between you and me is that Melody said yes and Daria is saying no. But you, Jaime, you did the same."

———

I ask Melody to visit me that same weekend. She does in a heartbeat, not even waiting for Friday. By Thursday, when I get back from school, I find her in my kitchen, making my favorite Italian chicken pot pie, designer bags spilling clothes on the dining table. She put music on her phone, and it's the favorite song "Maniac" from *Flashdance*. We used to dance to it like two loons when I was a kid.

When she sees me entering the room, she stops everything, straightens her spine, and wipes the last of the tomato sauce from her fingers onto her apron. I stand on the kitchen threshold, and for the first time in years, I see her for who she is.

A mother trying desperately to reconnect with her daughter but doesn't know how to because they've both made so many mistakes.

I plaster my forehead to the doorframe, taking a deep breath.

"What's wrong, Lovebug? Is everything okay?"

No. It's not. I've hurt her so much over the years, not communicating the frustration, fear, and jealousy I felt, and now we are like two strangers playing house. I walk into the kitchen and stand in front of her, dropping my backpack to the floor, just like I did that day in the studio when Via walked in and stole my thunder.

This time, Melody is not looking for anyone else.

She *sees* me.

"Our parents mold us into shapes," I start, trailing the granite counter with my fingers. "You, Melody, lost interest in me halfway through and moved on to another project. To a piece of art with the potential to be flawless. Her name was Via, and even though I've always been jealous of people for various things, my jealousy toward Sylvia Scully consumed me. Want to know why, Mel? You looked at her like I wished you'd look at me. Like she was already a fully formed, perfect piece of work, while I was barely even a canvas stretched on a wooden frame. I didn't see the whole picture. I didn't know where her fancy clothes came from. I didn't know why you let her get away with it on the days she *didn't* have proper clothing on while you berated all of us for less. I didn't know why you bought her favorite energy bars for her, or why you took her for a week in London, or why it was so important to you that she be there for every class."

Tears appear in her eyes, and they are like a mirror to what's going on inside her head. I see now, with a clarity I've never had before, the Melody Followhill that I wished to meet my entire childhood. The one who is not only an accomplished ballerina, an amazing teacher, and the talk of the town, but a simple girl—maybe even like me—struggling to do the right thing by her family.

"When Via disappeared and I knew it was my fault, I didn't even think I deserved your love anymore. You gave it anyway, though sparsely. We grew apart, further and further, maybe a couple of inches each year, until the first semester of senior year. I felt like you were doing things to purposely hurt me. To taunt me about how bad I was."

Melody shakes her head, pressing her fingertips to her mouth. "Never. I was frustrated and hurt and didn't know how to reach out to you. I kept waiting for you to snap out of it. One minute, I was trying to talk to you, being all submissive and fearful of my own daughter, and the next, I'd get angry and frustrated with you, losing my cool. At some point, when I recognized I had become so bad at it, I simply let you be. And when that happened, I watched your relationship with your father, and as much as I love my husband with my entire heart, I finally realized what it felt like to be you. Because not only was I jealous, Lovebug, I was absolutely *livid*.

"I never loved Via more than you. You were always my strongest, most natural love. But Sylvia needed help. She was poor, and abused, and neglected, and there was nothing I could do because I knew if I stepped in, things could get a lot worse for her. All I could do was help her by buying her gear, providing her with meals and support, and trying to enroll her in the Royal Ballet Academy. I cut her slack not because I was enchanted with her antics but because someone needed to. I took Penn and Via in without consulting you girls, and that was my biggest mistake yet. I was so focused on trying to atone for letting Via down when she disappeared, I hardly noticed I was stomping all over my own daughter. I'm so sorry you walked around feeling unworthy because of me. It's always been so hard for me to express my feelings, and I think this is something you inherited from me. I taught you how to act tough, assuming that you are. You became so good at the game, I bought it."

I laugh through my own tears, shaking my head and wiping them. "You really wanted me to stop trying to be a ballerina." I sigh.

"*Only* because I didn't want you to feel the same pressure I had when I was a preteen. You were always a natural."

"Liar." I snort, rolling my eyes, which only prompts more tears to fall.

She shakes her head and laughs, the sound bursting from her chest in relief. "Oh Marx, are you kidding me? You were always so amazing. I watched as you became more and more insecure as time passed, and I had no idea it was about me or Via. I thought you were just tired and bored."

"Tired and bored!" I screech. "Mom, I tried so freaking hard!"

We stop laughing. And crying. And breathing. Mel's eyes widen, and we both look at each other with amusement laced with shock. And gratitude. So much gratitude.

"You called me Mom."

"I did." I choke on the words. "I did. You are. You are my mom."

We meet halfway for a hug that squeezes out all the toxic hatred, frustration, misunderstandings, and miscommunication. The more time I spend in my mother's arms, the deeper I can breathe. We stand like this in the kitchen for twenty or maybe thirty minutes. Until my legs and arms hurt from standing like this, hugging in a weird position for a long time.

"Mom?" I'm the first one to speak.

"Yes, Lovebug?" I can hear the mirth in her voice, and it makes my heart sing.

"I think your chicken pot pie is burned."

CHAPTER TWENTY-EIGHT
PENN

Love is a battlefield.
And I think I fucking died.
(last entry)

GRADUATION DAY

The red gown and matching graduation cap make us look like a menstrual cycle. I shit you not, this thing is brutal. I don't know who thought of the idea to match our gowns to our football gear, but whoever they were, they need to lay off the crystal meth.

Kannon and Camilo trudge behind me in the long line on the stairway leading to the stage as our principal reads out our names.

"At least he shaved." Cam laughs, elbowing Kannon and jerking his chin toward me. His leg is healing, and though he still has a faint limp, he is surprisingly cool about it. I say surprisingly, but really, if there's one thing I learned this year, it's that you rise up to the circumstances when they are presented to you. We are so much stronger than we think we are. But sometimes, we go through decades without having a reason to be tested. The thing about life is, it always hits us. No one leads a charmed life. Even the blond, gorgeous, picture-perfect, popular rich girl harbors secrets. Even the football captain. Even the rich mother of two who married her hot millionaire ex-student. The ballet prodigy. Everyone's got a story, and we all have chapters we'd rather not read aloud.

"You look good, Penn." Camilo slaps my shoulder.

"I don't swing that way, Cam. Stop talking," I grunt.

"Are Melody and Jaime here?" Kannon asks, snickering some more. What's with those idiots? They act like it's the first time they've met me and I'm goddamn Taylor Swift. I adjust my stupid cap and let out a breath.

"Yeah, yeah. Bailey and Via too."

"Where are they?" Kannon asks.

"Somewhere in the crowd." Hundreds of seats are in front of the stage in our football stadium—red plastic ones, of course—but I never bothered to check because Mel texted me earlier telling me that they're going to grab a place in the back so we can slip out when it's all over for dinner. The last thing I want is to go on a family dinner, but I promised to play nice with Via, and so far, I've succeeded.

"You haven't even checked? That's cold." Camilo pretends to shudder, rubbing at his arms.

I turn around toward them sharply. "What's with you assholes? If this is about Via or Bailey, no, you can't hit on either of them. Bailey's not even fifteen, you goddamn pervs."

Kannon bursts into laughter that makes the girl behind him jam an elbow into his ribs while Camilo shakes his head on a smile, and says, "Just look for them in the crowd, you basic piece of shit."

Reluctantly, my eyes swipe over the rows of seats. The principal calls the girl two people away from me. I don't have time for this bullshit.

"Left, bro. Look left." Kannon is losing patience.

My eyes dart to the last row on the left side, and then a sharp sound of glass shatters in my ears and it's probably my heart.

Daria is there, sandwiched between Melody and Jaime. She is wearing a purple dress that makes her look like some kind of...I don't know, fairy or some shit. So pretty I can't blink because I'm afraid she's not even real. She is staring right back at me, throwing me a bone. A timid, unsure smile. I want my mouth to break into a shit-eating grin, but my brain has officially disconnected from the rest of my body and I can't function.

Function, Penn. Function. Don't be that creep. Smile back.

She stands because she can, because she is in the last row, because this, I understand now, was planned, and she is holding a sign in her hand. A generic brown piece of cardboard with one word written on it in black Sharpie.

Talk?

I nod, feeling the smile finally spreading across my face, letting loose.

Yes. Fuck. Yes.

"Penn Scully," Principal Howard yells for what seems to be the millionth time by the impatience in her voice. How long have I been standing here, ogling Daria?

"Penn Scully? One last chance to take your diploma. You'll need it if you want to attend Notre Dame." She sniffs, pushing her glasses up her nose. I stumble my way across the stage as people erupt in claps and whistles. My eyes are still on Daria. My eyes are always on Daria. Notre Dame, which I reluctantly agreed to after Jaime basically yelled at me that his daughter and I ain't happening, might have to take the back seat again.

I'll go wherever Daria goes. Even if it's straight to hell.

I take my diploma, mumble my thank you, hug the principal, and dart off the stage toward them. Technically, I need to go back to my seat like the rest of the students to throw my hat in the air. But technically, I've also been alive this last semester although anyone who knows me also knows it not to be true.

I run across the narrow row between the seats, knowing all eyes are on me, even though I don't have the greenest clue how she is going to respond when I stand in front of her.

She is still standing. Mel is in my way to her, and she doesn't make a move to stand or anything. So I just stand there, watching Daria watching me, trying not to notice the way everyone around us is grinning. I'm out of breath even though my cardio is on point.

"You're here." Evidently, I am still intellectually subpar even in comparison to wildlife when she's around.

She giggles into her palm, looking down at her feet. I can feel in the air that she has changed. I can feel in my gut that so have I. My eyes roam her face and body, trying to detect how else she is different. If she has a tan or a new tattoo or haircut or another fucking guy attached to her by the arm. But she just seems like good ole Daria.

"I'm here," she says.

"Thank you."

"I wouldn't have missed it for the world. You know that, right?"

No, I don't, and I'm trying to tell myself not to get my hopes up because they are slamming their little fists against the door of my brain's basement, wanting to gush out. She's just here to support me. Via's ceremony is next week, and maybe she wants to be there for the All Saints event too. But then why would I see her here, as a surprise, and not at home, where we'd just left a couple of hours ago?

She finally wants to talk. I have so much to say to her, I want to write it down in my phone so I don't forget the big stuff. But we have this stupid restaurant thing to go to. Food is for pussies. There's no way I can stomach anything right now that's not Daria's pussy juices. But I highly doubt her parents want to know that.

I turn to Melody and Jaime.

"Any chance we can have a rain check on that graduation dinner?"

"Not a chance in hell," Jaime replies dryly, his eyes still on his phone screen as he composes an email, his long legs crossed. His cigar pants ride up, revealing funny, colorful socks.

"Fuck," I say.

"Language," Mel singsongs, flipping through the program she got at the gate but not really reading it.

I turn back to Daria and take her hand even though Mel is between us. Daria tilts her head to the stage, her eyes never leaving my face.

"You better get back over there so you can throw your hat."

Last time we spoke to each other, she promised not to leave, but she did. I'm not taking any chances. She might as well file a restraining order because I'm not letting her out of my sight. I grin and tug her to me with Mel, Jaime, Via, and Bailey still around us. I squeeze her in a hug.

"Keep your embrace PG-13," Jaime coughs into his fist, and we both laugh.

The last thing I tell her before she pulls away is the truest thing I've ever said in my life.

"I missed you."

———————

Dinner is surreal.

Everyone exists like nothing happened, which can't be further from the truth. I high-key channel my inner Ted Bundy and stare at Daria the entire time and ponder the probability of Mel, Jaime, Bailey, and Via disappearing into thin air without notice. Shit's happened before. Mainly in paranormal movies, but still.

I watch the way Daria cuts her steak into pieces as though she invented utensils. Admire the way she steals glances at me to see if I'm still looking (I'm *always* looking), and how she pats the corners of her mouth with a napkin.

I watch everything. I eat nothing. They discuss the weather and town gossip when I ask Daria where she's been.

"Where do you live?" I'm aware of the crackling in my voice, but I left my pride at the door.

She looks up at me from her plate and smiles but doesn't say anything. I don't ask again.

The Followhills pay the check and pour out back to the street, stopping in front of Jaime's Tesla. I came here with the Prius because I had to get to school before them. I catch Daria's cardigan sleeve and clear my throat.

"Need a ride?"

Everyone goes silent for a moment. Daria throws a look at her parents, asking a question, and Jaime arches an eyebrow.

"Rephrase, kiddo."

"I apologize. Sir. Miss Followhill, will you do me the honor of getting into my cart? I have a hella big sword…"

Jaime chucks my head and laughs. He pushes an uncertain Daria toward me.

"Go. Talk. Fight. Blame your parents for everything. But when you're back home, I don't want any drama under my roof."

And just like that, she's in my car. As I throw it into drive, it occurs to me that she hasn't been here before. I never took her places. I never made an effort, period. I took the sea glass necklace, then her virginity, then taunted her about both before completely dumping her upon Via's request. Throughout, she thought I was messing around with Adriana. But I've never messed with Addy. By the time I noticed she was a woman, Rhett did too, and did something about it.

Rhett. That's a conversation starter.

"Rhett's dead," I say evenly as she chokes on her own saliva, coughing. I don't twist to look at her as I pat her back. I know exactly where I'm driving. Far away from here and to the only place I need to fix in her memory so she'll remember why we should still be together.

"What happened?"

"Overdose."

"That's sad."

"No, it's not." He was a rapist abuser who had beaten my entire family to a pulp, then proceeded to impregnate a young teenager.

Daria sniffs. "You're right. It's not. How'd you find out?"

"About three months ago, he started calling. Slurring about getting a retroactive payment for all the time I lived with him. He was trying to bleed your parents for money or something. Wanted to cut a deal with Jaime where they split my earnings if I made it to the NFL. By the time Jaime sent his lawyers to threaten Rhett, he didn't pick up the phone or answer the letters. So we went in person. His body stunk, but I guess you could say that about him even when he was alive."

I can't believe she is smiling at my stupid words, and I can't believe I'm saying them. I park outside Castle Hill Park and kill the engine. I round the car and open her door, drawing her outside, then we both walk in silence. Passing the bench where Adriana and I sat the day she watched us from across the park, I lead her deep into the woods. We don't stop or talk until we get to the broken tree trunk that's still there. To where we had sex the first time.

I lean against the trunk and cross my arms over my chest.

"You promised," I say quietly. Sometime between the graduation ceremony and entering the restaurant, I took off the blood gown, and now she can clearly see my black shirt, and the hole in it, and how not okay I am.

She nods, her hand diving into her hair as she massages the back of her skull.

"I know. I'm sorry. I'm so sorry."

She doesn't give me an excuse, which is a good start, but I don't know what the fuck that means.

"If you want to hear the second part of my secret, you have to promise me something."

"And what is that?"

"Yourself," I say quietly. "You were right, that day you told me you were trying to be mine but I never offered you myself. But now I am. And if you want my everything, you need to give me something. Let's start with a promise. A real one, this time."

She eyes me warily, and I consider the possibility that when she told me she wanted to talk, she meant for some closure or bullshit. I hold my breath in my lungs.

"I promise" comes the weakest, faintest voice I've ever heard. "I promise I am strong and good enough for you, and I want the rest of your secret. I want all your secrets. This past semester was horrible without you. How did I ever even live without you in my life? Bizarre." She rolls her eyes.

I look up and almost fall to my knees with joy.

This.

I take out the sea glass necklace I've been keeping for her, just in case, and throw it between us. She catches it.

"Do you want me to put my necklace on?" She cocks her brow.

Pushing off the trunk, I walk toward her, take the necklace from her palm, and secure it back on her neck.

"Where did we leave things with my secret?"

"First, I want you to tell me you haven't slept with anyone else since I've been gone." She turns her head around to face me, her body still tilted toward the trunk.

"I haven't even held another's hand. Even when I jacked off—it was to you. Hell, even my morning woods belonged to you."

She laughs, shaking her head. I missed her voice. Her laughter. *Her.*

"Thank you. Well, we left things off with your grandmother cursing you when you tore your shirt. What was the curse about again?"

"Eh." I take a moment to close my eyes and savor the scent of her hair. "So my grandmother is pissed, and she wants me to behave. She tells me that the only way to remove this spell, curse, whatever the hell it is, is for me to fall in love. That's some *Beauty and the Beast* bullshit, and I don't buy into it, but I'm thinking, even at five, that that's okay. I can fall in love a thousand times in an hour. Maybe not at five, but at thirteen or fourteen, sure. So of course, she puts a loophole."

I snort when I think about the first time I met Daria up close, after seeing her in and out of her ballet class for years.

"What's the loophole?" She turns around and holds my shoulders. *Escalation.*

I brush my thumb along her cheek, smiling.

"She said only true love would get rid of the curse. And it will have to be returned. And real. And for life. Most of all, she said it couldn't be just any girl. It needed to be a girl who can become a Scully, like us. But I was five, and dumb, and on pain meds, so what I heard was *Skull Eyes.* So I laughed and laughed and fucking laughed some more until she hit me with a broomstick. But wanna know what the weird thing is?"

Daria nods.

"When I saw you all broken and upset and finally mustered up the courage to talk to you, there really were skulls in your eyes. Like white marbles, bang, in the middle of your pupils."

Daria takes my hand and presses her lips to my palm. My heart quickens.

"Every time you called me that, you really called me the love of your life?" she asks quietly.

I smile.

"Now she is following. Where have you been this semester, *Skull Eyes?*"

"Waiting for you." It's her turn to grin. "Where I always knew you'd follow. In South Bend, Indiana. Notre Dame."

EPILOGUE
PENN/DARIA

PENN, NOTRE DAME, FRESHMAN YEAR

"Oh my Marx, my feet have blisters the size of your head, Penn. What's up?" Daria complains. In my defense, no one told her to wear those red-soled heels for our lengthy stroll. In her defense, this shit is pretty goddamn long. I can't see the end of it, and I'm pretty sure I should've packed water, Advil, and maybe even food for the road.

"Just a little bit more, baby."

She soldiers through it without questioning me or my motives. I said I preferred if she didn't ask any questions, and she trusts me. Why she does is beyond me, but she does. I hit the fucking jackpot on all counts when it comes to my girlfriend. She is hot, compassionate, funny, a spitfire, and her dad is willing to pay for our plane tickets when we come home for the holidays.

Daria releases air and starts whistling. She's bored. She's never been a power-walker or a jogger. She prefers to dance in the studio. She joined the cheer team at Notre Dame and doesn't even think about becoming team captain. She is much more content doing her own thing.

"Via said she is having fun at Santa Barbara."

My sister is attending community college and loving every minute of it. I think it's because it's so close to Mel, Jaime, and

Bailey. She doesn't like much exploring outside her territory and still needs some hand-holding. We've been getting better at the whole being twins thing, and Via and Daria have actually been keeping in touch. It's frosty, but it's there. At this point, I have no illusions or expectations about them becoming best buddies. If they can survive not killing each other over the holidays—which seems to be the case—I'm happy.

"Good. Good," I say. I'm too distracted by the insanity that's about to leave my mouth to care about Via.

"She's been dating this really sweet guy named Doug. I think she's bringing him to Thanksgiving dinner."

"Doug is an awful name, but anything is better than Gus."

"Okay, what's going on?" She stops. No. No. She can't stop. We have maybe ten feet left to complete the journey. I tug at her sleeve and practically drag her the rest of the way between the two lakes on campus in the shape of an eight.

"I said no questions."

"Fine! Can you release my hand, though? My palm is hella sweaty, and even though I love when you throw romantic crumbs at me, that's a bit needy, Penn."

I laugh and shake my head. "Eight more feet."

"Maaaaarx," she drawls. "You're killing me, Smalls."

When we reach the spot, I turn around and face her, releasing her hand.

"It's been said that if a male and female student hold hands and walk around the two lakes on campus in the shape of the figure eight, they will get married."

Seeing as we already live together in the apartment Daria's parents purchased for her, and we've been declared as the "it" couple on campus by every Tom, Dick, and Harry, I am trying to tell myself that it should not freak her out. But Daria takes a step back, cupping her mouth.

"Is this a proposal?"

"Nope"—I grin—"but it's a promise you'll be getting one before we graduate. Sound good?"

She nods. "Sounds…the best."

I let out a sigh of relief. Okay. Good. *Fuck.*

DARIA, NOTRE DAME, JUNIOR YEAR

I leave class and hug my psychology textbooks close to my chest. After much discussion with my mom, I finally decided what I want to do when I grow up. Become a school counselor and help little future Darias. My backpack with my MacBook, phone, purse, and the rest of my belongings is strapped on my shoulders, feeling light as a feather. I can't wait to see my superstar boyfriend playing against Navy tonight. Penn is all over political science. I think he wants to go back and make a difference in the neighborhoods that spat him and Gus and Via out into the world.

A smile hovers on my lips when I think about last night. About making love to him so long and hard he complained that he'd never have any strength for the game today. How, seemingly impossibly, our sex becomes even more intense and desperate and meaningful as time passes.

I'm about to exit Lyons Hall on campus, walking under the darkened arch on this autumn day, when a hand snakes behind me and tugs me to the corner of the arch. My back slams against the wall, and I let out a hysterical moan.

No. This is not happening. No.

A hand cups my mouth, and I'm thinking I should scream or bite it off when the man it belongs to stares at me from a few inches away. My boyfriend.

My soon-to-be dead *boyfriend.*

He removes his palm from my mouth with a cocky grin.

"What in the good heavens do you think you're—"

He shuts me up with a hard kiss, his lips grinding on mine roughly, and I melt and clasp the lapels of his tracksuit. I'm a fool for this guy. Stupid in love and embarrassingly hot for him. When we finally come up for air, he rears his head back, staring at me, dead calm and serious.

"I have something for you."

I bat my eyelashes as he produces a red apple from his duffel bag and tosses it into my hands. My eyes widen at the realization of what it is.

"Game over. You win. You conquered me even though it was me who marched into your territory unannounced."

I'm at a loss for words. So I choose to do the stupidest thing in the moment. I take a bite of the apple, press my lips to his, and we both bite it in the middle.

Lady and the Tramp style.

"Victories are sweeter when you celebrate them together," I whisper.

"All right. Take two. This time, I hope like hell that you'll get the hint because there's so much more on the line. According to traditional folklore around this neck of the woods, if two people of the opposite sex kiss under the Lyons Arch, it leads to marriage. You following this, Miss Followhill?"

I blink at him, biting down on my lip so I don't laugh hysterically. What does he mean, take two? When the hell was take one? My mouth drops into an O shape as the penny drops.

"You mean…?"

He gives me a sharp nod, closing his eyes.

"Had it in my pocket last year. Have it in my pocket now. I can't afford a diamond just yet, so it has—"

"Orange sea glass instead," I finish for him, my heart rioting in my chest.

He grins.

"Please, for the love of G...*Marx*, put me out of my fucking misery and tell me you'll be my wife. I'm not asking you to make the commitment this year. Or next year. Or maybe not even the next one. I'm asking you to make the commitment to *make* the commitment, and yes, I know how Dr. Phil that sounds."

I throw my arms around his neck and kiss him so hard I think our lips might fall off. He lifts me off the ground and into the air, kissing my cheeks, my nose, my forehead, then finally, my chin.

"Shiiiiit," he hisses. "You're still not giving me words, Skull Eyes."

His shirts are so perfectly whole these days. Mine too.

"Yes, Penn Scully. It would be an honor to be your wife."

"Thank fuck, I thought I was going to grow old and die behind this thing," I hear from the corner of the arch and cock my head. It's our entire football team, cheer team, Mom, Dad, Bailey, Via, Knight, Luna, Vaughn, and a girl I don't know but have heard all about. Adriana is there too, with Harper on her hip. Camilo has his arm wrapped around her shoulder, and they're smiling. Not just at us but also at each other.

Mom and Dad clap. Bailey jumps up and down. Knight gives us a thumbs-up, and Vaughn rolls his eyes but smiles. Luna, Addy, Harper, and Camilo look at us like they've won something. Happy in our happiness.

And that's what good friends and families do.

They pick you up and pull you out of the mud of your own mistakes.

And when you're not the best version of yourself? Well, they're still there, waiting, because we're all fucking human.

BONUS EPILOGUE
PENN

PENN BREAKING UP WITH DARIA AFTER VIA'S RETURN, FROM HIS POV

Meet me in Vaughn's pool house at noon.

I glare at the text message I sent Skull Eyes a few minutes ago. I'm eviscerated. Like someone plucked out my inner organs with a fucking spatula, and now I'm so empty, if I swallow a penny, it would rattle against the walls of my body. I want to fucking kill someone.

Problem is, that someone is my twin sister.

She'd deserve it. There's not one redeemable bone in her whole goddamn body. Too bad I feel like I owe her something—a pound of flesh. Logically, I understand that just because life handed her an even shittier hand of cards than mine doesn't mean I have to atone for making good choices. But logic has no place in love. That's why families are so messed up, I think. There's so much room for error when emotions are in charge of the wheel.

Plus, I just can't run the chance Via would act on her threat to tell Jaime and Mel what Daria did to her when they were fourteen. I'm not only doing this to satisfy my sister's bloodlust; I'm doing this to save Daria too.

I hike my gray sweatpants and pop the elastic over my shredded six-pack, shaking my head. *Snap out of it, asshole. Daria's just pussy.* Good pussy, no doubt, but pussy nonetheless. I yank two pieces of gum from a sleeve of Trident, shoving them into my mouth. My teeth grind it, spicy peppermint stinging my tongue, when my phone pings to life.

Daria: See you there. xoxo.

Shit. Shit. Shit. I really don't want to do this. But my wants have been taking the back seat ever since Sylvia reentered my life, shitting over every bit of progress I made since the Followhills took me in.

For real, asshole? Your own blood is now an inconvenience? *Have you forgotten what Daria Followhill did to you? To HER?*

But Daria did those things years ago, and it's not like her life is a picnic.

My dick and my mind aren't in agreement. I need to leave the confines of my room and find a distraction. My stomach grumbles. *Food,* it says, *is a good idea, asshole.*

I slam my bedroom door and take the stairs down two at a time. Everyone's already at the breakfast table. Via and Bailey talk ballet, lazily munching on wholegrain toast with a paper-thin layer of avocado. Daria is swirling a stripy pink-and-white straw inside her iced coffee, rolling her eyes at something Melody is saying. Jaime looks like he is drowning in estrogen, his eyes pleading for me to throw him a lifeline.

I take a seat next to him and pile bacon, scrambled eggs, and toast onto my plate, avoiding the anxious glares daggering at me from each side of the table. Via stares at me expectantly, like she wants me to break things off with Daria now. Skull Eyes sneaks nervous looks at me, trying to read the temperature after the party last night.

Jaime saves the day, pouring me some coffee and starting a conversation.

"Wanna catch the game today? Pats are built to destroy running quarterbacks. Should be a dark horse, big money game."

"You betting?" I lick the residual jam from the butter knife, my gaze slinging his way.

"Nah, just speculating." His eyebrows drop into a frown. "You gonna eat that jam–bacon–scrambled egg–avocado sandwich?"

Guess I was so busy trying to avoid eye contact with every vagina owner in the room, I created a culinary disaster greater than Brooklyn Beckham's stuff. "I'm a growing boy."

"Growing? Yeah. Dumbass? Not typically." Jaime narrows his eyes at me.

"Jaime!" Melody chides.

"Gross, Penn." Bailey wrinkles her nose.

"I need the calories."

"And the food poisoning." Via coughs into her fist. I ignore her. Just because I'm going to break up with Daria doesn't mean she and I are chummy now.

"Food poisoning is prompted by expired, rotten, or otherwise spoiled food. Not by weird combos," Bailey continues, being unnecessarily informative.

Mel is still talking to Daria, attempting to coax her into coming with them to New York.

Daria stands up abruptly, having had enough bullshit for one morning. "I'm not hungry. I'll catch y'all later."

Mel looks up, disappointed. "Where are you going?"

"Dunno." She flips her gloriously golden hair to one shoulder. "Drive around in my giant clitoris-looking car, looking for lives to ruin and souls to suck."

Fake news. Daria never accepted that godawful car. She's still driving her cherry-red convertible BMW.

"True story," Via mumbles under her breath.

Daria is out in a flash and my feet burn to chase her. My knee actually jerks violently, banging against the table, making utensils clatter and Bailey's milk glass spill over.

"Oh my Marx!" Bailey stands up to get paper towels and avoid a splash. "Close call."

"Shit, sorry," I hiss out.

"Pull yourself together," Via instructs coldly under her breath, her foot pressing over mine under the table. "Seriously."

Melody is up and walking around the kitchen, mainly to hide the tears in her eyes. "No biggie. I was going to mop the floor today anyway."

Only Jaime, blind to the apocalypse brewing inside these four walls, looks up from his paper and grins at me. "But if I were a betting man, I'd definitely put my money on the Packers."

I decide to go for a run before meeting Skull Eyes. I need to get some rage out, and plowing my fists into my sister's face is (sadly) not an option. I've never hurt a woman, and I'm not gonna start now.

You're about to hurt Daria a shit-ton, moron.

I run around the gated neighborhood shirtless. One mile. Two, then three. When I hit five miles, I glance at my phone to find out it's almost noon. Time to face the music. I detour and make my way to Vaughn's house, my spirit dying a slow, painful, violent death. I'm not in the habit of taking orders from anyone, and if it wasn't for Via being a hot mess and going through so much, I'd have told her to go stick her ultimatum where the sun don't shine.

When I slip into Vaughn's pool house, I find Daria in matching black panties and bra, waiting for me. She looks like my favorite dessert, and I'm famished. I have a vague recollection of eating my own weight in bacon and eggs this morning, but the hole inside me is so big, so vast, I think the food just melted inside me, dissipating through my pores or some shit.

One look at Skull Eyes, gorgeous and vulnerable and ready to be devoured, and I'm hit with the acute need to drop to my knees, kiss her perfect hot-pink toes, and beg her to pack her shit so we can both get out of here. Run. Live in Luna and Knight's tree house in the woods while we finish high school. I'll get a full ride in college. I'll take care of us. We just need to get over this hurdle.

But then Via's voice skulks through my cranium, like nerve toxin.

"She ruined us, Penn. So what if she's pretty? So what if she's broken? Her parents will superglue her back together, with therapists and positive affirmation and shopping sprees in Milan. We? We are scattered into miniscule pieces. Shattered Lego parts no one wants to play with. We won't be picked and fixed."

"Whoa" is the first thing to come out of my mouth. Though it's really more a whoosh of air leaving my lungs. "Put some clothes on, Daria. You're embarrassing yourself."

Her expression, soft and pliant—an expression I've only ever seen on her face when we're alone—liquifies like rain pierces through a fog. She frantically regroups. Moves around the room, putting on her Daisy Dukes, her top, and that padlocked, closed-off queen bitch expression. "What the hell, Penn?"

I force the next words out. Push them like they're dancing fire on my tongue.

"Nothing. I got what I wanted from you, and you got what you wanted from me. Time to cut the bullshit."

"Where's this coming from?" She toes into her Dior sandals, fully clothed now. Her face is as pink as her nails.

I shrug. "I'm bored of you, and it ain't worth the risk. Your parents are going to kick our asses if they find out. Besides, you have Prichard, and I have Adriana." And then, I say the words I've been wanting to tell her for years. The words I've dreamt of uttering every night, in my stupid-ass cot, in my stupid-ass dilapidated house, after brawling with Rhett. The words that should feel like triumph but now taste of venom. "Game over."

What I don't expect is the back and forth that comes after.

What I don't expect is her defiance.

What I don't expect is for her not to give up on me, even when I give up on *us*.

Aside from my football, I've never been use to anyone. But Daria is a force. Behind those dead eyes is a girl burning alive and determined to rewrite her own story.

We battle it out. She says things. I retort. When it becomes clear Daria isn't going down without a fight, I have no choice but to blurt out that Harper is my daughter. That Addy is coming with me to college. None of it is true. None of it is right. But I have to leave. Leave before I confess the truth and beg for forgiveness. Before I chicken out on Via's ultimatum. "I have a daughter. Now give it a rest."

Storming out before I can hear her reaction, I stomp on the freshly trimmed lawn of the Spencers. Clipped to perfection and the color of wild spearmint, this lawn, like its owners, drips privilege. Fuck the Californian drought—I've seen Baron Spencer turn on the sprinklers whenever his wife wasn't home to ensure his is the greenest grass in all of SoCal. He is a hedonist fuck who takes his backyard like he takes his coffee—Instagram-ready and obnoxiously perfect.

Which is probably why I hear the scary fucker barking at me from his spot on his bedroom balcony, lounging on a plush recliner, smoking a cigar. "Penn Fucking Scully, get off my grass before I shoot your ass with a rifle."

I've no doubt he'll make good on his promise. Fucker is just waiting for someone to trespass into his house so he can shoot them. "Gettin' out of your way now, sir."

"Not nearly fast enough. You're lucky Jaime is fond of your ass."

Not after he finds out how I treated his daughter.

I jog the remainder of my way out his wrought-iron gate. Then I start running. This time, I don't run around the neighborhood. I run aimlessly, trying to forget. I run even when my lungs are empty.

When my muscles are strained. When my body temperature is so high, I'm light-headed and nauseous. I run until I collapse in the woods, until I bury my face in mud. I taste the dirt and don't spit it out. I scream into muck and horseshit to muffle the sound, my fists pounding on chipped wood and cold stones.

I bury myself in the forest, closing my eyes, wishing I never wake up again.

SERIES INSPIRATION

Struggling to picture the characters? Here are the
physical inspirations for each character:

Daria Followhill—Nicola Peltz
Bailey Followhill—Chloë Grace Moretz
Penn Scully—Austin Butler
Knight Cole—Matthew Noszka
Luna Rexroth—Zendaya
Lev Cole—Patrick Schwarzenegger
Vaughn Spencer—Felix Mallard
Adriana Lima—Jenna Ortega
Sylvia Scully—Lily Rose Depp
Gus Bauer—Chase Mattson

BROKEN KNIGHT

KNIGHT, 9; LUNA, 10

I drove a fist into the oak tree, feeling the familiar sting of a fresh wound as my knuckles split open.

Bleeding helped me breathe better. I didn't know what it meant, but it made Mom cry in her bathroom when she thought no one could hear. Whenever she glanced at my permanently busted knuckles, the waterworks started. It had also earned me a trip to talk to this guy in a suit every week, who asked about my feelings.

My earbuds blocked out the sounds of birds, crickets, and crispy leaves under my feet. The world sucked. I was done listening to it. "Break Stuff" by Limp Bizkit was my designated ruin-shit anthem. Fred Durst might look like a ballsack in a cap, but he had a point.

Thump.

Thump.

Thump.

Most kids liked fighting each other. Not me. I only wanted to hurt myself. When my body ached, my heart didn't. Simple math and a pretty good deal.

A pine cone dropped on my head. I squinted up. My stupid neighbor Luna sat perched outside our tree house, bouncing another pine cone in her hand and dangling her toothpick legs from a thick branch.

"What was that for?" I tore the earbuds from my ears.

She motioned to me with her head to climb up. I made no move. She waved me up.

"Nah." I tried to gather phlegm, spitting sideways.

She arched an eyebrow, her way of asking what my problem was. Luna was nosy but just with me. It sucked.

"Vaughn stole my bike," I announced.

I'd have beaten the crap out of my so-called best friend, Vaughn, if I wasn't so sure I'd kill him by accident. He'd said he wanted me to lose my shit. *"Get it out of your system."* Whatever that meant. What's a system? What did he know about mine? About anger? His life was perfect. His parents were healthy. He didn't even have an annoying baby brother, like Lev.

Luna threw the second pine cone. This time I caught it, swung my arm like a baseball player, and threw it back at her, missing on purpose.

"I said *no*."

She produced a third pine cone (She kept a stash in the tree house in case intruders came upon us, which was honestly never.) and made a show of throwing it at me.

I finally snapped. "You're so dumb!"

She blinked at me.

"Stop looking at me that way!"

Another blink.

"Goddarn it, Luna!"

I didn't care what Vaughn said. I was never going to *want* to kiss this girl. God help me if she ever asked me to.

I climbed on the tire swing and up to our tiny tree house. Vaughn thought he was too cool for tree houses. Good. It was one more thing that was Luna's and mine that he wasn't a part of.

Luna jumped from the branch. She rolled on the ground, straightening up like a ninja and patting herself clean with a satisfied smile. Then she started running toward our neighborhood. Fast.

"Where are you going?" I yelled as if she was going to answer.

I watched her back disappear into a dot. I was always sad to see her go.

This was all so stupid anyway. I didn't know anyone who could talk Vaughn into doing anything. Luna couldn't even talk, period. Plus, I didn't need her help. I'd walked away from him because, if not, I knew he'd get what he wanted from me—a dirty fight. I wasn't like him. Pissing off my parents wasn't a lifetime goal.

Sometime later, Luna came back riding my bike. I stood up, shielding my eyes from the sinking sun. It always burned brighter when the ocean was about to swallow it.

She waved at me to come down.

I threw a pine cone at her shoulder in response. "Rexroth."

What? her quirked eyebrow said. She could tell me a thousand things with her eyebrows alone, this girl. Sometimes I wanted to shave them off just to spite her.

"I always get even. Remember that, cool?"

Cool, her eye roll huffed.

"Now, come up."

She motioned toward my bike, stomping her foot.

"Leave the stupid bike."

We huddled inside the tree house. Instead of thanking her, which I knew I should, I pulled out the pages I had printed earlier and arranged them on the wooden floor between us. Our foreheads stuck together with warm sweat as we both looked down. I was teaching her profanity in sign language—the stuff her father and therapist never would.

"Says here *dick* is a 'd' hand shape tapping the nose." I mimicked the picture on one of the pages, then flipped it on its back. "Oh, look. If you want to say *fuck you*, you can just give the person your middle finger and pout. Convenient."

I didn't look at her, but I felt her forehead resting against mine. Luna was a girl, but she was still really cool. Only downside was sometimes she asked too many questions with her eyes. Mom said it was because Luna cared about me. Not that I was going to admit it, but I cared about her too.

She tapped my shoulder. I flicked another page.

"Waving an open hand on the side of the chin, forward and back, means *slut*. Dude, your dad will kill me if he ever finds out I taught you this."

She tapped my shoulder harder, digging her fingernail into my skin.

I looked up, midread. "'Sup?"

"Are you okay?" she signed.

She didn't use sign language often. Luna didn't want to talk. Not in sign and not at all. She *could* talk. Technically, I mean. Not that I'd ever heard her say anything. But that's what our parents said—that it wasn't about her voice. It was about the world.

I got it. I hated the world too.

We just hated it differently.

I shrugged. "Sure."

"Friends don't let friends get upset over small stuff," she signed.

Whoa. An entire sentence. That was new.

I didn't understand the point of speaking sign language if she was planning not to speak *at all*, but I didn't want to make her feel bad and stuff.

"I don't care about the bike." I put the page down and scooted toward our branch, leaving. She followed, sitting beside me. I didn't even like riding my bike. It was cruel on my nuts and boring to the rest of my body. I only rode it so I could hang out with Luna. Same reason I colored. I *loathed* coloring.

She cocked her head to the side. A question.

"Mom's in the hospital again." I picked out a pine cone and threw it at the sinking sun, over the edge of the mountain our tree was rooted upon. I wondered if the pine cone made it to the ocean, if it was wet and cold now. If it hated me.

Luna put her hand over mine, staring down at our palms. Our hands were the same size, hers brown, mine white as fresh-fallen snow.

"I'm fine." I sniffed, choosing another pine cone. "It's fine."

"*I hate that word. Fine,*" Luna signed. "*It's not good. It's not bad. It's nothing.*"

She dropped her head down and took my hand, gave it a squeeze. Her touch was warm and sticky. Kind of gross. A few weeks ago, Vaughn told me he wanted to kiss Cara Hunting. I couldn't even imagine touching a girl like that.

Luna put my hand on her heart.

I rolled my eyes, embarrassed. "I know. You're here for me."

She shook her head and squeezed my hand harder. The intensity of her gaze freaked me out. "*Always. Whenever. Forever,*" she signed.

I breathed in her words. I wanted to smash my stupid bike on Vaughn's stupid face, then run away. Then die. I wanted to die in desolate sands, evaporate into dust, let the wind carry me nowhere and everywhere.

I wanted to die instead of Mom. I was pretty useless. But so many people were dependent on Ma.

Dad.

Lev.

Me.

Me.

Luna pointed at the sun in front of us.

"Sunset?" I sighed.

She frowned.

"Beach?"

She shook her head, rolling her eyes.

"*The sun will rise again tomorrow,*" she signed.

She leaned forward. For a moment, I thought she was going to jump. She took a safety pin from her checkered Vans and pierced the tip of her index finger. Wordlessly, she took my hand and pricked my finger too. She joined them together, and I stared as the blood meshed.

Her lips broke into a smile. Her teeth were uneven. A little pointy. A lot imperfect.

With our blood, she wrote the words *Ride or Die* on the back of my hand, ignoring the state of my knuckles.

I thought about the bike she'd retrieved for me and smirked.

She drew me into a hug. I sank into her arms.

I didn't want to kiss her.

I wanted to zip open my skin and tuck her into me.

Hide her from the world and keep her mine.

LUNA
KNIGHT, 12; LUNA, 13

I was named after the moon.

Dad said I'd been a plump, perfect thing. A light born into darkness. A child my mother didn't want and he hadn't known what to do with. He'd said that despite—or maybe *because* of—that, I was the most beautiful and enticing creature he'd ever laid eyes on.

"My heart broke, not because I was sad, but because it swelled so much at the sight of you, I needed more space in it," he once told me.

He said a lot of things to make me feel loved. He had good reasons, of course.

My mother left us before I turned two.

Over the years, she'd come knocking on the doors of my mind whenever I least expected her, barging through the gates with an army of memories and hidden photos I was never supposed to find. Her laugh—that laugh I could never unhear, no matter how hard I tried—rolled down my skin like tongues of fire.

What made everything worse was the fact that I knew she was

alive. She was living somewhere under the same sky, breathing the same air. Perhaps in Brazil, her home country. It really didn't matter, since wherever she was, she wasn't with me. And the one time she'd come back for me, she'd really wanted money.

I was five when it happened—around the time Dad had met Edie, my stepmom. Val, my mom, had asked for joint custody and enough child support to fund a small country. When she'd realized I wasn't going to make her rich, she'd bailed again.

At that point, I had made it a habit to tiptoe to the kitchen at night, where Dad and Edie had all their big talks. They never noticed me. I'd perfected the art of being invisible from the moment Val stopped seeing me.

"I don't want her anywhere near my kid," Dad had gritted out.

"Neither do I," Edie had replied.

My heart had melted into warm goo.

"But if she comes back, we need to consider it."

"What if she hurts her?"

"What if she *mends* her?"

Experience had taught me that time was good at two things: healing and killing. I waited for the healing part to come every single day. I sank my knees to the lacy pillows below my windowsill and cracked it open, praying the wind would swish away the memories of her.

I couldn't hate Valenciana Vasquez, the woman who'd packed up her things in front of my crib, while I'd cried, pleaded, *screamed* for her not to go, and left anyway.

I remembered the scene chillingly well. They say your earliest recollection can't be before the age of two, but I have a photographic memory, a 155 IQ, and a brain that's been put through enough tests to know that, for better or worse, I remember everything.

Everything bad.

Everything good.

And the in-between.

So the memory was still crisp in my head. The determination zinging in her tawny, slanted eyes. The cold sweat gathering under my pudgy arms. I'd racked my brain looking for the words, and when I finally found them, I screamed as loud as I possibly could.

"Mommy! Please! No!"

She'd paused at the door, her knuckles white from holding the doorframe tightly, not taking any chances in case something inspired her to turn around and hold me. I remembered how I didn't dare blink, too scared she'd disappear if I closed my eyes.

Then, for a split second, her motherly instincts won, and she did swivel to face me.

Her face had twisted, her mouth parting, her tongue sweeping over her scarlet lipstick. She'd been about to say something, but in the end, she just shook her head and left. The radio had played a melancholic tune. Val had often listened to the radio to drown out the sound of my crying. My parents hadn't lived together, but they'd shared custody. After Val had failed to answer Dad's many phone calls, he'd found me some hours later in my cot, my diaper so soiled it outweighed my tiny body.

I hadn't been crying. Not anymore.

Not when he'd picked me up.

Not when he'd taken me to the emergency room for a thorough checkup.

Not when he'd cooed and kissed and fawned over me.

Not when hot tears had silently run down his cheeks and he'd begged me to produce a sound.

Not at all.

Since that day, I'd become what they call a selective mute. Meaning I could speak, but I *chose* not to. Which, of course, was real stupid, since I didn't *want* to be different. I simply *was*. My not speaking wasn't a choice as much as it was a phobia. I'd been diagnosed with severe social anxiety and attended therapy twice a week since babyhood. Usually, selective mutism means a person can speak in certain situations where they feel comfortable. Not me.

The nameless tune on the radio that day had been burned into my brain like an angry scar. Now, it popped up on the radio, assaulting me again.

I was sitting in the car with Edie, my stepmom. Rain slapped the windows of her white Porsche Cayenne. The radio host announced that it was "Enjoy the Silence" by Depeche Mode. My mouth went dry at the irony—the same mouth that refused to utter words for no apparent reason other than the fact that when I'd spoken words aloud, they hadn't been enough for my mother. *I* wasn't enough.

As the music played, I wanted to crawl out of my skin and evaporate into thin air. Hurl myself out of the car. Run away from California. Leave Edie and Dad and Racer, my baby brother, behind—just take off and go somewhere else. *Anywhere* else. Somewhere people wouldn't poke and pity me. Where I wouldn't be the circus freak.

"Geez, it's been a decade. Can't she just, like, get over it?"

"Maybe it's not about the mom. Have you seen the dad? Parading his young mistress…"

"She's always been weird, the girl. Pretty but weird."

I wanted to bathe in my own loneliness, swim in the knowledge that my mother had looked me in the eye and decided I wasn't enough. Drown in my sorrow. Be left alone.

As I reached to turn the radio off, Edie pouted. "But it's my favorite song!"

Of course it was. Of course.

Slapping my window with my open palm, I let out a wrecked whimper. I shuddered violently at the unfamiliar sound of my own voice. Edie, behind the wheel, sliced her gaze to me, her mouth still curled with the faint smile that always hovered over her lips, like open arms offering a hug.

"Your dad grew up on Depeche Mode. It's one of his favorite bands," she explained, trying to distract me from whatever meltdown I was going through now.

I struck the passenger window harder, kicking my backpack at my feet. The song was digging into my body, slithering into my veins. I wanted out. I *needed* to get out of there. We rounded the corner toward our Mediterranean mansion, but it wasn't fast enough. I couldn't unhear the song. Unsee Valenciana leaving. Unfeel that huge, hollow hole in my heart that my biological mother stretched with her fist every time her memory struck me.

Edie turned off the radio at the same time I threw the door open, stumbling out of the slowing vehicle. I skidded over a puddle, then sped toward the house.

The garage door rolled up while thunder sliced the sky, cracking it open, inviting more furious rain. I heard Edie's cries through her open window, but they were swallowed by the rare SoCal storm. Rain soaked my socks, making my legs heavy, and my feet burned from running as I grabbed my bike from the garage, flung one leg over it, and launched toward the street. Edie parked, tripping out of the vehicle. She chased after me, calling my name.

I pedaled fast, cycling away from the cul-de-sac...zipping past the Followhill house...the Spencers' mansion darkening my path ahead with its formidable size. The Coles' house, my favorite, was sandwiched between my house and the Followhills'.

"Luna!" Knight Cole's voice boomed behind my back.

I wasn't even surprised.

Our bedroom windows faced each other, and we always kept the curtains open. When I wasn't in my room, Knight usually looked for me. And vice versa.

It was more difficult to ignore Knight than my stepmother, and not because I didn't love Edie. I did. I loved her with the ferocity only a nonbiological child could feel—hungry, visceral love, only better because it was dipped in gratitude and awe.

Knight wasn't exactly like a brother, but he didn't feel like less than family either. He put Band-Aids on my scraped knees and shooed the bullies away when they taunted me, even if they were twice his size. He'd given me pep talks before I'd known what they were and that I needed them.

The only bad thing about Knight was it felt like he held a piece of my heart hostage. So I always wondered where he was. His well-being was tangled with mine. As I rolled down the hill on my bike, toward the black, wrought-iron gate enclosing our lush neighborhood, I wondered if he felt that invisible thread attaching us too, if he chased me because I tugged at it. Because it hurt when one of us got too far away.

"Hey! Hey! Hey!" Knight screamed behind my back.

Edie had caught up with him. It sounded like they were arguing.

"I'll calm her down."

"But, Knight—"

"I know what she needs."

"You don't, honey. You're just a kid."

"You're just an adult. Now *go*!"

Knight wasn't afraid to get confrontational with adults. Me, I followed rules. As long as I wasn't expected to utter actual words, I did everything by the book—from being a straight-A student to helping strangers. I picked up trash on the street even when it wasn't mine and donated a selection of my gifts every Christmas to those who really needed them.

But my motives weren't pure. I always felt less-than, so I tried to be more. Daria Followhill, another neighbor my age, called me Saint Luna.

She wasn't wrong. I played the role of a saint because Val had made me feel like a sinner.

ACKNOWLEDGMENTS

I always rewrite my books, but this one took three drafts to get right. No, wait…four. Yes. Four, completely different versions of Daria's story. And all of them were read by Charleigh Rose and Tijuana Turner, so suffice to say, they should be the first to get acknowledged for this book.

Also, to Lana Kart, Melissa Panio-Petersen, Sarah Grim Sentz, Amy Halter, and Ava Harrison: Thanks for not hating me. I appreciate it.

To Angela Marshall Smith, Paige Smith, and Jenny Sims, my wonderful editors—I cannot thank you for not hating me, for I do not know it to be true, but thank you for always being patient with me. I appreciate it too.

To Letitia Hasser and Stacey Blake, who always make my books pretty. Thank you for being so incredibly talented. And to Lin Tahel Cohen, my PA, for doing everything short of breathing for me. I am so awfully dependent on you.

To Helena Hunting—thanks for holding my hand. Jenn Watson—thanks for existing. And my agent, Kimberly Brower, who made this series happen even before I started writing it. You're wow. All of you.

Special thanks to the Sassy Sparrows group, my favorite group in the universe, and to my wonderful street team, that is continuously growing, so I simply decided to start dedicating my books to them to show my appreciation, two people at a time.

I would also like to thank the bloggers who took the time to read this book for no other reason than their love for the written word, and to you, the reader, for allowing me to do what I love. Please consider leaving a brief, honest review if you have time.

Always grateful,
L.J. Shen

ABOUT THE AUTHOR

L.J. Shen is a *USA Today*, *WSJ*, *Washington Post*, and #1 Amazon Kindle Store bestselling author of contemporary romance books. She writes angsty books, unredeemable antiheroes who are in Elon Musk's tax bracket, and sassy heroines who bring them to their knees (for more reasons than one). HEAs and groveling are guaranteed. She lives in Florida with her husband, three sons, and a disturbingly active imagination.

Website: authorljshen.com/
Facebook: authorljshen
Instagram: @authorljshen
Twitter: @lj_shen
TikTok: @authorljshen
Pinterest: @authorljshen